Rainie Daze

Melody Muckenfuss

For Mr. Swanson, Florie, Faye and Virginia.

My life has been enriched with knowing you

Chapter One

Life is full of questions. Like: what do you want to be when you grow up? Do you want to go to college? Do you want to get married?

And then there are the really *important* questions. Such as: What am I doing here? How in the hell did I get myself into this situation?

I suppose everyone asked themselves those questions now and then. Maybe on a bad date, or in the midst of a party full of obnoxious people you suddenly realize you don't want to waste your time with. I remember asking myself that shortly before the demise of my marriage.

This, however, was no social situation. This was a matter of life and death: mine, as a matter of fact. And although my life had its share of warts and blemishes and unsightly bumps, for the most part I found it rather attractive. I was not ready to give it up yet.

So here I was, cowering under a car in a rain saturated parking lot, protected from the pounding rain, but not from the growing rivulets of water that were flowing under and around me, soaking into my jeans and my T shirt, gathering in a rather deep puddle right under my belly. The left side of my face and my left shoulder felt like someone had taken a belt sander to them, but that was still low on my list of concerns.

I stared out into the night, listening intently for the scrape of boots on wet asphalt, trying to make out the slightly darker shadows of my pursuers' legs against the shimmering blackness of the nocturnal downpour.

I heard something behind me, and I jerked my head around, smacking my skull against the undercarriage of the car, causing a shower of wet rust particles to sift down on me. I closed my eyes instinctively to protect them from the tiny fragments, but then promptly opened them again, fearing my elusive pursuers more than possible blindness.

I stared into the blackness at the other end of the car; I couldn't see anything but the glare of the parking lot floodlights against the wet pavement, but then I couldn't really get a good view of anything directly behind me. My chest constricted with renewed terror as I waited for a hand to grasp my ankle, dragging me from under my fiberglass and steel sanctuary.

A long moment went by with no further sound, and no deadly grip on my lower limb. I forced myself to take a deep breath, trying to slow the rapid hammering of my heart. The small voice in the back of my head, the one that often went off on inappropriate tangents at the oddest of times, was waxing poetic once again. That little voice was remarking on the poetic dissonance of the pounding but steady rhythm of my heart playing counterpoint to the chaotic pulses of the wind-driven rain.

In spite of the dire circumstances I liked the image, and had I not been wet and cold and terrified and if I had access to pen and paper, I might have jotted a note, a reminder for a poem to be written later. I write a lot of poetry, but of course there's no money to be made with that vocation, which was perhaps one small part of the reason I was in my present circumstance. My poetry was rarely published, and when it was it didn't pay well.

But all that was irrelevant, at least at the moment, so I told that little voice in my head to shut up.

I had to think, had to come up with some sort of plan or I was going to die here, under a non-descript Buick with an apparent gas leak and rusty muffler system.

I had scrambled under here without much thought, seeking a moment's safety, but I knew they were out there, and they knew I was still somewhere in the dark lot. It was just a matter of time until one or the other of them looked under this car, and then it would all be over.

I had no weapons, no means of defense but my bare hands and sneakered-feet. I knew basic self-defense. I knew to aim for the eyes or the crotch, to make contact with any vulnerable body part that made itself available, but I doubted that I would get much chance to use that theoretical knowledge when faced with the point-and-shoot power of a loaded gun.

So again I ask myself: how in the hell did I get in this situation?

The answer to that goes back a couple of months, to a night of poker and the loss of Max.

Chapter Two

My name is Rainie. That's short for Rainbow, and that should give you a pretty good idea of how I was raised. I've been recycling since before it was the politically correct thing to do, I see nothing wrong with hugging a tree, and many of my family members partake of certain herbs that might be frowned upon by the police.

I was a tomboy, and in a lot of ways I still am. I'm not squeamish about spiders and I prefer playing poker to doing handicrafts and James Bond movies to chick flicks. Most of my friends are men, except for Thelma, who is technically not really a friend, but one of my bosses...but I'll explain that later.

I am 5'6". I weigh 140 pounds through sheer determination. There was a time I carried an additional 75 pounds around with me. In fact, I'd carried them for so long that they considered themselves to have a legitimate claim on me, and were left behind in the sweat of a stationary bike with stubborn, ugly reluctance.

So here I was, driving along to work, thinking about stopping at the little roadside park ahead to have a cigarette.

Oh, did I forget to mention that I smoke? Okay, so healthy living isn't my strongest virtue. It's not like I chain smoke, yellowing my curtains and staining my teeth a dull amber color. Actually, I only smoke a pack of cigarettes every four days or so, and then never in my house and rarely in my car. I have *some* discipline, but face it, I need something to substitute for that fancy ice cream that used to fill my evenings and my stomach.

My biggest fault seems to be the inability to stick with any one thing for long. I went to college, but could never decide on a major, so after two years of basic courses I dropped out and started a chain of low paying jobs.

I never have found a job that would hold my interest for a full forty hour work week. Unfortunately, I've also never found a job that paid well enough to allow me to work only part time. I solved that dilemma by working multiple part time jobs. In the past I have waited tables and clerked in bookstores, but for the last couple of years I have settled into a type of work I would never have thought I was suited for.

I take care of elderly people in their homes. Believe it or not, there are a number of retired folks out there who can no longer (or at least *should* no longer) drive, cook, or perform other tasks of daily life that most of us take for granted. I fill that gap by becoming their "companion." I drive them to the grocery store and doctor appointments, do a little light housekeeping, cook their meals and remind them to eat, shower and take their medicines. It's often a frustrating job, especially when you're dealing with Alzheimer's patients who more often than not can't remember their kids' names, yet alone mine, but most of the time it's fun and a bit rewarding. After all, without someone like me around, those people would be in a nursing home, and no one deserves to be consigned to one of those. While I'm sure there are a few good facilities out there, most of them resemble something from biblical descriptions of Hell, complete with the wailing and gnashing of teeth promised by the Holy Roller religions.

I decided to skip the smoke, and went on to work. Monday, Wednesday and Friday, I spent the mornings with a sweet lady named Mabel, who was afflicted with the first stages of dementia. Today was Saturday, but Mabel's daughter was out of town, so I'd agreed to come over. It was only three hours, but those were very important hours for Mabel.

Mabel let me in, a big smile on her wrinkled old face. She called her wrinkles a road map of her life, much easier to read than palm lines. She had 85 years of lines, a complicated network of creases and crow's feet that testified to some rough days in the past. But when Mabel smiled, her whole face shifted and seemed to smooth out, or maybe it was just that it was hard to see anything else past that wide, sunny grin. Either way, I always found myself smiling back, no matter what mood I was in when I arrived.

I fixed Mabel's breakfast: half of a grapefruit and cereal with banana, a glass of water and her morning pills. It never varied, but hey, she had lived this long, who was I to change a system that obviously worked?

"Are we going shopping today?"

"Yes, Mable, for groceries."

"Oh good, because I think I'm out of milk."

"Almost. We need to get some soup, too."

I read the headline on the morning paper: "Spring Taxes Have Sprung." How revoltingly cutesy could they try to be?

"Are we going shopping today?"

"Yes, Mable, for groceries."

"Oh good, because I think I'm out of milk."

No, I wasn't trapped in a time loop like Bill Murray or the intrepid cast of Star Trek. It's just that Mabel, while quite intelligent and full of a good sense of humor, has difficulties with short term memory retention. The shopping question would be asked and answered at least a dozen more times before she finished her half of a grapefruit and miniscule bowl of cereal. I might vary the words of my answer a little, ("yes, we're going grocery shopping," or "yes, we need milk,") but I tried always to maintain the same patient tone. After all, Mabel had no idea she'd already asked me the same question eleven times, and it certainly wasn't her fault. I would be old someday, and I feared dementia like some people feared global warming or nuclear war. (Come to think of it, I was kind of afraid of those things, too.) With any luck, being kind to Mabel would build up some karma for me and I would have someone patient to answer my repeated questions without wanting to slap me upside the head.

I came across an article in the paper about the county parks. Mabel used to work for the park system as a dispatcher, so I read the article aloud to her. Mabel was still quite interested in current events, even if she couldn't remember them very well, and reading had become a challenge. Her mind just didn't want to retain the words anymore.

Hearing the words was a different story, and we had a brief but lively discussion about the state of the park system while Mabel finished her breakfast.

Besides Mabel, I had also been going three afternoons a week to care for an eighty year old guy named Max, who in his former life, I'm told, was a warm, imaginative and well-loved teacher of English. I have to take his family's word for all that; in the two months I'd known him he had been totally immersed in that merciless and cruel world of Alzheimer's, which starts by stealthily stealing a person's memory and then moves on to suck out their ability to care for themselves or even remember that they *should* take care of themselves. It is a slow, torturous disease that no human being deserves to suffer through, yet too often people react to it with a shudder and future avoidance of the victim. There are pink ribbons for breast cancer and book after book written about brave cancer survivors, but there is very little done to publicize sufferers of Alzeimers. Maybe because there are no survivors, or maybe because no one knows quite what to make of it. Or maybe because people see a potential future for themselves that they aren't ready to face.

Regardless, now and then I saw flashes of the humor-filled Max that once was, but for the most part our time together was stressful, even adversarial. He did not like strangers in his house, and each time I came I was a stranger anew to him. He barely remembered his own daughter, whom he'd loved and spent time with for fifty years; he could hardly be expected to remember a woman who had been coming to his house three times a week for two months.

My cell phone rang, and I checked the readout. Mabel was frowning at me curiously; some days she couldn't quite understand the concept of a phone you kept in your pocket.

The caller was Joe Mead, Max's son-in-law. "Excuse me Mabel, but I think I should answer this."

"Of course," she nodded dubiously, still not certain exactly what kind of gadget I wanted to answer. "Go right ahead."

Joe was calling with sad news. Max had fallen and broken his hip. He was in the hospital, and not expected to be allowed to go back home.

This was rough news. It was bad enough to have dementia, but to have to be confused in a place that would *never* look familiar was just too much. Still, sometimes there was little choice. Twenty-four hour home care could easily run a couple of thousand bucks a week or more, way out of reach for most folks.

I told Joe how sorry I was, and to call me if anything changed.

It wasn't until after I hung up that it occurred to me that Max's tragedy was also, to a much smaller degree, mine. I had a mortgage to pay. I supposed I would have to get my ad back into the paper soon.

I left Mabel's house at 11:00 and headed home. I felt a little guilty that in spite of the bad news about Max, I was in an excellent mood. The thing was, not only was it Saturday, it was poker night.

We played the first Saturday of every month, dollar limit on raises, so we could play for hours with twenty bucks unless we'd done something to really piss off Lady Luck. Of course, the truth was I had no business risking even twenty bucks; my mortgage payment was creeping up on me. Nonetheless, it was poker night, and I was loath to give it up.

The players varied once in a while if someone had family obligations or they tripped off a cliff or whatever, but for the most part it was me, Eddie, Mason, Charlie, Riley and Jeff.

Yeah, I was usually the only female. Even though Jeff and Mason had wives, they were allowed to come and play with me. Apparently I wasn't considered much of a threat.

This might have to do with the fact that I was married to a gay man for five years. I think everyone assumed from that fact that I wasn't much interested in sex. Besides, I struggle mightily to maintain my size twelve body. I have been described as "big-boned" and been told that I had hips absolutely designed to give birth. I've never tested that theory, which considering my track record with men is definitely a good thing. I am content with George, my pet iguana. What more does a girl need?

I said hello to George when I came in, and filled a bowl with fresh fruits and veggies for him. I put them up on the shelf over his cage and opened the top so he could climb out.

I got George when he was only six inches long, a miniature dinosaur with a voracious appetite. He was growing accordingly, and was now two and a half feet long from the tip of his scaly nose to the end of his long spiny tail. He now lived in a cage that dominated one wall of my living room. It was eight feet long, three feet deep, and five feet tall, and nicely furnished with tropical plants that helped keep his environment humidified. Special lights provided the benefits of sunlight that he would enjoy basking in his natural habitat, and one end of his cage featured a filtered pool for swimming.

Yes, I spend a lot of time and money on George, but what the hell, he's all I've got. I don't see another marriage in my future, and at thirty two I'm running out of child bearing years at a good clip.

George climbed eagerly out of his cage and on to the shelf above it, where he raised his head and looked around regally, master of all he surveyed. He was a rather gentle reptile most of the time, but now and then someone would piss him off, and then that tail would lash like a bullwhip, raising welts on unprotected flesh that wouldn't be forgotten any time too soon.

With my pet-owner duties tended to, I turned to setting up for poker.

I sliced up a plate full of cheese and salami and set out a couple sleeves of crackers and emptied a bag of chips into a bowl. I had French onion dip still in its plastic tub that I would add to the buffet when the guys showed up. Now, I know all about the domestic thing. I *could* have laid the cheese out in fancy little circles or put the chips and dip in one of those dishes with the separate compartment for the gooey stuff, but hey, this was just the guys. I was more or less one of them; I wasn't expected to be Martha Stewart, and in fact I think it might have creeped them out a bit if I behaved too much like a girl.

My front door opened and I heard a voice call out.

"Hey Rainie!"

"Hey Mason!" I yelled back, not bothering to go greet him. He knew his way around my house as well as I did. Most of my poker buddies had been Tommy's friends before the shocking announcement of his true sexual orientation. I suppose that in most cases male friends would stick with the husband in a divorce, but in this case the guys were a little freaked out. All the bawdy jokes they'd made all those years had taken on a new tone once they discovered Tommy preferred the company of men for more than having a few beers or playing poker. So I lucked out; I lost all my credit references, but I'd kept custody of our friends.

Mason came into the kitchen carrying a six pack of beer and a canvas grocery sack. The beer went in the fridge, minus one that he twisted the top off of. He pulled nacho chips and a small pan out of the sack.

"Nacho dip."

"Yum. Thank Pam for us."

Mason grinned, revealing teeth that would be perfect if not for one incisor that was nearly sideways. His wife was definitely domestic, and she was always sending some new snack she'd whipped up out of "whatever she had on hand." If this was true, she must have a pantry the size of an average grocery store, because her recipes always included exotic ingredients I'd never heard of.

"Where is everyone?" Mason leaned his tall but too-thin frame against the kitchen counter and took a long pull on his beer, eager to put the week behind him. He was a computer geek, his job involving software and hardware in combinations that meant nothing to me. He was pale from too much time spent in his home office, from which he performed his magic for a company based in Utah. The kitchen light reflected off his round, gold framed glasses, concealing intelligent brown eyes that reacted readily to a joke or tragic news, his emotions as easy to read as a newspaper headline.

"It seems everyone else is fashionably late." I took a chip and scooped up a small glob of the taco dip. Damn, I didn't know what all was in the slightly pink mixture, but there was definitely cream cheese involved. This was bad. I had a hard time resisting cream cheese, but if I ate it I might just as well take a block of it and tuck it into my jeans; it would end up on my hips one way or another. With a sigh I turned away from the yummy dip and snatched a carrot out of the fridge.

"Hey, are we playing poker or what?"

That would be Jeff. He joined us in the kitchen, tending to his own beer. Jeff was just about at the six foot mark, the shortest of the men in our group. Standing around with the guys was the only time I ever felt small; at five foot six, I was a full head shorter than any of them. We'd speculated on that fact in the past: did tall people automatically gravitate to other tall people? Did their higher perspective on the world change their perceptions so that they preferred the company of others with the same outlook? The conclusion had been that, if that were the case, then I was exempt because I was female and therefore my perceptions were so alien that the height factor was negated.

Jeff's hair, as usual, was an unruly blonde mop. But it suited his slightly rounded, open face. He'd spread a few inches across the middle, his "badge of contentment" according to him. His wife, Julie, was also a good cook. Sometimes I wondered if Mason and Jeff had married for love or domestic help.

Although none of our group was lacking intelligence, Jeff was our acknowledged resident genius, working a desk job while he completed his Masters degree in physics. No one quite knew what he intended to do with the degree when he got it, but we were somewhat awed by the prospect just the same.

He took a short sip of his beer. "So how are the book sales going?"

I believe I mentioned that I'm a poet. Of course, poets don't tend to get noticed these days like the Brownings or the Frosts, so we take work where we can get it. I've been known to write poems on bathroom walls, just so they get read, but that's not really the kind of publishing credit you can claim to a publisher. (Although on subsequent trips to the bathroom I often discover that many women, while perched to pee, can also multitask as critics.) So in order to actually get my stuff in print, I sometimes contribute to those sappy "I love you because..." books or "Mothers are wonderful," you know, the ones that people give to other people when they can't think of a *real* gift. I'd made the mistake of mentioning that some of my work would be featured in just such an upcoming tome, and for some reason Jeff kept bringing it up.

I shrugged and wrinkled my nose. "Oh, you know. A few sales here and there. It'll probably be a decent seller come Mother's Day."

"What's this one called?" Mason asked as if he was really interested.

"Notes to Mother."

"Hmm. Maybe I'll pick up a copy for my mom. It'll go nice with the flowers I usually get for her."

"Don't you think you should read it first, to be sure the sentiment fits?"

"I'm sure it will. Maybe there's something in there like: Roses are red, violets are blue, I love my mom, so I bought this book."

"Uh, dude," Jeff shook his head. "That doesn't even rhyme."

"That's because I'm not a big shot poet like Rainie is."

"I hate to tell you this, but most of my poetry doesn't rhyme either."

"Yeah, I know." Mason shook his head. "It's all metaphors and commentary on the human condition. Hell, I can't even figure out my own condition, yet alone the state of humankind."

"Speaking of kind of human, is Brad coming tonight?"

"Be nice, Jeff!" I laughed in spite of myself. Brad was my boyfriend, but not particularly popular with the guys. "And no, he's not coming."

"Of course he's not," Mason rolled his eyes. "He's much too busy selling McMansions and lake front vacation homes to hang out with the riffraff."

"Come on, that's not why he doesn't come."

"Sure it is, Rainie. He's always thought we were a bit beneath him, even back in high school."

"Then why do you suppose he hangs around me? I'm sure not from his side of the tracks."

"You have the advantage of being a pretty girl; that sort of thing can transcend financial barriers."

"Since when do you think I'm a pretty girl?"

Jeff grinned. "Hey, don't let it go to your head. I mean, you're not my type- I like leggy blondes. But I can see that Brad might find you kind of cute."

"Besides, dating you has got to really piss off his mom."

"Oh I see." I turned on Mason, hands on hips, giving him my best outraged glare. "So you think he's dating the town freak just to irritate his mother?"

"Being the offspring of hippies doesn't make you a freak; just a little weird."

"Now you think I'm weird?"

"*I* don't," Mason protested. "But the Murphy Matriarch probably thinks so."

"And so Brad dates me just to get under her skin."

"Nah, not really." Mason laughed. "I was just trying to get under yours."

Jeff apparently decided it was time for a change of subject. "Hey, did you hear the President's speech today? Damn, what a toad!"

That kicked them off. Our group was a mixture of republican, democrat, independent and who-gives-a-shit-they're-all-crooks. We rarely agreed on any matter of national policy, which meant any mention of one got us off to a rousing discussion. I was never sure if we remained friends because of or in spite of our differences.

I let them argue, busying myself at the kitchen sink, where there was nothing to be done. I knew Mason had been kidding, but I couldn't help but wonder if maybe he wasn't at least a little bit right. It was true, Brad's family was of the wealthy variety, and in high school he wouldn't have taken the time to piss on me if I were on fire. Was it possible I was just a tool intended to crack the seemingly unshakable pedestal on which his mother stood, ruling over the family with an iron hand?

Before I could go much further with that line of internal inquiry Riley ambled into the kitchen. Riley always ambled, or sauntered, or in some way took the best advantage of his long, lean limbs when he moved. Riley was a good looking guy, and he knew it. We often teased him about his arrogance, but he didn't mind at all. He admitted to it freely, and believed it was justified. It was difficult to fault him for it; he was charming and good looking, and underneath his arrogance he was warm and sensitive, a fact that I, being a girl, acknowledged. The guys just knew that they liked Riley, and that they could count on him in a pinch. Men tended to simplify things like that, which was one reason I got along so well with them. I might recognize sensitivity, but I didn't want to particularly belabor the issue.

Mason and Jeff got into an animated discussion of some new software that had been released among great fanfare. It was a program I had no interest in, and apparently it didn't intrigue Riley either, because he took a slight step away from them, toward me, and spoke in a serious tone, his voice low.

"Can I ask you something?"

"Sure, Riley. What's up?"

"You know, a guy needs to know he's got a couple of people he can really count on."

"Yeah, of course. Is something up?"

"Nah." Riley took a swallow of his beer. "I was just thinking, you know. It was one of those nights last night when I couldn't sleep, and I was just thinking."

It occurred to me that this was not Riley's first beer of the evening. His eyes were a bit glassy, and his words a little blurry. He only lived a few blocks away, and the weather was decent; I hoped he'd opted to walk over.

"And you came up with what?"

"Well, suppose someday I needed an alibi. You know, suppose I did something I thought was totally justified, but the law wouldn't see it that way. I'd need to have an alibi all ready and waiting, you know?"

"I never thought about it."

"Most people don't, but it's a good idea. So, I'm just wondering, should the cops ever come around asking about me, about a particular night, would you just tell them I was here? You know, playing cards."

I laughed, thinking Riley had to be messing with me.

"Hey, I'm serious. I need to know you'd do this."

Okay, this was weird. Riley was not a scary guy. He was straightforward, honest, and generally abhorred violence. What in the world could he be considering that he'd need an alibi?

"Uh, you got a plan here I should know about?"

"No! Nothing like that." Riley grinned. "It's just in case, you know. I mean, it might not come up for years, but if ever I just have to take action on something I want to know that's taken care of. So, will you do it?"

I realized he was completely serious. This was like someone asking you to be a godparent, but in the traditional sense, when you actually promise to raise their children in the event of their demise. This was *huge*. Nonetheless, I was still hoping it was just the alcohol talking, so I grinned and asked the obvious question.

"I don't know. I mean, do you have plans to kill someone?"

"Well I don't have any *plans*," he answered with a perfectly straight face. "But a person never knows when it might be necessary to take someone out."

"I suppose that's true." The smile on my face was flickering doubtfully, but I finally nodded. "All right, if the cops ever ask, you were with me."

He nodded in satisfaction. I thought I might have future reason to worry about that promise, but what the hell. Riley was my friend, and I trusted him completely. I doubted if he would take advantage and use me as an alibi for a random, unprovoked murder, so it was all good.

Mason and Jeff finished their impromptu software consultation and Jeff went to the fridge for another beer.

"How about we play a couple rounds of five card draw to get warmed up while we wait for Eddie?"

We all agreed that sounded good, so we headed for the dining room. I had a ceiling fan complete with light kit hung over the table for good lighting and air recirculation, although the fan wasn't as necessary as it had once been now that several of us had quit smoking and the remaining holdouts now smoked only outside. Sometimes I hated this new century with its emphasis on health. No smoking, no fats, no white bread, no tap water. Sometimes I wondered how earlier generations had ever survived to breed the next one.

We played a couple of hands and I won a couple bucks, but then lost half of that in the next hand. We were dealing out another round when Eddie showed up. He stopped at the archway to the dining room on his way to the kitchen to say hello.

"Hi Eddie!" I was happy to see him, and I think Eddie was pleased to see us, but it was a little hard to tell these days. Eddie was the only member of the group that I had been friends with pre-Tommy. We lived in a small town, so Eddie, Jeff, Tommy and I had all gone to school together, but back then Jeff moved in different circles.

Eddie had been the class clown back in our high school days, finding humor in situations both tragic and comic. His family had been, to be politically correct, "under-privileged." His lack of opportunities had led him to join the army the same month he turned eighteen, and after a brief stint the army, in its infinite wisdom, apparently saw something in Eddie we'd never discerned, and recruited him for Special Forces. By the time they sent him back to us Eddie was a changed man.

The changes weren't just physical, although there were plenty of those. He'd gone from an average built teenager to a lean, hard bodied man, all his baby fat chiseled away in favor of muscle, and his once long locks had been shorn to a recruit's buzz that he still maintained, even four years out of the service. But the real change was far more dramatic and troubling than a few muscles and a new hairdo. Eddie still joked around, but his humor was darker, often sarcastic bordering on cynical. And although he still had his big goofy Eddie smile that split the bottom half of his face with seemingly whole-hearted good humor, that smile rarely reached his eyes. They remained dark and sorrow-filled, as if he was constantly watching some internal movie filled with horrors beyond my comprehension. That was bad enough, but now and then there was a spark of something that closely resembled bitterness, maybe even rage. It was a spooky contrast, and sometimes I worried about Eddie, but I loved him just the same.

"Hey, I brought Jack along, is that okay?"

"Sure!" I answered with enthusiasm. It was actually more than okay, it was *fine*. *Jack* was fine. He had been in the Special Forces with Eddie, and now they worked together at B&E, a security company based in Niles. Eddie told me the owners set up shop there because the rent was cheap, but it was just a couple hours from Chicago, where their biggest clients came from. They provided everything from private investigator services to body guards, and let me tell you, Jack could guard my body any time- although, to be honest, Jack also scared me just a little bit. For one thing, there was his name: Jack Jones. I mean, really, is there a more obvious fake name out there? I asked Eddie once if Jack was on the lam, but he had only laughed.

"Come on, Rainie, does Jack look dumb to you? If he were hiding from something would he pick a stupid alias like that? Obviously it's his real name."

He was taller than Eddie, maybe 6'2", and like Eddie there wasn't an ounce of fat on his tightly muscled, lean frame. He could amble or saunter even better than Riley, but his best moves made him look like a sleek jungle cat weaving through the underbrush, slick enough to never disturb a single leaf. He had dark brown, almost black eyes and always looked as though his tan came fresh from a Miami beach, even in the chill of a Southern Michigan winter. A critical person might point out that he kept his hair buzzed short to conceal that it was thinning on top, but the truth is some men simply didn't need hair. Jack was one of those men; I would cheerfully run my fingers over that bald spot and consider myself one lucky girl.

"Hey." Jack stepped in behind Eddie, and I felt a little piece of my tummy melt down to a spot somewhere between my legs.

"Hi Jack." I think I managed to sound casual, and I doubted if anyone knew I was having my own private sexual experience right there at the table.

Eddie moved on to the kitchen with his six pack of beer, which I knew he'd only drink two or three of; he took his physical condition seriously. Jack took a seat at the table, a bottle of water in his hand. I had never seen Jack drink. I don't think it was just a matter of physical health, but a matter of keeping all his senses alert at every minute. I wondered how he ever managed to sleep. I suspected he did it with his eyes half open, always watching for a sneak attack. The thought of him sleeping brought to mind an image of him in bed, and I almost gasped aloud at the rush I felt. I shut the thought out and reached for my cards. What the hell was the matter with me? I had a boyfriend; I wasn't supposed to be having these thoughts about another man, was I? It must be hormonal.

The doorbell rang, and for the briefest moment I was actually puzzled. Who would bother to ring the bell on poker night? Besides, everyone was already here.

I went to answer it, hoping it wasn't Jehovah's Witnesses or some other bible thumping do-gooder. I could slam a door in their faces with the best of them, but they always left me with a sour taste in my mouth just the same, as if I'd actually tasted their sanctimonious ignorance.

"Brad!" I opened the door, genuinely surprised to see him. "What are you doing here?"

"Isn't it poker night?"

"Well yeah, why?"

He frowned. "You told me I'm always welcome to join you. Is the invitation still valid?"

"Well, um, sure." I finally stepped back from the door. "Come on in."

"You're sure I'm not intruding?"

"Of course not, I'm just surprised is all."

Brad kissed me on the cheek and handed me a chilled bottle of wine. "I brought refreshments."

"Sure." I looked at the bottle dubiously. "Usually we just drink beer."

"Oh sure." Brad shrugged like he played low-ante poker every night. "You can put that away for another occasion."

I led the way back to the dining room. "Hey, look who's here!"

"Hey, Brad!" Most of the guys greeted him cheerily enough. If the smiles were false and masking grimaces of distaste they weren't obvious about it.

Brad grabbed an extra chair from against the wall and put it next to mine.

Eddie came back in and dropped into a chair, looking at me with his sad eyes. "I heard about Max. You doing okay?"

I didn't ask how he knew so quickly. As I mentioned, we live in a small town. You could play the Kevin Bacon game with anyone in Buchanan and find a connection to any other resident with maybe three degrees of separation.

I shrugged and nodded. Max had been cranky, but even so somewhat endearing in his own confused, crotchety old man way. I'd only been taking care of him for a couple of months, so losing him wasn't quite as devastating as some had been. Nonetheless, his absence left a little hole in my heart- and, to be honest, in my paychecks. I chose to leave the emotional part out of my reply to Eddie. He seemed to have enough loss in his memory to last any four people a lifetime. Instead I mentioned the financial part, keeping my tone light.

"I'll miss the old dude, but my biggest concern right now is paying my mortgage. He was a twenty hour a week client, and I don't have any good prospects right now."

"That's the problem with your chosen career. You can't live paycheck to paycheck when you never know when someone's going to die on you."

I wanted to be irritated at Eddie's callousness, but he said it in such a matter of fact tone, and the truth was, he was right.

"There's not much I can do about that."

"You could get something steadier. You know, something that doesn't involve clients with one foot in the grave and the other on a banana peel."

I looked at Jack, surprised by this corny old cliché coming from his oh-so-sensual mouth. He was watching me, his expression neutral, as if he'd not intended to be funny at all. Maybe he hadn't been.

"True, but I hate factory work and supermodels have to travel too much."

"That does limit your choices," he agreed with the slightest hint of a smile. "Maybe you should think about a job with B&E."

I looked at Jack, sweeping my eyes across his broad shoulders, and then cut a glance toward Eddie and his lethal-weapon body. I then pointedly looked down at my own less-than-athletic frame. "You think I can be a body guard?"

"Probably, if you put your mind to it," Jack answered with all seriousness. "But I had in mind you might start out a little slower. Say, as an investigative assistant to one of our P.I.s."

"That's ridiculous!" Brad protested. "Rainie is hardly cut out to be a private investigator!"

"No, wait, that's not a bad idea." Eddie had been looking at Jack like he'd taken leave of his senses in a big way, but now he was nodding enthusiastically. "It's not a bad job. You'd be mostly helping out with background checks. You just run a few computer checks, do a few interviews, find out if a person has any skeletons in their closets."

"Isn't that a P.I.'s job?"

"Yeah, but you have to be licensed to actually be a P.I., and to get a license you have to have at least three years experience or a college degree."

"So I do their job for less pay."

Jack grinned. "Hey, it's the way of the world, babe. Shit rolls downhill, so you either need a big shovel or a sturdy ladder to get to the top."

"Besides, the job isn't all that hard." Eddie jumped back in. " Like I said, it's mostly background checks, maybe running down a dead beat dad or two, but you'd just be doing the preliminary stuff. The down and dirty work gets handled by a regular P.I. And the pay is the same as you get for your old people- fifteen bucks an hour."

I winced at the "old people" thing, but didn't correct him.

"Yeah?" I was a little intrigued. It would be different, and I'd been feeling a bit restless lately. "I wouldn't want to give up my clients though," I said doubtfully. "Especially Thelma."

"No problem," Eddie assured me. "You can pretty much make your own hours. They have lots of part timers."

"Hmm, that might not be bad. I could maybe work two or three days a week, have some steady money coming in."

"Rainie, you're not actually considering this, are you?" Brad sounded outraged.

"Why not?" I shrugged. "It sounds interesting."

34

"Come on by the office Monday morning. I'll introduce you to Harry Baker." Now that the idea was out there, Eddie was making it his own. It didn't surprise me that he was ignoring Brad's protests; he made no secret of his dislike. Eddie had always been somewhat protective of me, more so than my own brother, who had problems enough of his own without worrying about me.

Regardless, none of that mattered. What mattered was that I had a job prospect, and with any luck I'd collect a paycheck before my mortgage was in serious arrears.

Cheered by the thought, I bet a buck on a pair of nines and we got down to some serious poker.

Chapter Three

On Monday I went straight from Mabel's to B&E. Harry Baker, The "B" of B&E, was ex-military and all business. He was in his fifties, and in spite of his well-tailored suit looked fit enough – and tough enough – to take on a small platoon single-handed.

He hired me after the briefest interview I'd ever been subjected to, taking Eddie's word for my character. He turned me over to Belinda, who promptly pulled out a pile of paperwork for me to fill out.

Belinda was an attractive woman, her makeup well done and understated, her business suit well cut and professional looking but unable to hide her inborn sex appeal. She was tall - nearly six feet in heels - and while certainly not fat, no one would ever describe her as a waif. She had red hair that likely came from a bottle - highlights and all - that she piled high on her head, as if trying to make a point of her height. I wondered if she had spent her high school years trying to pretend she was shorter than all the guys, and finally at some point gave it up and went all out with the tall thing.

Belinda had at one time done the same job I'd just been hired for - background checks. She had worked at it full time for nearly ten years before getting burned out and turning in her resignation. Mr. Baker, it seemed, didn't want her to go, so he'd hired her as his assistant and all-around office person.

"I've been doing this for two years and I'm still not really sure what my job description is," Belinda admitted with a laugh. "I answer the phones when the receptionist goes on break, I do a little filing, I handle the paperwork for new hires and more or less train them, and pretty much do whatever else Mr. Baker asks me to do." She laughed. "Of course, I mean office related things; there's nothing off about it, you know?"

I smiled and nodded. I didn't care if she was sleeping with the boss, but somehow I couldn't see it. Any woman who could wear those heals and that hairstyle had to have a strong sense of self, and I couldn't see her debasing herself for any man.

This is when I discovered that even a great reference would only take me so far; first off, I had to sign papers authorizing a complete background check. I hesitated only a moment. There were some things in my past I'd rather not have brought to light, but nothing that should make me ineligible for the job. I only hoped whoever dug around in my past would be discreet.

The paperwork finished, I was done and out the door. There wouldn't even be a tour until my background check cleared. Free for the day, I stopped at the grocery store and did a quick run through the deli and produce department and headed for home.

Home is the cute little two bedroom house Tommy and I had picked out together. The front porch is wide and covered, perfect for watching thunderstorms roll in. The front door opens directly into a modestly furnished living room. One door leads to the kitchen; an archway gave way to the dining room. On the other side a short hallway accesses the two bedrooms, one of which was a seldom used office furnished with a tiny desk and a futon, and the bathroom. There's another bathroom off the "master" bedroom; Tommy had remodeled a spacious walk in closet while he was still in residence. The house is only blocks away from the house I grew up in, the house where my mother and her long-time boyfriend, my sister and her daughter still lived. In spite of that proximity to a lot of memories I'd just as soon forget, I liked the area. It would have been a nice place to raise children, if one were so inclined.

I parked in the driveway and came in through the back door, first into a small back porch sometimes known as a "mud room," then through another door into the kitchen. I called hello to George and stopped to put the groceries away. I pulled out a bowl of veggies and another of fruit, already cut up into bite sized pieces, and filled a bowl for George.

"Hey buddy, you ready to stretch?" George, being an iguana and therefore incapable of speech, didn't answer, but he climbed on to the top branch, anticipating my next move.

I put the bowl up on the shelf over his cage and opened the top so he could climb out.

Eddie had once raised the suspicion that George was the reason I didn't have any girlfriends. Well, not the iguana itself, you understand, but the mere fact that I preferred a cold-blooded, prehistoric looking reptile to a cuddly puppy. The truth is, I like dogs - love them in fact - but no dog would tolerate my crazed schedule, with me coming and going at all hours of the day and night. George would simply wait patiently in his cage with his pelleted iguana food and wait for me to get there with the good stuff and to let him out on his shelf. What would a dog do, cross its little canine legs until I got home to take it outside?

I spent the rest of the day cleaning house and catching up on my laundry. Monday had been one of my days with Max. I found myself thinking of him frequently, and a quiet melancholy overtook me as the day wore on. It was funny how attached I tended to get to even the most difficult of my clients. Maybe it was just that I understood their sometimes rude, even mean behavior was an outlet for their frustration. I sure wouldn't want to be dependent on someone else for the most basic needs of life. I doubted I would keep my patience long if I had to rely on someone else to take me to the bathroom or to wash my hair. After eight or nine decades of life, most of them spent working just like me or the next guy, it seemed that there should be a more dignified downward spiral into death.

By six o'clock my house was spotless and my laundry hamper empty. I grabbed a bowl of high fiber cereal for dinner and sat down on the couch to eat it while watching *Jeopardy*. Cereal was a common meal for me. I kept a half dozen varieties in the cupboard, only one of them an overly sugared brand, and I selected a different one depending on my mood. For even more variety, I would sometimes slice fruit into the cereal, or just munch an apple with it. This is the sort of thing that happened to single people: cooking for one, and worse, cleaning up after one, was just too much work to be worth the effort. With my abbreviated menu, a quick rinse of the bowl and spoon and into the dishwasher was all that was required to put my kitchen back in order.

Besides, the cereal diet seemed to be helping me keep the pounds off, and that was one fight where I needed all the help I could get.

Long before Tommy came forward about his true sexual orientation, our sex life hit the skids and never recovered. Our sex life was never all that great, but to tell you the truth I'd never had great sex, and in spite of the movies and magazines telling me that I should *demand* the orgasm which I was *owed*, I never worried a lot about it.

But when the sex stopped altogether, I guess I did miss it. Not consciously, you understand, but without realizing it I started substituting the orgiastic experience of premium ice cream and expensive boxed chocolates for bedroom intimacy. Although now and then the time I spent in my darkened living room with a bag of chips and a bucket of dip, topped off with an icy cold Dr Pepper and followed by a pint of Ben & Jerry's felt a bit intimate. The nice thing about substituting food for sex is that you don't need to shower afterwards, and potato chips never snore or take all the covers afterwards.

Nonetheless, my decadence of choice caused me to blow up to a whopping 225 pounds, a fact Tommy was kind enough to never point out.

The day the divorce was finalized I joined a gym, and cussing and swearing all the way I knocked myself back down to 140 pounds. I am content here. I will tolerate 143 with water weight gain, and I am ecstatic on those rare occasions when the little needle on my scale stops jiggling at 138. Even better, as long as I walk every day and hit the gym at least twice a week, the cellulite on my thighs doesn't jiggle, either.

I was half way through my cereal when my phone rang. The answering machine was on a little table by the front door; I decided to let it pick it up. In spite of registering on the "no-call" list, I still got more than my share of phone solicitations. I know those people just needed a job, but that still didn't give them a right to intrude on my dinner; I was rarely civil to them.

The machine picked up, and I heard myself say in my perkiest tone: "Hey! Leave a message!" There was the usual beep, then an explosion of noise out of the tiny little speaker: loud music, many loud voices, then one voice, clearer, shouting to be heard over the noise. "This is Bob, the bartender at Larry's. Your brother is here, and I really think someone ought to come and get him."

With a sigh I set my cereal aside and hurried to the phone, snatching it up before Bob ended the call and instead dialed the cops.

"I'm here, Bob. What's up?"

"We've got a new bartender, and she's been serving your brother shots at a steady clip since 3:00."

"Oh boy."

"Oh boy, yeah right. Listen, can you come get him?"

"Sure, I'll be right there. Oh, and thanks Bob. I appreciate you calling."

"No problem. I like your brother when he's sober or just beer drunk. But get him on the hard stuff..."

"Yeah, I know. I'll be there shortly."

I hung up and grabbed my keys off the table just inside the door. I didn't bother with shoes; I had a pair of sandals in the car.

My brother wasn't a drunk. He was a smart, hardworking man and a good father to his two kids, but he had a tendency to get restless and bored and then he would do things like this. My mom thought his soul was in search of something it was missing, something as essential to his spiritual self as his beating heart was to his physical self. Whatever, I would leave the search for his soul to my mother. I was only concerned with getting his physical self home in one piece.

I parked a couple of doors down from the bar. There were plenty of available spaces on a Monday night. Besides the bar, there was an art gallery featuring local talent, a small corner diner that only served the breakfast and lunch crowd, and two empty store fronts.

I hurried into the bar to find Bob, the bartender, trying to hold my brother in place on a bar stool, with little success.

"I gotta go," my brother slurred. "Gotta go to a *party*, where things are *happenin'*."

"Just hang on, Jason. Your sister's coming, she'll take you to the party."

"My sister? Rainie's coming?"

"Rainie's here." I moved over to Jason's other side and slipped his arm over my shoulder. "Come on, Jason, let's go." I gave him a slight tug to get him on his feet.

"Rainie!" Jason pulled his other arm away from the bartender and threw it around me in drunken glee. "S'good to see ya."

I grunted with effort as his weight fell against me. Bob backed away, done with drunk duty, happy to leave it to me.

I grabbed Jason's hand to keep it over my shoulder and started for the door. We made about five steps before Jason suddenly stopped.

"Whoa, there, where'r we goin'?"

"Someplace else," I answered vaguely, knowing that when he was this drunk he had no interest in going home.

"To a party?"

"Sure."

"Oh boy!" Jason took a drunken spin away from me, eager to get to the party, and promptly fell over his own feet, crashing to the scuffed, beer-stained wooden floor.

"Oops!' He lay there, unhurt, giggling like a drunken schoolgirl - or at least, the way I assumed a drunken schoolgirl would giggle. I'd never actually seen one, though I admit I'd probably been one. But that's an issue for another day. I stared down at Jason, my hands on my hips, wondering how the hell I was going to get him back on his feet. He wasn't a particularly big guy, maybe five ten, 190 pounds. Big enough that I couldn't dead lift him, that's for sure. With a sigh, I reached down and grabbed one limp arm and gave a good tug.

"Come on, Jason, you've got to get up."

"Sure, sure...jus' a min..." he tried valiantly to get to his feet, but managed only to fall back on his butt, laughing hysterically.

"Hey, Bob..."

"Yeah, yeah." Irritated that his duty to the drunk was not yet done, Bob came and grabbed an arm, and together we heaved my brother off the floor. I once again slung Jason's arm over my shoulder and managed to maneuver him out the door.

We made it almost half way to the car before Jason toppled again, this time onto unforgiving pavement, but whatever saint it was that was supposed to watch out for drunks and fools must have been paying attention, because Jason seemed none the worse for the fall. He lay on his back, laughing.

"Whoo! There I go again." He struggled to sit up, and I knelt down to grab hold of him again. When I did, he threw an arm around my shoulders, and as abruptly as a faucet turning on, he was bawling like a baby.

"I'm sorry, Sis!" He sobbed into my shoulder, his tone truly remorseful. "I don' mean to get like this. Poor Raini, havin' to come get me...what kinda big brother has to have his kid sister take care of him?"

"It's okay. You'd do the same for me."

"Yeah, 'cept you're not this dumb. You don' do things like this...I'm such a loser."

"Come on, let's go home. We'll talk about this later."

"Don' wanna go home!"

Suddenly a pair of white gym shoes topped by a pair of tight jeans came into my view. My eyes traveled quickly up over a gym-sculpted body and looked straight into the oh-so-blue, smiling eyes of Tommy, my ex-husband.

"You need some help?" He didn't wait for an answer, but bent down and slung my brother's free arm over his broad shoulders. He lifted him to his feet with only a slight grunt of effort. "Where's your car?"

Too surprised by his unexpected but fortuitous arrival to say anything, I pointed dumbly towards my weather-beaten Escort. Tommy swung Jason around in the right direction and headed that way.

"Hey, I know you!" Jason seemed amazed by Tommy's presence. "I really liked you. Why'd ya haf to go and hurt my sis like that?"

I moved ahead of them and opened the car door, still too surprised to say anything. Other than brief glimpses on the street, I hadn't seen Tommy since the day our divorce was finalized three years before. He still looked good; better, in fact. He had obviously upped his gym workouts, although he'd avoided the 'roid plumped, over-inflated musculature of the true fanatic. His hair was a little longer, and he no longer wore the mustache that he'd so carefully trimmed every morning of our married life. Otherwise, he looked like the same old Tommy I'd been so damned fond of, right until the day he announced that he was gay, that he was so sorry he'd tried to fool me along with himself, and that he was moving out.

Tommy deposited Jason into the front seat and buckled him in. Jason laid his head back against the seat and promptly started snoring.

"Are you taking him to his place?" Tommy asked as he shut the car door.

"Yeah."

"He still live over on Third?"

"Uh huh." That's me, always a great conversationalist in awkward situations.

"Okay, I'll meet you over there."

"What?"

"I'll come over and help you get him into the house."

"You don't have to do that."

"But I want to. How are you going to get him up those stairs by yourself?"

That was a good question. Unable to come up with a good answer to match it, I just shrugged.

"So, I'll meet you there." Tommy turned and walked away to his own car, confident that the matter was settled. I could think of no good reason to argue, other than the fact that he'd broken my heart and left me crushed and vulnerable, believing that I was inadequate to the task of keeping a man interested enough to hang around, or even remain heterosexual.

But that had been three years ago. Since then, I've come to accept the fact that it wasn't my failure; actually, it wasn't anyone's. I happen to believe that a person is born gay, that it is a genetic thing, not a lifestyle choice. Tommy had lived in denial for years, and I was quite sure it hadn't been easy for him to come out. He'd lost all his friends, and at least for a while, his family, who had been adamantly opposed to his announcement - as if he'd decided to join the PLO or some such thing, and could be talked out of it if only he was willing to see reason.

I got into my car and made my way the few short blocks to my brother's apartment. At least he had the sense to drink locally. He had probably walked to the bar, knowing in his still sober state that he would be in no condition to drive home later.

As I drove, my brother's soft snoring and the whine of the Escort's little engine the only background noise, I thought some more about Tommy.

He'd tried to make things right with me. He had left me everything: the house, the furniture, even the Escort, which had been in better condition back then. He had even helped make the mortgage payments for the first year, knowing that it would take some doing on my part to survive on one income. Every month for a year a check would arrive in the mail, with no note until the eleventh one. That one had a brief explanation, in Tommy's small, neat handwriting, that he was buying another house, and there would be only one more check coming.

No doubt, Tommy had been more than generous about the whole thing.

I pulled up in front of the house where my brother rented a second floor apartment. There was an open staircase on the side leading up to his door. The steps were steep and creaked ominously, but so far no one had fallen through them.

Tommy pulled in behind me by the time I'd moved around and opened the passenger side door. Jason woke up and squinted drunkenly at us. "You're Tommy, right?"

"Yep, that's me." He helped Jason out of the car and moved toward the house.

"You goin' to the party, too?"

"Sure." Tommy grinned as he guided my brother to the stairs.

"Gonna be like old times!" My brother declared this with a wide grin. He really had liked Tommy, although he'd been a bit freaked out when he'd first heard that he was - as Jason put it - "light in the loafers."

"That's right, buddy, just like old times." Tommy got Jason up the stairs, and after some confusion Jason produced his keys and I unlocked the door. Tommy half-carried Jason into the bedroom and settled him on the bed. I pulled off his shoes and we pushed him onto his side. I put a pillow against his back: the standard recovery position, in case he threw up in his sleep, he wouldn't choke. By the time I threw a quilt over him he was softly snoring again.

We left him to sleep it off in peace. I left his keys on the kitchen table and locked the door behind me on the way out. Tommy followed me silently to the car. Just as I was opening the door, he spoke up.

"So, Rainie, how have you been?"

"Okay," I answered automatically. "How about you?"

"Pretty good." He swallowed and stared hard at the street, suddenly shy. "I've missed you though."

"What?" I frowned. That was the last thing I expected to hear.

"Well, you know...I mean the marriage thing was obviously not so good, but..." He trailed off and now stared down the street, as if the right words would come driving out of the dark, headlights blazing. "We were good together. I mean, as friends."

I considered that statement in silence. It was true, we had a lot in common. We liked the same books, the same foods, picnics and blues festivals, the same movies. In fact, I'd all but given up one of my favorite things, watching action-adventure movies, the kind where the hero pulls off outrageously impossible stunts, over and over again. I was a junky when it came to James Bond, Indiana Jones, and more recently, the *Transporter* movies. But they didn't have the same fun-filled appeal that they'd had when I watched them with Tommy. None of my friends had the same appreciation for the sheer enjoyment of the ridiculous.

Tommy wasn't sure how to take my silence, so he blundered on.

"Look, I know I hurt you. I'm really sorry. But I really miss you."

"You do?"

"Yeah. You know, I watched those movies, the *Transporter*? They were great, but the whole time, I kept thinking how much more fun it would be to watch them with you."

I couldn't help a small smile. We had often had the same thoughts back when we were married, a closeness usually shared by twins or those who had been wed for fifty-plus years.

"That Jason Statham is pretty hot." The comment popped out of my mouth without planning. Tommy grinned.

"You got *that* right."

I couldn't help but laugh. Here was yet another thing Tommy and I had in common: our taste in men.

"So, I was thinking, maybe I could call you some time? We could go out for coffee, or a beer, or...whatever. Just hang out for a while."

Now it was my turn to stare off down the road. Hang out with my ex-husband? Wasn't that a little weird? And had I forgiven him? Could I really just be friends with the man who had shared my bed for five long years? Who had made me the subject of much tsking and whispered gossip, the poor little thing who hadn't *known* her own husband's true nature?

Then again, what harm was there in a cup of coffee? I did miss Tommy, so why the hell not give it a try?

"Okay, sure. Why not?"

Tommy broke into a wide grin. "Hey, that's great. Really. So I'll call you then, in a couple of days?"

"Okay." I nodded and grinned back.

"This is great." Tommy was grinning so wide it seemed his face might split. He backed away, moving towards his car, half-laughing, shaking his head, as if he'd just been told he'd won the lottery and couldn't quite believe it. "This is so awesome." He laughed again and then turned and jogged towards his car. I couldn't believe how happy he'd seemed.

I got into my own car, feeling pretty good myself.

Chapter Four

Bright and early on Tuesday morning I headed for Thelma's.

Thelma had been a steady client for two years, although to tell you the truth she needed a caregiver less than I did.

She had read my ad in the paper, and called out of curiosity. She couldn't understand why someone had to hire a companion. Were these people such losers they couldn't make friends of their own?

I arrived at her house, a rambling old Victorian structure on a block that had been designated historical but which was, in spite of the efforts of the Historical Society, going downhill rapidly. She greeted me at the door wearing jeans and a faded Aerosmith T-shirt, five foot four inches and 120 pounds of teenager packed into a 74 year old body.

I hid my astonishment and followed her into the parlor, where she served tea from a delicate antique tea set and offered me tiny cookies from a matching plate. The elegance of the room and the serving set were a sharp contrast to Thelma in all her denim glory.

She grilled me sharply on just what duties I could perform if she hired me. I explained that I could run errands for her, take her to doctor's appointments or wherever she needed to go, fix meals for her and do light housekeeping.

She listened carefully, and then shook her head. "I have a chauffeur; haven't driven a car in years. I also have a girl that comes in and cleans twice a week, and I can do my own damned cooking. What else you got?"

"I'm afraid there's not much else. I guess my services aren't what you require right now."

I stood to go, but she waved me back to my seat.

"Oh, sit down, don't go yet. What about the "companion" part. Can you keep me company?"

"Well sure, I mean...well, being a companion is just sort of a sideline to my real work. I mean, obviously I'm keeping someone company when I drive them around or whatever."

"So, keep me company." Thelma offered me another cookie. "I'm kind of bored today."

I shrugged and settled back. I didn't have any other plans for that day, and besides, I kind of liked Thelma, even if it was clear this interview wasn't going to end up with me being hired.

We chatted for a while, at first about general topics, but then Thelma got going on religion, and that's when we hit it off.

Thelma had been raised Baptist, but over the years she'd seen too many examples of the Jim and Tammy Baker variety, and her views had turned outrageously cynical. Since I shared much of the same opinion, believing religion to just be a legally and socially acceptable mass scam, we were able to tear into the subject with relish.

Religion led us to politics, which somehow led us to music (Thelma listened to everything from Aerosmith to Glen Miller, depending on her mood) and before I knew it two hours had passed.

Thelma cleared the tea away and looked at her watch. "Well dear, that's two hours you've worked for me. Let's see, you charge fifteen dollars an hour so..."

"No, wait!" I stood, appalled that she wanted to pay me for simply passing a lonely morning with her. "I wasn't working, we were just chatting!"

"Yes, exactly, and a grand time I had!" Thelma was grinning, her eyes sparkling and so lively that her clothing seemed quite appropriate. "This is a real kick, hiring a friend. I never thought I'd see the day!" She pulled a wad of money out of the front pocket of her jeans and peeled off a fifty. "I don't have anything smaller, so I guess you'll have to owe me an hour. Consider the other five a bonus for a job well done. When can you come again?"

"Well I don't know," I hesitated, looking at the fifty in my hand. "I mean, there's usually paperwork to sign, and I'm not usually paid in cash..."

"What, you want to let the government in on this deal? What are you, a closet conservative? You sounded pretty liberal, even independent when we were talking, but maybe you're hiding some Republican tendencies. If you are, you'd better let me know now. It might not be a deal breaker, but I have a right to know up front."

"No! I'm not a Republican!" In fact, I was mortally offended by the suggestion. "But I do tend to be law abiding."

"Law abiding! You know what laws are for? They're for controlling the population; the only ones who benefit from laws are the lawyers and the government. Especially when it comes to paying taxes. Why do you want to give your hard earned money to some bureaucrat so he can line his silk pockets?"

I could see her point, but then again I did think I benefited from *some* laws. I mean, it was kind of nice that the annoyed clerk in the store wasn't legally allowed to hit me over the head with the pair of shoes I was trying to return or just pull out a gun and shoot me if she was having a bad day. Not that that sort of thing didn't still happen, but the laws at least served as some deterrent.

The taxes though. Hmm. I did already pay an awful lot of those.

Thelma read my hesitation and grinned again, shoving the wad of money back in her pocket. "All right then, I guess we have a deal. What days are you available?"

"I have Tuesdays and Thursdays open completely, and half days on Fridays."

"I think two days will be enough." Thelma nodded in satisfaction. "Let's make it easy. How about 8 to 4?"

"Okay." I still wasn't sure what my job was going to be, but what the heck? I liked Thelma, and I did need to fill in those days.

That was two years ago. Since then I've learned a lot about Thelma: she outlived three brothers, two husbands and one daughter who had produced no grandchildren. She had a niece who lived in Florida and called on Christmas - according to Thelma, just to remind her that she did still have one living heir.

"Actually she called me on my birthday the last two years, too. After all, my family isn't known for its longevity. I think she's hoping I'm getting to the last of my birthdays."

"Oh Thelma, surely not!"

She laughed at my outrage. "Honey, I might not dress rich or live in a mansion, but that doesn't mean I don't have money! I've got lots of it, more than I'd be able to spend if I lived the next ten years on life support in the Mayo Clinic! Believe me, Candy is hoping I kick off early enough to leave her middle age on easy street."

"You look plenty healthy enough to me," I assured her, and I wasn't lying to make her feel better. In some ways I think Thelma was in better physical shape than I was. I could barely keep up when we went for a walk. "I think Candy better be making more tangible plans for her future."

"Nice to think so," Thelma nodded. "But you know, my brother was still running his farm at the age of seventy one, getting out on the tractor at the crack of dawn every morning, cutting and hauling his own wood, as strong as the horses he kept. Then one night he went to bed and whammo. Heart attack. Never woke up so far as we could tell. So don't be renting any halls for my 75th birthday; probably wouldn't get your deposit back."

I never knew what to say when Thelma said things like that. She talked about dying as casually as I talked about lunch. In fact, with less passion than I used ordering a cheeseburger and fries, and with a lot less trepidation.

I walked in without knocking and called out to let Thelma know I'd arrived. I heard a muffled answer from the back of the house.

"In the kitchen!" This was followed by a string of four letter words and a loud clank.

"Are you all right?" I hurried through the entryway and down the long hall to the heavy walnut door and pushed through it to the old fashioned but well-kept kitchen. No Thelma.

Then I saw a pair of denim-clad legs sticking out from under the kitchen sink.

"Thelma?"

"Clogged pipe." The two word explanation was followed by another clank and an inventive sentence that called into question the parentage of the pipes she was obviously struggling with.

"Can I help?"

"Almost...got...ouch!" Thelma cussed again, and then there was mostly silence, punctuated by a grunt or two. I waited quietly. I'd made the offer to help; if she needed me, she would let me know.

Finally she squirmed out from under the cabinet, her hair awry and her face smudged with something sticky and dark, but her expression clearly satisfied.

"There, that's got it."

"You say it was clogged?"

"Yeah, that damned elbow joint. I don't hold with chemicals, so the easiest way is just to take it off and flush it out."

"That's the easy way?" I grinned and held out a hand to pull her to her feet. As always I was surprised by the strength in her aged hand.

"Maybe not so easy as it was a few years ago," she admitted.

"You could call a plumber."

"What, and wait around for two days without being able to use the sink?"

"I suppose you're right, that's a handy skill to have."

"You want to learn how?"

"Sure."

"Well, come on down!" Thelma squatted and waved for me to join her on the floor.

"Now?"

"Honey, at my age now might be all I've got. We'd better not waste it."

As always unable to refute that logic, I joined her on the floor and got my first plumbing lesson.

Thelma and I sat down to chicken salad sandwiches at noon. We took them out to the back porch, a lovely old wrap-around structure obscured by thick ivy.

"Do you remember me mentioning Tommy?" I asked Thelma.

"Remember? I couldn't forget if I was in the last stages of Alzheimer's. You talk about him all the time."

"I do?"

"Sure. 'Tommy used to like this,' and 'Tommy said that.' I almost feel like I know the guy."

"Huh." I thought about that for a minute. I hadn't known I still thought about him that much, much less talked about him.

"So what about him?" Thelma prompted.

"I ran into him the other night, and he called me yesterday. He wants to meet for coffee tonight."

"Yeah? That's cool."

"You think so?"

"Are you looking for approval?"

"Not exactly." Though I thought maybe I was. "It's just...well, you don't think people will think it's too weird, me hanging out with my ex-husband?"

Thelma shook her head. "What people? Look girl, as I'm always trying to remind you, we have a finite number of years on this planet. At the end of them, who do you want to have pleased? Your neighbors? Or yourself?"

"Well, I don't care much about my neighbors..."

"You shouldn't care what anyone thinks, as long as you're not out to deliberately hurt them. You need to live your life as if it matters to you, or else it won't."

Wow. That was kind of profound. We sat in silence for a few minutes while I absorbed that bit of wisdom.

"So are you going to meet him?"

"Yeah, I guess. We're supposed to meet at Borders at four-thirty."

"Nice neutral place." Thelma nodded approval. "I'm real happy to hear that. You have a good time."

I smiled, thinking of Tommy's eagerness to rekindle our friendship. "I think I will."

And I did.

It was only awkward for the first few minutes, while we ordered coffee and decided where to sit. Then there were a few moments of "well," and "So, how have you been?" before the conversation really took off. From then on, it was as if the bad times, when the marriage was coming apart and there was nothing but hurt between us, just fell away. I found myself laughing and teasing Tommy with the same old ease we'd enjoyed in our happy years. In fact, it seemed somehow better, as if that painful secret he'd held had somehow been a shadowy presence that we'd felt but not acknowledged.

Tommy had blossomed in the light once he'd come out of the closet. His sense of humor allowed him to acknowledge the stigma of being gay without letting it mark him like an ugly brand.

I went up for a second cup of coffee, reluctant to end the encounter.

"Interesting date."

I turned at the familiar voice. I knew who it was before I saw his face; I could tell by the flash of heat in my belly.

"Hey, Jack."

His smile was slow and crooked. He flicked a glance back toward the table where Tommy sat waiting.

"I couldn't help noticing that that is *not* Brad."

"Uh no, it's not." Duh! I gave myself a mental smack on the forehead. Why was it every time I talked to Jack I sounded either like a six year old or a highly functioning moron? "That's Tommy."

"Tommy?" Jack arched one dark eyebrow. "You mean as in your gay ex Tommy?"

"Yep. We're having coffee." I help up my empty cup as proof, and mentally gave myself another "duh."

"So I see. Well, just thought I'd say hello." Jack gave me another crooked smile that seemed to say something that I couldn't quite grasp. "See you around."

Jack turned and walked away, and I stood watching him, blinking stupidly. It occurred to me to wonder what Jack was doing here. He didn't seem the bookish type. In fact, watching him walk away in his tight black jeans and t shirt, I couldn't help thinking it was like seeing a polar bear walking through a pine forest. It was incongruous somehow. I noticed other people - mostly women - noticing him, and I wondered if he got that wherever he went, or just in civilized places.

"Can I help you?" The girl at the counter sounded impatient, as if she'd been waiting for me to acknowledge her for a long time. Blushing for no good reason I could think of, I thrust my empty cup at her.

"Coffee. Black."

"Right."

I paid for the fresh cup and went back to Tommy.

61

"Who was that you were talking to?"

"That was Jack, a friend of Eddie's."

"Yeah? He looked like he wanted to be your friend." Tommy grinned and wiggled his eyebrows up and down. "If you know what I mean."

"Oh come on!" I blushed again. "Jack is way out of my league!"

"What, are you kidding?" Tommy shook his head. "Girl, you never did think enough of yourself."

"I like myself just fine."

"Maybe, but you have a poor self-image."

"Sometimes I still see myself as a two hundred and twenty pound behemoth."

"You were *never* a behemoth!" Tommy protested. "And even when you were heavy you were a pretty girl. Besides, it's what's inside that matters."

"Nice platitudes." I rolled my eyes.

"Just the truth. I mean, I should know, I married you, and you weren't even my type!"

I laughed. I wasn't even the right *font*."

"Oh, a writer's joke. That's cute." Tommy smiled, but he looked a little wistful. "I worry sometimes that I hurt your self-esteem. I mean, you do know that the whole marriage/divorce thing was all my fault, right?"

"Are you asking if I worry that I wasn't woman enough to keep you straight?"

Tommy laughed. "Something like that."

"I won't say the thought hasn't crossed my mind," I admitted. "But really, I know better."

"Good." Tommy reached out and squeezed my hand. "So, there's a bluegrass festival in three weeks at Riverfront Park. You want to go?"

"Sure!" And with that, I knew that Tommy and I were going to be friends again.

Life was good.

Chapter Five

It took only a few days for B&E to get the results of my background check. There was no mention of unearthed facts such as random promiscuity or drunken binges on school roofs, so either they didn't talk to the right people or they considered my early indiscretions to be not worth mentioning. Relieved, I showed up on a Wednesday afternoon to go over the basics with Belinda.

Belinda greeted me in all her towering glory, this time dressed in a lime green suit with a skirt that ended a few inches above her knees, showing off well-defined calf and thigh muscles. I couldn't help a spark of envy. As a "big girl" I was usually only jealous of the petite little size twos that paraded around in crop-tops and tiny shorts, but here was Belinda with her relatively large frame and exceptional height, as sexy as any woman I'd even seen on the street or the screen. I had dressed carefully that morning myself, in a swirling skirt and form-fitting T-shirt, and strappy sandals that were as close to bare feet as I could get without my soles touching the plush carpeting of the B&E offices. I had looked in my mirror this morning and pronounced myself "looking good." Now I wanted to retreat to the perpetual slouch that I'd acquired when my weight had topped the two hundred mark. Next to Belinda I felt like a cow.

Belinda didn't seem to notice my discomfort. She grinned cheerfully when she saw me, had me sign a couple of last minute papers, explained the confidentiality contract I was signing, and took me on a tour.

There was one large room full of small cubicles, each outfitted with a small desk, a chair and a computer.

"You can use a computer any time; just sign in here." She showed me a book full of names and times. "Each computer has a number." She showed me where the numbers were written on the side of each monitor. "Just write down which computer, sign your time in, and sign your time out when you leave. You'll spend a lot of time in here; the internet is a wealth of information if you know how to look."

I nodded as if I knew just where to look, though to tell you the truth I didn't have a clue. Belinda must have seen right through my bluff, because she grinned and said, "I'll help you out the first few times. You'll go to the same sites over and over again."

Next she showed me the library, where there were all sorts of useful books, such as directories for every major city I could think of and many for smaller communities I'd never heard of. There were cross directories, where you could find an address if you had a phone number, and vice versa. "Of course, you can find most of that on line now, but sometimes these older directories help you find stuff from way back. Like, say you want to know who a guy's neighbors were back in 1978. If you know his address from that time you can cross check tax records and such and find out who lived on his block."

I nodded, intrigued. This might be more interesting that I'd expected.

"We don't use time clocks around here; there's too much time spent out in the field. So use this to track your hours." Belinda handed me a spiral notebook, about 3x5 inches. "It's pretty self-explanatory: just fill in the spaces with the date, time, what you were doing, mileage. You don't have to be too specific about the 'what,' just a couple words, like 'interview,' 'library research,' whatever." She handed me another notebook of similar size. "This is your field book. Keep good notes; you'll not only use them to write up reports, but if accounting has any questions about your time you can fill in details from this.

"You'll spend a lot of time knocking on doors," Belinda went on. "You'll need to speak to each reference in person. The trick is to try to get them to give you other names, ones that aren't listed on the references. Childhood friends, old neighbors or teachers, people like that. Ex-spouses are good, but always take whatever they say with a grain of salt; sometimes they're just bitter, and they'll say anything to get back at their ex."

"Unless of course, they still happen to be friends with them." Jack was leaning in the doorway.

66

"Hi Jack!" Belinda eyed him boldly, a flirtatious challenge in her eyes. I wanted to wince at her temerity; Jack didn't strike me as a particularly playful guy. But he grinned back and made a point of checking her out, head to toe.

"You are looking *fine* today, Belinda. What are those, six inch stilettos? Probably illegal in twenty two states."

"Only if they're concealed." Belinda cocked a foot to display the lime green heels. "Besides, they're only four inches. Just like a man to overestimate by a third."

"The problem is, you've been talking to men who want to *talk* about length. You need a man who isn't afraid to *show* you."

I couldn't believe what I was hearing. Where was serious Jack, the man I'd come to know and lust? Since when did he stand around making low-brow locker room jokes with executive assistants? And why didn't he ever flirt with *me* that way?

"That's just it, Jack. I'm looking for a guy who isn't afraid. Know any?"

"Sorry. You scare me to death, and I'm fearless." Jack turned his attention to me. "I have a couple of free days. I thought I'd take you around, show you the ropes."

"Oh." Wow, talk about brilliant repartee. But I couldn't help it; the thought of spending a couple of days in close proximity to Jack made my mouth dry and my stomach flutter. "Um, why?"

There, that was better. Two syllables that time. Next time I'd go for three, and prove what a hopeless moron I was.

Jack shrugged. "Why not? I got you into this, I figured the least I could do was get you off to a good start."

"And Harry is okay with this?" Belinda looked skeptical. "I mean, you're a pretty expensive employee to be wasted training on door-to-doors."

"Harry can afford it. Besides, if he'd said no I would have done it for free."

He threw a casual arm around my shoulders, and I felt a wave of heat cascade from the top of my head to the soles of my thinly shod feet. I'm not good at casual touching. My family never hugged when I was little, so I never knew how such things were done. How tight did you squeeze? How long did you hold it? And now I stood with my arms stiffly at my sides, wondering what I was supposed to do. Sling an arm around his waist? Grab the hand that was so casually dangling past my shoulder and very nearly brushing my right breast? I was afraid that if I moved my hands would make contact with his more private parts, or his would make contact with mine, so I stood perfectly still, barely breathing, as animated as a parking meter.

As if suddenly sensing my popsicle-like stance, Jack glanced at me, his grin fading, and removed his arm. I was relieved and disappointed at the same time. I was pretty good at the mixed emotions thing, and I wondered if that was a woman's thing or if everybody suffered from it.

"Well, she couldn't get better training." Belinda shrugged and held out a thin folder. "Here's her first run. I was going to have Pete take her around but I'll let him know he's free for the day."

Jack opened the folder and glanced at it briefly, then handed it to me. "Okay, let's go." He turned abruptly and walked out of the room. Startled, it took me a moment to grab up my purse and follow him out, with a brief wave to Belinda.

We headed toward my car, and I pulled my keys out. Jack squinted at the dented Escort with its rusty embellishments but politely declined to say he didn't want to be caught dead in it.

"Let's take my truck. You can navigate."

I shrugged, not really caring. I liked to drive because I preferred to feel like I was in control of my own destiny. I guess if I was going to die in a fiery crash I somehow thought it would be better if I was the one responsible. I wasn't fanatical about it, though, so I followed him to his truck.

He drove a shiny black Toyota pickup, with big lights on the roof that I associated with spotlighting deer, and a large, heavy duty metal box affixed to the bed, right behind the seats.

There was an excellent stereo system, and the dashboard looked like it would be comfortable sitting in the front of a small but well-designed airplane. He started the truck and turned down the stereo, which had been set to blast level, and looked at me expectantly.

"Well, this is your show. Where to first?"

"Um, I'm not sure." I blinked, for the moment completely at a loss. I mean, how the hell was I supposed to know where to start? He was the one training me, right?

Then I remembered the folder clutched in my hands, likely filled with a list of references to be interviewed. Duh, I thought. Okay, just open it and pretend you just hadn't decided which interview to start with. Jack never has to know the depth of your denseness.

Or so I told myself, but I caught his little grin as I fumbled the folder open and scanned the first page. It was a summary of the "case" we were working on.

We would be checking references for Haley Nieswonger, a woman who had applied to be the nanny for a wealthy couple's children.

I flipped to the next page and found the list of people I was supposed to interview, complete with their addresses, names and phone numbers. We're not talking the standard three personal references you find on an application for a department store job. This woman had no less than twelve personal references.

The next sheet was a list of standard questions I should ask of each reference, including how long they'd known Haley, in what capacity, and if she'd been an employee, would they hire her again.

The rest of the folder contained brief notes about the individual references: where they worked, what hours, whether or not they were available to be interviewed during working hours. I assumed Belinda had put the folder together, and my estimation of her efficiency went up yet another notch.

We spent the afternoon going from one interview to the next. Jack said little, letting me take the lead. I asked every question on the list provided and dutifully wrote the answers down in my little notebook.

The references were all accessible, seemingly eager to discuss Miss Nieswonger, and every one of them gave a glowing review. Haley was smart, witty, capable, compassionate, a gem with children, a great cook who kept a spotless house, able to leap tall buildings with a single bound...

Okay, I made that last thing up, but you see what I mean. According to her references, Haley Nieswonger was *perfect*, a super woman who could cook, clean, teach and play with children, walk the dog and invent a cure for cancer, all while writing a novel and keeping every hair on her head in place.

"You know, I'm having a hard time believing in this woman." I confessed this to Jack once we were back in the privacy of the truck, after the fifth recitation of Haley Nieswonger's considerable virtues.

"Yeah? Why's that?"

"Because she's too good to be true, to borrow on an old cliché. I mean, everybody pisses people off once in a while. This woman seems to be a modern day Mother Theresa."

""I'm sure she's pissed people off, but maybe never bad enough that these people consider it worth mentioning."

"So do you think this is legitimate? Have you had other reference checks go this smoothly?"

"Sure. Let's face it, you wouldn't give someone as a reference if you thought they were going to trash you."

"Then isn't this all just a waste of time?"

"It could be." Jack was watching me intently. I felt as if he were trying to telegraph a message to me without saying the words. "But it's usually possible to get the true background out of people, even if they are trying to sugarcoat things."

"How?"

Jack gave me a tiny smile. "Ah, so the student finally thinks to ask the master for advice."

I blushed. I *had* been more or less moving forward without consulting him, but I figured he'd let me know if I was screwing up. "Hey, I didn't know I had to ask! I thought you'd just jump in when I needed help."

"I thought it would be better if you figured out some basic truths for yourself. Actually, you caught on to this pretty quick. Back when I trained a lot, some investigators took weeks to figure out that the question list is basically just an introductory tool, but virtually useless for getting any real information."

"So, what do you recommend?"

"Conversation. Get them talking, first about things in general, then Haley in particular. And don't always be talking. People hate silence. If you keep quiet, they'll usually rush to fill the void, and that's when they let slip the more interesting information."

"Anything else you can suggest?"

"Plenty." The emphasis Jack put on the word, combined with the look in his eyes, made me blush. Oh my god! Was he flirting with me?

Before I could process that thought all the way, he shook his head. "I think the rest can wait. Try the conversation and silence first. When you get that down pat, we'll work on other methods."

"Fair enough." I consulted the folder, eager to move on to the sixth name on the list. I was ready to dig in my heels, determined to find the flaw in this seemingly perfect gem.

The next name on the list was Jacob Bryant, the president of a local bank, also a long time friend of Haley Nieswonger. Mr. Bryant was home that day, willing to meet us between a late business lunch and a round of golf. We arrived at his home at 3:30, prepared to listen to him sing the praises of Miss Nieswonger. I was wondering if the Pope had heard of her; surely she was being considered for sainthood.

A plump maid in a spotless, well pressed uniform answered the door and led me through the foyer to a side room that I thought might be a "parlor." I'm not really sure about that. I have trouble distinguishing between parlors, morning rooms and sitting rooms in rich people's houses. The library I can usually figure out, clued by the wall to wall books, but the rest of them all seem pretty much the same to me. Why can't they just have a living room and a family room like normal (poor) people?

In any case the room the maid abandoned us in was huge, the ceilings towering higher than the roof of my single story house. There was a large fireplace, with a polished mantel holding shiny objects that I feared to get too near to, as if my coarse, unrefined breath might knock a priceless vase to the floor. The furniture was understated and mismatched in a clearly carefully thought out way. If I tried decorating like that, my living room would end up looking like it was furnished with garage sale cast offs. Come to think of it, my living room *was* furnished from garage sales.

On a side table there was a group of photographs in matching heavy wooden frames. There was an older couple on the deck of a boat (a yacht? I wasn't any better at identifying boats than I was at naming parlors) that I guessed would be Bryant's parents, or perhaps his in-laws. There were two children pictured separately and then together, and another photo with a younger couple and those same two children, posing with the ocean for a backdrop, smiling as if they were the proud owners of that body of water. I guessed it was Bryant with his wife and children. The kids were nicely tanned; the wife, also browned to perfection, was slim and fit in a one piece bathing suit and a lacy cover-up, her blonde hair blowing in the breeze. The picture could have been used in a glossy magazine ad for any number of vacation destinations or sun products.

Mr. Bryant breezed into the room after several minutes, dressed casually in slacks and golf shirt, perhaps as a reminder to us that he had a tee time coming up.

"Hello!" He greeted us enthusiastically enough, with a bright smile that was obviously enhanced by expensive hours spent in a dentist's chair. He had a deep tan, the color enhancing the blonde hair on his lean but fit-looking forearms. "I'm Jacob Bryant. And you are Lovingston, I presume?"

I grimaced inwardly at the tired old joke, and managed to shape my lips into what I thought was a convincing smile. "That's right, and this is Jack Jones. We're just following up Miss Nieswonger's references."

"So you said on the phone." He managed to make that sound like a reprimand, as though he wasn't pleased with me wasting his time by repeating information. "I was rather surprised," he went on, waving me toward a chair while he perched on the edge of an ornate loveseat. "I thought my letter of recommendation was quite thorough. I didn't expect an in-person interview."

"It's standard procedure," I assured him. "I hope it isn't a problem?"

"Oh no! Of course not!" He was vehement in his denial. "I'm happy to do whatever I can for Haley. She's a wonderful person."

"That's what we've heard so far." I nodded agreeably and pulled out my trusty notebook and pen, where I'd jotted the highlights of Mr. Bryant's letter. "I understand you've known Miss Nieswonger for twenty-two years?"

"Whew, that long?" He laughed. "Makes me sound old, having friends from so far back."

I made a non-committal sound and waited for him to go on. Jack had wandered to the fireplace, behind Mr. Bryant, and stood examining the displayed objects, not contributing to the interview. Now and then he turned and glanced at me, his expression neutral.

"I've known her since college." With that opening sentence, it seemed almost as if he had begun a prepared speech. For the next several minutes he went on non-stop, singing the woman's praises much as the previous references had done. I sat with my pen poised, ready to make a note on the off chance he said anything useful, nodding now and then to demonstrate my attentiveness to his narrative.

I waited for him to wind down, annoyed at this canned speech, which sounded nearly identical to the letter he'd written. I wondered if he'd memorized it, or if it was a standard form he used when any of his friends requested a reference. There was one point that interested me, and that was his first sentence.

"So you went to college with Miss Nieswonger?"

"Oh no, I'm sorry, did I give that impression? Actually she went to school with my wife. I met them both at about the same time."

"I see. Were they roommates?"

"No, Haley lived off-campus."

"Did she live alone?"

"Uh no." Abruptly Bryant blushed, and I wondered what was so embarrassing about a roommate. "She shared a house with another young lady."

"And her name was?"

"Oh, uh...let me think," Bryant was looking away from me, staring out the window, stalling for time. Now *this* was getting interesting. "Her name was Kathy, or Katie, something like that."

"Hm. Well, I'm sure I can find that out elsewhere."

"But why?" He frowned at me. "We haven't seen Katherine since graduation, I'm sure she has nothing to add."

"Katherine? So you do remember her name?"

"It just came to me." Bryant looked angry, whether at my pressing the point or his own slip, I wasn't sure. "In any event, I don't see the point in looking her up. I'm sure Haley provided plenty of good references."

"Yes, she did," I agreed. "But B&E prides itself on the thoroughness of our background checks. No stone left unturned, as they say. Of course, if you think Katherine might try to sabotage Miss Nieswonger, say, because of some bitterness from the past, I'll be sure to keep that in mind when I interview her."

As if suddenly realizing he was protesting too much, Bryant abruptly shook his head.

"No, of course not. I'm sure Katherine has nothing but fond memories of our college days. By all means, look her up, interview her. Haley has nothing to hide."

"That's good to know. I don't suppose you've suddenly remembered Katherine's last name?"

"As a matter of fact, yes." Suddenly he was once again the spirit of cooperation. "Matherly, Katherine Matherly."

"Thank you." I made a note of the name. "Do you happen to have any idea where Miss Matherly lives these days?"

"Sorry, I've no idea. We haven't kept in touch. Probably still back east. We were there for college, but so far as I know that was Katherine's home town. She wasn't a student, just a roommate."

"I see." I waited to see if he would add any more. Jack gave me a tiny nod of approval from behind Bryant's back, maintaining his own silence.

Movement outside the huge bay windows caught my eye, and I looked out to see a woman in a well-pressed pantsuit leading two children toward the pool. So much for the silent treatment. My curiosity forced me to speak.

"Is that your wife?"

"No, that's Bridget, our nanny."

"Oh?" I looked back at him with some surprise. "If you don't mind my asking, if you know of such a wonderful nanny like Miss Nieswonger, why didn't you hire her?"

Again, the deep blush, the cutting away of his gaze. "Well, er…"

I stared at him, waiting for him to go on. Had he actually said "er?" This man was a bank president, a college educated businessman who was now resorting to stalling tactics normally reserved for a six year old caught with a stolen candy bar.

How could a successful businessman like this not know how to lie? I could have come up with a half dozen plausible explanations on the spot, although I wasn't very good at delivering the lies; I blushed too easily. But top of the list would have been that Bridget had already been hired and was doing a fine job. There was no justification for firing her, even to replace her with Saint Haley.

Bryant fumbled for another few seconds, and then blinked as an idea connected in his brain.

"It would have been awkward, her being a friend and all." He nodded once as if agreeing with himself, and his eyes finally met mine again. "I mean, no matter how good she is, in the case of the employer/employee relationship there always comes some occasion for the employer to mete out discipline." At this, Bryant flushed again. This time he came up out of his seat and moved to the fireplace, his movements too studied to be natural. Jack stepped neatly aside, as if trying to remain as unobtrusive as possible. Bryant didn't seem to notice him. "We just didn't want anything to come between us...our friendship, that is."

Uh huh.

I sat and stared at him, my intuition buzzing frantically. Something was off here. Way off.

"I can see how it would be difficult, having to *discipline* a friend."

I emphasized discipline, since that seemed to be the word that set him off the first time, but if it had been, he now had it well under control. Perhaps it was having the massive fireplace as a backdrop, or maybe it was the crystal paper weight he had picked up from the mantel and now bounced casually in his palm, but once again Bryant was every bit the successful business man, his confidence and arrogance back in place as firmly as if he'd donned it like a close-fitting wetsuit.

"Yes, quite awkward. Now, if you don't mind, three of a potential foursome are likely already waiting at the club, and I did warn you I had a limited time." His tone of dismissal wasn't nearly as warm and hearty as his welcoming "hello."

"Sure. I think I got everything I needed, anyway." I stood and closed my notebook, sliding it into my purse. "We appreciate your time, Mr. Bryant."

"No problem." He smiled and extended his hand, but there was still no warmth there. "If I can do anything else, let me know. Believe me, whoever hires Haley is getting one hell of a great nanny."

I nodded and murmured my good bye. He walked us to the front door, belatedly shaking Jack's hand, and closed it behind us with nearly enough of a slam to indicate we'd been given the bum's rush, but not so much that we could actually protest his rudeness.

Jack and I strolled back to his truck, not saying anything. As we pulled out of the long drive, a little red Mercedes convertible pulled in, driven by a tanned, fit looking blonde whose makeup looked like it had been applied by a professional. I recognized her from the photo: definitely the wife. She would look perfect clinging to Jacob's arm, like Barbie and Ken.

I looked at Jack as we pulled out of the driveway.

"So, I think maybe we need to talk to Katherine Matherly."

Jack grinned. "You're taking to this stuff like a duck to water. That was good work, Rainie."

"Yeah, well we'll see if it gets us anywhere."

There was no Katherine Matherly listed in the college town Bryant had gone to, but there were three within a one hundred mile radius. Unfortunately, none of them were anywhere near the right age. One was in a nursing home, one in high school, and the other not yet out of diapers. By the time I finished that cumbersome computer search the offices of B&E were closing down and Jack had to leave for an appointment. (Maybe a date? He didn't say, and I sure wasn't going to ask him!) I would have to wait to ask Belinda for some further search tips.

Chapter Six

When I arrived the next morning at Thelma's, she was in a mood to clean. Her old house had five bedrooms, four of which hadn't been used in years. She'd kept them pretty much closed off, but one of them had become a junk room, filled nearly to bursting with cast-off furniture, wheelchairs and other accessories from her second husband's long decline into ill health, and a variety of stuff that, at the time it had been stored, was too good to just be thrown out with the trash.

Thelma wanted to empty it out, determine what could be donated for continued use, and what could now be officially determined as trash.

We dug in, Thelma grunting and lifting right beside me. I had given up a long time ago on trying to get her to take it easy with such activities. She had strong bones, and surprisingly good musculature for a woman her age. She seldom needed more than an Ibuprofen or two in order to combat her aches and pains.

We worked steadily until almost two o'clock before Thelma abruptly dropped a box of her husband's old clothes and arched her back, stretching a sore muscle.

"Okay, that's enough of that. I'm hungry. How about we run out for a burger?"

"Sounds good to me!" I had been enjoying myself; cleaning a room of forty years accumulation is a lot like a treasure hunt. We'd come across things that might be of historical interest to some people, and other things that neither of us knew the actual use of. I'd been having so much fun I hadn't realized we'd skipped lunch. Now that Thelma mentioned burgers, my stomach growled its demand to be filled.

We rinsed the dust from our faces and hands and got in the car.

"Where do you want to eat?"

"How about Casey's?"

I grinned and started the car. Casey's was a neighborhood bar, and on the weekends it was notorious for drunken brawls and loud, rocking country music. During the week it was just a dark, quiet bar with the biggest, greasiest, absolutely best burgers in town. Thelma got no argument from me, although I knew I'd need to spend some extra time on my bike to work off the fat calories. Oh well; a Casey's pub burger was well worth the added sweat.

The bar, as usual, was dark, but not smoky this time of day. Bars were the last refuge for smokers who didn't want to stand outside for their habit, on display like animated dinosaurs for the self-righteous to tsk at and shake their heads over. But soon enough the smoking ban would reach even these dark havens, and I supposed that eventually us last holdouts would have to hide in our homes or creep into back alleys to get our nicotine fix, like heroin addicts. Or maybe it would be like the Prohibition days, and we'd be giving a secret knock on the door of a speakeasy, where black market cigarettes would be sold, and flashing red lights would warn of an impending DEA bust.

Thelma and I sat at one of a dozen empty tables, the lunch rush long over. A few people sat at the bar, shadowy figures in the low light. The TV was on behind the bar, broadcasting CNN; the jukebox was silent.

We ordered burgers with the works. I asked for Diet Coke, ignoring the irony, and Thelma ordered a draft beer. While we waited for the drinks a woman walked in, took a quick glance around as if searching the nearly deserted room for someone, then moved towards the bar. Even in the dim light I could see that she was stunning. She had blonde hair that fell in shining waves half way to her tiny waist, which was offset by a set of boobs that any plastic surgeon would be pleased to use as an "after" model and hips that flared out just enough to fill her tight jeans to perfection.

I grimaced and looked away from her. I didn't need any reminders of how imperfect I am.

We sipped our drinks as we waited for the coveted burgers and chatted easily. Over the past two years Thelma and I had become much more than client and caregiver. I considered her a true friend. In fact, that relationship had been bothering me more and more as of late. It didn't seem right to be accepting money from her every week.

Knowing she would balk, I waited until we'd finished our burgers to bring the subject up. Thelma was sipping at her second beer, and I thought between the carbs and the alcohol she might be properly mellow.

"You know Thelma, I've been thinking..."

"Uh oh. You look serious. I think you think too much."

"Look, you never really needed a caregiver in the first place, right?"

"Of course. I hired you to be my companion."

"And I've loved doing it, but that's the point. I consider you a real friend now. I mean, we hang out together outside of "working hours" as it is. I don't think you should pay me anymore."

Thelma was vigorously shaking her head. "Don't be ridiculous. Of course I'll keep paying you."

"But Thelma..."

"If I don't pay you, you'll have to get another client on Tuesday and Thursday right?"

"Well...yeah, I guess so." I did, after all, have bills to pay.

"Then what am I going to do on those days? You want me to go back to wandering the house, bored to tears? The truth is, I *do* need you. All of my friends have either died off or gotten so wrapped up in their health miseries that they might as well be dead. Hell, it's all I can do to get three other people together for a game of Euchre without someone begging off because of arthritis or just plain forgetfulness. I like our time together!"

"So do I, and we'd still hang out..."

"When you had time between jobs. That's not enough for me. The week stretches mighty long when you don't work, honey. And it's not like I can't afford to pay you. I told you more than once, I'm loaded! What do you think I'm going to do with all that money if I don't spend it? You think I want to save it for that greedy niece of mine? And you know how I feel about charities: there's not a one whose CEO doesn't live rich off a large percentage of donated funds. I'm sure not going to leave my money to someone who'll spend it on air conditioned dog houses."

"But Thelma, I feel bad taking money from you."

"Why, because you like your job?" Thelma grinned. "There's some people who would appreciate having a job that didn't suck."

"Still..."

"Now wait honey," Thelma's smile faded, and she gave me one of her rare serious expressions. "You know, some day my body might figure out it's damned near eighty years old. I hope not; I hope to just go *bang*! like my brother did. But it's always possible I'll go slow, and if that happens I don't want a nursing home. I hope I'll have the wherewithal to do myself in, but if I'm too cowardly to do that, I don't want strangers tending me, I want a friend. So when that time comes, you'll be earning your money right enough."

I felt hot tears prick the backs of my eyeballs at this frank statement. Of course I knew the reality of aging; hadn't it been my chosen career for some years now? But to think of Thelma, who was perhaps the best friend I had, helpless in bed, unable to get to the toilet herself...

"Now Rainie, don't get all mushy on me." The twinkle was back in Thelma's eye. "You know, maybe it won't happen that way. Maybe tomorrow you'll get hit by a bus and get a head injury or something, and I'll have to take care of you!"

I couldn't help but laugh. "Thanks Thelma. You always know how to look on the bright side."

"Damned straight!" She took a long drink of her beer. "That's one fine brew!" She announced, licking her lips in exaggerated enjoyment. Obviously the serious talk was over.

We moved on to other topics as we sipped our drinks, reluctant to end the afternoon. I was pleasantly tired from the morning's labors and well satisfied by the pub burger (which I had eaten to the last, juicy bite.) The waitress, after being assured we didn't need anything else, brought our check with the cheerful reminder that she was done for the day, and if we needed anything else we'd need to go to the bartender. I understood, having waited tables for many a night myself, that this was a hint she wanted to be tipped before she left. I reached for my wallet, but of course Thelma waved me away.

"Oh no, you don't." Thelma pulled her usual wad of cash from her pocket and peeled off enough to pay the tab, with a generous amount left over. "Keep the change."

With a genuinely grateful smile, the waitress left us to finish our drinks in peace.

A man walked through the front door, silhouetted by the blinding light outside. I blinked and turned my gaze away, but looked back after the door swung shut. He was wearing jeans that looked like they'd been ironed, and a pale blue polo shirt. Like the woman who'd come in earlier, he paused and glanced around the dim bar, but I noted the light of recognition on his face as he moved to the bar to sit next to the gorgeous woman.

Belatedly I realized who the man was: Jacob Bryant, the man I'd interviewed as a reference for Haley Nieswonger. I didn't know who the woman was, but it sure wasn't the blond wife I'd seen pulling into the driveway.

"What's up, Rainie?" Thelma was peering at me curiously. "That's some smirk you have on your face." She turned to see what I was looking at. "Hmm. Someone you know?"

"Sort of. I interviewed him yesterday for a reference check. I'd sure like to know who his friend is."

"Yeah?" Thelma looked thoughtful. "You think it's important to your investigation?"

I shrugged, smiling at Thelma's eagerness. She loved the idea of me being a private eye, even if I was just a lowly assistant. "I doubt it, but I *am* curious. I'm pretty sure that isn't his wife."

"Huh." Thelma looked back at the couple again, and I could practically see the gears turning in her head.

"What are you thinking about?"

"I was just noticing she's kind of careless. Look how her purse is just hanging open on the back of her chair."

I peered closely, wondering at Thelma's keen eyesight. Sure enough, the woman's purse, made with some sort of dark metallic material, was slung by its strap over the back of the barstool, and she'd neglected to snap it. I could see the dark gap where it hung open.

"Someone ought to tell her about it." She flashed me a big grin that held more than a hint of mischief in it. "I think I need to pee."

Abruptly she stood up and slung her big purse over her shoulder. She wove in and out of the tables, heading in the general direction of the restroom, but also moving much closer than necessary toward the end of the bar where the couple in question was sitting. I watched her, curious but not overly concerned. I mean, what could she do, go up and ask him who the chippy was?

Boy, was I underestimating her.

She got to the couple and suddenly stumbled, catching herself on the back of the woman's bar stool, and dislodged the purse strap, knocking it to the floor. In the same motion, her own purse, mysteriously open, fell to the floor, spilling its copious contents onto the dark floor.

"Oh my! Excuse me!" Thelma's voice was high pitched and tremulous, as if she'd suddenly turned frail in her trek across the room.

The woman turned, annoyed; Jacob Bryant at least had the decency to look concerned, and started to get up.

"Oh no, don't get up! I'll get it!" Thelma patted at his chest, looking befuddled and embarrassed. "It's my fault, I'm so clumsy anymore!" She knelt down and hurriedly began scooping up the spilled contents, shoving them into her purse with embarrassed haste.

"I'm so sorry! I hope I didn't soil your pretty bag." She picked up the woman's purse and brushed it off, then hung it back on the bar stool.

"I'm sure it's fine." The woman's voice was that of an ice queen, cool and imperious.

"Are you sure you're all right?" Jacob Bryant no longer looked concerned; his question was asked by rote, the proper thing to say in an awkward encounter with an obviously confused old woman.

"Yes, I'm fine, just fine young man." Thelma patted his shoulder as if to soothe his false concern. She swung her purse back over her shoulder and turned toward the front door, her shoulders hunched. "I guess I'd better get home. My soap's coming on soon, don't want to miss that." She kept up a mumbling dialogue with herself as she made it to the front door and out.

I blinked, for the moment taken aback by her abrupt departure. Then an ugly suspicion filled my mind. As casually as possible, I took a last sip of my Coke and got up, glad that Jacob's back was to me. I grabbed my own purse and went to the door, fighting the urge to run.

Thelma was already in the car, gesturing for me to hurry up. I ran to the Escort and jumped in, hurriedly starting the car and taking off so fast I nearly popped the clutch and killed the engine.

"Is that any way to make a casual getaway?" Thelma admonished me.

"Getaway from what? What did you do?"

"Do? I didn't do anything. I'm just a poor old lady, stumbling around in that dark bar, why I ought to sue them for maintaining such dangerous conditions..."

"Thelma..."

"All right, all right. Don't get so testy." She rooted around in her bag for a minute. She fixed her face in a comically false expression of amazement. "Well, will you look at that!" She held up a slim black, metallic wallet. "I must have accidentally picked up that young woman's wallet! Why in the dark, with all the confusion..."

I felt the blood drain from my face, even as a flush of heat ran from my head to my tingling toes. "Oh my god! You stole her wallet!"

"Stole it? Don't be ridiculous. Do I look like a thief? Like I said, it was dark and..."

"Save it for the cops, Thelma!"

"Cops! What, are you going to call them?"

"Of course not, but she will!"

"Not to worry. She won't notice for a while yet. A girl that pretty, she won't be taking out her wallet to pay for any drinks, I can promise you. By the time she notices it missing, I'll have it in a Fed Ex office, on its way back to her via overnight service, complete with a note about how *sorry* this old lady is for the inconvenience. Of course, to do that, I'll just have to open it up, and check for her name and address, right?"

I hated to admit it, but it would probably work. I was fairly certain Jacob Bryant hadn't seen me, and so wouldn't connect me to the clumsy old lady. And if the woman got her wallet back intact, with nothing missing, she probably wouldn't make much of a fuss.

I took a deep breath to calm myself. "I can't believe you did this."

"Ah, this was nothing." Thelma had already opened the wallet to peer at the woman's driver's license. "It was plenty dark in there, an easy snatch. Nothing like trying to cop smokes from under the nose of old lady Meyers at the corner grocery store. She kept that place lit up like Time's Square, but I still managed to get my Lucky Strikes!"

I couldn't help but grin at this image of Thelma as a juvenile delinquent, filching cigarettes, probably hanging out on a street corner with her hoodlum friends, smoking and acting like they owned the world.

"Have you got a pen?"

"Yeah, and a notebook, in my purse."

Thelma went into my bag, and not for the first time I marveled at the dexterity of her aging fingers as she plucked out the pen and paper and wrote down the woman's name and address. "It's an Indiana license. Katherine Matherly. 1642 South Maple, South Bend, Indiana."

"Katherine Matherly?" I practically squeaked in surprise.

"You know her?"

"As a matter of fact, I've been looking for her. Jacob Bryant knew her back in college, out on the east coast. According to him, he hasn't seen her in twenty years."

"Huh. Strange coincidence, this sudden reunion."

"You bet it is! I've got to call Jack."

"Okay, but first take me by the Fed Ex office before it closes. I want to get this on its way home as soon as possible." She had tucked the driver's license back into the wallet and shoved it back in her purse.

"No problem." I headed toward the mall, eager to get this business done so I could call Jack.

"Hey, I'm pretty good at this stuff." Thelma was grinning, as excited as I'd ever seen her. "Maybe I should see about getting a part time job with this B&E."

I laughed. "They'd probably be lucky to have you Thelma, but there's one big problem: you don't drive."

"So, I could be partners with you!"

I shook my head, hoping this was just a passing fancy. "I don't know if the world is ready for Thelma: P.I."

"Sounds like a great title for a TV show." Thelma held out her arms, one hand in the classic shape of a gun, the other supporting it in a standard shooting stance right out of the movies. "I could be the next *Police Woman*. Maybe get a blond wig, I'd look just like Angie Dickenson!"

I glanced over at her slight frame, comparing it to the lush figure of Dickenson. "You think?"

"Well, I'll bet I look as good as she does *now*!"

Unable to think of an argument for that, I just laughed and drove on.

We mailed the package and I dropped Thelma off at home with a promise to fill her in as soon as I knew something. I suppose there were some privacy issues I was violating, but hey, Thelma had, through some risk to herself, gotten the information. It seemed only fair to keep her in the loop.

I called Jack as soon as I had the car back on the road.

"Hey Rainie." He answered after one ring. I was pleasantly surprised that he knew who was calling; it was always flattering to be added to someone's call list, but to be on *Jacks*... "What's up?"

"I found Katherine Matherly."

"Yeah? How'd you do that?"

I hesitated. Did I really want to tell him? I mean, it *was* illegal and all. "Um...a friend got the information for me."

There was a moment of silence as Jack digested my obvious evasion.

"Should we be talking about this on the cell?"

"Maybe not."

"Okay, where are you?"

"I just left Thelma's, I'm heading home." Immediately I wanted to kick myself. So much for keeping my "friend" anonymous.

"Thelma?" Jack sounded more than a bit curious. "Okay. I'll be at your place in fifteen minutes."

The connection was broken, and I closed my phone. That was Jack for you: when he was done talking, he was done.

When I pulled into my driveway I saw Jack on my front porch, lounging on my wicker recliner like he didn't have a care in the world. He didn't move as I approached him, and with his sunglasses on I couldn't tell if he was watching me. His long legs were crossed at the ankles, his arms folded across his chest. He might well have been sound asleep.

He wasn't, of course. As soon as I started up the two sort steps to the porch he unfolded himself and stood with languid grace. "Hey."

"Hey back." I nearly had to brush against him to get to the front door; I couldn't help the little shiver of pleasure I felt at this close proximity. Damn, I had it bad. But I might as well have been lusting after Harrison Ford or Jason Statham: like those celebrities, Jack was way out of my league.

Jack followed me into the house and stopped just inside the door.

"Well?" His abruptness reminded me that this was not a social call, a reality check to bring me out of my lustful longings.

I quickly explained being in the bar and seeing Jacob Bryant. I tried to gloss over Thelma's part, reporting only that I had seen Katherine Matherly with Bryant, but Jack wasn't fooled for a minute.

"How did you know who she was?"

"Um...well, Thelma figured it out."

"Figured it out? How, with amazing Sherlock Holmes type deductions?"

"Not exactly."

"Are you going to make me squeeze the info out of you drop by drop?"

I gulped. I certainly wouldn't mind being squeezed by Jack, but not in the manner his tone indicated he would use to extract information. He looked annoyed, and Jack, when annoyed, was a very scary looking guy.

I licked my lips, suddenly just a little bit afraid of Jack. But that was silly; he wouldn't really hurt me over Thelma's little escapade, would he?

He was staring at me impatiently, his sunglasses off, his eyes dark and unreadable. Finally I took a deep breath, feeling like I was about to plunge into an unfamiliar lake, and let the whole story out. My words came fast, tumbling over one another, some events slipping out early, causing me to backtrack, and I wondered if I really sounded as much like a blithering idiot as I thought I did.

When I was done, I noticed Jack was no longer looking at me. He was staring at the floor, as though the pattern of my worn carpet held some sort of hidden meaning he was trying to decipher. We stood in silence for a long moment. Jack's jaw was working, flexing and relaxing, as though he'd bitten on something distasteful.

Finally he looked up at me, and with a wave of relief I saw the humor in his eyes that he'd worked so hard to keep from his lips.

"Let me get this straight. Thelma, that sweet old lady you go to the zoo with, is a *pickpocket*?"

"Apparently. And a pretty good one, if you ask me."

Now Jack did smile. "She's bold, I'll give her that. And quick thinking; maybe she should get a job with B&E."

I groaned. "Please, don't say that in front of her. She's already considering it."

Jack laughed outright. "You could be a team, like Cagney and Lacey."

"Actually, Thelma sees herself as more of the Angie Dickenson type."

Jack laughed again. "She probably does look a lot like her now."

"That's just what Thelma said."

"I think I like that old lady. So, where does this Katherine live?"

"So you think it'll be all right, the way we got this information?"

"All right?" Jack shrugged. "Apart from the fact that you committed a crime, I don't see a problem. After all, you didn't get caught. That's rule number one in the PI business."

"Are you saying you break the law in the course of doing your job?"

"Me?" Jack assumed a wide-eyed stance of innocence. "Don't be ridiculous. And as long as I never get caught, I'm sticking to that story."

"Katherine lives in South Bend, not more than fifteen miles from here."

"Huh. That's interesting."

"So, shall we go see her?"

"Not quite yet. Boot up your computer; let's check her out."

"From here? But I don't have the data bases..."

"You don't need them; we'll just type her name into a search engine, see what pops up."

"You think that'll get us anywhere?"

"Sweetheart, everything is on the internet nowadays. Haven't you ever searched your own name?"

"No. Why would I?"

"So you know what everybody else can find out about you with a few keystrokes." He was already walking toward my guestroom/office, and he pressed the on button for my computer. "You'd be amazed what makes it into public domain."

"I'll be there in just a minute. I need to let George out."

By the time I reached the office he had the computer online, and Jack directed me to a particular search sight. I typed in Katherine's name and we waited the few seconds for the search to be complete.

There were a lot of entries that featured Katherine Matherly's name. We scanned them quickly, looking for something with a local reference. It didn't take long to find one: a newspaper article that reported one Katherine Matherly had been arrested for prostitution during a raid on a massage parlor in Niles, Michigan the year before. Niles was only a few miles from Buchanan, a small town trying hard to become a big city.

"Whoa. Paydirt."

"Maybe." Jack frowned. "So she's a working girl; that doesn't mean all that much. It would certainly explain why Jacob Bryant doesn't want us to know he still has a connection to her."

"You think he uses her services?"

"Maybe." Jack was still scanning the article. "This says it's alleged that Katherine was the owner of the massage parlor, so she's not just a hooker, she's a madam." He clicked on an icon and a photograph of Katherine Matherly came up. No doubt it was the same woman I saw in the bar. In the photo her hair was pulled back. There was a small dot under her left eye that with her perfect features served as a beauty mark; on someone less attractive it would likely be termed a mole.

"So, what next? Do we go talk to her?"

"Ah, you're so direct." Jack shook his head. "That's refreshing, but frankly not always useful when it comes to this stuff. I think we'll try a back door approach." He pointed farther down the article. "There's two men listed here who were busted at the same time- "clients." I think we should start by talking to them, see what they know about our Madam Matherly."

"So you think they'll talk to us?"

Jack smiled a mean little smile. "Oh yeah. They'll talk."

Next we typed one of the client's names, Phillip Howard, into the search engine. Besides the article we'd already seen on his arrest, he was also listed as having won an award from the state, for charitable work. Phillip Howard was an accountant, and he'd devoted a number of hours the year before doing free taxes for the poor.

"An accountant." Jack considered this information for a moment. "I think we'll wait until tomorrow to talk to him. I'd like to catch him in his office."

"Why?"

"I just think the conversation we're going to have would be best kept away from the wife - at least in the beginning."

"You'd go to his wife about this?" I was genuinely shocked.

"You're so damned cute when your being naïve." Jack grinned and patted my cheek. "I'll pick you up at eight."

"Wait! I can't go that early; I have to go to Mabel's."

"Damn, I keep forgetting about your other work. What time will you be done?"

"Eleven."

"Fine. I'll pick you up at eleven-thirty."

Jack left without another word.

I fed George and then flipped the TV on, searching for the five o'clock news. I'm not much of a TV watcher. I don't even bother with cable, but I try to catch the news a couple of times a week, just to be sure there's no imminent threat of nuclear missiles heading toward Southwest Michigan or talk of a Communist takeover in Washington.

I turned to channel sixteen in time to hear of yet another meth lab exploding in a rural area, followed by the news that two people had been shot to death in separate incidents in South Bend over the weekend. The little town I lived in was closer to South Bend than any big city in Michigan, so most of our local news involved incidents south of the border. For that matter, except for a couple of decent grocery stores and one big box store, any shopping we did was in Indiana. The whole area was called Michiana, and a lot of people lived in one state and worked in the other.

I was spared any more bad news by my phone ringing. I let it ring twice before picking it up; I didn't want whoever it was to think I was just sitting by myself, bored to tears and hoping for any kind of distraction.

"Hi Rainie, it's me."

"Hi Brad. What's up?"

"Not much. I was just thinking, what with you not having Max tomorrow, that maybe we could have lunch."

"I can't. Jack is picking me up at eleven-thirty."

"Jack?" Brad's tone lost some of its warmth. "What does he want?"

"We're working together."

There was a long moment of silence.

"Why?" His tone had chilled yet a few more degrees.

"He's training me."

"Training you? To search data bases and interview references? I thought Jack was some sort of big shot ex- Navy Seal -bodyguard- P.I. Why is he training an assistant?"

"I dunno. He offered, so what the heck?"

"I don't like Jack."

"Oh." I didn't know what else to say to that.

"I don't like the idea of you working with him."

Now it was my turn to be silent. He didn't like it? So damn what?

"Rainie, are you there?"

"I'm here." I unclenched my teeth to answer. "But I've got to go. I have something burning."

"You're cooking?"

"Don't sound so shocked! I know how to cook."

"So take the phone with you. It's cordless, isn't it?"

"I think it'll take two hands. Talk to you later."

I hung up, knowing he would be livid at the abrupt disconnect, but not really caring. Who the hell did he think he was? We'd been dating pretty seriously for about six months, but there was no ring on my finger or leash on my neck. I suppose I should have told him so, but I wasn't particularly in the mood for a fight.

I shut off the TV and went in to take a long, hot bath. That, my friends, is yet another of the simple pleasures of living alone; I could soak until I pruned and no one would be knocking on the door, saying they had to pee. Of course, on the downside, if I slipped and fell and knocked myself out, no one would find me for days. I could be lying in a coma until poker night. Then Mason or Jeff or Riley would wander in and find me, cold and naked on the floor...eew! That was an image I did not need! Sometimes I hate having such a vivid imagination.

I was extra careful climbing into the tub.

Chapter Seven

Mabel was having a rough day. She couldn't find a hundred dollars in cash she'd gotten out of the bank two days before, and was convinced someone had broken into her house and taken it.

"I can't imagine anyone got in, what with the alarm and all." I smiled and put a soothing hand on Mabel's shoulder to keep her from pacing across the kitchen yet again. "You know Mabel, sometimes you hide your money, and more than once you've hidden it so well even you couldn't find it."

"Not this time." Mabel shook her head adamantly and held her empty wallet out to me. "It was in here, and I had the wallet under my pillow. Someone came right into my *room*!" Her eyes widened in fear at the thought.

"Before you panic, can we at least go look?"

Mabel grimaced, but I could see she was giving in. She relied on me for a lot, and with that reliance came a certain trust. "All right, but you'll see, it's gone."

I led the way back to her bedroom and began a methodical search of all Mabel's usual hiding spots: the sock drawer, under the liner in her underwear drawer, between the mattress and box spring on her bed. I moved to the huge walk-in closet and checked the purses neatly hung on hooks. No cash. I stood with my fists on my hips and stared around the room, trying to think like Mabel. If it was late at night and I was stuck here, and suddenly paranoid that someone would take something from me, where would I hide it?

The room was neat as a pin, with very little clutter. No books to tuck dollars into, no clever little containers to stuff full of green.

My eyes fell on the neat row of shoes on the closet floor, every toe lined up evenly with the one next to it. One of the dressier shoes, a glossy black pair with a low, sensible heel, was slightly out of line with the rest. I pounced on the shoe like a cat on a startled mouse, and sure enough, there was the hundred dollars, neatly folded and pushed into the pointy toe. I held the money up with a triumphant smile.

"Here it is!"

"Oh my!" Mabel looked embarrassed. "How could it have gotten there? I've never hidden money in a shoe before!"

"There's a first time for everything."

Mabel sighed. "I'm a little old for starting new habits. Whatever would I do without you?" She hugged me, grateful tears in her eyes. "I'm afraid I might be going crazy!"

"Not crazy, just forgetful." I assured her.

"I think maybe it's getting worse, though."

I had to agree, but I didn't want to worry her; she was upset enough for one morning. I would call her daughter later in the day. There had been a few more incidents lately, and I was thinking it was time for Mabel to have more than part time help. For now, I smiled cheerfully and shook my head.

"Mabel, you're fine. You probably put that money in there when you were half asleep. Anyone could have forgotten about that."

"Maybe you're right. It's a good thing I have you. You're quite the detective!"

In light of my new job, I found that comment rather funny, and I laughed. "Come on, Mabel, let's have breakfast, and we can run to the grocery store."

"Oh good. Maybe they have some of that nice soup in the deli."

I smiled at her good humor, wondering why it was that in our thirties we seem to lose the ability to be so delighted over small pleasures. It seemed to be a gift given only to the very young or old.

I was sitting on the porch, smoking a cigarette, when Jack pulled into my driveway, promptly at 11:30. I stubbed the smoke out in the ashtray and hurried to his truck, part of me anxious to see him, the other part of me nervous about this excursion. I had no idea how this interview was going to go. I hoped Jack was planning to take the lead.

"Hey."

"Hey."

I was getting used to our usual chatty greeting. Jack always looked good, but today instead of his customary black jeans and painted-on T-shirt he was wearing well pressed black slacks and a form fitting black dress shirt with a maroon tie so dark it almost blended with the black.

He flicked a glance in my direction that managed to travel, lightning quick, from my head to my toes. I was dressed in a long, colorful skirt and a blue T-shirt that stopped just at the waist, and of course my thin sandals. If he thought my outfit inappropriate to the task at hand he didn't say so; in fact, he didn't say anything.

He backed out of the driveway before speaking again. "I figure this accountant will probably go to lunch at noon, so we might as well get something to eat before we go see him."

"Oh, okay."

"Something wrong?"

"No, huh uh." There went again with the sparkling conversation. I didn't want to tell him that having lunch was too close to a date kind of thing; I mean, hadn't I turned down my boyfriend's invitation to lunch so I could work? Of course, I was sure Jack wasn't thinking of it that way at all. He was just a practical kind of guy.

"Any place in particular you want to eat?"

"Any where is fine."

"How about Casey's?"

I thought about that wonderful greasy cheeseburger. It seemed everyone loved that place. I shook my head.

"Not Casey's. I had my allotment of cheeseburgers for the month yesterday."

"I could eat one of his cheeseburgers everyday."

"So could I, if I wanted to buy my clothes at Omar the Tentmakers. I think I'd better stick to a salad today."

"Okay, how about Pepe's? They serve a great taco salad."

"Sounds good." That is, it sounded good until I realized I'd have to have it without the deep fried tortilla bowl and ground beef and sour cream...I kept that to myself.

Pepe's was filling up with the coming noon hour, but we found a table at the back and ordered lunch. Jack ordered enough to feed three hungry men, and shook his head over my request for a small salad, no croutons, no cheese, dressing on the side.

"How do you expect to get through the afternoon on a few bites of rabbit food?"

"I'll be fine. I'll eat an apple or something later."

"What, are you in training for that supermodel career you mentioned? I thought you said they travel too much."

"Yeah, but I decided I wanted to see Paris before I died."

"Don't need to starve yourself to do that. I'll take you next time I go."

"Yeah? You go to Paris often?"

"Actually I'm rather fond of a small town a couple hundred miles from there, but hey, once I get you to France you can take a bus, right?"

I laughed. "Fair enough."

"Great. I'll let you know next time I go."

I laughed again and ate my salad. I could never quite put my finger on this guy. I knew he was kidding, and yet he seemed so matter of fact about

107

the idea, as if he really might call me next month and tell me to pack my bags.

"So how do we approach this Phillip Howard?" I thought it was time to get back to business.

"I think I'll take the lead on this one." Jack grinned, and it wasn't a "hey, I'm just a nice guy" kind of smile. The grin made him look as if he ate cute little puppies for lunch and picked his teeth with kitten claws when he was done. "He might need a little push to tell us what we need to know."

"Just how hard a push?"

"Now, don't get squeamish on me. I promise, no broken bones; not even a bent fingernail. I'm just going to ask him some questions, put a little pressure on."

"Uh huh. Pressure as in telling his wife about his visit to a hooker?"

"Don't you think his wife has a right to know?"

I thought about that. Finally I shrugged. "I suppose she does. Then again, maybe she doesn't want to know."

"Ignorance is bliss?"

I thought about my marriage, and how I'd never even guessed at Tommy's little secret. "Nah. In that context ignorance is just stupidity with a fancy name. Besides, it was written up in the paper. Don't you think she already knows?"

"I doubt it." Jack waved for the check. "I took some time to research Phillip Howard last night, and I discovered an interesting fact that might just help our cause."

"How interesting?"

"I found out the name of his wife. One Chastity Wannamaker."

"Wannamaker..." I felt my eyes widen; sometimes I'm hyper aware of such things. "As is the old money, politically connected all over Indiana and parts of Washington Wannamakers?"

"That would be the one. She's the daughter of William Wayne Wannamaker III, and she obviously married far below her station when she tied the knot with Phillip Howard. I tried to imagine why she would do such a thing; I mean, she had to have plenty of men vying for her fortune. That is, her hand in marriage."

"And what conclusion did you come up with?"

"Well, I suppose it's possible it was true love." Jack laughed, showing what he thought of that idea. "Or it could have been an accident - you know, of the nine months to a squalling rugrat variety - but they don't have any children." Jack handed the waitress the bill and some money, waving me away when I reached for my own wallet. I hesitated. Once again, that made it seem more like a date. Then again, if I kept mooching lunch from people I'd definitely have enough to make the mortgage payment. With only a little twinge of guilt I dropped the wallet back in my purse.

"Okay, you've shot down my two best ideas. So what else?"

"Simple, dear Rainie. Miss Wannamaker comes from a long line of hard-nosed boss-type people. Her father, especially, is known for his need to always, in every situation, have his own way. Her mother serves as chairwoman of a dozen different committees at any one time- note I said "chairwoman," not member. On the other hand, Little Chastity failed to finish college, and she doesn't serve on anything much more than a tennis court. Ergo, she's probably never had anyone to boss around except the servants, and what's the fun in that?"

"And so you think she married beneath her so she could have someone to boss around?"

"Even if I'm wrong, I can pretty much guarantee that ole Phil isn't going to want a tawdry scandal like this to get back to the wife; I'm sure there's a prenup in there somewhere, and I doubt if hookers are allowed in the agreement." Jack glanced at his watch and stood up. "Come on, by the time we get to his office he should be back from lunch."

Phillip Howard was a partner in a firm named, with clever originality, Burns, Howard and Getz. The office was located in a long strip of buildings that also housed an outlet for hospital scrubs, (which pretty much everyone but doctors seemed to wear nowadays) a dentist that specialized in children and an office equipment firm.

The display windows for Burns, Howard and Getz were covered with heavy drapes; only their names adorned the front door.

Jack and I stepped into the reception area, a nicely decorated room that could have been the front for a doctor. A young, slim woman sat behind a chest-high counter, manning a multi-line phone, a discreet attachment plugged into her ear to allow her to answer hands-free. As we approached the desk she pressed a button with one carefully manicured nail and looked up with a practiced smile.

Jack smiled back, and I moved a few inches back, giving him room to work.

"May I help you?" The young woman's smile warmed a little when her eyes met Jack's. He flicked a glance at the nameplate in front of her computer terminal: Jasmine.

"I'm sure you can, Jasmine." Jack's voice had the smoky quality of a man with sex on his mind. Jasmine's smile warmed even more; other parts of me warmed. "I need to see Mr. Howard."

"Of course. Do you have an appointment?"

"No, I don't," Jack sighed regretfully and leaned against the counter, closing the gap between them. "Nonetheless, I do need to see him. It's rather urgent."

"I'm sorry, I don't recognize you," Jasmine did look genuinely regretful. "Are you a long time client?"

"Again, I'm afraid the answer is no. But trust me on this. Mr. Howard wants to see me as much as I want to see him. He just doesn't know it yet."

Jasmine's smile faltered a little. This statement seemed to be a bit over her head.

"And may I tell him what this is in regards to?"

Jack managed to look sheepish, and I nearly laughed aloud. Talk about your wolf in sheep's clothing!

"I'm afraid I can't reveal that either. It's of a rather...personal nature."

"Personal?" Jasmine looked taken aback by that, as if Mr. Howard never, ever had any personal business. His life, as far as his receptionist knew, began and ended at the office.

"Very." Jack leaned closer and nearly whispered to her. Jasmine leaned toward him, probably completely unaware she was doing it. I could sympathize. I'd been pulled in by the Jack magnet myself more than once. There was just something about him that made a girl want to sidle up to him, maybe even plaster herself against him...

I pulled my mind back to the matter at hand. Jack had pulled out his ID and was now holding it out for Jasmine to read.

"You're a private investigator?" Her eyes widened. "Whatever could you want with Mr. Howard?"

"I'd prefer to tell him, if that's okay." Jack straightened up, and as if an elastic band had been severed between them, so did Jasmine. She looked disconcerted by the abrupt change of mood.

"Um, sure, okay. Please have a seat, I'll see if he has a moment."

"Thank you, Jasmine."

Jack moved to one of the padded chairs, and I silently followed. We waited only a moment before Jasmine stood.

"Mr. Howard says he has a moment between clients, but it will have to be quick."

"Fair enough."

Jasmine indicated we should follow her. She led us through a side door and into a carpeted hallway. There were numerous doors, several of them open, and I glanced in a couple as we passed. Each was occupied by a man or woman behind identical cheap wooden desks, staring at computer screens, oblivious to anyone or anything but whatever was on the screen in front of them.

Phillip Howard's door was closed, his name, followed by an impressive array of letters that I assumed meant he was well educated, embossed on a plate on the door. Jasmine gave two short taps and opened it.

"Mr. Howard, this is Mr. Jones and..." she faltered. She had completely forgotten to ask me my name. In fact, I think she had forgotten my presence until she turned and saw me standing next to Jack.

"My associate, Miss Lovingston." Jack filled in smoothly and moved past the receptionist.

Phillip Howard was so much the epitome of an accountant he might have been a character actor in an old movie. He was pale and thin, medium height, balding, wearing thick black framed glasses. The frames did happen to be small and stylish, but they weren't stylish enough to keep from screaming "accountant!" at even a casual observer. He wore a white shirt and a conservative tie under what looked like an expensive, well-tailored suit coat.

Unlike the underlings we'd passed, Mr. Howard's desk was of the expensive variety, and nearly six feet long. It was well ordered, holding the usual pen set and name plate and a huge blotter, in the middle of which sat a sheaf of papers that Mr. Howard was apparently working on. To one side, turned so that it was visible both to Mr.

Howard and any visitors, was a framed professional photograph. It featured a woman in her late thirties who probably would be called plain (though likely not to her face.) Her hair was carefully styled, and her makeup looked professionally applied. It reminded Rainie of the "Glamour Shots" people had done at the mall. The woman's expression was no less than imperious. This then, must be Chastity Wannamaker, the heir apparent herself.

Phillip Howard didn't stand up when we came in.

He waited for Jasmine to back out the door and then remained silent until the door swung closed.

"What can I do for you, Mr. *Jones*?" His sarcastic emphasis on Jack's name left no doubt he thought it an alias; I wondered how often Jack got that reaction.

"I need some information regarding a little incident you were involved in last year. At the massage parlor?"

Howard's face went through an abrupt color change, first to deep red, then back to its original pale and beyond to a distinctly unhealthy looking white. He did an admirable job of holding his tone steady.

"And your interest would be?"

"We actually aren't interested in your part; we know all about it. We are however interested on a further bit of information on the...service providers."

"That business is long over and done with." Howard was recovering his composure. "I have no interest in talking about it."

"Fine. Then maybe your wife will answer our questions." Jack turned and jerked his head toward the door, indicating I should follow. That got a reaction from Howard. He literally jumped to his feet, sending his big chair back so hard and fast it crashed into the credenza behind him, setting off a minor earthquake among the various framed awards showcased there.

"Now just a minute, there's no need to involve her in this!"

"Oh? You mean she doesn't know? Doesn't your wife read the papers?"

"It only came out in the Michigan papers. She never saw it." Howard opened a cabinet and revealed a well stocked bar. He poured himself a drink; straight amber liquid of some kind, no ice. He tossed it back in one gulp and poured another. The red flush came back to his face, creeping up from his neck.

"All right, maybe we don't need to speak to her." Jack shrugged. "That is, if you're willing to tell us what we need to know."

"And what would that be?"

"We just want to talk about the woman in charge of the...massage parlor."

"You're investigating Mistress Holly? Why, did she finally go too far and kill someone?"

Mistress Holly? I wondered who the hell that was. Jack didn't blink.

"Does Mistress Holly have a temper?"

"A temper?" Howard laughed harshly. "Hell, she doesn't have to be *mad* to do what she does! She loves every minute of it." He tossed the second drink down and I saw his eyes gloss over. It was obvious he couldn't hold his liquor. He swayed slightly while he poured one more, but he just held on to this one, not drinking.

Jack smiled almost triumphantly, and I wondered what he had picked up from Howard's words that I obviously wasn't getting.

"I take it you don't enjoy Mistress Holly's services?"

"Me? No way. She's way beyond what I like. I mean, a little corporal punishment is one thing, but hell, that bitch dishes out debilitating *pain*! I knew a guy had to take a week off work after a session with her. Who needs that shit?"

Suddenly I got it. It was just like the cartoons, when a little light bulb appears over a character's head. I almost glanced up to see if there was one hovering over me. S&M. Mistress Holly. Not just a wet massage with a happy ending; this whole thing smelled of kink. Obviously when Jack told Mr. Howard we knew all about it, he thought we knew *all* about it. This was juicy stuff.

Jack was playing it cool, as if none of this was news to him.

"So you prefer Miss Matherly?"

"Who?" Howard looked genuinely perplexed.

"The tall one with the blonde hair, has a cute little mole right under her left eye?"

"Oh, Mistress Kate. Yes, I would say so. But then, you already know that, don't you?" There was a flicker of alarm in the man's eyes, as if it had suddenly occurred to him he'd revealed too much.

"Of course. It's all in the public record."

"So what do you need me for?"

"I'd like to speak to Miss Matherly, but she seems to have relocated. Do you know where that is?"

"No, I don't." Howard tossed back his third drink, and properly fortified made his way back to his chair. He was none too steady, and his words were starting to slur a bit.

"What, you've found a new outlet for your...needs?"

Howard flushed. "One arrest was enough. I'm not going anywhere near that place again. I mean, the others had the money to keep their names out of the paper, but I..." He waved an arm around his modest office. "I can't afford that kind of publicity." Hmm. Miss Wannamaker must be a little tight with the purse strings. That went a long way toward proving Jack's assumption of a prenuptial agreement.

"How did you find the place the first time?" Jack was relentless.

"A friend told me about it."

"So ask the friend where they've moved to."

"What? No!" Mr. Howard lurched to his feet, trying to appear bold and fearless, but the alcohol tripped him up. He fell against his desk and had to thrust out both hands to steady himself.

"But why not, Mr. Howard? If you aren't involved anymore..."

117

"But my friend is! I won't risk him getting arrested..."

"We're not cops, Mr. Howard." Jack suddenly dropped the calm, businesslike tone. He set his own hands on the desk and leaned into the accountant, but this time there was nothing flirtatious in his tone. His expression hardened; his biceps flexed. This was the Jack that could kill a man fourteen different ways with his bare hands, the Jack that looked like he could reach down your throat and pull out your heart without breaking a sweat, and do it with that same I-ate-a-puppy-for-lunch-smile.

"If we were cops, you wouldn't have much to worry about. All that stuff about warrants and such. I have no such restrictions." Jack lowered his voice and leaned in an inch closer. I stepped back, my mouth suddenly dry and my palms sweaty. I feared he might very well reach out and do something gruesome and painful to the little accountant. "You *will* tell me what I want to know."

Phillip Howard swallowed, and I heard it from where I stood. I had never known what was meant when a writer said someone "swallowed audibly." Now I knew, and I kind of wished I didn't. Howard's face was a mottled mess of unnaturally pale flesh and random patches of red. His eyes had widened until the whites were visible all the way around, his nostrils flared, and his mouth was opening and closing on rapid gulps of air. I feared that even if Jack didn't do something to him, the man might just die of fright anyway.

"Th-there's a club..." Howard shut his mouth and worked up some spit, swallowed and tried again. "A health club, I mean...the basement...you can't just go there though...they'd never let you in."

"Where?"

"J-just outside of N-Niles. On the main road. Quickfit, all one word."

"And the festivities take place in the basement?"

Howard nodded. "But they won't let you in!" He gulped again. "No one would believe you're...I mean, who would believe you want to be..."

"Spanked? Is that the word you're looking for?" Abruptly Jack leaned back and grinned, amused. "Don't worry, I'll get in. Especially since you're going to tell me the password."

"The what?" Howard licked his lips, his eyes flicking away, trying to find anything to look at but Jack's not-nice smile.

"The password, Mr. Howard. I'm sure the basement door is kept locked, probably guarded, right? But they need new customers. They'll take recommendations, won't they?"

"Sure, but..."

"Well, I doubt if they expect you to walk in there with the buddy you recommend. So they'd give you a password, or a phrase, something to indicate that you're in the know, that you've been invited. So what is it?"

"I told you I'm not involved in that..."

"Fine. Let's go Rainie. We'll just see what Chastity knows..."

"No! You can't do that!" Howard lurched to his feet again, panic in his eyes. He stared around the office, his eyes falling on the picture of his wife. He groaned aloud and fell back into his chair, dropping his head onto his arms. From the cradle of his arms, barely audible, he mumbled. "Ask for Mandy Hurley, the personal trainer."

"What was that?"

Howard lifted his head. "I said you ask for Mandy Hurley, the personal trainer."

"And that's it?"

"That will get you to the basement door. Then you tell the guy there that you need to see the manager about a billing problem."

"That's it?"

"Yes. That's it." Howard's eyes flicked toward his wife's picture. He looked so totally forlorn, I wanted to go and put my arms around him, tell him everything would be all right.

Jack turned as if to go, but stopped and spun back toward Howard so fast the accountant fell against the back of his chair as if he'd been pushed. "By the way, Mr. Howard, don't call your buddy with a warning. If you do, I'll know it was you, and then I'll have to come back here. On the other hand, keep your mouth shut and you'll never see me again. Okay?"

Howard nodded vigorously. "Okay, yeah, not a word."

Jack nodded and headed for the door, me a shaking step behind.

"That was kind of nasty." I clicked my seatbelt closed and wished for something to drink. The whole experience had left a bad taste in my mouth.

"I didn't think it was so bad." Jack grinned. "Anyway, Phil is into pain and humiliation. The whole scenario probably turned him on."

"Eew!" I grimaced with distaste. "That was an image I didn't need."

Jack laughed. "So, Grasshopper, what have we learned today?"

"That behind every mousy accountant there's a dark shadow no one wants to see?"

"I meant what have we learned relevant to our Saint Haley?"

I frowned and thought about it. "Not all that much, really. Just that she has a friend who's a dominatrix."

"And?"

I thought some more. "And that her good friend the banker doesn't like to associate the word 'discipline' with her." I was finally getting the full picture, like an old Polaroid slowly developing. "You think Saint Haley works for Mistress Kate on the side?"

"There's only one way to find out. You'll have to make a trip to the fitness club."

"Me?" The word came out in an astonished squeak, as if I'd been goosed.

"Of course, you. Phillip was right about that; I don't think anyone would buy me as a customer."

"And you think they'll believe I like to be spanked? What about me gives you that wrongheaded idea?"

"Nothing. I can't imagine you'd like it, so I promise not to try it. But they might believe you like to dish it out."

"Me, a dominatrix?" I laughed. "That's rich!"

"By the time we're done shopping, you might actually believe it yourself."

"Shopping?"

"Let's head for the mall. Don't worry, it'll all go into expenses."

"All what?"

"Your leather boots and bustiere."

"My what? Are you nuts?"

"Don't you want to find out the truth about Haley?"

"Sure, but I thought I was just supposed to interview people and stuff. No one said anything about infiltrating an S&M club!"

"Okay." Jack's tone was flat. "So I'll drop you back at the office and you can do some more computer searching."

He made it sound like I wanted to go to the park and clean up dog poop.

"I was told that was what the job was all about." I wanted to defend myself, but I thought I just sounded petulant.

"That is how a lot of people do it. I just expected more from you."

"Why? I'm a caregiver and part time poet for God's sake! This was just supposed to be a way to pay my mortgage, not a lifestyle change."

Jack's jaw was set. He didn't say anything.

"Are you actually pissed off at me?"

"No. Just disappointed." Jack shrugged. "Like I said, I thought you were going to bring more to this job than just a clerical attitude."

Now, here's the thing. If Jack was mad at me, I think I could have gotten mad right back, and to hell with him. But having him disappointed in me was another story. Okay, I know my sense of self-worth should all come from within and all that, but the truth is I was enjoying the attention this very macho, kind of dangerous guy has been giving me. I hated the thought that he'd be so disgusted with me that he wouldn't come around anymore. So I did a stupid thing. I caved in to his desires, always a bad habit when it comes to dealing with men, even more so when that man has as strong a personality as Jack Jones.

"Do you really think I can pull this off?"

"No sweat, sweetheart." Already he'd relaxed his jaw and the warmth had returned to his eyes. All right, I know it was stupid, but I was happy to have pleased him. "So on to the mall?"

"I guess I'm with you."

With a slight nod he turned at the next corner and I jumped in to his scheme with both feet. I just hope I can touch bottom.

Chapter Eight

Jack parked at the mall and led us directly to Victoria's Secret. He had no need to check the mall map; I suspected he'd been there before. A petite salesclerk with carefully applied makeup and a great haircut approached us as soon as we entered. She immediately focused on Jack, and I realized she knew him.

"What can I do for you today?" From her tone I didn't think there was much she *wouldn't* do for him. Damn, did every woman flirt with Jack?

"Hey, Susan, this is Rainie. We need an outfit put together for her. Something in leather."

"Ah." Susan smiled, revealing crooked teeth. Apparently her cosmetic budget didn't cover extensive orthodontics. The smile seemed genuine, though, and I felt myself warm up to her a little, in spite of the familiar way she had her hand resting on Jack's arm. "You have a little project going on or is this for a special date?"

"It's for a project, but who knows?" Jack shifted a bit and slung an arm around my shoulders. "Maybe someday Rainie will succumb to my boyish charms."

Susan rolled her eyes. "We all do, Jack. Well come on, Rainie, let's see what we can find. You're what, a size twelve?"

"Wow, that's pretty good."

"My life calling," Susan answered wryly.

She led the way to a rack of leather bustieres and flipped through them. She came out with a size twelve. It was black leather, complete with laces to tighten past all hope of taking a deep breath.

"How much leather do you want?" She asked Jack.

"Enough to be noticed, but not so much she can't walk down a public street without getting arrested."

"Okay, then we'll go with a jacket over this. Pants or skirt?"

"I prefer skirts."

Susan looked at my long, colorful skirt and smirked. "We might have to go with a different style."

She led us to another rack, and quickly came up with a leather mini skirt that might have covered my butt cheeks, with a little tugging and a lot of prayer.

"Uh, no, I don't think so." I blushed at the thought of walking anywhere in that tiny thing, even my own bedroom, let alone a public street!

"All right, pants it is."

Within moments Susan had selected everything she thought I needed and hustled me to a dressing room. I squeezed into the ensemble. Even in my size the leather fit pretty tight. I stared at myself in the mirror, not sure if I wanted to laugh or cry.

My breasts were pushed up and together, creating a lot more cleavage than I ever thought to reveal. The pants fit like a second skin, and no matter how much I tugged I could see a little skin between the waistband and the top. And it wasn't just skin, it was a small but obvious roll of fat. I think younger girls referred to it as a "muffin top," and some seemed to think it was kind of cute. I thought it just looked like one too many of Casey's cheeseburgers.

The pants tapered down to ankle high black leather boots with four inch spiked heels and laces to match the bustiere. The jacket was short, black but not leather. It was made of something silky and shiny looking, and I had to admit it softened the look just a little.

No way was I going out in this get up.

"Rainie, you about ready?"

"I don't think I'll ever be ready for this, Jack. The *world* isn't ready for this!"

"Come on, I'm sure you look great. Step out so I can see."

"No."

"No? Do I have to come in after you?"

"You wouldn't dare!" But even as I said it I wondered if maybe he would dare.

"Was that a challenge?' I heard the laughter in his voice, but I still wasn't sure he was kidding. Besides, maybe it was best to let him see me. When he saw how ridiculous I looked he'd probably give up on this whole stupid idea and I could go back to my computer searches.

I stepped out.

Jack grinned and made a twirling motion with his finger, indicating I should turn and show him the back.

I did, blushing furiously, tottering a bit on the heels. I definitely preferred my whole foot touching the ground.

"Damn. They'll be lining up to feel the burn."

"Very funny." I stood, hands on hips, not believing he still wanted me to go through with this. "Did you hear my description of Katherine Matherly? That woman is *hot*! I don't think I'm the type they're looking for."

Jack looked to Susan for an opinion. "What do you think?"

"Not sure what you're after, but it looks good to me. If I tried that outfit I'd look like a mad munchkin gone bad."

Jack took another thorough look, head to toe. "Put a whip in your hand and you might even get *me* to my knees." There was something in his eyes that made it seem like he meant it.

I felt a warm flush wash over me. I blew out a hard breath, not easy when I couldn't inhale more than a sip of air at a time.

"Fine, if I'm not talking you out of this, let's get on with it. I'll go change."

"Maybe you should leave it on. Looks like you could use some practice on those heels."

"I am not walking around in this stuff any longer than I have to!" I took a step toward the dressing room and nearly turned my ankle. "Maybe you're right about the heels though. I'll leave them on. My skirt will mostly cover them anyway."

I went to change while Jack went to pay. I didn't know how B&E would react to these items on the expense account, but Jack didn't seem concerned. Maybe all the P.I.'s shopped Victoria's Secret on a regular basis.

"So when are we going to do this?" Back in Jack's truck, back in my own familiar clothes, this whole situation was beginning to feel unreal, like a bad dream where you saw yourself sliding toward an abyss but had no way to stop yourself. In dreams I always woke up before I got to the edge. I didn't think a well-timed period of wakefulness was going to save me this time.

"I figured we might as well do it tonight."

"Tonight? Wouldn't the weekend be more likely?"

"People don't just have sex on the weekends. Some people like it a little more regular than that."

I wasn't about to ask him how frequently *he* liked it. I didn't care to know. Really, I didn't.

"That doesn't give me much time to get used to these heels."

"Also doesn't give you much time to chicken out." Jack smiled that crooked little smile of his, and I knew I was willing to follow him anywhere. Wow, was I a sucker.

"We'll stop by the office, pick up some supplies."

"Supplies?"

"Spy stuff." Jack grinned again. "We have a guy, just like 007 had Q."

"I think I'm more the Agent 86 type."

"You, Maxwell Smart?" Jack shook his head. "I'd think you'd rather be 99."

"Obviously I'm not. She was the smart one."

"But Max was the lucky one, and sometimes that counts for more."

B&E really did have a gadget guy, but his name was Melvin Krantz, not Q. And he didn't work in a laboratory full of cool high tech gadgets being tested in every corner. Instead he had a large basement room filled with shelves, stocked with the latest spy gear, and a big book that he used to sign items out at the request of the P.I.s. There was also a catalogue on the counter. Jack flipped it open and perused it, searching for what he needed.

"I need one of these," he pointed at a heavy medallion on a gold chain, "and one of these." He pointed to what looked like a tiny transmitter. "And give me one of these, too."

"Okay." Melvin filled out some numbers on a line in his book and spun it toward Jack. "Sign for it while I get it."

He disappeared into the warren of shelves and returned a short time later carrying a small cardboard box.

"Happy spying."

"Happy spying?"

"Good luck? Have a nice day?"

Jack laughed. "Keep working on it, Melvin. You're bound to come up with a good exit line one of these days."

We went back to my house and carried in the shopping bags and the little cardboard box of spy gear. The afternoon was gone and evening was coming on fast. Too fast for my liking. I hit the play button on my answering machine and let George out of his cage while I listened.

There was a computerized sales call, followed by a hang up. Hm, no heavy breathing, maybe a wrong number. Then there was another sales call. The last message was my mom.

"Hi Rainbow, this is mom."

"Rainbow?" Jack laughed. "What are your other siblings named, Moonglow and Sunflower?"

"Actually Jason and Brenda. They were born before my folks moved to the commune."

"Seriously? You grew up in a commune?"

"Only the first few years. Hey, let me listen, okay?"

My mom was still talking."...hate these machines. So impersonal. You know our whole world is being overtaken by machinery. Why, a baby could be born in a test tube and between vending machines, the internet and cell phones go its whole life without personal contact with another human being, and you know that's no good, you can't get good vibes to feed your aura from a machine. I know I didn't hug you when you were little, but I didn't know any better. That's probably what's wrong with Jason and Brenda. You have to touch people, feel their essence, feed each other's spirits or your soul will starve and then we'll all be empty shells, no different than the machines. Of course, sometimes I think that's what we're becoming. We're programmed by the government from earliest childhood in school, which starts earlier and earlier, and of course the media only reports what the government wants us to hear, so it's almost impossible to see the truth and form an individual opinion. I mean, how many real individuals do you know? Everyone dresses like everyone else in their group...I guess that's some diversity, that we have so many different types of people, I mean yuppies and rappers and hippies and..." There was a long moment of silence. Jack started to say something, but I held up a hand.

"Wait. She's probably not done."

Sure enough, her voice came back on, a little hesitant. "Um, sweetie, I guess I forgot why I called. Well, anyway, I love you!" there was a click and a beep.

"Wow. Did you follow all that?"

"That's just how my mom talks. You shouldn't make fun of her."

"I'm not." But Jack wasn't even trying to hide his grin.

Time to change the subject. "I'd offer you something to eat, but I don't have much on hand."

"I'm hungry enough to make do with just about anything. Mind if I scrounge?"

"Help yourself. You know where the kitchen is." I checked the timers on Geroge's heater and light, looked to see if his water was still clean, and then went to the fridge to get George some fresh goodies. Jack was holding the bowl of chopped fruit and veggies.

"Looks like the iguana eats better than you do."

131

"He doesn't like cereal."

"Cereal. That's no kind of dinner."

"It works for me. I think there might be some chicken in the freezer."

"At least that's meat." Jack opened the freezer door and blinked at the contents. I was right, there was some chicken: two skinless, boneless breasts wrapped separately so I could thaw them one at a time. There was also a bin full of ice from the automatic ice maker, and nothing else.

"You don't cook much, do you?"

"I cook for my clients all the time."

"What about cooking for yourself?"

"Not really. Do you?"

"Sure, I like to cook. It's soothing."

"Soothing? What, is it a Zen thing?"

"Sort of. Something about the order of it. Taking individual ingredients and combining them to create something new. Besides, I like to eat. It seemed like a good idea to learn how to cook."

"I like to eat, too, but I don't feel a need to create anything when there are three pizza joints in town that deliver."

"Do you have any flour? Eggs? Breadcrumbs?"

I shook my head. "What would I need all that stuff for?"

Jack sighed. "All right, pizza it is."

"I want just cheese and veggies on my half." I plucked the bowl of goodies out of his hand and went to feed George while Jack made the call.

We watched the local news while waiting for the pizza, then the national news while we ate. We didn't talk much. I was too nervous about the upcoming events; I don't know what Jack was thinking.

We threw the leftover pizza in the fridge, box and all, and I rinsed our plates and stuck them in the dishwasher. Clean up done. Pizza was almost as efficient as a bowl of cereal.

"Oh man, I almost forgot, I have to call Jenny."

"Who's that?"

"Mabel's daughter. Give me a minute." I called up the number on my cell, and Jenny picked up the phone on the second ring.

"Hello?"

"Hi Jenny, it's Rainie. I wanted to talk to you about your mom."

"Uh oh, is it bad?"

"I think maybe her cognitive ability is slipping." I told her about the recent incidents that worried me, concluding with the lost money.

Jenny sighed. "You know, I've been wondering. Last weekend when I stopped by I could have sworn she didn't recognize me at first. She insists she did, but there was something in her eyes..." Jenny sighed. "You think she's in danger being alone?"

"Well, nothing immediate. Having the electric circuit cut to her stove was pretty smart; at least she won't burn the house down. But I'd worry about other stuff - leaving the water running, letting strangers in, that sort of thing."

"I knew this was coming. I guess we'd better have someone full time. So you think she needs someone around the clock?"

133

"I don't think yet. I mean, she still gets around pretty good, and she sleeps well most of the time, so she's probably okay over night."

"So are you available full time? The day shift at least?"

"Well, I have Thelma on Tuesdays and Thursdays."

"That's right. Well, what about Monday, Wednesday and Friday?"

I hesitated, thinking about B&E. So far it had been kind of interesting, although this business tonight was making me rethink it. Still, being a caregiver full time could be emotionally draining. I thought I should at least give the B&E thing a fair shot.

"You know I love Mabel, and I'd like to, but I sort of started another job recently, and I want to see how it shakes out."

"Oh. Sure, I understand." I could hear the disappointment in Jenny's voice. "I just hate to start all over with people I don't know."

"I don't blame you. Listen, I know someone who might be perfect for you. I worked with her before, she did overnights for a client that needed twenty-four hour care, and she was really good. Do you want her number?"

"Sure!" Jenny brightened a little at the prospect of a recommendation. It was hell trying to sort out strangers to find one you trusted with your mom. I gave her the number and we hung up after promising to keep in touch, and my assurance that I would still be with Mabel part time until Jenny got someone else in place.

No more time left. Jack looked at me expectantly.
"Well?'
"Well what?"
"You need to get changed."

I took a deep breath, considering trying one more time to talk him out of this. He still hadn't really explained the plan to me; could I even pull it off?

I went into the bedroom, not bothering to argue.

When I came out ten minutes later in my leather-biker-chick-from-hell outfit, Jack nodded approvingly and held up the gold medallion. I noticed there was a black jewel in the center of it.

"Latest technology. There's a camera in the jewel. Here, hold your hair out of the way."

Jack fastened the medallion on. It rested just above my enhanced cleavage.

"There's a button on the side, here. You see it?" I nodded; the button was barely raised from the beveled edge of the medallion. "Just push it to take a picture. It's got a decent wide angle lens. As long as you're facing your subject you should get good results."

"My subject?"

"You're going into the basement. Hopefully Miss Nieswonger will be there, looking something like you. Get pictures, and you're out of there."

"And if she's not there?"

"Then we'll think of something else." Jack pulled another gadget out of the box.

"This is a transmitter." He held up a tiny plastic square not much bigger than one of the newest MP3 players. "There's a wireless ear bud." He fitted a tiny object in my ear, and then took a moment to look at my outfit, the transmitter cradled in the palm of his hand.

"Hmm, this might be a problem. There's not much storage space in those pants, is there?"

"Very funny. I told you this would never work..."

"Calm down, Rainie, I was just kidding. I think it'll fit in the waistband." He tugged at the tight pants and managed to slide the transmitter between the leather and my skin. My skin, or at least the modest layer of fat under it, gave way, and surprisingly the transmitter didn't show at all.

"Very nice." Jack's fingers lingered a little longer than necessary at my waist, long enough to make me uncomfortable. I stepped back a pace, careful not to fall off the high heels.

"Okay, so I can hear you. What if I need you to hear me?"

Jack pulled a heavy bracelet out that matched the medallion with the camera. "There's a microphone in this; just press on the jewel to activate it. But keep in mind that it looks suspicious when people talk to their jewelry. Only use it if things go bad and you really need me."

"How far away will you be?"

"I'll be in the club. I'm going to go in and inquire about a membership." He held up one arm, flexing his bicep in that age-old gesture of machismo. "I think I could use a little buffing up, don't you?"

I rolled my eyes and didn't answer that.

"Anyway, I should be able to hear you, unless the basement walls are too thick."

"What if they are?"

"Just whip anyone who gets in your way and run like hell!"

"You think I'll be in danger?"

"Not really. I mean, what they're doing is illegal, and certainly Haley has plenty of financial reasons to conceal the nature of their business, but I don't think they'd kill to keep the secret."

I couldn't help a hard gulp at the word kill. Jack obviously read the terror in my eyes and he smiled encouragingly.

"Come on, cops hardly ever die busting a brothel."

"But I'm not a cop!"

"Even so, I think you'll be fine. Come on, let's get going. We're going to swing by Belinda's place so you can borrow her car."

"Why?"

"Because we need to show up separately, and I don't think your Escort is going to cut it. Just in case someone sees you arrive, you want to look like you're good enough to earn some money at this."

One last hard swallow, and I followed him outside.

Chapter Nine

Belinda's car was an '87 cherry red Camaro, buffed to a glistening shine right down to the chrome wheels. It was beautiful, strong and sexy, and suited Belinda to a T.

"Just take good care of her," Belinda admonished me when she handed over the keys.

"I'm only driving it a couple of miles, what could happen?"

Belinda flashed a look at Jack. "Lots of things, when you're with him."

I looked from her to Jack, thinking she sounded like she was speaking from experience. "Should I be worried?"

"No, you'll be fine." She patted me on the shoulder and looked me up and down. "That is one fine outfit!"

"Yeah, it's great if you're into sweating and not breathing too hard."

"Honey, in that outfit I could accomplish both quite happily."

There didn't seem to be much to say to that, so I just turned and went out the door.

Belinda's car was a great, rumbling, powerful ride. I could see where it had a few advantages over my little Escort, although I did miss my stick shift.

Quickfit was in a storefront, part of a strip mall on a busy corner. The whole front of the fitness center was plate glass windows, no shades, and the inside of the place was well lighted, so you had a clear view of the sweating people on a row of exercise bikes and stairclimbers across the front. I guess it was to guilt the people comfortably ensconced in their passing cars. They could cruise by, sucking on a 32 ounce cola and chewing on a burger from a fast food joint, see the people working out, and think "Hey, I should be doing that!"

I parked in the middle row, sliding in between two SUVs, and sat for a long moment staring at the front door of Quickfit, my sweaty palms tight on the steering wheel. No way could I go through with this. No way could I walk in there and...

"Hey babe, what are you waiting for?"

Jack spoke softly, but through the ear bud it sounded as if he were shouting. I nearly jumped out the window.

"Asshole." I muttered the word, knowing he couldn't hear me. Then I pushed the clunky jewel on the bracelet. "I don't think I can do this."

"Sure you can, and do it soon. You don't want anyone to see you out here having second thoughts. You're supposed to be tough, right? Think leather whips and mamma's boys tied to chairs, just waiting for you to..."

"All right!" I pressed the jewel again and hissed at him. "I'm going. Where are you?"

"Don't turn around, but I'm in the lot two spaces over, in the back. Go on in, I'll be along shortly."

I took as deep a breath as the leather laces allowed and got out of the car, stepping carefully on the high heels. I think I had the walking down pretty good, once I was moving, but getting to my feet still felt like a circus act.

I walked into Quickfit, trying to look masterful. I paused inside the door, concentrating on not hyperventilating, and took a moment to get the lay of the land.

I found myself in a brightly lit foyer. There were several doors, clearly marked with their function. To the left was the workout room, obviously the one you could see from the street. Ahead was a door marked Pool/Locker Rooms. Both had key card readers on them, so that only card-carrying members could access them. Great. I didn't see any door marked "basement S&M room."

To my right was a short curved counter. A perky young thing in a shiny leotard and short skirt sat behind the counter. She looked up and smiled cheerfully at me. If she thought my outfit a little much for an evening workout, her expression didn't show it.

"May I help you?" Her voice practically squeaked with perkiness.

"I'm here to see Mandy Hurley, the personal trainer." I impressed the hell out of myself with how normal my voice sounded. I bet the little cheerleader chick had no idea I was about to pass out from fright.

"Oh, sure." Perky girl jumped off her stool, and for a minute I thought she'd break out the pom poms and rattle off an old school cheer, but instead she just raised a short section of the counter and motioned me through.

Huh, really? It was going to be that easy?

I followed her through a door behind the counter and down a short hall. A large man in a t shirt that was struggling mightily to contain his bulging biceps stood in front of another door, his arms crossed over his considerable chest. He watched us approach, absolutely no expression on his well-tanned face. Maybe he wasn't a real man; maybe he was just an oak carving set up for decorative intimidation.

"She's here to see Mandy Hurley," Perky girl told the oak carving.

No, it was a real man, after all. I knew this because his eyes shifted and looked at me. Nothing else on him moved. He didn't say anything.

I stared back at him. Perky girl stood there being perky, looking at me expectantly.

The silence stretched out. What the hell?

"Um...so is she in?"

Still he just stared at me. What did he want? Why wasn't he saying anything?

Finally it hit me, and I nearly slapped myself on the forehead. Of course; there was another line in the password for me to speak. Naturally Perky and Oak weren't going to prompt me!

I cleared my throat. "Um, I need to see the manager about a billing problem."

Oak nodded once, a bare movement of his head. Maybe the muscles were too overdeveloped to allow any more motion than that. Perky said "Okay, then!" and scampered back down the hall. Oak unfolded his arms and reached behind him, swiped a key card through a slot on the door, and pushed it open, all without turning his back to me.

I saw a dimly lit stairwell beyond the door. It was utterly silent down there. Silent and kind of dark.

I looked at the stairs and back at Oak. He was holding the door ajar and staring at me, not saying a word. Maybe they'd cut his tongue out to assure secrecy. Maybe the steroids had eaten away the part of his brain that controlled speech.

Maybe I was just stalling with all this mental speculation and I should just get on with it.

I nodded at Oak and stepped past him into the stairwell. As soon as I'd cleared the door he let it swing shut behind me.

I tried to be nonchalant about clutching the railing while I negotiated the stairs. I should have practiced doing steps before I went wandering into uncharted territory in four inch heels. I managed to make it without mishap, and I was feeling pretty cocky when I reached the bottom. Well, not cocky exactly, more like confident. Or maybe just not like I was about to throw up. Yep, that was it.

At the bottom of the stairs was another foyer, much smaller than the one upstairs. The walls were painted a deep forest green, and there was a ridiculously plush carpet to match. There was indirect lighting coming from the ceiling, but not a lot; the room was pretty dim.

A nice looking young woman sat behind a desk, the only furniture in the room. It was one of those open front things that look more like a small dining room table than a desk. The inlaid surface was devoid of paperwork or pens or any other accoutrements of office work except for a multi-line phone that managed to look sleek and elegant. There was a heavy looking door behind her, its polished wood surface gleaming even in the low light.

The woman behind the desk was wearing a lot of makeup. Dark eye shadow and thick but smoothly applied mascara emphasized her large eyes. Her skin was too smooth and free of imperfections not to be covered with foundation, but it was imperceptible beyond the fact that I knew it had to be there. Quite a trick; if I tried that much makeup I'd look like a clown on her way to entertain at a birthday party.

The receptionist had long, well formed legs under a short skirt, and the open fronted desk allowed her to showcase them for anyone who entered her little space. She uncrossed them and sat forward a bit when I came in, her knees primly together. Apparently I wasn't worth posing for.

"May I help you?" her voice was soft and slightly husky.

"I'm here to see Mistress Kate."

The receptionist raised both perfectly sculpted eyebrows and looked at me for what seemed a long moment. I resisted the urge to fidget.

"Do you have an appointment?"

"Uh, no." I took a deep breath to stop myself from stammering, but it didn't help much. "A friend suggested...I mean, he thought she might be hiring."

"You're here to apply for a job?"

I knew I was blushing and still stammering in a very un-dominating way, but I couldn't help it. My knees were trembling so hard I was pretty sure the tight leather pants were the only thing keeping my legs from shaking apart at the joints.

"Yes, that's right." I think the calm tone I managed was worth the small delay in answering.

"One moment, please." The receptionist picked up her phone and pushed a button with one long, perfectly manicured finger. I supposed, with no paperwork to do all day, she had plenty of time to work on them.

I glanced around. There were no visitor's chairs to sit in, no pictures on the walls to gaze at. There was nothing whatsoever to do but stand in front of the desk and stare at a random spot on the wall over the receptionist's head while she made the call.

The walls must have been very well insulated. There was no sound of clanking weights from above, no cracking whips or cries of pain from behind the heavy door. The receptionist's softly spoken conversation reached my ears as a murmured undertone. I couldn't pick up a single word of what she was saying. Once she glanced over at me, a quick flick of her eyes moving from top to bottom, then she spoke into the phone again. Shortly afterwards she hung up the phone.

"You may go in. Mistress Kate will meet with you." She stood and opened the door for me, holding it much the same way Oak had held the door upstairs.

I stood where I was as if my spike heels had nailed themselves to the thick carpet. Actually I was just stunned; I had expected to be turned away with scornful laughter.

I swallowed a sudden lump in my throat and nodded, at whom I don't know. Maybe I was just trying to jump start my brain with a little friction.

The receptionist stood holding the door, looking at me with what might have been curiosity.

Finally I managed to get one heel unstuck from the carpet and I took a step, which was fortunately followed by another and then another until I'd passed the receptionist and stepped into another dimly lit hallway.

This hall was carpeted with the same thick, dark green expanse, the walls the same deep forest green. The lighting came from low-wattage bulbs expertly fashioned to resemble medieval candle holders, one beside each of eight doors lining the hall, four to a side. At the very end was another door, without a sconce.

The receptionist let the door close behind me, and I stood in almost pure silence; it was disrupted by the sound of my own breathing, which still sounded a little harsher than I liked. So much for the cool, ready-to-mete-out-punishment dominatrix. I realized I hadn't heard from Jack since the parking lot. Was it because he hadn't said anything or could the transmitter not pick him up through the thick walls? Was I really completely alone down here?

I pushed that thought aside, fearing an epic panic attack. Instead I thought of what my next move should be. There was no sign of Mistress Kate.

What to do? Maybe open the nearest door and start snapping medallion pictures at whoever - or whatever - was in there?

Before I could do anything so boldly intrusive the door two down and to the right opened, and out stepped Saint Haley!

Only she didn't look so holy at the moment.

Her leather bustiere was cinched smaller at the waist than mine, and her breasts were far more generous and far less contained. She wore no jacket, exposing thin but sleekly muscled arms with silver bands circling the biceps. She wore a short, skin tight leather skirt over black fishnet stockings and glossy black leather boots that pulled up over her knees. Like the receptionist, her makeup was liberally but expertly applied, except in Haley's case she'd used a lot of eyeliner, giving her a dark, somehow mysterious look.

She was holding a short leather crop in one hand. Through the open door I heard someone sobbing. She glanced at me and pulled the door shut, cutting off the sound.

I couldn't believe it. What had I been so worried about? This spy stuff was so easy a child could do it!

I quickly pulled the medallion from its nest of cleavage and started snapping pictures.

"What are you doing?" Haley sounded more curious than anything. I kept snapping, holding the medallion at different angles to be sure I got a good shot.

The door at the end of the hall opened and Katherine Matherly stepped out, dressed in a conservative business suit. I had nearly forgotten about her in my excitement over finding Haley.

"Hey Kate, who is this woman?"

"A new prospect." Katherine answered Haley calmly, not having noticed anything amiss.

"Well, what the hell is she doing?"

Belatedly it occurred to me that my secret camera was hardly a secret with me waving it around like that. I was supposed to be subtle with it, just reach up and touch the shutter release a few times, not wave it around in the air like a bejeweled and be-leathered paparazzi.

"What is that? Is that a camera?" Haley started for me, crop raised. Katherine, abruptly catching on that all was not well, picked up her pace.

"Who are you? What the hell are you doing here?"

I didn't think it prudent to answer. I yelped and spun on my heel to make a fast exit.

At least, that's what I pictured doing. Instead my heel had managed to once again bury itself in the deep pile of the carpet, and while my body turned, my foot didn't.

I cried out in pain and fell against the door behind me.

"You bitch! How dare you!" Haley snatched at my hair and pulled my head back so I was looking at her from an awkward sideways and nearly upside down angle. Nope, this was definitely not Saint Haley, Super Substitute Mommy. This was demon Haley, whose red, uber-sharp nails could cut your heart out while she licked her blood-red lips with glee.

Behind her Katherine was coming at a run, no longer looking professional even with her well-tailored suit. Like Haley, she seemed to have no problem keeping her heels from hanging up on the carpet; it must be an inborn talent, like the ability to sink unerring free throws or run the hundred yard dash in record time.

I quickly figured out that I had two options. I could try to talk these two bitches from hell into a calm and friendly demeanor, or I could fight them off. Haley's dagger-like nails were reaching for my face. No time for peace talks.

I swung my arm as hard as I could, deflecting the nails, and rolled over onto my back. Haley's hand came loose from my head clutching an alarming amount of torn hair. I screeched in pain and kicked her. My heel landed somewhere near her ovaries, and in spite of all the leather she grunted and fell back a step.

Katherine immediately filled the gap, coming at me with nails painted more sedately but honed just as sharply as Haley's.

I kicked again, this time with the foot I'd twisted, but I wasn't really thinking about current pain just then. I was thinking about pain to come, and the permanent scarring that might come with it.

I kicked high just as Katherine was bending over. I caught her in the side of the head, a pretty solid blow, and she fell to the floor. I hurriedly scrambled to my feet in time to meet Haley's renewed attack.

She swung her crop at me, hitting me a good one on the cheek.

"Ow! That hurt!" I swung at her, a looping backhand, and caught her on the side of the face with the clunky microphone/bracelet. At last it had a use!

"OH!" Haley cried out and dropped back a pace, her hand going to her face as tears sprang up in her eyes. Apparently she couldn't take pain, only give it.

I didn't take time to criticize her. I grabbed for the doorknob and jerked the door open, staggering on my right ankle when I tried to run. Great. I hope it was only sprained and not broken. Either way, I had to keep moving. Although it seemed I'd smacked the fight right out of Haley, Katherine was getting up, and she really looked pissed.

I went for the stairs with a sort of hopping, hobbling gait, hurrying the best I could past the startled receptionist. I was sure the carpet was made of something far more sinister than wool or polyester; maybe quicksand.

I made it to the bottom of the steps and grabbed the railing to go up just as Katherine reached me.

"Stop!" I yelled with what I thought sounded like authority and held up the arm with the bracelet. I pressed the jewel. "There's a whole platoon of cops upstairs! One word from me and you'll be awash in a sea of blue uniforms!"

I heard Jack's amused voice in my ear. "A platoon? Hey, I'm good, but come on…"

I ignored him, and stared at Katherine.

Her perfect bun was in disarray, a button missing from her suit coat. She was breathing hard, and the grimace on her face was seriously detracting from her good looks.

"The cops?" She flashed a hand signal at the receptionist, who nodded and reached for something under the desk. The lights flashed three times in rapid succession; I assumed it was a signal for the people in the back rooms to cease and desist.

"I'm not interested in your little operation." I was dragging up lines from old Starsky and Hutch episodes, trying to sound like a cool undercover cop, but with my wheezing, gasping breath behind the words I probably sounded more like a wimpy Darth Vader. "I got what I came for. Now back off and I leave, no one the wiser."

"I don't think you're a cop." Katherine's eyes narrowed suspiciously. "You're too dumb to be a cop."

"Hey, you want me to kick you again?"

I heard a muffled cry followed by a loud thump at the top of the stairs. Katherine and I both looked up in time to see the door open. Jack stood there, staring down.

"The cops are here!" He shouted.

Katherine blinked once, then turned and hurried across the foyer and through the door, closing it with a solid but muted thump.

I looked up at Jack, who stood grinning down at me. At last, the cavalry had arrived.

Jack's grin faded when he got a good look at me. I'm not sure what bothered him the most: the bald spot where Haley had torn my hair out or the big red welt where she'd gotten me with the crop.

"You okay?"

"Just peachy." I grumbled and sat on the bottom step to remove my boots. No way was I going to maneuver up the stairs with those stilts and a sprained ankle now that the charade was over.

"Did you get what we came for?"

"Oh yeah, I got what *we* came for."

"Hey, I was here! Is it my fault I don't have any cleavage?"

I muttered something unflattering and wrenched at my right boot. The ankle was swelling rapidly, making it difficult to get it off.

"That doesn't look so good, Rainie." Jack shook his head when he saw the swelling.

"I just twisted it. I'll be fine." I dropped the boots and stood up on my left foot. I grabbed the railing and hopped up a step.

"Here, let me carry you."

"No! I'm not some sissy girl that needs to be rescued. I'll be fine!" I gritted my teeth and hopped up another step. Jack shrugged and picked up my boots.

At the top of the stairs I did relent and throw an arm around his shoulders. He was kind enough to lean down a little so I could reach, and he did make a pretty solid crutch.

Oak man was lying in the middle of the hall, oblivious to our passing. I didn't ask Jack about him; his condition was pretty self-explanatory.

Jack led me to his truck.

"Wait, what about Belinda's car?"

"I'll call and have her pick it up. No way you can drive with your foot like that."

He called Belinda on the way back to my house and briefly explained the problem. I couldn't hear her side of the conversation, but I could tell from Jack's end that she wasn't very happy.

"Hey, things happen, you know?" He was quiet for a minute while she vented some more. "I'll make it up to you...I don't know, I'll think of something." Jack glanced over at me and grinned. "Hey, how would you like a barely used bustier and some leather pants? The boots? Size 8 I think. Uh huh. I'm expensing them off, no one will miss them. Sure. Okay." He listened again, and looked over at me.

"Belinda wants to know if you need to go to the ER. If so she'll fax over some paperwork."

"No way! I'm not going anywhere in this outfit. Just take me home."

"You heard that?" Jack spoke into the phone again. "Yeah, I'll call if I think she needs to go. Okay. See you tomorrow."

He disconnected, looking satisfied. "That worked out well."

"You mean she *wants* this outfit? What for?"

"Why do you think she wants it?"

"Eew!"

"Don't knock it until you've tried it."

"I've never tried chewing gum I found stuck under a theatre seat, but I don't thing I need to try it to know I wouldn't like it."

Jack dropped me off at home. He offered to help me inside, but I turned him down. Being around Jack seemed to keep me in a high state of alert. Part of me lusted after him, part of me admired him, but a significant part of me still feared him. He wasn't just a Bad Boy, the type your mother warned you about. He was Dangerous, clear and simple. He was not only capable of killing in more ways than I could probably imagine, there was something about him that made me think that not only would he not hesitate to kill, but that he might even enjoy it. Eddie had that hard, lost look in his eyes; Jack had the hardness, without the lost part. Maybe he'd never had any goodness in him to lose.

Then again, maybe I was just tired and sore and bitchy.

Either way, I was relieved to get out of the leather and into some flannel pajama pants. I settled on my sofa with my foot on the coffee table, cushioned by a throw pillow.

I leaned my head on the back of the couch and tried to think about something besides the throbbing coming from my ankle. I was wishing I had a glass of water. Maybe a piece of fruit to nibble on. Both were in the kitchen, too far away to hop to in my current condition. I tried to put it out of my mind.

The phone rang. Luckily the cordless handset was on the coffee table, and I didn't have to get up to answer it.

It was Brad.

"Rainie, where the hell have you been?"

"Excuse me?"

"I've been calling all evening. Why weren't you answering your cell?"

"I didn't have it on. Jack and I were working."

"Jack? You stood me up to hang out with Jack Jones?"

"Stood you up?"

"Yes, Rainie. We were supposed to go to my sister's for dinner, remember? We set it up two weeks ago!"

"Oh god, I completely forgot! I'm sorry Brad."

"Sorry? That's it?"

"What do you want me to say?"

"You could start by telling me what the hell you were doing with Jack that was more important than meeting me!"

"I told you I was working."

"Working? God damn it, I told you I don't like you working with him..."

"Brad, this isn't a good time."

"Not a good time?" Brad was full out shouting now, and I held the phone away from my ear. I really did not need this. I put the phone back to my face long enough to get in a few words.

"Call me tomorrow, Brad." And I hung up. Who the hell did he think he was, telling me what to do? Maybe hanging up on him wasn't the best way to deal with him, but he'd get over it.

Or would he?

Actually, I thought it quite possible he wouldn't. I wasn't sure how I felt about that. I was exhausted, and in a lot of pain. I just wanted to sleep.

I had just dozed off when someone rang the doorbell.

I opened my eyes and glared at the door. "Who is it?"

"It's Brad."

I sighed. The door was only ten feet away, but I was finally comfortable, and ten feet was a long way to hop. Besides, I really didn't feel like fighting with Brad. On the other hand, if I refused to let him in, our relationship would definitely be over. Did I want that?

Apparently not. I yelled "Just a minute!" and swung my foot off the pillow.

Dropping the foot to the floor caused all kinds of new pain, and mentally I was creating new swear words to describe my current mood. Nonetheless I hopped to the door and unlocked it, blinking back tears. I pulled the door open.

"Come on in." I was clinging to the wall for support. Brad stepped in, frowning and looking ready to continue where he'd left off on the phone. Then he got a good look at me.

"Jesus, Rainie, what happened to you?"

"It was all in the line of duty."

"Who hit you?'

"Super Nanny."

"Who?"

"It's a long story." I turned to hop back to the couch.

"Whoa, what happened to your foot?"

"Twisted my ankle."

"Hang on, hang on!" Brad grabbed me and swept me up in his arms. Sometimes I forgot just how strong he was; he spent a lot of time at his health club. He carried me to the couch, suddenly full of solicitude. I wanted to protest, to tell him I was fine, but to tell you the truth my ankle really *hurt*, and I was grateful not to have to hop back to the couch.

"You're a real mess! What kind of interview were you conducting?" Brad lightly brushed at my hair, where the (thankfully) small bald spot still showed; I would figure out a way tomorrow to brush my hair to cover it. He took in the welt on my cheek, and then looked back at my ankle. "Just what did that Jones guy get you into?"

I wanted to defend Jack, I really did. But the truth was he *had* gotten me into this. The throbbing in my ankle seemed to be moving up my leg. I was beginning to question this new job. Besides, what did it matter what Haley's sexual inclinations were? Did being a dominatrix necessarily make her a bad nanny?

"It's a really long story, and to tell you the truth I don't feel much like talking. I'm really tired."

"I'll bet you are." Brad smoothed my hair back, and I closed my eyes with a grateful sigh.

This was a side of him I'd never seen. I wasn't usually much into being coddled, but right now it felt kind of nice.

"Let's get you settled into bed. You can tell me about it in the morning."

"No, really, I'd rather sleep right here. I don't feel like hobbling to the bedroom."

"Nonsense." Brad was already scooping me up again. "You'll sleep better in your own bed."

Too tired to argue, I allowed myself to be carried. Okay, so I like to feel small and protected *once* in a while. So sue me; and don't be saying that's a girl thing. There are plenty of men out there that want to be mothered, and if that's not seeking the ultimate protection, I don't know what is. I mean, why do you think men get married? They want someone to feed them and clothe them and kiss them nighty-night, and most wives provide those services, even if they work full time outside the home.

Now it was my turn. I let him put me in bed and prop up my foot and pull the covers over me. I think I might have mumbled thanks; I'm not sure, because a moment later I was sound asleep.

Chapter Ten

I woke up alone the next day to the smell of fresh brewed coffee. Brad must have set the timer on the pot before he left.

My ankle felt much better. I found I could hobble around within reason, with the aid of a couple over-the-counter pain killers. I sat at the counter and drank a cup of coffee, and took a second cup to the bathroom with me while I showered and dressed for the day. My foot was too swollen even for my simple sandals. It was a good thing I was going to Thelma's; she wouldn't care if I was barefooted.

George was sound asleep on his shelf, basking under his light that had come on automatically at seven a.m. I said his name on my way over to pick him up; it's not a good idea to startle even a friendly iguana with an eighteen inch leathery whip for a tail. I put him down in his cage and locked the top.

I drove to Thelma's, glad that it wasn't my left foot I'd injured. I never would have managed the clutch. Just as I pulled up in front of her house Jack called.

"The pictures came out pretty good. A few odd angles on some of them, but overall they show what we need them to show."

"So Super Nanny is out of a job."

"You sound like you feel sorry for her."

"Not really. It just seems...I don't know, dirty somehow, digging into her private life."

"You really think a dominatrix should be in charge of a child's upbringing?"

"I don't think I'm up to a discussion of ethics right now."

"Oh." Jack sounded a little puzzled. I guess I was being a little churlish, but yesterday had not been my idea of a good time.

"So are you coming in tomorrow? Belinda should have something new for you. I could ride along again."

"Um, I think maybe I can handle the next one myself. I mean, I appreciate your help and all, but I think I get the idea of what I'm supposed to do."

"Okay." His tone had gotten a bit cool. "Fine. You need anything give me a call. Good luck."

"Thanks." But I was talking to dead air. Jack had already hung up. Great. Now I had the big scary guy mad at me. This was really turning into a great week.

With a sigh I got out of the car and limped up to Thelma's door.

She was waiting for me, and her face lightened with a big grin when she got a load of my limp and the bruise on my cheek.

159

"Woo wee! Looks like you had some fun last night! Come on in and tell me all about it, and don't leave out one juicy detail!"

Somehow Thelma's enthusiasm was contagious. As I told my tale, it started to seem less like a woeful disaster and more like an outrageous adventure. By the time I got to the part with me waving the camera around I was laughing right along with Thelma.

"Damn, I wish I'd thought to be a P.I. back when. Would have been a hell of a lot more fun than selling women's clothes or being a housewife."

"I don't know, you've told me some pretty funny stories about your time as a saleswoman."

"That's because I liked to mess with them, all those snooty bitches with their fru-fru dogs and designer handbags, insisting we say they were a size six when they were on the far side of sixteen! Probably a good thing I married my Herbie when I did, or I might have snapped and tossed one of those little dogs down the garbage shoot!"

I laughed. "That's not fair, Thelma! It wasn't the dog's fault they were fru-fru!"

"Maybe not, but I couldn't have fit any of those ladies' fat butts into the hopper."

My cell phone rang, and I checked the caller ID. It was Tommy. I must have smiled, because Thelma said "Hot guy?"

"Hot gay," I corrected with a laugh.

"Oh, answer it. Invite him over, I want to meet him."

"Well..." I hesitated to promise, but answered the call.

160

"Hi Tommy, what's up?"

"I hope it's okay I called. I know you're with Thelma, but she's cool right?"

"Very cool," I laughed. "In fact, she wants to meet you."

"Yeah? I'd like that. Maybe I could buy you guys some lunch today."

Huh, another free lunch. I was on a roll. Maybe I should start ordering enough to take doggie bags, and I'd never have to shop for groceries again.

"I don't know, let me ask." I asked Thelma, who of course was enthusiastic about the idea.

"Cool. I have a quick errand to run downtown, you want to meet at Caseys?"

I almost groaned aloud. Was it a conspiracy, was everyone in town trying to get me to eat those cheeseburgers?

"Actually we just ate there a couple days ago. How about the BW Inn?"

"Sounds good to me. I'll meet you there in about an hour then?"

I glanced at the clock on the wall. "Okay, 12:30 it is."

I hung up, only then wondering why Tommy had called in the first place. Certainly he hadn't planned to invite us to lunch, had he? Well, whatever, he'd tell me when I saw him.

The BW Inn wasn't much, just a quiet bar on a side street in Buchanan, which had karaoke some weekends but otherwise was just a pleasant place for a meal. Tommy was already there when we arrived, sipping a beer and browsing the menu.

161

He stood when we walked up to the table, grinned and shook Thelma's hand when I introduced them, and gave me a brief kiss on the cheek - the one without the bruise. When we were seated, it was the first thing he asked me about, with a worried frown.

"Who did that?"

"A dominatrix!" Thelma informed him with glee. "That's a crop mark!"

"What?" Tommy stared at me, open-mouthed, obviously thinking a lot had changed with me in the past three years.

"It was in the line of duty." I laughed at his expression, and gave him a brief explanation.

"Huh. That Jack Jones sounds like trouble. What's the matter with him, dragging you into that kind of crap?"

"Watch it, Tommy, you're starting to sound like Brad. Really, I'm a big girl. I can take care of myself. Besides, I sort of gave Jack the brush off this morning. From now on, it's strictly dull interviews and computer searches."

"Good girl." Tommy nodded with satisfaction, and I felt a slight twinge of annoyance. What was it with the guys in my life, who seemed to think it their place to approve or disapprove of my lifestyle?

A waitress came over to get our orders, and I was saved the need to voice my irritation. We talked for a while about nothing in particular, Tommy and Thelma trying to get to know each other. It was clear from the first few minutes they were going to hit it off. They both had a good sense of humor, and neither one cared to fit into a ready mold. It was as if they were simpatico with each other's quirks; come to think of it, I had a few myself. Maybe that's why we'd ended up here together in the first place.

We talked until our lunches were served, thick steaks smothered in mushrooms and onions for Tommy and Thelma, a chef's salad for me. Half way through Tommy finally remembered that he'd called me for a reason.

"I know you've got a lot going on with all your clients and now this P.I. stuff, but do you have any more hours you need to fill? I know it's usually feast or famine for you."

True enough. I worked for myself, taking jobs through word of mouth. Sometimes I could go months with hardly anything, which was when I resorted to waiting tables. Other times I had people calling me when I was already too busy, and those I passed on to other caregivers I knew.

Now I thought about losing Mabel, but just shrugged. She was only nine hours a week, and I was thinking I might try to fill them with work at B&E, if I could. I needed a little break from the caregiving. Still, I didn't want to shut Tommy down without hearing him out.

"I might, why?"

"Well, you remember my Aunt Georgia?"

"Sure, how could I forget? She practically raised you."

"Thank God," Tommy said. "Who knows what a mess I'd be if it had all been up to my mom. Anyway, Aunt Georgia has a very dear friend who needs a caregiver for her mother, just a few hours a week. She's been doing it all herself, but Miss Ida isn't so young herself any more. She doesn't want just anybody coming into her house though, you know? So when I told Aunt Georgia I was hanging out with you again, she wanted me to ask if you're available."

"That kind of surprises me," I admitted. "I never thought your aunt liked me much."

"I think she always liked you fine. It's just that Aunt Georgia had better insight into my preferences than I did. I think she was just worried you'd get hurt in the end."

"Huh, smart woman." Thelma piped up. "But she should have told you what she suspected."

"She might accept that I'm gay, but it's not something people talked about openly back in her day. Besides, maybe she was hoping I'd get over it."

Thelma laughed. "You mean like a bad case of acne?"

"Something like that," Tommy agreed with a grin.

"I'm kind of flattered she thought of me," I tried to get them back to the point. "I do have a few open mornings, but I'm not sure I want to get into anything too deep right now. How bad off is her mom?"

"I don't know for sure, but I get the impression not too bad. She's kind of frail, needs help bathing and such, maybe some companionship while her daughter is out running errands."

"Any dementia? Does she get mean?"

"Dementia maybe, but Aunt Georgia didn't say anything about any mean spells. Miss Ida could tell you more."

I sipped at my Diet Coke and thought about it. With Max and Mabel gone, Thelma would be my only client, and she wasn't exactly one, either. I didn't want to give up the caregiving altogether; there was a certain satisfaction at the end of the day that I think my self-esteem needed. Besides, I couldn't be sure that B&E would let me get any more hours in, especially when I was still mostly unproven.

"I guess I could at least talk to her."

"Hey, that's great Rainie! Aunt Georgia will really appreciate it. Maybe we could run over there Saturday, and I can introduce you."

"Okay, call me, we'll set a time."

"Just remember Rainie, you're not available Tuesdays and Thursdays."

"No problem, Thelma. I'm not likely to forget about you."

I got home to find Eddie sitting on my front porch. He raised a hand in greeting and gave me one of his strange smiles, so cheerful, if only his eyes weren't so dark and sad.

"What's up, Eddie?"

"Does something have to be up for me to come see you?" But his smile had already faded. He looked down at my swollen foot, and he frowned.

"Of course not." I unlocked the door and led the way into the house. Eddie moved over to George's cage and opened the top, as comfortable with the little green guy as I was.

"You want a beer?"

"No thanks. I just stopped by to check on you. I heard you got into a thing with Jack."

"Nothing serious. Just checking references."

"How's your foot?"

"It's okay, just a little sore. I twisted my ankle. Can you picture me in four inch heels?"

That made him smile again. "Not really. That must have been Jack's idea."

"Sure wasn't mine." I agreed.

"Jack's a good guy, but sometimes he forgets not everyone had Special Forces training. He shouldn't have taken you into that situation."

I plopped on the couch and put my foot up on the table, hiding a grimace of relief.

"It wasn't that big a deal."

"Like you said, it was a reference check. You never should have been hurt."

"I don't think Jack expected me to get involved in a catfight with a couple of crazy dominatrixes. Wait, that's not right; what's plural for dominatrix?"

"Ask Mason or Jeff; they're the college graduates." Eddie flashed a quick grin. "The point is, Jack had no right to expect you to get involved like that. I'm going to have a talk with him..."

"Whoa, wait a minute," I leaned forward, instantly on the defensive. "I don't need you to talk to him, Eddie. I can take care of myself."

"You don't seem to get it. Jack doesn't stop to think of what a person's limitations are. He figures

166

if you want to do something, you just do it, like he always has."

"And you think I'm that limited?"

"No, of course not. But you aren't a P.I., you're a caregiver."

"I'm a caregiver by choice. Maybe now I'm choosing to be a P.I. Maybe Jack's right, and I *can* do whatever I set out to do."

What the hell was I thinking, defending Jack? Wasn't I just as pissed at him for getting me into that mess? Hadn't I already blown him off so he couldn't do it again? Yet somehow the idea of someone telling me I couldn't do it really got my stubborn up.

Eddie was looking at me, his expression unreadable.

"So you're saying you want to do that kind of stuff? That Jack didn't just suck you in over your head?"

Of course, that was exactly what Jack had done. But was I going to admit it? Hell no.

"Actually it was kind of a kick. You know me, I get bored easily. One thing I can say about Jack, he isn't boring."

"That's probably what they'll write on his tombstone." Eddie smiled wryly. "I won't say anything else about it then, to you or him, but promise you'll remember what I told you. I know you're tough and stubborn, but Jack will never think of physical limitations, or how much training you've had. So when he comes up with a plan, take a hard look at it, okay? Make sure you aren't trying to do a job better left to a platoon of marines."

"That sounds like the voice of experience."

This time Eddie's smile almost reached his eyes. "Jack pulled me into a few of his crazier stunts. When he gets rolling it's hard not to just ride on the momentum. We once rescued five marines, and all we had for weapons was one hand grenade and a couple of big sticks. Now *that* was good fun!"

"No kidding? Now that's a story I'd like to hear."

"Sure, why not. Think I'll have a beer after all. You want one?"

"Sounds good."

Eddie grabbed a couple bottles of beer from the fridge and launched into his story. Good fun indeed!

Chapter Eleven

On Friday morning I met Jenny and Lila, the caregiver I'd recommended, at Mabel's. We all thought it was a good idea for Lila to get to know her in familiar company rather than just dumping them together.

We spent a pleasant morning chatting, although Mabel made it clear she wasn't too sure about a new caregiver, and even less sure she needed someone around so many hours a day.

"I'm not a child you know." She said it almost petulantly. "I can still look after myself."

"Of course you can, Mom, but you said yourself the days are awfully lonely, with me working full time and hardly any of your friends able to drive any more. Lila can take you to the Senior Center to play cards, or pick up one of your friends to go have lunch, maybe do a little shopping. You'll have fun."

"Maybe." She didn't look convinced, and in fact she was glaring at Lila a bit suspiciously.

"I've known Lila for a long time," I assured Mabel. "She's lots of fun to be around. At least give her a chance."

Mabel sniffed and shrugged. "All right, guess it won't hurt to give it a try. Do you like the Symphony?" This last was directed at Lila, sounding much like a challenge.

"I've never been to the Symphony," Lila answered honestly. "But I love most music. I'd love to go someday."

"They're doing a lunch series at the Morris Civic Center over the next couple of months. Would you be willing to drive a few old ladies over there?"

"Sure, if you can find some old ladies. Sounds like fun."

"Okay then." Mabel smiled, for the first time treating Lila to the full bright wattage. "You might work out okay."

My guilt over leaving Mabel was greatly assuaged by that smile. I left amid a few tears and promises to keep in touch and headed for B&E.

Belinda was wearing the black leather ankle boots and the silky jacket, but not, thankfully, the leather pants or bustiere. Instead she wore the spike heels with a tapered pair of black slacks and a white blouse under the jacket. She had managed to take pieces of what I considered a trashy outfit and fill them with just the right touch of class.

"You have a new assignment for me?"

"A couple, actually. Harry was pretty impressed with the job you did with the S&M nanny. He thinks you can handle some meatier assignments."

"Uh, well...you know, that was mostly Jack."

"Jack might have put you up to it, but you handled it fine yourself. Besides, none of these are much; a couple more references checks, really. But this one might be a little tougher." Brenda handed me a file folder. "Dead beat dad. He owes his kids almost 20,000 dollars, but on the rare occasions they find him to haul into court he always pleads no money, no job."

I was outraged. I didn't have any kids, but if I did I'd sure want their dad to help with the support. "Why don't they throw him in jail?"

"They probably will, next time they find him, but right now he's in the wind. We have a P.I. looking for him, but you need to run these data checks, make sure he doesn't have any hidden assets for when they do get him to court."

"So I don't actually have to confront the guy?"

"Nope. Just research him, send the reports to Greg Hopper, the P.I. on the case."

"Doesn't sound so meaty to me."

"Maybe I exaggerated a little," Belinda grinned. "But hey, Harry really was impressed."

"That and a buck will get me a burger at McDonalds."

Belinda nodded in agreement. "If you need any help getting started let me know."

I glanced at the file folder and scowled at the name: Ken Gripe.

"What, do you know him?"

"Yeah, I'm afraid I do. He was a bully all through school, picked on little kids, substitute teachers, probably even kicked his own dog for sport."

"I know the type," Belinda nodded. "Is he local?"

"Buchanan. I haven't seen him or even heard his name in years."

"Still, you might know someone who still knows him. If you do, check it out, see if you can find out where he hangs his hat these days and pass it on to Hopper."

"Sure, won't hurt to make a few calls." I retreated to the computer room. I commandeered one of the small desks to make use of a phone.

I scheduled two interviews for the following Monday, to check references on a management prospect for a local chain of grocery stores. That done, I called Gina Hendricks, an old friend from school. We didn't hang out much since she'd gotten married and settled into motherhood, but we still had a connection from our younger, considerably wilder days.

"Hi Rainie!" She sounded enthused to hear from me. In the background I could hear screaming, and I feared that maybe a serial killer had broken into her home, but she assured me it was just her seven and nine year old boys fighting over a remote control.

"Nothing to worry about." She raised her voice to be heard over them. "I give them a bit to work it out. They're pretty evenly matched, so unless I hear bones breaking or see blood spurting I figure it's best to let them have their little power struggles. Kind of like a flock of chickens: they need to straighten out their pecking order."

"I see," I said, though I had no idea if that was the best way to handle it or not. The only experience I had with kids was when Jason had his for the weekend and brought them to visit me. Then I was "Aunt Rainie," the fun aunt (so they told me) and I never bothered with any kind of discipline. Then again, I'd never heard them caterwauling like Gina's kids. If they ever did, I think I'd be inclined to lock them in the garage until it stopped.

Gina and I spent a few minutes catching up. We hadn't spoken for several months, and she felt a need to fill me in on the doings of several people we went to school with, none of whom I cared about even a little bit. Still, I wanted to be polite, so I interjected a few times with "really?" and "no kidding?" and "Huh, that's a shame," where appropriate.

Gina finally ran out of gossip, and I got around to why I'd called.

"Do you remember Ken Gripe?"

"Yuk. Yeah, I do, but why?"

"I was just wondering if you had any idea who he's hanging around with lately."

Gina was quiet for a long moment, and so, thankfully, were her boys. Apparently they'd either settled their argument or killed each other.

Gina finally spoke, sounding guarded.

"Why do you want to know about Ken?"

Now it was my turn to hesitate. If I told her why I was looking, it was very possible most of Buchanan would know by dinner time, and Ken might get the word and split. I didn't want to lie to Gina, but hey, I was looking out for Ken's kids, right? The problem is I hate to lie. I know how it's done, and I can always think of plenty of them, but I'm lousy at actually telling them. I'm always sure that the truth is right there for everyone to see in

173

my eyes or on my blushing cheeks, and someone will call me on it. My self-esteem can't take the humiliation. Nonetheless, I was amazed to hear the untruths roll off my tongue like ball bearings off a roof. Maybe it was the distance provided by the telephone.

"I'm not so much looking for Ken as I am his sister, Kim. Remember her?"

"Sure, mousy little thing, always sat in the back of the room, never said much?"

"That's the one. I heard she moved to Texas, but I'm not sure exactly where. Anyway, I was cleaning out my mom's attic the other day and I found some old pics I took for the yearbook, ones that never got published. There are several really good shots of Kim, one with Bobby Price, and I thought she might like them."

"Really? Kim and Bobby Price? I can't imagine them standing close enough together to be in the same photo."

"He's even got his arm around her shoulder." I touched the tip of my nose just to be sure it wasn't growing. Nope, same perky little nub on the end.

"Well you're right, I think she'd love to see those!"

"So anyway, I figured I'd mail them to her if I could get her address, and the only way I could think to do that was to call Ken."

"Hm, I suppose you're right. I can't think of any friends she left here in town that would still keep in touch with her. She was such a loner." Gina fell silent again, but this time I thought she might be trying to remember something. My patience was rewarded.

"Last I heard Ken still spent most of his time with Jim Freman."

"Jim, the greasemonkey?"

"Yep, Mr. Autoshop himself. Still does nothing but work on cars. He's got a little shop behind the carwash next to the tracks, but he doesn't keep regular hours. Best I can suggest is stop by and see if you can catch him there."

"Isn't he listed in the book?"

"The business isn't near that structured. He just sort of works word of mouth. You know, someone's car will break down, and someone else will say take it to Jim, and they'll run over there and if he has time he'll fix it."

"Huh. Can't make much of a living that way."

"You wouldn't think, but Jim drives a pretty nice car, and he always seems to have cash for the bar, so who knows?"

"Not me. Well, thanks Gina. I appreciate the help."

"Sure." I heard the kids hollering again. Gina sighed. "Let me know how it turns out, all right? I'm always interested in news from the outside world."

I spent the rest of the afternoon staring at the computer, running through data bases, taking longer than I probably would have if I really knew what I was doing. It was sort of interesting at first. I was amazed by how much detailed information there was about any given person in the public domain. A little scary, really; I thought maybe I'd take a day, soon, and research my own name to see what people could find out about me.

By five o'clock my eyes felt like I'd rubbed them with sandpaper, and I couldn't seem to stop yawning. As I exited the last data base and collected my stuff to go home, I had to admit to myself that this was really pretty dull work. Maybe I shouldn't have been so quick to shut Jack down; working with him had certainly been a lot more fun.

Tommy picked me up at 9 o'clock Saturday morning and we went to meet his aunt's friend. Fortunately the welt on my cheek had faded to a barely noticeable pink, and I wasn't limping much at all.

Tommy stopped in front of an old three story house that had likely once been structured in the Victorian style, but which had long since been transformed through a combination of neglect and low-cost repairs to a rambling gray structure with no particular form or style.

There was a deep porch, many of the boards warped and faded from too many years of sun, rain and scuffling feet, and mismatched windows of varying size, some still bordered by charming gingerbread scrollwork that now looked foolish and out of place. There was a wooden gate across the porch steps, at the moment standing open. A metal ramp, just wide enough for a wheelchair, covered half the steps.

The yard was mowed, but otherwise little maintained. There were brown patches and bare spots here and there, and the grass was creeping over the concrete sidewalk, narrowing it to half its size in places. Once decorative shrubs now grew untamed, crowding the lower-level windows, an invitation to peeping toms and other unsavory folk who might want to get near an accessible window without being spied from the road.

In stark contrast to the general air of casual neglect, two flower boxes attached to the porch railings were carefully planted in a variety of well-pruned flowers that Rainie couldn't name. She inhaled deeply of their rich scent as they mounted the two short risers to the porch, wistfully thinking how much she'd like to have a whole bed of such beauties in her own yard. One of these days she was definitely going to forego her pragmatic bent for growing edibles and plant something totally useless.

Tommy rang the bell next to the heavy front door. It was likely made of oak, probably beautiful somewhere under the top coat of army pea-coat green.

There was only a short delay before the door was opened by a woman somewhere in her late sixties. Her hair, teased and puffed into a full helmet to be envied by any NFL player, was dyed a color of red that might not be unattractive - on a teenager. Her makeup was heavily applied over surprisingly smooth features, the wrinkles relegated to the areas directly east and west of her generous, brightly painted lips and her blue shaded eyes.

"Tommy, my dear boy! Come in!" The woman smiled widely, clearly delighted to see him, and she pushed the screen door open to engulf him in a warm, heavily perfumed hug.

"Miss Ida, it's good to see you!" Tommy hugged her back enthusiastically. Rainie took a wary step back, not wanting to be accidentally drenched by the effusive wave of affection. She hoped Miss Ida was not the type to hug first and exchange names later; Rainie was just as content with a simple handshake.

Tommy, bless his heart, saved her from the dread possibility by keeping one long arm casually looped around Miss Ida's shoulders as he turned to introduce her.

"Miss Ida, this is Rainie, my ex-wife."

Miss Ida's smile faltered only slightly. "I don't understand why you let sweet Tommy go. Any woman should be proud to have a husband of his caliber. And I sure don't understand you two staying friends. Why, in my day, people only got divorced when things got *ugly*- if you know what I mean. None of this 'irreconcilable differences,' which is just a euphemism for 'I just want to sleep with someone else now.' But it's not for me to judge, I suppose." She clucked her tongue in judgment just the same, and held out a slim hand, lightly dusted with age spots and heavily adorned with gaudy rings.

"It's a pleasure to meet you." Rainie shook the hand gently and smiled. It wasn't her place to point out Tommy's sexual preferences to the last person in town to not be aware of them.

"Come in then, meet my friend and my mother."

Miss Ida led them into a long, dim hallway. Scarred but polished pocket doors concealed two rooms, and there was a narrow set of stairs that took a sharp turn after the first six risers, obscuring any view of the upstairs. Miss Ida led them through a third set of open pocket doors.

This was a formal dining room, furnished with a long, cherry wood table polished to such a sheen Rainie was sure Miss Ida could see her reflection in it well enough to apply her makeup. The sideboard and china cabinet were as well maintained, and the carpet, though somewhat threadbare in spots, was scrupulously clean. It seemed that whatever energies the ladies had for maintaining their home was spent indoors.

We passed through the dining room and through a swinging door into a large, cozy kitchen. The well-worn appliances were outdated by a good twenty years, the counter tops flecked green Formica straight out of the seventies, but everything was clean, if slightly cluttered. The kitchen table held unopened mail, the newspaper, and an odd assortment of household items that had apparently congregated there of their own free will. This was clearly the room in which the women spent most of their time.

Two women were at the table, one ensconced in a wheelchair. The other stood when they came in, pushing up from the table on arms that looked surprisingly strong for a woman on the far side of seventy.

"This is my friend, Frieda." Miss Ida indicated the older woman, whose traditional no-nonsense tightly-in-a-bun gray hair and un-rouged, chubby cheeks gave her the appearance of being the Standard Grandma, one on which every fairy tale grandma was based. Her smile revealed neat, slightly yellowing teeth that were likely original, considering the slight gaps and imperfections that in no way took away from the warmth of her infectious grin.

"And you must be *little* Tommy," Frieda giggled like a young girl as she said this, craning her neck to look up at his full height. In sensible heels, the old woman stood no more than five feet two. "And you are his wife, Rainie, right?"

"Ex-wife, actually." Rainie smiled and held out a hand for shaking. Frieda shook it firmly, no indication that arthritis bothered her grip in any way. "Pleased to meet you."

"And this is my mother, Virginia Gains." Miss Ida swept her hand toward the woman in the wheelchair, in a gesture curiously like one of Bob Barker's models pointing out a new car on the Price is Right.

The woman in the wheelchair was not just old; she was, after all, the mother of a woman already past retirement age. Virginia Gains was a dry husk of wrinkled flesh, hunched in her wheelchair like a desiccated carrot left too long in the root cellar.

Her hair was pure white and wispy, carefully combed to cover the worst of the bald spots. She stared at a point somewhere between me and Tommy, but her focus seemed to be at a distance somewhere beyond the Milky Way. I thought of that old song: "the lights are on, but you're not home."

I am not in the habit of making fun of my elders, but the fact is I have to maintain a sense of humor in my work or the tragic nature of it all will push me to the depths of despair. Such random thoughts are, of course, always kept between me and my little inner voice.

I greeted her politely.

"It's nice to meet you, Mrs. Gains."

The woman stared silently, not acknowledging me.

"Momma, did you hear?" Miss Ida bent down to speak directly at the old woman. "This is Rainie. We're thinking of hiring her to look after you. Wouldn't you like to meet her?"

Mrs. Gains blinked and slowly shifted her gaze to her daughter's face.

"I don't care for meat. Just give me some vegetables, maybe a nice soup."

"No Momma, I wasn't talking about lunch. I want you to meet Rainie." Miss Ida pointed at me.

"Rainie? Like the weather is kind of rainy? What did you do to your mamma to get saddled with a name like that?"

"It's short for Rainbow."

"Huh. Imagine that. Doesn't anyone name their girls Jane or Barbara anymore? Everything has to be so damned clever."

181

"Momma, please don't swear." Miss Ida's cheeks might have flushed with embarrassment, but it was difficult to tell under the heavy rouge.

"I can swear all I like! I'm ninety-four years old, and I spent a good ninety of those years watching my tongue. Now I'm going to get it all out! Damn, shit, Hell...Fuck! How's that?"

The old woman grinned triumphantly, and I couldn't help but laugh. Dementia might be creeping up on the old lady as surely as the grass was obscuring the sidewalk out front, but her mind hadn't yet been completely swallowed up.

Mrs. Gains turned her red-rimmed eyes on me. "Well, at least this one has a sense of humor. So, sit down, let's talk. You ever take care of an old lady before?"

"Yes please, everyone sit." Miss Ida indicated the extra chairs pulled up to the table. "Would anyone like tea?"

"No thank you." I chose the chair closest to Mrs. Gains. Tommy sat across from her.

"I'd love some, Miss Ida."

"I've been taking care of elderly people for a few years now." I belatedly answered Mrs. Gains' question. The old woman, however, seemed to have forgotten not only the question, but my presence as well. Once again she was staring off into the ether, oblivious to everyone.

"Don't mind Momma; she's like that, especially on overcast days. She was always a sunny day person. Those are her flowers in the boxes on the porch. Hand her a trowel and a few seeds on a sunny day and she's an absolute genius."

Miss Ida placed a cup of tea in front of Tommy. We left Mrs. Gains to her mental wanderings while we sat and got acquainted, talking about general things before we got down to anything resembling a formal interview.

"Well, you certainly seem to be every bit as sweet as Tommy claimed you to be." Miss Ida patted Tommy's arm. "Now, you said you were available three days a week?"

"Yes ma'am, Monday, Wednesday and Friday, but only half days."

"Well, to tell the truth I just need someone two days a week for a few hours. You know, so Frieda and I can get out and run errands, get our hair done, things like that."

"Can't leave me alone with the homeless guys upstairs." Mrs. Gains suddenly spoke, her rheumy eyes again in sharp focus. "Probably psychopathic killers, the both of them!"

"Now Momma, they aren't homeless. They live here." Miss Ida smiled indulgently at her mother and explained to me and Tommy. "We're renting a couple of rooms out upstairs. You know, to help ends meet."

"Two *seedy* looking men!" Mrs. Gains supplied. "If they weren't homeless, you tell me why they were each wearing six layers of clothes when they got here, not a suitcase between them, and neither one familiar with a shower or soap!"

"Now Momma, they weren't that bad." Miss Ida's tone was still calm, but there was a slight edge to it as she hurriedly moved to change the subject.

"So maybe Monday and Wednesday morning…"

"That tall one, he wanders through here, arguing with himself, I swear sometimes there's two people. And you think *I* need a babysitter…"

"Momma, please. Rainie and Tommy don't care about our boarders." There was a definite note of irritation in Miss Ida's voice now. She leaned toward me and whispered, "It's the dementia. She forgets what she had for breakfast, but then remembers things that never happened."

I was intrigued. While it was true dementia could manifest itself in just the way Miss Ida described, Mrs. Gains sounded quite lucid and sure of herself, and her description certainly befitted a homeless man, likely one afflicted with schizophrenia or some other delusional illness. But why would these women, who both seemed sensible enough, allow two less-than-wholesome sounding homeless men to live in their worn but scrupulously clean home?

"Maybe they should care. Someone should! This is still my home, you know, even if I did let you move in and take over. I think I have a right to speak up when I don't like the occupants, don't I? And I damn well don't like those two, especially the Debater."

"Then maybe you would be more comfortable staying back in your room more, Momma." The anger was carefully smoothed from Miss Ida's voice. "I'm sorry you don't like them, but we really need the rent money. It isn't cheap maintaining this old moose of a house, you know."

"Well I *know* that!" Mrs. Gains' quavering voice dripped sarcasm. "But did you have to take renters off the *street*?"

Miss Ida blew out a careful breath. "Momma, please."

"All right, all right." Mrs. Gains waved an impatient hand. "I know, they were just travel weary. Flew in overnight on the red eye, lost their luggage, no time to shave...for the last six months." Abruptly her bony hands reached for the oversized wheels of her chair and she pushed away from the table. "I've heard enough. This one's just fine with me." She waved at me. "Come on, I'll show you my room...we'll likely spend a lot of time there, avoiding Debater and the Scarecrow."

I stood, looking uncertainly at Miss Ida. The woman shrugged and waved me on. "That's fine, whatever. Let's plan on Monday morning, say eight a.m.?"

"Okay, I'll help her get settled in her room. I'll be back in a few minutes Tommy."

He nodded at me, his expression bemused.

That afternoon I went to visit my mom, which also included a visit to my older sister, Brenda, since she still lived at home. I had never really gotten along well with Brenda. She was too needy, too much of a "poor me I never catch a break" kind of person.

She worked full time as a medical receptionist, making good money, some of which she supposedly contributed to the household. The vast majority of her earnings, however, went to clothes.

Brenda had taken over the entire top floor of the house as living quarters for her and her daughter Sierra, a brilliant ten year old who might well be the best of our gene pool. Brenda had converted one of the four bedrooms to a sitting room, wired with cable and high speed internet feeding a computer (for on-line shopping) and a flat screen TV (for the home shopping networks.)

Another bedroom had been converted to a closet. Seriously. It was full of racks upon racks of clothes, many with the tags still on them. One wall was nothing but floor to ceiling shelves to display her hundreds of pairs of shoes. She had pointy heels and dressy flats and running shoes and sandals and Birkenstocks and boots and many styles I couldn't name. Clearly her shopping was an addiction, the outward manifestation of something, maybe depression, maybe obsessive compulsive disorder. Mom and I had tried to talk to her about it many times, but had at last given up. At least she was functional, and spending time in her "closet" seemed to make her happy.

The house was located right at the edge of town, just before the road wound out into farmers' fields. It had once been owned by a wealthy business owner from Chicago, who had come to Buchanan in search of new investments. He and his family had moved away years before, the house left to fall almost into ruin before my mother and Jedediah bought it. The house came with two acres of property surrounded by an ancient wrought iron fence. Over the years ivy had grown and entwined with the fence so thoroughly that it was like a privacy fence, and you had to look hard to see the actual wrought iron underneath.

I went in through the front door, which as usual wasn't locked. The house was neat, the windows all thrown open to the fresh air. I glanced into the living room, which had a big, overstuffed sofa and a lot of pillows, and a plush rug on the floor, my mom's favorite spot to sit. There was no TV, but there was a nice stereo, complete with a turntable to play their many vinyl record albums, now sitting silent.

I walked down the quiet hall, past family pictures and group photos dating back to the commune days. There was a big one of a lot of teenagers dressed in long skirts or torn jeans, the boys shirtless, the girls braless, everyone with long hair and many with granny glasses or love beads strung around their necks, all of them waving the peace sign at the camera. I'd met most of the people in that picture, all of them older now. Some still dressed the same, but others had entered the very establishment they wanted to bring down, dressing in ties and bringing home real pay checks. My mom still loved them all, even the ones who had "dropped back in."

I went through the kitchen, which was worn but neat, with a lovely old cast iron woodstove with a cook top and an oven. Mom had electricity, and she had a conventional furnace, but such things were used sparingly. She and Jedediah were trying hard to go "off grid."

I found Mom in the back yard, working on her vegetable garden, which as always was extensive and flourishing. My mom had learned a lot about organic gardening back at the commune.

She stood and brushed dirt off her hands when she saw me. No gloves for my mother; a person needed direct contact with the earth to maintain inner harmony.

"Hi Rainbow," she gave me a tight, extended hug. I still hadn't gotten used to this behavior, and my hug back was awkward. We hadn't been much of a hugging family when I was little, but my mother had many friends who practiced different forms of spiritualism, and one had convinced her that she had to "touch people to be in touch with them." As for me, I'd hug Eddie now and then, and my brother when he was drunk, but for the most part I didn't really care for people to invade my personal space.

"Hi mom. The garden's looking good."

"Yes, it is, isn't it?" She gazed back at the lush greenery with a fondness usually reserved for new-born babies. "And you should see the greenhouse. Best crop in years."

"You always say that, Mom." I grinned. The greenhouse was where she grew her favorite crops, the ones that might get her into trouble. She grew very little, only enough for her and Jedidiah, her long-time live in boyfriend, and a few friends that stopped by now and then for a beer and a smoke. Harmless, but it worried me, knowing that she could go to jail for twenty-five years if she got caught.

"Where's Brenda?" I asked, not really caring, but wanting to be polite.

"In the house." Mom frowned. "I wish she'd spend more time outside. How can she expect her aura to heal if she never gets out in the sun or digs her toes in the earth?"

I smiled down at my mom's bare, dirty feet, peeking out from under the long granny-style dress she was wearing. Of course, my feet were just as bare, though not as dirty. Neither one of us could understand my sister's fascination with shoes.

"Hey Ma, you out here?" My brother hollered from inside the house.

"In the garden!"

Jason came out the back door, carrying a cardboard box.

"I met the Fed-ex guy at the porch on my way in. I signed for this."

He handed the box to my mom, who smiled happily at the return address. "Oh, my bat guano. My little babies will be so happy!" She turned to take the box back to the greenhouse. I knew enough about growing herbs to know that bat guano was a prized fertilizer, but very pricey. My mother took very good care of her plants.

"So you two tell me what you've been up to." Mom spoke over her shoulder, assuming we'd follow her, which we did.

"Not much," Jason answered. "Working's about all. But from what I hear Rainie's been real busy."

"Doing what?"

I looked at Jason, wondering what he'd heard. Buchanan was a small town. Word got around fast, good or bad.

"I'm not sure what he means. I've just been working, too."

"Yeah? Not what I hear. I hear you've been out to lunch not only with your ex, but with some mysterious man in black."

"What?" My mom stopped and turned to face me. "You've been out with Tommy? And what man in black?"

I gave myself a mental head slap. Did I really think I could go to the local bars without everyone in town knowing when, where and with whom?

"Tommy and I ran into each other a couple weeks ago, and we've been hanging out a little, no big deal."

"It seems like I saw Tommy recently..." Jason frowned, but apparently couldn't recall that Tommy had helped carry him home from the bar.

"Well, I don't know if that's such a good idea," my mom shook her head. "That whole thing with Tommy... some bad karma, don't you think? Your aura was bruised for months after that mess."

"My aura is fine mom." I didn't crack a smile. My mother was very serious about damage to auras and such, and I would never let on that I didn't believe in them. Besides, whether it was auras or just body language my mother read, she was an amazing judge of people's moods. "Tommy and I were good friends, and that's what we're trying to be now. Didn't you always say our auras blended so well?"

"In the beginning, sure, but...I'll tell you what, you bring Tommy over here, let me do a reading. I want to be sure your auras aren't clashing."

"I don't know if Tommy will agree to that."

"If he only has your best interests at heart, he will." Mom put a hand on my arm, and she stared at me, the concern in her eyes so genuine I could almost believe my aura was in mortal danger. "Please, Rainie, this is important."

"All right, Mom, I'll ask him."

Satisfied, Mom turned to go into the greenhouse.

Jason nudged me and grinned. "Poor Tommy doesn't know what's coming."

He spoke softly, but not softly enough. My mom turned back and looked him up and down.

"Speaking of auras, yours could use a good cleansing. Let me finish up here, and we'll take care of that."

"Oh Ma..." Jason rolled his eyes, looking like he wanted to run, but I knew he wouldn't. This meant too much to her, and avoiding it would be like telling her you hated her company. My mom's cleansing rituals included drinking lots of odd tasting teas while in a room saturated with strong incense, chants and prayers to the elemental spirits, and a good sprinkling of scented oils and waters. I didn't know how much good it did cleansing the aura, but it sure emptied your digestive system and your sinuses.

"I wish I could stay for that, but I've got to run." I spoke quickly, before she could discern any suspicious smudges on my aura. "I just stopped to say hi, but I've got to get home to take care of George."

I knew that was the only excuse that would get me out of there with no ill-will; my mother wouldn't tolerate neglect of an animal.

I said good bye, hiding a grin at Jason's glare, and made my escape.

Chapter Twelve

The rest of my weekend was pretty much routine. I went out to dinner Saturday night with Brad, and he came back to my place to watch a movie and stayed over. We shared a leisurely breakfast Sunday morning, and we sat on the porch in the early warmth and read the paper. He left around noon, leaving me free for the day.

I noodled around with a little poetry, but it didn't go well. I felt antsy somehow, like I wanted to be doing something, but I wasn't sure what. I finally got my bike out, the one with two wheels, and took a long ride around town.

I spent the rest of the day reading and cleaning the house, admitting to myself that all in all, I was pretty bored.

I spent Monday morning with Mrs. Gains, who after a very short time insisted I call her Virginia. I made French toast for her breakfast, which she said was her favorite.

"Always seem to be craving something sweet," she explained. "Not much else tastes good anymore."

"That isn't unusual," I assured her. "When we're born the first taste buds to develop are for sweet, and as we age it's the last one we lose."

"Huh. Maybe I ought to sprinkle a little sugar on my meat and vegetables. Might make them taste like something besides cardboard."

I laughed. "It would probably just make them taste like cardboard with sugar on it, but we could try if you'd like."

She started to laugh with me, then abruptly cut it off, glaring towards the kitchen door. I turned to see a rather scruffy old guy standing there, swaying a little, hanging on to the door jamb for support. He was wearing worn but clean dress slacks at least two sizes too big, cinched tight with a brand new but cheap-looking leather belt. He had a flannel shirt tucked into the pants, and the shirt fit well enough to show he had a rather sunken chest. His face was gaunt, and there were two little pieces of tissue stuck to his cheeks where he'd obviously cut himself shaving. I assumed this was the one Virginia called the "Scarecrow."

He stared at us with rheumy eyes, blinking as if the light was painful.

"Good morning." I spoke cheerfully but not too loudly. He seemed almost feral, and I didn't want to scare him off.

His eyes flicked toward Virginia's plate, where a few bites of French toast and a little pool of syrup remained. He licked his lips and finally spoke.

"Hungry."

"Oh." I looked at Virginia, who was still glaring at him but hadn't said a word. I was more than happy

194

to give the guy some food, but I was new around here. I didn't want to overstep my bounds. "Does your daughter usually fix breakfast for the boarders?"

Virginia shook her head. "They've got hot plates in their rooms."

"Oh." I wasn't sure what to do next. The old guy looked at Virginia, then at me.

"I ain't got nothin' to eat. Ate my last can of soup two days ago."

I looked back at Virginia, whose glare had lightened up a little.

"Well damn it, why don't you stock up a little better?"

"No money 'til the third of the month. Ran out."

Virginia scowled, but then waved a hand at me.

"Guess you better feed him. No one ever starved under my roof before, not going to let it happen now."

Relieved, I quickly made up a plate of French toast and put it on the table. The old guy stood there another long minute, swaying, staring at the food as if it were a mirage that would dissipate if he moved towards it.

"Well, go on then! Sit down and eat it!" Virginia snapped.

He jerked as if she'd pulled a string in his neck, and finally tottered to the table. He poured a generous amount of syrup over the toast and dug in as if it were his last meal. I caught a whiff of stale urine and alcohol. Virginia was right about the man's bathing habits.

"It's not right. Just not right." Virginia was mumbling. I turned to ask her what she meant, but I saw the faraway look in her eyes and knew she'd gone away again. Her head slowly tipped forward and she drifted off, still mumbling.

I spoke to the Scarecrow instead.

"My name's Rainie."

He looked up at me, a dribble of syrup on his razor burned chin. There was a long pause as he processed this information and decided on a proper response.

"I'm Doug."

"Nice to meet you. Have you been living here long?"

Doug shrugged. "Not sure."

Now it was my turn to pause and process. It wasn't too hard to believe that he suffered some form of dementia, but why would Ida take in someone who had such special needs? Didn't she have enough taking care of her own mother?

"How did you come to live here? Did you see an ad in the paper?"

He snorted, an ugly sound that seemed to involve a lot of mucus deep in his throat. "Don't read the paper. Use it as a blanket sometimes, but don't read it. Miss Ida found me. Asked did I need a place to stay. Took me to a doctor, got me these nice clothes, gave me a regular mattress to sleep on. Nice lady."

"Very nice," I agreed. So, Virginia was right; he was a homeless guy right off the street. Tommy had always said Miss Ida was a sweetheart.

Apparently her good nature extended to charitable works. "It was good of her to rent you a room."

"Rent?" Doug shook his head. "Don't pay no rent. Only got Social Security, three hundred forty-five bucks a month, barely feeds me and pays for…other stuff. Miss Ida said I could stay here for free." He pushed his now empty plate away and looked at me, concern in his red-rimmed eyes. "Is she gonna want money? 'Cause I can't pay…that's why I was sleepin' in the alley in the first place!"

"No, no, I'm sure she won't. I was just making conversation. I'm new around here. I'm helping out with Virginia."

Doug looked at the old lady, who was now snoring softly.

"She never liked me. Surprised she let me eat." He pushed himself slowly to his feet. "I better go 'fore she wakes up and remembers she hates me." He tottered to the door, and I wondered if he had started the morning with a bit of a cocktail.

Not my business. I had no idea why Miss Ida would claim she was renting for the money when in actuality she was just being charitable. Maybe she just wanted to keep it quiet; some people were embarrassed by their own good works. It was none of my business. I was here for Virginia.

I picked up the empty plates and washed them, waiting for her to wake up.

For a couple of weeks life settled into dull routine. That's the way with life: we tend to remember the excitement, the joy and the pain, as if that was what made up our lives. But that isn't true. If life was a wall we built, each day a brick, it would be a mostly gray wall, with a few colorful bricks thrown in now and then. Even Evil Kneivel, for all his amazing stunts, had to have just hung around the house many days, watching TV, cutting his toenails, or tending to business. He couldn't jump canyons *every* day.

Even the new job seemed old after only a few days. I searched the same websites over and over, filled out reports so similar to each other that I could have used a fill-in-the-blanks form. I saw Jack now and then, but he was busy doing his thing and didn't include me in any of it. There were no surprises in the personal interviews, no psychopaths threatening to slice me up or perverts wanting to tie me up.

Wait a minute, was I complaining? I didn't mean to be. I mean, I'm not really into having my life threatened on a regular basis. I didn't miss Jack's brand of detecting.

Really, I didn't.

Another Monday. Virginia would be expecting me for the morning, and then I had an afternoon of interviews and searches for B&E.

I left Virginia at noon when Miss Ida and Frieda returned, their hair freshly coiffed and their arms full of shopping bags. I stopped by the Subway and grabbed a veggie sub on whole wheat bread to eat on the road. My first reference interview was scheduled for one 'o clock on the west side of South Bend. It promised to be routine, just an in-person rehash of a reference letter. The main focus was to be on the guy's honesty and work ethic; I doubt anyone cared what his sexual practices were. I swung on to the bypass and got there by 12:45. I took a moment in the parking lot to go over my notes.

I was in and out in less than a half hour, not surprised by anything I'd learned. I headed back to the B&E offices for more computer searches. My second interview wasn't scheduled until four o'clock.

I got off the bypass, planning to turn east toward Niles, but on an impulse I turned toward Buchanan instead. I had been driving by Jim "Autoshop" Freman's shop now and then, hoping to catch him in, but so far no luck. I really wanted to help the P.I. find Ken Gripe. He'd been getting away with crap all his life, and I'd never been in a position to do anything about it. I liked the idea of being instrumental in getting him to pay child support.

I drove in on the main road, my speed dropping from 45, to 35, all the way to 25 when I hit the town limits. I crossed the tracks and pulled into the carwash parking lot, then swung around back, where a small, hand painted sign over a garage door read simply "Jim's." I was just getting out of the car when I heard a car start up behind me. I turned in time to see Jim pulling away in a very cherry dark green Charger. I shouted and waved, but he didn't hear me, and kept on going.

I jumped back into my car, figuring it wouldn't be too hard to just follow him wherever he was going, maybe home, maybe out to a late lunch.

I followed him through town, an easy trick at 25 miles an hour, but he reached the outskirts and kept going, running up to 60 as soon as he passed the town limit. At that point I probably should have given up, but I wasn't sure how long it would take to run into him again, so I stayed behind him. He was probably heading home. He seemed like the type who'd prefer living in the country.

We went out a few miles and he abruptly turned to the left, without benefit of a turn signal. Fortunately I wasn't following too closely, having no fear of losing him on the familiar roads. A few miles later he turned right onto a dirt road and finally slowed down. We must be approaching home.

Sure enough, he pulled into a long dirt driveway that cut between a rusting wire fence. By the time I got there the Charger had disappeared around a curve. I pulled in, not hurrying, but I wanted to catch him before he got in the house. It had suddenly occurred to me that there weren't any neighbors within hollering distance out here, and I really didn't know much about what kind of person Jim had turned out to be after high school.

The driveway was deeply rutted and narrow, the weeds growing tall on both sides and even in the middle. Jim must not get much company out here, and he sure didn't spend any time on yard work.

I came around the curve and saw the Charger parked up tight against the house. I got a quick glance at the house, which I was surprised to see looked long abandoned. I had time only for a quick impression before there was a loud ping followed by the crack of a pistol shot.

"Hey!" I saw a paint chip fly off the hood of my car. What the hell, did he just shoot at me?

I slammed in the clutch and frantically shoved the car into reverse. There was a grinding as I missed, punctuated by yet another shot, this one off the roof of my car.

"What the hell?" I finally hit reverse and swung in a wide circle into the yard, which was knee high in weeds. I heard a crunch when my back bumper made contact with something solid hidden in the tall growth, but I wasn't worried about dents in my car right now. Another bullet slammed into the car, this one apparently catching the passenger's side. I didn't know much about the power of bullets or how much it took to punch through aging Detroit metal (if the Escort even was metal, and not all fiberglass) but I wasn't about to hang around and test the limits. I'd leave that to the Myth Busters on the Discovery Channel. I pushed the gear shift into first and slewed out of the weeds, hitting the rutted driveway too fast, moving up to second gear, jouncing so hard I bit my tongue and tasted blood. One more shot hit the back of the car and then I was around the curve and racing for the road as fast as my little four-cylinder would take me.

I pulled on to the dirt road without checking for traffic or cows and was up to fifth gear before I reached the cross road. I barely slowed for the turn, careening over into the far lane and narrowly missing a pickup truck heading south. The truck blared its horn at me and I saw a finger wave out the window, but I just kept going.

I was shaking, swallowing the blood from my abused tongue between loud gasps for breath. "Oh my god, oh my god..." I kept sobbing those three words over and over, nearly incoherent from terror. I finally thought to look in my rearview mirror. There was no green Charger in pursuit, no one on the twisty road but me.

I forced myself to back off the gas, only then realizing my little car was shuddering mightily at nearly 90 miles per hour. I backed off to 60 and fumbled in the console for a cigarette. I dropped the pack on the passenger seat, recovered it, dropped the lighter twice when I tried to lift my shaking hand to my mouth. I reached down and retrieved it from the floor, swerving dangerously, and slowed down some more. Finally I had the cigarette lit, and I took a deep, soothing drag just as I reached the town limits.

I was still shaking, and it was all I could do to slow down to the posted limit. I looked behind me again: no sign of Jim Freman. I turned down a side street, went a block and turned again, and pulled over to the curb. I sat there, puffing on the cigarette like it was my last ever, and tried to get my brain back into thinking mode.

What the hell had just happened? Why had Jim shot at me? I just wanted to ask him a simple question.

I got out of my car and walked slowly around it, looking at the bullet holes. Two had gone in, one straight through the trunk. One had glanced off the hood, another off the roof, leaving long, shiny furrows where the paint had been scraped away.

I spent the longest time looking at the hole in the passenger side door. It looked like it went all the way through. I opened it, and sure enough there was a hole on the inside, and another punched through the side of the passenger side seat.

A wave of dizziness washed over me and I grasped the door frame tightly, wondering if for the first time in my life I was going to pass out. A few inches higher, and that bullet would have kept moving, right into me!

After a few minutes I felt steady enough to move back around and get in to the driver's seat again. I wasn't sure what to do next. Just go on to work? No, I had to tell someone about this.

Duh. I'd been shot at. Obviously I had to tell the cops!

That was easy enough. The police station was right down town, only a few blocks away. I started the car and slowly made my way there.

I pulled into the lot and sat for another minute, considering what I was about to do.

See, I'd never actually been in jail, but that didn't mean I'd never dealt with the Buchanan cops before. My family had never exactly been considered model citizens. Back in the day my mother had done a few month-long stints in the county lock up, back when getting caught with pot got you a slap on the wrist or short time. I'd been picked up as a juvenile once or twice, but mom had always bailed me out before I was processed into a holding cell. That was a good thing, since even the *thought* of being locked up caused me to break out in a cold sweat. I remember sitting on a bench outside a cell, staring at the bleak interior. All I could think about was how I was going to kill myself using just a metal cot and a seat-less toilet bowl. Could I drown myself? Smash my head against the wall? Choke on a mattress button?

Fortunately they never actually locked me in there, but I still spent the occasional sleepless night imagining I could hear the metal clang of the cell door slamming.

My brother had been picked up for drunk and disorderly a number of times, and once for domestic assault, although the charges were later dropped when it became clear it was his ex-wife doing the assaulting.

Still, I couldn't say the cops were likely to have warm and fuzzy feelings towards me. In a small town reputations were often made by the most insignificant incidents. Once the story was spread from one backyard fence to one local bartender to the lady that works the counter at the gas station it became bigger than life. A mistake that might be laughed off and forgotten in a city with 50,000 people would instead define you in a town with 5,000. I probably rated somewhere above white trash, but well below respectable.

But I had been shot at. I had to report it.

I took a deep breath and got out of my car. At least the worst of the shaking had stopped.

I went into the police station, which was housed in a small white brick building, a historical site that had once been the city founder's house or some such thing. I went up the steps to the little porch. A short ramp came up one side, a token attempt to conform to accessibility laws. It was nice that a wheelchair could make it to the porch, but good luck maneuvering around in the tiny space and managing the front door, which was heavy and definitely not automated.

Inside the floors were hardwood but creaky with age, the plaster walls covered in worn but still lovely wainscoting up to about waist level. The entryways were all framed with the same dark wood that covered the floors. At one time this had obviously been a beautiful, welcoming home.

Directly inside the door was a counter blocking access to the rest of the building, leaving me trapped in an area about four feet by eight. There were no chairs on this side of the counter; petitioners probably weren't expected to have to wait long to report their crimes.

Behind the counter a woman sat at a desk, not wearing a uniform, so I assumed she was a civilian receptionist. To the right there was an open door leading to an office; on the desk I saw a placard that read "Chief of Police."

I stepped up to the counter, knowing a buzzer on the door had announced my arrival, and waited for the woman behind the counter to look up and acknowledge me.

After a long moment she did.

"Can I help you?" Her tone sounded anything but helpful, but I plunged in anyway.

"I was just shot at and I want to report it."

Her eyebrows went up at this. "Shot at?"

That got the attention of the guy in the office. He stood up and sauntered over to his door. He was a portly man in a neat uniform, his gray hair cropped close. It didn't seem strange to me that the chief of police would take an interest in a report of shots fired. This was after all, a town of only 5,000 people, and he was chief over no more than ten officers, a few of them part time.

"Are you hurt, ma'am?"

"No, he didn't hit me, just my car."

"Aren't you one of the Lovingston girls?" The receptionist piped up, clearly more interested in my parentage than my well-being.

"Yeah, I'm Rainie."

"Rainbow, right?"

I nodded, and the police chief smirked. "Rainbow? That some kind of hippie name?"

I bit back a sigh. "I suppose. But my name doesn't have anything to do with this."

"Maybe, maybe not." The chief shrugged. "So tell me what happened."

"Well, I was following this guy to his house..."

"Following him? Why?"

"I wanted to ask him a question."

"So why didn't you call him?"

"I don't know if he even has a phone. If he does it isn't listed."

"So you don't know this guy too well?"

"I don't really know him at all, except by reputation in high school."

"So why were you following him?"

I took a deep breath, suppressing the urge to scream. Was this guy being deliberately obtuse?

"I told you, I wanted to ask him a question."

"What question?"

"I'm looking for a friend of his. I wanted to know if he knew where he was."

"Why are you looking for the friend?"

"It's my job. He's a deadbeat dad…"

"Who, the guy you were following?"

"No! His friend!"

"Hey, no need to raise your voice, young lady. I'm just trying to get to the truth here."

"And I'm trying to tell it, if you'll just listen."

"Fine, go ahead."

"So I saw him, and I followed him home so I could ask my question, and when I pulled into his driveway he jumped out of his car and started shooting at me!"

"Where was this?"

"Out on Garr Road."

"That's clear out in the township. You followed him way out there?"

"I didn't know we'd go that far until I got there."

"Uh huh. So let's see, you follow this guy to Hell and gone, in the middle of nowhere, and as you yourself admit, you follow him into his driveway and accost him on his own private property and he takes a shot at you? Hell, under those circumstances I might of taken a shot myself. You were trespassing, after all."

Again I squelched the urge to scream. If nothing else, I wanted to correct his English: it is might *have* not *of* you ignorant oaf! Living in a small

Midwestern town didn't give him an excuse to talk like a hick; he was, supposedly, educated. I mean, cops at least had to graduate high school, right?

Okay, so it wasn't that bad, it was really just a regional idiosyncrasy of the language. I knew I was guilty of much worse. I was just pissed off that this guy was blowing me off. I mean, I had just been the target of live gun fire! Apparently that was just run of the mill stuff for the good ol' boys out in the township, nothing to get upset about missy, now run along.

"Look, this may not seem like much to you, but damn it, I was shot at!"

"Yeah?" the cop gave me an irritated look. "And you know where I just came from? An assault with a deadly weapon, a block from the high school. A sixteen year old girl stabbed a fifteen year old girl for flirting with her boyfriend. And last week, a cop the next town over got run down by a drunk driver while doing a routine traffic stop, and I worked the shift so his buddies could go to the funeral. You may think I'm just some dumb hick cop that don't know a crime when it bites me in the ass, but honey, I've seen my share of crime. Your little tussle just don't quite get my blood boiling, you see?"

I did see. I admit I was rather surprised by his impassioned speech. I didn't think small town police had to deal with that kind of stuff. On the other hand, I didn't think shots fired should be ignored, especially when those shots were aimed at *me*.

"So you're saying you don't care who shot at me, you don't want to see the bullet holes in my car, you don't even want to take a report?"

"Not my jurisdiction anyway," he said with another infuriating smirk. "Outside town limits, that's county patrol, or maybe the state boys from over to Niles will be interested."

I closed my eyes and took a deep breath, working hard on containing my temper. So this dickhead had just put me through all this, knowing he couldn't help me anyway?

"Thanks for your time," I forced the words out past gritted teeth, doubting he could recognize the sarcasm, and turned to go.

"By the way, who did you say shot at you?"

I turned to look back at him, incredulous. So he wouldn't help me, but he wanted a name for the rumor mill? Uh uh, no way.

"Why don't you call the county police and ask them after I've made my report?"

With that I turned and left.

In the end I didn't make a report at all. By the time I drove the fifteen minutes to Niles I had calmed down considerably, and decided I really didn't want to go through all that again. What if the county cops agreed that I'd deserved to be shot at? I didn't need that humiliation twice in one day.

So I headed back to B&E to run some data and kill time until my fouro'clock interview. I decided I'd give Jim Freman's name to the P.I. on the case and let him dodge the bullets. That's what he was paid for, after all.

Belinda informed me that Hopper was in Chicago on a job, and wouldn't be back before Friday. I left him a message stating that I had some info on the Gripe case and left it at that.

At least, I planned to leave it at that.

The problem was, as the day went on and the whole incident kept playing over in my mind, I started asking myself a few questions.

First of all, was that really Jim's house? Did he really live in a place with boarded up windows? I had gotten only a brief glimpse, but I'd almost swear that even the front door was boarded over.

So if it wasn't his house, why did he pull in there? Had he seen me following him? If so, why would he care? Unless he had something to hide.

Something he wanted to keep hidden so badly he was willing to kill me to do it.

Huh.

I tried to put the whole thing out of my mind, but I couldn't leave it alone. I kept picking at it like an old scab.

I was still running it around in my head when I got home. I let George out and went to see what there was for dinner.

I had gone shopping over the weekend, so I was pretty well stocked. There was milk for cereal, peanut butter and jelly and whole grain bread, some fruit, some carrot sticks and a bowl of salad made up with romaine lettuce, fresh spinach, shredded carrots and cabbage. There was also a piece of chicken breast left over from the weekend. I threw a big handful of salad in a bowl, tore up the chicken to go over it, sliced a tomato for color, and sprinkled Catalina dressing over the whole mess. Yumm.

I put some Pink Floyd on the stereo and sat at the dining room table to eat, the newspaper spread out in front of me.

I couldn't concentrate on the paper. Wars and robberies had no appeal tonight. I wanted to know what was up with that house, and why Jim Freman had shot at me.

The first part of that question was simple enough to answer. I just needed to go back out there and look around.

"Oh, you are nuts!" I spoke the admonishment out loud, as I was prone to do when my inner voice came up with particularly stupid ideas.

Who cares about the house? Not me.

But of course I cared. I'd been shot at, and the answer to why might be in that house. I had to know.

"Well at least don't go alone." There, that was more sensible. Never, ever let your inner voice run unchecked!

I pulled out my cell phone and ran down the contacts list until I got to Eddie. He answered on the second ring.

"Hi Rainie, what's up?"

"Not much, just sitting here reading the paper. Oh, I did get shot at today."

"Yeah?" Eddie laughed. "Single shot or automatic?"

"Single. Big enough to punch through the door of my car."

Eddie was silent, digesting this information.

"Rainie, are you serious? Were you really shot at today?"

"Yep." I was trying to keep it light, but somewhere deep down I felt a little flutter of fear when I remembered that hole in the upholstery.

"What the hell happened?"

I laid it out for him, right up to the point where I'd left the police station, humiliated and pissed.

"Damned small town cops. They're good enough at their jobs when they want to be, but it's a lot like high school; they only want to take care of the in crowd."

"That's kind of how I felt. So here's why I called. I want to know what, if anything, was going on out there. I mean, maybe he just pulled in there so he'd have a quiet place to shoot at me, but it seemed he was driving with a purpose, you know? I want to go back out there, but I want someone to go with me. Will you?"

"Hell, Rainie, you know I would, but I'm kind of in the middle of this thing out in LaPorte."

"Well, that's okay, I understand."

"I'll be done with this by Saturday, we could do it then."

"That's all right. Hopper will be back by Friday. Maybe he'll go check it out."

"You're not just saying that, are you? You're not going to be stupid and go out there alone just to satisfy your curiosity?"

"Of course not!" But that, naturally, was exactly what I was thinking. I mean, it was just an abandoned house, no different than I'd partied in a hundred times when I was a teenager. What was the big deal?

"Shit." Eddie had obviously seen right through me. We had, after all, been friends for a long time. We'd suffered puberty and oddball parents together, had gotten drunk and climbed the school roof and groped each other (although we were both glad we'd never gone any further.)

"I can't believe I'm saying this, but I think you should call Jack."

"You mean ask him to go with me?"

"Yeah, seeing as how you're determined to go. He probably won't get you in any more trouble than you'll get yourself."

"I don't know, he kind of scares me."

"He scares everyone, but don't let that worry you. He's a good guy, and as long as he's watching your back you never have to look over your shoulder, you know what I mean?"

"Maybe I'll just let Hopper handle it."

"That would be best, but just in case, do you have Jack's number?"

"Yeah."

"All right then. Look, I've got to go. Don't go out alone, right?"

"Right. Thanks Eddie."

"Love ya, Rainie." And he hung up.

I stared at the phone for a long minute. That was weird. I mean, I knew Eddie loved me, and I loved him, sometimes I thought maybe more than I loved my own brother, but he'd never said it before.

Huh. Wonder what was up with Eddie.

I tried to go back to the paper, but I might as well have been reading Sanskrit. I couldn't concentrate well enough to make any sense of it. I gave up and tossed the paper into the recycling bin, rinsed my salad bowl, and wandered around the house, picking up what little clutter there was, trying to make myself forget about Jim Freman.

I just couldn't do it. I couldn't ignore the fact that someone had shot at me.

I could just run out there, see if there were any lights.

No, that wouldn't do it. I needed to look in the house.

I couldn't imagine that Jack would agree to this, but what the heck. Eddie was right, it wasn't a good idea to go out there alone. Besides, when it came right down to it I wasn't that brave.

I dialed Jack's number, but after one ring it went to voicemail. So fine, he probably had it turned off, and wasn't available anyway. So if Eddie asked, I could honestly tell him I tried.

I was kind of relieved. Going out to the boonies with Jack was almost as scary as going alone.

So who else could I ask? Tommy? Our renewed friendship still seemed a little fragile. This might be too much to ask so soon.

I went through my other choices: Not Mason and Jeff. Even if they were willing, I doubted if their wives would allow them to take a late night excursion with me. Riley might, and he sort of owed me for promising to be his alibi, didn't he?

My cell rang, and I checked the readout: Jack. Oh boy. Did I really want to answer it?

I debated for three rings.

"Hi, Jack."

"Hey. You called?"

"Um, yeah, but...well, it was nothing really. I've changed my mind."

"Oh? Now you've got to at least tell me what you were thinking."

"It was just this thing I was going to do, and Eddie suggested I call you, but I've decided it was a stupid idea."

"Yeah?" Jack didn't say anything more, and after a moment, like a suspect being sweated, I spoke to fill the silence.

"I got shot at today by some bozo I wanted to interview. I followed him out to a house in the country, but it looked abandoned. I was thinking about going out there, see if there's anything up."

"Sounds like a great time. We should probably wait until midnight. Less traffic on the roads, not much chance of being noticed. Wear something dark. I'll bring the flashlights."

"Uh..."

"What, you have your own favorite flashlight?"

"No, but I..." Oh hell, what was I hesitating for? I really did want to go. "No, yours will be fine."

" I'll see you about 11:30."

He clicked off, and that was that. I was committed to it now.

Chapter Thirteen

So what does a person wear for sneaking into an abandoned house in the middle of the night?

Something dark, Jack said. That made sense. I chose a pair of loose fitting black jeans and a baggy old black sweatshirt.

Jack showed up promptly at 11:30, dressed much as I was, but his jeans were tight, and instead of a sweatshirt he had a long-sleeved, form-fitting black T-shirt.

"Are those your stealth clothes?" He asked with a grin.

"I dressed for night."

"I would prefer to see you wearing something a little tighter."

I couldn't stop myself from blushing. "I'm going to break into an abandoned house, not seduce the residents. Besides, the sight of me in tight clothes isn't going to attract much but pitying gawks."

"You're way too hard on yourself." Jack looked me up and down, his gaze frankly appraising. "You'd look damned fine in a tight pair of jeans. You shouldn't buy into society's ridiculous ideas about thin equating with sex appeal."

"Yeah, well I'm not seeing many size twelve's cavorting in beer commercials."

"Any guy who equates drinking beer with having a fulfilling sex life likely isn't going to give you must satisfaction anyway." Jack grinned. "Personally, I like a little meat on my women. Hell, you don't even dare shower with one of those really skinny chicks, for fear they'll slip right down the drain."

I reddened further at an unbidden image of showering with Jack. I really wanted to change the subject.

"I didn't call you for a fashion consultation."

"True enough. Actually I was more concerned with the practicality of your clothes: if you get in a tight situation, you don't want any loose ends hanging out that could get you caught up - literally."

"Ah," I nodded, as if I'd known what he meant all along. "Unfortunately, I don't have anything else, so I'll have to make do."

"Got gloves?" He asked me while pulling on a sleek looking pair of leather gloves.

"No."

"All right, just try not to touch anything."

Jack held the door for me. "And try not to climb under any chain link fencing or run through any thorny thickets. I'd hate to have to cut your clothes off to free you."

His tone made it sound like he wouldn't hate it at all, but I kept my eyes averted and told myself not to be ridiculous. A drop dead gorgeous hunk of man like Jack simply would not be interested in a

217

not-so-svelte   thirty-something
poet/detective/caregiver.

The moon was nearly full when we stepped outside. It gave everything a surreal look, as if it were daylight in an old black and white movie.

We took Jack's truck, and I gave him directions to the old house. He drove at a steady 45 miles per hour on the approach, not too fast, but not so slow as to attract attention. He drove past the overgrown driveway without slowing. There wasn't much to see. The house was past a curve in the driveway, hidden by trees.

He kept going another 150 yards or so before pulling over to the shoulder.

"We'll go cross-country from here, try to come up from the side."

"I use to play in the woods a lot when I was a kid. It's pretty easy to get turned around, even in daylight. You sure we won't get lost?"

Jack grinned. "I have an inborn sense of direction, don't worry."

I decided I'd worry as much as I wanted to, but I kept that to myself.

He stepped cautiously into the woods, his nostrils flaring like a wolf seeking a scent.

"What are you doing?"

"Shh, whispers only. We're sneaking, remember?"

"Sorry." I lowered my voice. "But what are you doing?"

"Smelling for stagnant water. This is lowland; there'll be a lot of swamps. I think we're okay here."

He moved off into the trees slowly but steadily, weaving around objects I couldn't see. I wondered if the military installed special cat's eyes in him while they were perfecting the rest of his physique. Maybe they'd even given him new olfactory nerves to allow him to smell swamps. He could be the modern day Six Million Dollar Man, and maybe those luscious glutes and bulging biceps were just molded polymers over mechanical tendons.

I shushed my inner voice, which was once again running off on a tangent, fueled by my tension. I concentrated on following Jack, who now seemed little more than another shadow among the trees. The full moon was of little help under the lush canopy of the woods.

It seemed we walked for hours, constantly getting scratched by the green thorny vines that grew everywhere they found a few inches of space. The horrid things grew everywhere around here, the first to green up in the spring, the last to die off in the winter. They easily pierced cotton fabric and tore at tender skin, sticking like Velcro when you peeled them off.

At last Jack stopped and whispered to me, very softly.

"I see a light." He pointed through the trees. I moved my head to the side a little and finally saw what he saw, a bare strip of light shining through the boarded up windows. So the house wasn't abandoned after all!

I felt vindicated, but at the same time my heart started pounding a little harder. So I had been right, there was something here to hide, but did I really need to know more? Was it worth the risk of being shot?

I'd come this far. Might as well get a peek.

"Let's move, but try to be a little quieter from here on out."

"I'm already whispering as softly as I can."

"I mean when you walk. You don't have to step on *every* dry stick, you know."

I was glad he couldn't see my cheeks coloring in the dark. "Who do I look like, Daniel Boone?"

"I thought you said you spent a lot of time in the woods when you were a kid."

"Yeah, but I was *playing*, not *sneaking*."

"Whatever. Just set your feet down softly. If you feel a stick under your shoe, don't step on it, okay?"

"Aye, Captain!" I snapped off a sloppy salute. He turned and kept walking. I followed, trying to pay attention to where my feet landed, but if I concentrated too hard on that I couldn't avoid the branches slapping at my face. I tried slowing down, but then I lost sight of Jack. In a panic, I took a few hurried steps to catch up.

He grabbed my arm in the dark, and fortunately clapped a hand over my mouth at the same time, or they would have heard my screech of terror back in town.

"Hey!" He hissed at me, working hard to keep his own voice soft. "We're being quiet, remember?"

"I can't be quiet unless I move slow. You're going too fast."

He blew out an impatient breath and started moving again, this time at such a slow pace I almost tripped on him. Boy, we were quite a team, working as smoothly together as a well-oiled machine.

We finally reached the edge of the clearing around the house, and Jack crouched down. I got down beside him and peered at the building.

There was plenty of light in there. It was shining through cracks in the plywood covering the windows, cracks that were likely big enough to give us a glimpse in.

Jack put his mouth to my ear. "You wait here, I'll go check it out."

I shook my head angrily and grabbed his arm so I could get close to his ear.

"No way, this is my thing! You're just the backup!"

Jack flashed me a quick grin and shrugged. Then he started pointing and gesturing, some sort of complicated hand signals that were probably supposed to explain his plan to me. It looked like something right out of the movies. All he needed was camouflage paint on his face and a pack on his back. I almost giggled, but bit my lip and nodded as if I understood instead.

He started across the clearing, keeping low, heading for the side window. That looked easy enough, so I followed him, maybe not as gracefully, but I thought I was getting the quiet thing down pretty good.

I reached the window to find him already peeking through a crack. He glanced at me, looking slightly annoyed, and I guessed I had misread the finger-signed plan. Oh well, who died and made him boss, anyway?

I nudged him aside so I could get a look.

The house was a long way past habitable. The floor was a shaky looking mess of missing tiles and warped floorboards, in some spots with the boards missing altogether. The sheetrock was covered in graffiti where it wasn't torn away, the ceiling coming down in thick sheets of wet plaster.

Even so, the place was occupied.

Three men lounged around the rotting room, leaning against broken counters, drinking beer. A dirty Styrofoam cooler rested on the floor at the feet of one of the men. I recognized him: Jim "Autoshop" Freman. It took me a minute to figure why the guy next to him looked familiar, but then it came to me. Ken Gripe, deadbeat dad, a little heavier than he'd been in high school and a lot balder, but it was definitely him. I didn't know who the third guy was.

They were laughing and talking, gesturing now and then at what looked like an elaborate but poorly funded science experiment laid out on a table in the middle of the room. The table was nothing more than an old door propped across some rickety looking sawhorses. The experiment seemed to involve a lot of liquids in glass jars and a few cans of Sterno. I got a whiff of something that smelled like a wet baby diaper left too long in a hot parking lot.

Then I got it. Duh. Science experiment, smell of ammonia, three beer swilling dirt bags in the middle of nowhere.

Meth lab.

With a grimace of distaste I looked at Jack, who gestured with his head for me to follow him back across the clearing. That gesture I could read.

Still crouching, I followed him back, relieved to reach the trees so I could stand upright. He led me a ways into the trees before he stopped.

"Now I know why he was shooting at me." I remembered to whisper.

"Yep, that'll do it." Jack grinned. "So, you want to take them out?"

"Take them out?" I stared at him, aghast. "Just me and you?"

"Sure, why not? There's only three of them, and we've got surprise on our side."

"But they've got guns!" I was having a hard time keeping my voice down. "Did you see what he did to my car?"

"I've got guns, too." Jack lifted his shirt to reveal a black gun snugged tight into the waistband of his pants. How stylish, a weapon to match his outfit. "I've got one for you, too." He pulled up his pant leg to show me a smaller gun strapped to his ankle.

"What do you want me to do with that, shoot myself? Because that's probably what I'd do. I've never handled a gun in my life!"

"It's easy, I'll show you…"

"No you won't. I'm a caregiver, not a marine!"

"Then what are we doing out here?"

"I wanted to know why he shot at me."

223

"So now you know, so that's it? You'll just go home to bed and sleep comfortably because your curiosity is satisfied? That's enough for you?"

"Yes it is. It has to be. I'm not skilled enough to go in and bust up a meth ring."

"I don't know that this counts as a meth ring, just three guys hanging out drinking beer."

"And cooking meth. With guns! Don't forget the guns!"

"So you think we should just let them keep cooking in peace?"

"Of course not. I'll call the cops - the county cops. Let them handle it."

"Yeah, okay. They'll probably send a guy right out. He'll be careful, being way out here, all alone, but a part of him will be wondering if it's a false tip, and he might pull right into the driveway. Those guys inside see the headlights and come out shooting. The cop might get lucky and get away like you did, buy maybe they'll aim higher, or better. Could end up one dead cop, and they'll just move the operation somewhere else."

I stared at him, unable to read his expression in the dark, wondering how accurate his scenario was. Would they really just send one cop to check it out? Would Jim and the boys really shoot at a cop if they did?

Drug penalties in Michigan were pretty stiff. They might think it was worth it to shoot first, ask questions later to avoid spending a good portion of their lives in prison.

All of that didn't change the fact that I was *still* not a marine. I didn't even play shoot 'em up video games. No way was I going in there.

And yet I caught myself asking Jack: "Just what did you have in mind?"

He grinned again, his teeth a sudden white flash in the dark.

"What, are you crazy, Rainie? You've never even handled a gun before! You don't really thing I want to go in there, just the two of us?"

I wanted to hit him. Now it was my turn to hiss.

"What the hell was that all about? The element of surprise crap, the dead cop scenario..."

"Hey, I was just curious to know if you'd go for it." He grinned again. "You're an interesting woman, Rainie."

Interesting? Like a lab rat?

Jack was really weird, there was just no doubt about it.

I caught a flash of light from the corner of my eye. Someone had opened the back door. We both ducked, though it wasn't necessary. We were far enough into the woods to remain unseen.

We heard voices, then the deep, rumbling bass bark of a big dog.

"Uh oh."

"Let's move," Jack grabbed my arm, but it was clearly too late. The dog raced across the clearing and into the woods, straight toward us.

The guy at the door yelled back into the house, "Hey, I think someone's out there!"

"C'mon Ken, that damned dog of yours is always..."

I couldn't hear any more over the crashing noise the dog was making as he barreled towards us. I'd barely run five steps before the beast was on us, leaping on Jack.

Jack spun to fight it off, but it was huge, something like a cross between a Great Dane and a Saint Bernard, and Jack went down from the impact.

I hurried back, not sure what I could do to help, only to find Jack sputtering and spitting.

The dog was trying to lick him to death.

"Crazy mutt!" Jack heaved the dog off him and bounded to his feet. Behind us there was plenty of activity at the house, which I assumed was the crazy guys with the guns. I didn't think they were going to be nearly as friendly as the dog.

"Move! Run!" Jack gave me a light shove, and I did just that, no longer caring about stealth, just wanting to outdistance the bullets, or at least the limit of their aim.

The dog came with us, romping happily along, overjoyed at a game of catch-me in the dark woods.

Several shots rang out, and I heard someone yell, "Hey, don't shoot my dog!"

Great. At least the meth-head loves his dog. Not his kids, certainly not two strangers in the woods, but he cared about his dog.

There was no trail. I ran headlong, seeming to find every low-hanging branch on every tree. The branches slapped at my face and tangled in my hair, pulling every bit as hard as a certain dominatrix I'd recently dealt with. The thorny vines kept snagging my jeans and tearing at my hands, but I kept running.

The dog was next to me now, nipping at my heels, barking excitedly, so damned pleased that someone wanted to have a midnight romp in the woods. It might have been funny if not for the fact that he was serving as a beacon to the men behind us, as surely as if they'd tagged us with a GPS finder.

"To the left, Rainie!" Jack whispered loudly, right behind me. I veered left, hoping he knew where he was going. The woods out here were pretty extensive. We could run in circles in the dark for miles without ever coming across a road or another house.

Behind us the shooting had stopped but I could hear the guys crashing along, yelling back and forth to each other.

"Where the hell did they go?"

"Follow Brutus, he's on 'em!"

I swatted at Brutus. "Bad dog! Go home!" But that only made the big lug leap at me, and he damn near knocked me over. I was beginning to think of a few more reasons to defend my preference of an iguana over a dog.

"Which way to the car?" I didn't even try to keep my voice down, not that it came out all that loud between my gasping sucks of air. I really needed to quit smoking if I was going to hang out with Jack.

"The road is straight ahead. See how it lightens up?"

I didn't see any such thing. I ran on, trusting him because I didn't have a better idea, Brutus

227

bounding along beside me, his bark acting like a buoy in the dark seas, drawing the armed men right to us. At least, from the amount of cursing going on behind us, they weren't making any better progress than we were. I hoped maybe they'd had enough brews to slow them down even more.

Finally I saw what Jack saw: a barely perceptible lighter space up ahead that very well might be the moon reflecting off the road. I put on a burst of speed.

And ran full tilt into a swamp.

The first step sank my foot up to the ankle in thick muck. My second step plunged me headlong into the stinking, stagnant water.

I think I cried out just before my face went under water.

An instant later I felt Jack grab a handful of my sweatshirt and haul me to my feet. He had reflexes to match his cat's eyes, and of course he had managed to stop before going into the water.

I came up, sputtering and gagging. The water smelled like the rotting carcasses of a few dozen deer mixed with the oh-so-inviting odor of an overripe septic tank.

I scrubbed at my face with my mud-slimed hands. "Ew! That really stinks! How the hell did you not smell *that* coming!"

"No time for that, we've got to move!"

I suddenly remembered the meth-heads with guns, and with a final sob of disgust I followed Jack back to solid ground and started moving again.

Brutus was gone. Apparently his idea of fun did not include swimming in swamps. Go figure, a big dumb dog like that being too fastidious to get his paws dirty.

Jack was moving to the left again, and I stayed tight on his heels, trying to step where he stepped. It was only then that I realized I'd lost a shoe to the sucking mud. I have thick calluses from going barefoot so often, but even so I tried to step carefully with the bare foot.

Behind us, Brutus had apparently returned to his master. I heard Ken yelling at him to settle down.

"Damn it, where'd they go?"

"I don't know, can't see a damned thing. Send the dog back after them."

"He's not a bloodhound!"

"Hey, they must have a car at the road. We can get 'em there!"

Great, just what I needed, quick thinking drunken meth heads.

"Damn." Jack muttered and stepped up the pace. "I was hoping it would take them a little longer to figure that out. We'd better hurry."

We finally came out to the road. The moonlight glinted off the superb wax job on Jack's truck, about fifty yards away.

We started off at a slow jog, my gait made strange by the one shoe I still wore. It occurred to me I should probably take it off, but back the way we'd come I heard a car start. No time now. We sped up.

"Aw shit!" I felt the crunch and peculiar pressure of punctured skin just before I felt the pain.

"I stepped on something!" I stopped to remove the offending object, but I heard another engine start and engines revving. They were coming; we were out of time.

"Never mind, I'll get it later!" I started hobbling toward the truck on one shoe and the toes of my bare foot.

"Let me carry you..."

"Don't you dare!" I was amazed at the vehemence of my warning. Jack must have been impressed too, because he didn't argue. Instead he moved ahead and beeped the truck doors unlocked.

He was already in, the engine running, by the time I pulled myself into the passenger seat. Ahead I saw headlights as the first car pulled out of the weedy driveway, hesitating while the driver looked to see where we were.

Jack left the lights off and swung into a u-turn before I even had my door shut. The driver must have seen the flash of the interior lights. He fishtailed onto the road in pursuit. Jack turned on the headlights and hit the gas.

I reached for my seat belt, frantically trying to buckle it while the truck rapidly picked up speed. Ahead I saw the reflection of a sign at a crossroad. Barely touching the brakes, Jack swung left, slewing onto the dirt road, his expression as bland as if we weren't about to die in a high-speed chase.

I looked behind us and saw headlights come around the turn, followed closely by another set.

Then I saw a muzzle flash and heard the report: one of the meth heads was leaning out of the car window, shooting at us!

I turned back to give Jack this new information - in case he didn't already know -just in time to see the startled eyes of a deer standing in the middle of the road.

I opened my mouth to scream, but it was too late. We barreled right past her, missing by inches as she leaped away.

I had barely taken a relieved breath when I heard the crash behind us and turned to look.

Here's the thing. There are lots of deer in Michigan. In fact, Michigan has the distinction of being the #2 state in the nation for most deer/car accidents.

Here's the other thing. Deer travel in herds, so if you see one, there's probably another one right behind it.

Jim's beautiful green Charger came to a sudden halt, but Jim didn't. Apparently he'd been in the kitchen getting a beer when the public service message came on warning people to buckle up, because there he was, diving through the windshield and over the hood of his car in a gruesomely graceful motion.

A second later there was another crash as his buddies rear ended him.

At that point, I admit it, I closed my eyes tight, not wanting to see any more, but I managed not to squeal like a little girl. Okay, maybe a little squeal - more of a squeak.

Jack slowed but didn't stop.

"Jack, wait! We have to stop and help!"

"And take a chance one of them can still fire a gun? No way. We call 911, let the cops handle it."

"Okay." I started to fumble my phone from my pocket, but Jack shook his head.

"Not that one. Grab a phone from the glove box."

"What?"

"There are a couple of disposable cells in there for just this kind of emergency. You don't want 911 to get your caller ID. I don't particularly want to answer questions about this, do you?"

I grabbed a phone and fumbled for a minute for the on switch until Jack reached over and did it for me. I dialed 911 and made the report.

"We're on Madron Lake Road, somewhere between Pardee and Walkins. You'd better hurry. One of the guys came right through his windshield!"

The operator asked my name again, and I ended the call without answering him.

"All right, wipe it and toss it." Jack told me.

"I thought you said it was untraceable?"

"Still don't want to use the same one again."

Sheesh, he was paranoid. But hey, it wasn't my phone, what did I care? I started to wipe it on my jeans, only then remembering how slimy I was.

Jack grinned and took the phone, still wearing his gloves. He wiped it on his T-shirt, front and back, then opened the window and gave it a hard toss. It landed in the woods, just another piece of plastic for some archeologist to excavate a few hundred years from now.

Jack turned onto a paved road, his pace sedate now, just another driver travelling from here to there.

"How's your foot?"

Funny, I'd forgotten all about my cut foot along with my slimy clothes, but now that he mentioned it, it really hurt! I crossed the foot up over my knee to get a look at it, and turned on the map light.

There was a rather sizable piece of glass protruding from the arch of my foot. It was obviously from a beer bottle. A portion of the thick bottom was still attached, which is likely why it was sticking up for me to step on in the first place. There was a fair amount of blood oozing around the glass, mixing with the mud in a sort of grayish maroon goop, sort of like lava.

"Got any napkins?"

Jack looked over at my foot, and his eyes might have widened just a bit.

"Don't you mean a towel and a needle and thread?"

"No stitches. I don't have insurance, and an emergency room would charge a thousand bucks. I'm not officially on the job, remember?"

"You were looking for Gripe's friend..."

"Look, we'll argue it later." I didn't want to admit that I was really scared to death of stitches. The thought ranked right up there with getting locked in a closet or getting shot. My brain sometimes did a bad job of prioritizing fear. "Right now I'd like to pull this glass out, but I need something to stop the bleeding when I do." I had never been squeamish about doctoring myself. It was better than putting my fragile flesh in some stranger's hands.

"You're taking this rather calmly." Jack pointed out.

"What should I do? Squeal and faint?"

"No, but even I would probably at least wince at the sight of half a beer bottle sticking out of my foot."

I rolled my eyes. Men sure liked to exaggerate size. "It's no more than two, three inches, maybe an inch actually in my foot."

"Still." Jack grimaced. What a sissy.

I glanced around the truck cab in search of a napkin, but there was nothing, not even a tiny scrap of a gas receipt. Damn, he kept a clean truck.

"Give me your shirt."

"My shirt?"

"What, it's not like an Armani or something, is it?"

"No, I was just hoping you'd use yours." He gave me a sly grin.

"You're a strange man, Jack."

"If you think I'm strange because I want to see a woman take her shirt off, you were definitely married to Tommy too long."

"Very funny. Your shirt, please."

"All right, hold the wheel."

I grasped the steering wheel and steadied it while he pulled the shirt over his head and handed it to me. If I hadn't been in pain and still freaked out from being chased through the woods and witnessing a likely fatal car accident, I might have enjoyed seeing him without his shirt.

Okay, actually, I did enjoy it, but only for a few seconds. I got my mind back on the business at hand.

I folded the shirt into a thick pad, set my jaw, took a deep breath, and yanked the glass out. I clamped the shirt over the fresh flow of blood, pleased that I'd managed to not even whimper.

Jack pulled into my driveway and I squished out of his truck. I looked back at the upholstery and grimaced. "Sorry about your truck."

Jack shrugged and came around and to help me hobble to the door. I didn't argue this time. I was emotionally and physically drained.

"They'll have to hose it down to get that mess out."

"Probably." Jack looked at my hair, then down the rest of me. I was covered in green slime, scratches on every piece of visible skin, my hair matted and tangled. "You could use a good hose down yourself."

I nodded as I unlocked my door. "I'm headed straight for the shower."

"Want me to help?"

"No!" I blushed furiously at the suggestion. Just what I needed, Jack soaping up my cellulite. Hell no.

"Just offering. Let me at least help you to the bathroom."

That I allowed, since I wanted to keep my bloody foot off the carpet. I made it to the tile, thanked him politely, and shut the door.

I showered until the hot water ran out, even used some flowery smelling soap someone had given me for Christmas a couple of years before, but I could still smell that underlying reek of stagnant water and dead animals.

My foot was still bleeding, but not as bad. Fortunately I have an extensive first aid kit. People without insurance were wise to invest in lots of over the counter medical supplies.

I used a couple strips of tape to pull the wound closed, and then covered it with several folded gauze pads. I wound tape around my foot to hold it in place, then cut a piece off an ace bandage and added that to the top. There. That should keep the blood off my carpet until it clotted.

I threw on an oversized T-shirt, my preferred pajamas, and limped into the living room.

Jack was lounging on my sofa, his feet up on the coffee table, reading the newspaper.

"Hey, you feeling okay?"

"I thought you'd left." I tugged at the hem of my shirt, making sure everything was covered down there.

"Wanted to be sure you're all right." He looked me over, taking in the wild tangle of my hair, which I hadn't yet combed. I wasn't expecting company. His gaze lingered on my face, which I knew was covered with a crosshatch of scratches, as were my arms and even my legs. Maybe I should have kept the leather pants for traipsing through the woods. Those persistent thorns had torn right through my jeans. Finally he looked at my bandaged foot.

"Did the bleeding stop?"

"More or less." I dropped onto the couch and put my own feet up.

"You always this tough?"

"I'm not tough, I'm practical."

"That wound needs stitches."

"Why? I'm not likely to bleed out from it, even if it takes a while to stop bleeding. The only other reason to get stitches is to lessen the scar, and what do I care about a scar on the bottom of my foot?"

"What if you meet a really great guy with a foot fetish someday?"

"I think I'll risk it."

"Damn, you do like to live on the edge." Jack grinned and got up. "Well, thanks for inviting me. I had a great time." He said it as if I'd hosted a great party and he was the last guest leaving.

"Yeah, this was loads of fun. I got shot at, almost drowned in sewer water, and I watched a man die horribly. Fun night."

"Not bad for a Monday. Call me anytime." He gave me a little wave and left.

Chapter Fourteen

The next morning I arrived at Thelma's to find her sitting on the back porch with Tommy, drinking coffee. They were laughing uproariously about something. I hadn't expected to see Tommy here. So they were friends now? I supposed that was okay, but this was my day with Thelma. I couldn't help a little twinge of jealousy.

"Well, you two are certainly getting along well."

"Good morning, Rainie." Thelma peered at me over the rim of her coffee cup. "Rough night?"

I had finally managed to tame my hair, but my face was still a mess of scratches, and of course my foot was still bandaged.

"Did you participate in Monday Night Football?"

"Very funny, Tommy. No, I just ran out to get a gallon of milk and stopped to bust up a meth ring on the way home. You know, the usual."

"This new job is too much." Tommy was frowning. "I think you should reconsider your options."

"What, are you kidding?" Thelma protested. "She's having a great time!"

"Are you sure it's not just you having fun living vicariously through her reports?"

"Well, that too," Thelma admitted. "But hey, you wouldn't deny a little old lady some fun in her last days?"

"Oh, brother." Tommy rolled his eyes.

"Just never mind, young man." Thelma poured a cup of coffee from a carafe and waved me to a chair. "Come on, sit down and tell us all about it."

Thelma's coffee was always strong and delicious. I might not give my right arm for a cup, but telling a story was a more than fair exchange. I settled at the table and started talking.

Jack called me later that day to give me an update on the meth heads.

"Jim Freman was DOA at the scene." I wasn't terribly surprised. "Ken Gripe must have had the presence of mind to fasten his seat belt, because he was nowhere to be found when the emergency crews arrived. The third guy was his cousin, Les Trainor. He was the one shooting at us, so he wasn't belted in either. He was ejected from the car and he's in a coma at Lakeland Hospital, not expected to make it."

"How do you know all this? The 12:00 news just reported a two car accident, no names released."

"I've got friends. Anyway, I made an anonymous call about the operation out at the house. They probably have hazmat crews out there already to clean it up."

"Good to know. Thanks for the update."

"No problem. Like I said, you ever get it in your head for another midnight run somewhere, give me a call."

I was about to say good bye and hang up when a thought occurred to me. "Hey, what about Brutus?"

"Brutus? You mean the dog?"

"Yeah. Was he in the car with Ken?"

"Hell, I don't know. No one mentioned the dog."

"So he might be out at that abandoned house? Left to fend for himself?"

"Rainie, he wasn't exactly a helpless pup. The thing was the size of a small pony."

"A big, dumb pony, you mean. He can't survive out there by himself!"

"So what do you want to do about it?"

That was a good question. Just what did I want to do about it? I couldn't very well bring the beast home, even if I could find him. But what was the alternative? Besides, he was kind of cute, wanting to play, blissfully unaware of the danger around him. Leaving him out there might not be as bad as leaving a little kid, but it felt damned close.

"I guess I'll go look for him."

Jack was silent for a good ten seconds. I waited him out. He hadn't said no right away, so I gave him some time to probe his conscience. It worked.

"All right, I'll take you out there. Can you wear shoes yet?"

"I've got a pair of thick-soled leather sandals I can fit over the bandage."

"All right. I'll pick you up in a half hour."

I hesitated before climbing into the truck, but miraculously the seats looked spotless.

"How did you get the seat cleaned so fast?"

"I know a guy."

"A guy that runs an all-night carwash?"

"You can get anything done at any time if you know the right people."

"Huh." I climbed in and didn't ask any more questions.

The driveway to the meth house was blocked by a fire truck, and we could see flashing lights through the trees. Jack cruised on past. We'd have to park up the road and head across country again.

We were saved the trek when Brutus came out of the woods ahead and stopped in the middle of the road, looking to the right and left as if deciding which way to go.

"There he is!"

"Great." Jack didn't sound like he thought it was all that great. He stopped the truck just short of Brutus, who hadn't bothered to move out of the road but was instead watching us approach with his head cocked, as if about to ask us a question.

"Dumb dog doesn't even know enough to get out of the road."

"Which is why we had to come back for him." I pointed out righteously. I got out of the truck, and after one tentative sniff, Brutus bounded toward me, a big grin on his dumb face, ready to continue our game of catch-me from last night.

"Whoa, buddy! Stop it!" I raised my arms to fend him off, but he was all over me, his big slobbery tongue on my cheeks and in my ears, and I wanted to be mad, but instead I giggled. It kind of tickled.

He had me up against the truck, his paws on my shoulders. Damn, but he was a big dog! I tried in vain to push him away, but he was having none of it. Jack was no help, still sitting behind the wheel of the truck with a huge grin on his face.

"That's it, Rainie, you've got him now!"

Finally my annoyance overwhelmed my pleasure at seeing the cumbersome beast safe and sound, and I managed a firm tone. "Down, Brutus!"

To my surprise, it worked. Brutus dropped away from me and sat in the road, staring up at me with huge brown adoring eyes.

Now what? He couldn't possibly fit in the cab of the truck, so I went to the back and dropped the tailgate. Brutus followed, once again prancing and leaping in hopes of some playtime.

"Up here, buddy." I patted the tailgate, and Brutus jumped up eagerly. He ran to the side and hung his head over the side of the bed, looking forward. Obviously he'd ridden in the back of a pickup before, and it was on his list of fun things to do. I shut the gate and jumped back into the cab.

"Well, that was simple enough."

"Yeah, but the real fun has just begun." Jack put the truck in drive and started off slowly, giving Brutus a chance to set his feet. I glanced back. The dog was still looking forward, that big goofy grin on his face, lapping at the air as it rushed past his slobbery tongue. "How do you think George will like him?"

"I'm not going to keep him!"

"No? Then what are you going to do? Turn him over to the animal shelter? If they don't adopt him out..." Jack drew a finger across his throat and spoke in a really poor imitation of an old movie gangster. "It's curtains!"

"I'll find him a home. Who can resist that cute face?"

"Me? You? Anyone else with half a brain that doesn't want to get saddled with a rowdy, poorly behaved pony who thinks he's a house pet?"

I looked back at Brutus, who was chomping happily on something that must have blown into his mouth, saliva running from his floppy jowls.

Jack might have a pretty good point.

I talked Jack into stopping by a pet store on the way home. Brutus was wearing a collar, but I needed a leash and some dog food. I picked out the heaviest nylon lead my budget would allow and a ten pound bag of a national brand of dog food that didn't cost more than my own grocery budget for a week.

Jack dropped us off at home, looking way too amused as he watched me struggling up the walk carrying the dog food, all the while with Brutus pulling on his leash and nearly jerking me off my feet. I noticed Jack didn't offer to help. I suspected he was just having fun watching me, and I added another point to the weirdo-meter. I wondered if he amused himself in the winter by parking near an icy spot on the sidewalk and watching people slip on their butts all day.

I fumbled for my keys, finally dropping the dog food to free a hand, Brutus now bouncing between jumping on me and the door. At long last I made it inside, and released the big mutt from the lead.

Immediately he started scrambling around the house, stopping at every piece of furniture for a sniff. Figuring he'd been without a meal for at least twenty-four hours, I went straight to the kitchen and dug out a couple of cereal bowls. I filled one with kibble and one with water.

Obviously familiar with the sound, Brutus galloped in through the swinging door and dove into the food. I took advantage of his distraction to go let George out.

I had barely gotten the cage opened and turned back to the kitchen when Brutus came racing out, his muzzle still dripping from a drink of water. Wow, he was fast.

He saw George, and his eyes seemed to light up. He gave his rumbling play bark and jumped up on the cage.

"No Brutus! Down!"

But it was too late. Quick as a flash George lashed out with that long spiked tail and whipped Brutus right across the face.

Brutus yelped and ran behind the couch. George leaped for the drapes, fell, scurried across the floor and up onto the dining room table. He slid across its polished surface with a screech of sharp nails and somehow managed to get himself onto the back of a chair, and from there leaped to the drapes and climbed to the top.

George stared at me accusingly from the curtain rod.

Brutus peeked around the corner of the couch and stared at me with big, frightened, puppy dog eyes, obviously wondering what sort of hellish place I'd brought him to where the toys fought back.

I had planned to have dinner before calling around to find a home for Brutus. Now I realized I had no time to waste; I picked up the phone and started to dial.

An hour later I hung up the phone, ready to admit defeat.

Mason pleaded allergies, Jeff pointed out he didn't have a fenced yard, and Riley just laughed. He managed to stop guffawing long enough to gasp "no way!"

I didn't bother calling Eddie. He often went out of town for weeks at a time, and couldn't even keep a houseplant alive. I left a message on Tommy's machine to call me, but I didn't have much hope.

I stared at Brutus, who stared back at me, his whole body quivering and ready for action. He reminded me of one of those little toys you wind up and they walk across the floor, only if you hold them in your hand they shudder and shake instead.

Brutus seemed to be constantly fully wound.

My phone rang, and I snatched it up eagerly, hoping it was Tommy.

It was the bartender at Larry's, once again asking me to come and get my brother. This was getting old, but what could I do? I couldn't let them call the cops and have him arrested. I know all about tough love, but I wasn't about to let my brother face my worst nightmare.

I promised the bartender I'd be right there. I hung up and looked at Brutus, who reacted to my renewed attention by bounding around and barking.

"Down!" Brutus jumped again, so I repeated the command. He sat, still quivering.

I couldn't take him with me. It would be hard enough to handle my drunken brother. No way could I leave him loose without knowing what his house manners were.

I put him on the back porch with a fresh bowl of water and an old blanket to use as a bed. He woofed when I closed the door, but I ignored him and hurried out the front door to my car.

I returned home to find Brutus jumping at the front door, greeting me with his great bass bark.

"How did you get out?" He only leaped a little higher, not answering. Of course, he could no more talk than he could operate a doorknob. Yet here he was, off the porch.

I went to the kitchen and froze in horror.

He had chewed right through the porch door. It looked like an oversized cartoon mouse hole.

I stared at the hole, at Brutus, and back again, the classic double-take, my mouth hanging open in disbelief. If this had been a sitcom I would likely have been panned for overacting, but what could I say? I really was stunned speechless.

For just a moment I considered taking the beast back and dumping him on the country road I'd found him on. I mean, did I need this? Did I deserve this?

I took a deep breath and calmed myself. My mother always said there were no bad dogs, only poorly communicative human companions.

"Hey, my mom!" I didn't mean to shout, but I couldn't believe I hadn't thought of her in the first place. Brutus flinched as if I'd yelled at him.

"Sorry, pup. I'm hardly even mad." I patted the dog, and glanced back at the big hole. "Okay, I'm a lot mad, but it probably isn't your fault. My mom would say I just didn't make it clear what I wanted you to do."

I wasn't so sure I believed that, but my mother had never met a dog she couldn't handle. She claimed they were our spirit brothers, intended to share our lives, not be dominated in them. Given the proper respect any dog would behave like a valued member of the family.

Too bad that same philosophy didn't seem to work with human beings, like my siblings.

I grabbed the phone and called my mom. I explained about Brutus, right up to the point where he ate my door.

"Oh, honey, did you explain to him that you wanted him to wait there for you? For that matter, why didn't you just give him the run of the house and explain the rules to him?"

"I didn't have time. I had an errand to run." I didn't want to tell her I'd had to go get Jason from the bar again. She would just call him over for another aura cleansing, and I didn't think he could survive two in one week.

"If you don't have time for a dog you shouldn't have one."

247

"I know that, Mom." In fact, that's where the conversation had started, but I didn't point that out. "I was hoping you might take him."

"Of course I will! But remember we're going on the Retreat next weekend, so you'll have to take care of him then."

"No problem." I was nearly faint with relief. "Can I bring him now?"

"I think you'd better. I'll see you soon."

Watching my mother with Brutus is was easy to believe he really was her spirit brother. I brought him around to the back yard, struggling mightily with the leash.

"Rainie, why ever would you chain that beautiful animal? Let him go!"

I unsnapped the leash, and Brutus raced across the yard to my mother. She allowed him to leap up and give her some exuberant licks, but then she spoke to him. I couldn't quite make out the words as I came across the yard at a more sedate pace, but after a moment Brutus dropped to all fours and went racing off around the perimeter of the yard.

"What did you say to him?"

"I greeted him, of course." My mother was watching him fondly as he cut across the grass, full tilt. "Then I explained to him that he was welcome to run off some energy so long as he didn't run into my garden."

"And you think he'll listen?"

"Why wouldn't he?"

Here's the thing about my mom. She says things like that with such a guileless expression and so much sincerity that you can't help but wonder why you doubted her in the first place.

"I really appreciate you taking him in like this."

"I'm happy to have him. Just remember I'll need you to keep him this weekend."

"No problem."

"We'll sit and have a talk before you take him. Okay? We'll go over the ground rules at your house so you won't need to leave him penned on that little porch."

"Sure, okay." I was picturing my entire house being chewed up if I dared leave the beast roam for even an hour, but I wasn't going to argue with my mom. After all, Brutus had already made several circuits of the yard, and hadn't once stepped into her garden. It *had* to be a coincidence and yet... well, my mom never ceased to amaze me.

"I'd better get going. I need to get George back to his own shelf. When I left he was still clinging to the drapes."

"All right, Rainbow." She grabbed me for a big hug. I turned to go, and she said, "By the way, thanks for looking after your brother."

"What?" I blinked at her, not sure what to say. How did she know? Not for the first time, I wondered if she could read my mind.

She smiled. "I smelled liquor when I hugged you, and I've never known you to drink much besides a beer or two. I guess the cleansing didn't help him much, did it?"

"I guess not."

She sighed. "I love that boy, but I don't know how to get through to him."

"No one can, mom. It's a choice he makes for himself."

She gazed toward the house and stared up at the second story, where I suppose my sister was sequestered in her over-sized closet.

"Was I such a bad mom, Rainbow? Your brother drinking like he does, your sister obsessive-compulsive, and you..." her gaze came back to me and she suddenly smiled. "Well, you're not all that messed up, other than having bad luck with men. Are you?"

"No mom, at least I don't think so. And you did a fine job raising us. You know Brenda's problem is just a mental disorder, some screwed up chemicals in her brain, and you know Jason drinks mostly because he's bored. You can't blame yourself."

"I still wonder if I left the commune too soon. It was so hard to keep everything organic for you kids. All those chemicals you ate and breathed, it's no wonder everyone's heads are messed up."

"That's probably it, mom. Thanks again for taking Brutus in. I'll call you tomorrow."

The rest of the week went by with no incident. My brother seemed to be avoiding the bars for a change, and Jack was apparently busy getting someone else into life-threatening scrapes.

Eddie came back from LaPorte on Friday, only for the day. His business there was going to take longer than he'd expected. He listened with amusement to my account of our little expedition.

"You aren't mad?"

"What's the point? You've always done your own thing, and besides, I'm not your parent."

"I wish you'd talk to Brad. He sure doesn't see it that way."

"Brad doesn't see anything but what Brad wants to see."

"Why don't you like him?"

"Because he's all wrong for you."

"Maybe, but Mr. Right isn't exactly hiding under my bed. I know, I've looked."

"You're definitely looking in the wrong place. Who would want a guy that hides under beds?" Eddie stood to go. "By the way, Jack isn't a very good choice either."

"Jack?" I felt myself blushing. "We just work together."

"Yeah. Well, I told you he's a good guy in a fight, but I don't think he's really boyfriend material."

"Whatever." I rolled my eyes to prove how ridiculous I thought the idea was. "Besides, I have a boyfriend, remember?"

Eddie gave me his sweet-sad smile.

"Okay. I'm going over to B&E to pick up a couple of things. Maybe you should come along, we can spend a little time on the shooting range."

"Why?"

"Because you should at least be somewhat familiar with guns if you're going to hang out with Jack. You never know when he might toss one across the room at you. You should at least know which end the bullets come from."

"I don't think I want to know. Guns only serve one purpose, and I can't imagine I'll ever want to shoot someone."

"No? What about meth heads who are about to shoot you?"

"Well, I suppose that might feel justified. Still, to just shoot someone in cold blood..."

"That's not what I'm talking about. I just want you to know how to defend yourself."

"Maybe it would be better if I just stayed away from people who point guns at me."

"You're right, that would be better. Should I call Jack and tell him to lose your number?"

"That isn't necessary."

"Fine, then let's go."

I sighed and considered my reluctance. Guns were as common as fast food places were scarce in Buchanan. Every other person hunted, and it seemed that having rifles around just led to having handguns. It wasn't unusual to hear gunfire all day long in the outlying areas, especially on the weekend, when people gathered for target shooting in their back yards.

I don't want you to get the impression that every country boy in Buchanan was running around with a loaded weapon ready to blow your head off. Most of them were responsible gun owners, serious about safety, passing the knowledge on to their kids and grandkids and pretty much anyone else who wanted to learn. I, however, had been raised by pacifists, by a mother who had actually been arrested in war protests. I had a well-ingrained distrust of war machines.

What the heck, it was only shooting at targets, and it would make Eddie happy. I went along with him.

B&E had a target range in the basement, laid out exactly like I expected. There were long lanes with paper targets at the end, each capped with a little booth surrounded by heavy duty Plexiglas that cut down on the noise.

Eddie put four guns on the shelf in front of us.

"Why so many?"

"I wanted you to get the feel of different ones. Three automatics, one revolver, all different calibers so you can feel the various kicks."

"Kicks?"

"Yeah, when you fire a gun you release a lot of forward energy, but there has to be something behind it, and you're going to feel that. You have to be prepared for it, and you have to hold the gun steady, because it will have a tendency to jump up."

"You make it sound like it has a life of its own."

"Hardly. It's just a tool, an inanimate object with no morals or conscience. But it will do what it's designed to do the way it's supposed to do it, and if you don't understand that you'll likely shoot yourself in the foot or just put a few rounds into the ceiling."

I stared at the guns, wondering once again if I really wanted to even touch one.

"Look Rainie, there's no need to be afraid of them. Like I said, it's a tool, like a hammer or a screwdriver. Those can be used as weapons, too, if the handler chooses to use them that way."

"But guns can't help build a house."

"True. But if you know the safety features and handle them properly they're no more dangerous than carrying around a hammer."

"Okay." I sighed. "Which one do we start with?"

We spent an hour going carefully over each gun. Eddie had me break them down and put them back together. He had me load each one and unload it, and then go down the row to check that each one really was clear. He showed me how a bullet could be chambered in some guns, so that even without the clip it was loaded. He made me find and work the safety catches over and over again, until I could close my eyes and tell by the feel which one I held and work the switch.

By the time he actually got around to having me fire the first one I no longer feared that one might suddenly turn on me of its own accord. He was right, they were just tools.

Eddie handed me a pair of earplugs and showed me how to work them in my fingers to soften them before I shoved them into my ears. He pointed at the revolver. "So, try it." He pointed at the target, which was about fifteen feet away. "Aim for the torso."

I raised the gun and pointed it at the target. Eddie stood close behind me, and adjusted my arms the way he wanted them, the left hand supporting the right arm.

"Okay, now squeeze slow and steady."

I did, and at first nothing seemed to be happening. The trigger was a lot stiffer than I'd expected. I squeezed harder, and suddenly the gun bucked in my hands and there was a bang so loud I nearly dropped it.

"Oh my god!" I stared at Eddie, wide eyed. He held onto my right arm, keeping me from flailing around wildly with the loaded weapon. My heart was pounding and my mouth was suddenly dry. "Why didn't you warn me? That hurt!"

"Hurt?"

"Yeah, my hand stings like I slapped a frozen car hood."

"You probably just didn't have a good grip on it. I told you to hold it steady."

"Nice you can be so calm!"

"You will be, too." Eddie gently turned me back to face the target. "Now remember, hold it steady and squeeze gently..."

"No way! I can't do that again. It's like deliberately blowing up a balloon too far, knowing it's about to pop. The anticipation is too nerve racking."

"It's just a noise. Now come on, take a stance."

I did, but I felt my insides fluttering. I took a deep breath, then another. He was right, it was just a little noise, and it hadn't hurt that much. In fact, the sting was already gone.

I aimed, took one last deep breath and pulled the trigger.

I'm not sure, but I think I put the bullet somewhere in the ceiling.

Eddie sighed and repositioned my arm. "This might take a while."

We fired the guns until my arms were so weary they felt like overcooked noodles, and I finally cried uncle. I simply couldn't do anymore.

Eddie agreed, but promised to talk to Jack and have him continue the lessons while he was out of town.

Terrific. Just what I needed.

I Left Eddie and drove straight to my mother's house to pick up Brutus. Before we left mom sat down and had a long talk with us. She made me state the rules of my house, speaking clearly directly to Brutus. I felt silly, but what the heck, he still hadn't run into my mother's garden.

"I suppose you'll have to use the leash to take him for walks," my mother frowned at the thought. "Your yard isn't big enough to contain all his energy." She looked at Brutus and spoke solemnly. "I know you don't like the leash; no one would. But without it the authorities could pick you up, and you'd like that even less. It's only for a couple of days, and then you'll be back here, okay?" Brutus gave her a big sloppy lick up the side of her face. Seeming to take that as a yes, my mother handed me a canvas bag filled with toys and the organic food she cooked up for Brutus and waved farewell.

Chapter Fifteen

Friday night went surprisingly well. Brutus stayed well away from George, and except for the fact that he tried to hog the whole couch when we watched Jeopardy we got along fine. Brad called and wanted to go out, but I begged off, saying I was just too tired. We made plans to meet on Sunday afternoon instead, but I could tell he wasn't happy with me.

Saturday morning I snapped the leash on Brutus and took him for a walk. In spite of my mother's talk with him, he was not interested in following my rules.

I suppose mom would say I was just expecting him to perform outside the parameters of his normal behavior. Whatever. All I knew was that I had to hang on to the lead with both hands as the big lummox pranced and lunged and started and stopped like a jack rabbit with Tourette's Syndrome.

He peed on a fire hydrant, then on a tree, a bush and a stop sign. He stopped to sniff every scrap of litter and lunged after every wind-blown leaf. He peed some more, tried to run, got caught up short by the leash and peed and sniffed some more.

I admit his behavior was annoying, but it was also somewhat endearing. He was as curious and rambunctious as a two-year-old without the tantrums and dirty diapers.

I let him choose the route, and he turned at nearly every block, weaving through the neighborhood as if determined to map the whole place out.

At long last he sniffed out a spot near a juniper bush and assumed that familiar hunched posture. I politely looked away, thinking with distaste of having to pick up his leavings - which were, unfortunately, appropriately large for a canine pony. I had three plastic bags, one tucked inside the other, to handle the unpleasantness with no fear of actual contact. I never use plastic bags, having been raised by hippies, so I had to borrow the bags from my neighbor. I only hoped my mom didn't find out I was using them.

"Hey! What are you doing with my dog!"

I spun toward the sound of the angry voice, stunned to see Ken Gripe coming toward me with long, aggressive strides.

His eyes were blackened and a dirty piece of white tape was stretched across his nose. He must have broken it in the accident, or maybe someone had popped him one for general principals.

I stared at him, speechless. He stopped within three feet of me, pointing at Brutus.

"I asked you a question, lady! Why do you have my dog?"

Several things occurred to me almost simultaneously. First of all, he didn't know who I was. He had no idea he'd been shooting at me just a few nights before.

Secondly, what kind of an ass was he, to be so pissed off before he knew the facts? What if I was one of those nice (but usually slightly crazy) ladies from a rescue shelter that had taken his dog in out of the kindness of my heart in hopes of finding his true owner?

And third, although I realized Brutus was somewhat preoccupied, he showed no enthusiasm for the sight of his long-lost master. Not a whimper or a bark, not the least twitch of his considerable tail.

Now there's one thing I know about dogs: they're extremely loyal. Even beaten and half-starved they will come back to their human masters, ready to forgive.

Maybe Ken wasn't human. Or at least didn't qualify by Brutus' standards.

"Give me that leash!" Ken reached for it, but I backed away a quick step.

"Back off, man! What makes you think this is your dog?" I had finally recalled the power of speech, and apparently with it the ability to hedge around the truth.

Ken pointed at Brutus, who was still finishing his project and seemed to be staring off at a point somewhere between us, as if embarrassed.

"That's the collar I put on him."

"I don't see any tags."

"So? It's still my dog."

"Yeah? Is he licensed? Up to date on his shots?" Actually, the shots were up to date, thanks to my mom, but she would never consider a license. That would be like getting government permission to own someone.

Ken hesitated only a minute. "That's none of your business! Give me my dog!" He made another move for the leash and I took a big step back, this time moving behind Brutus. Brutus had completed his task and stepped rather daintily to the side of his leavings.

"You bitch! Give me my goddamned dog!"

He took a swing at me, and I tried to duck but he'd taken me by surprise. His fist connected and I saw stars.

Now Brutus seemed to recognize Ken. With a vicious snarl I would never have believed he could produce he launched himself at Ken and took him down.

"Brutus, no!' I snatched at his collar and pulled at him. Even though the attack was justified I was afraid animal control might take Brutus in as a dangerous animal. They took dog bites pretty seriously in Buchanan.

Brutus lifted his head, coming away with a huge chunk of Ken's shirt, but I didn't think there was any flesh.

Screaming (like a girl, I thought) Ken rolled away.

And right through Brutus' pile.

I should have seen it coming. It was like it was scripted, right out of an Adam Sandler movie. I burst out laughing, but Ken didn't seem to get it. He got to his feet and took a step toward me.

"What's so damned funny, bitch?"

Brutus lunged for him with a snarl, and Ken backed off.

"Fine, keep him for now, but you haven't heard the last of this." He pointed a finger at me, which caused Brutus to lunge again. He cast a last hate-filled look at the dog, but he was all out of bravado. He turned and hurried away.

I wondered how long it would be before he realized he had a large, sticky mound of Brutus crap on the back of his shirt. I hoped not before he sat in his favorite chair or in his car.

And the best part was I no longer had to pick it up and carry it home.

On Sunday afternoon I ran to the grocery store, trusting Brutus (who was now my hero) not to eat my house while I was gone.

I grabbed a canvas bag. My grocery bags were all hand-sewn by my mother, who had started using them long before our nation learned the familiar phrase "paper or plastic." Back when I was a kid the baggers would look at us with annoyance; now we were just one of many. Who knew back-to-the-land hippies were so progressive?

I was walking to my car with my little bag of groceries when I saw Gina just getting out of hers.

"Hi Rainie." She waved, and I could actually see her eyes widen when she got a look at my black eye.

"Who hit you?"

"What makes you so sure I didn't run into a door?"

That made Gina pause; I wasn't exactly known for my grace and athleticism. "Did you?"

"No! I'm not *that* clumsy."

"So who hit you?"

"Actually, it was Ken Gripe."

"Ken!" Gina frowned, suddenly suspicious. "Why would he hit you? What did you do?"

"I didn't do anything. Is that what you think, that Ken's wife earned her beatings?"

"Of course not." Gina had the good grace to blush. "It's just that you were asking about him, and then I heard a rumor you were working for some private detective, and I thought maybe you stuck your nose in where it didn't belong."

"Thanks a lot, Gina."

Annoyed, I turned to stalk off, but she grabbed my arm.

"Wait, Rainie, I'm sorry. I didn't mean it that way. I was just a little pissed off that you got information from me under false pretenses. I mean, that was kind of dirty."

Hm, she had me there. "I didn't think you'd tell me if you knew why I was looking."

"So why were you looking?"

I wanted to shrug and walk away. I hated to feed the local gossip mill. Then again, it was a great source of info, so who was I to starve it to death? I might need Gina again someday.

"I was looking for him because he's way behind in child support, but when I found him he was running a meth lab."

"Meth!" Gina's blush had faded, and now she looked a little pale. "Isn't that stuff dangerous to make?"

"Of course it is. There are all kinds of dangerous fumes. They practically have to gut a house to get rid of the hazardous chemicals."

Now there was no question, she was definitely pale, and chewing on her lower lip like she meant to have it for a snack.

"Why, Gina? Do you know something?"

"Well damn, Rainie, Ken was always a jerk, but he's a local, you know? I don't feel right turning him in..."

"For what? Gina, tell me!"

"I – um - I know where he is. What if he's cooking meth there? I know there are a lot of kids..."

"Where?"

"If anyone finds out I told..."

"No way anyone can find out. I'll turn it over to the P.I. as an anonymous tip, there'll be no connection to you. Now where is he?"

"He's staying at the Red Bud Apartments."

"Right here in town?" No wonder he'd seen me walking Brutus. That was right around the corner. Of course, almost everything was right around the corner in Buchanan. "Do you know what apartment?"

"No - um, he's not really renting. Remember they started the renovation on the fourth floor last year?"

"Yeah, but they stopped because of a problem with state funding."

"Right, so the top floor isn't lived in right now. He's kind of squatting up there."

"I'll be damned." Gina was right to be concerned about the meth. Those apartments were for low-income residents, and it was a mixture of some elderly, but mostly families with young children.

"Thanks, Gina. Really."

"You think he's cooking up there?"

"I don't know, but we'll find out."

"We?"

I hadn't even realized I'd said that until she repeated it back to me.

"I meant 'they.' I'll pass the word along."

"Okay. Hey, you never did tell me exactly why Ken hit you."

"Oh. It's because I took his dog."

"Yeah? Well good for you. He obviously doesn't deserve one."

"That's what his dog said." I grinned and waved good bye, already reaching for my phone to call Jack.

Even as I was punching up Jack's number it occurred to me to wonder why. I mean, this wasn't really his case. I should be calling Hopper. But it was Sunday, and the office was closed, and I didn't have Hopper's number. I could call the emergency service number, but did this really qualify as an emergency?

Besides, Jack would probably want to know. He had helped flush out the first meth lab so he had a personal interest. I would just tell him what I'd learned, and let him decide if I should bother Hopper on a Sunday.

He picked up after one ring. "Hey."

"I have some news."

"Yeah?"

"I know where Ken Gripe is hiding."

"You going to tell me, or are you just being a tease?" His tone made my palms sweat. Be still, my heart! Stick to business.

"He's squatting at the Red Bud Apartments. The fourth floor is vacant, waiting on renovations."

"Huh, good spot. So you want to check it out?"

"I was thinking maybe I should tell Hopper."

"Hopper is back in Chicago on another gig, won't be back until middle of next week."

"If he's always out of town how is he supposed to find Ken?"

"Deadbeat dads aren't top priority."

"Why did they take the case if they can't complete it?"

"They'll complete it, but they've only had it for a week and a half."

"Yeah, and in that time I've found him three times!"

Jack laughed. "You're good. But hey, when was the third time?"

"I ran into him yesterday while I was walking Brutus. He wanted him back."

"You still have the dog?"

"No, my mother took him, but I'm dog watching for the weekend."

"You didn't give the dog back to Ken, did you?"

"No." I lightly touched my eye, remembering the punch, and I felt the anger swell all over again. "But I owe him one."

"Great, so I'll pick you up about midnight?"

"Wait a minute, I didn't say I wanted to go."

"No? Then why did you call me?"

"I don't know. I just..." I just what? I touched my eye again, wincing. I just wanted to kick Ken's ass, that's what.

"So what if we find him there? What do we do with him?"

"Take him into custody. There's a bench warrant out on him."

I took a deep breath and let it out. What the hell was I thinking? Let Jack go. He was the private eye/bounty hunter/body guard extraordinaire. I was...

I was just pissed. So what the hell.

"All right, I'll see you at midnight."

"Great. And hey, don't bring the dog."

Jack clicked off. I sat for another minute, looking at the sunshine glaring on the cracked surface of the parking lot. People were coming and going with their groceries, going about ordinary lives.

And me, I was making plans to confront a crazy, armed meth head in his own den.

Is this a great life, or what?

I took Brutus back to my mother, who was exceptionally mellow after the weekend retreat. I wasn't terribly surprised. She'd taken me to one when I was eighteen, and all I really remember is smoking a lot of pot and lying in hammocks

266

listening to the birds. There was some talk about meditation and getting in touch with your inner self, but all I wanted to get in touch with was the fridge.

After I dropped the dog off I met Brad at the park in Niles. He was on a new fitness kick that involved a lot of walking, and he was trying to get me to join him.

Instead of "Hi" he said: "Hey, where'd you get the black eye?"

"I ran into a lamppost."

"Very funny. Is this more of that P.I. crap? Have you been working with Jack again?"

"It isn't crap, it's my job, and Jack is my co-worker. Besides, he had nothing to do with this. I got in an argument with a guy over a dog."

"You got in an argument and some guy punched you? Did you call the cops?"

"No, I didn't think it was necessary. Can we drop it?"

"Drop it? My girlfriend shows up with a black eye and I'm not even allowed to talk about it?"

"Maybe later. Right now I thought we were here to walk, so let's go."

The new Riverwalk had just opened, a paved path that ran for two miles along the St. Joe River. Brad's new kick was to walk it twice a day. I took off at a brisk pace so he'd either follow me or leave me alone. Right then I didn't much care.

He followed me, his silence speaking volumes.

I hiked the first four mile round trip with him, but then I insisted on stopping off at a picnic table for a long drink from my water bottle. It was hot out, and I admit I was getting a little cranky.

"That's enough for me. I'm heading home for a shower."

"Four miles? Come on, Rainie, you're in better shape than that."

"If you want me to walk eight miles you're going to have to start in the morning. I hate this heat."

"Sweating is good for you. It takes off the weight."

"Is that what this is all about? You think I'm fat?"

"Hey, you're the one that's always obsessing about your weight. I'm just trying to help."

Right, by agreeing it was a problem instead of telling me I was fine the way I was, like Jack did. Okay, forget Jack. He was just a smooth talker, not to be taken seriously. I decided not to be mad at Brad anyway. It was too damned hot for that nonsense.

"I can watch my own weight, I don't need any help."

"Fine." He sighed, the much put-upon boyfriend. "Let's just head back to your house for lunch."

"What are you bringing?"

"Won't you cook?"

"I've got some lettuce and some peanut butter."

He wrinkled his nose in distaste. "I'll stop off at Subway."

"Great. I'll have a veggie sub with sweet onion sauce and extra pickles." I got up and headed for my car before he could change his mind.

By the time Brad got there I had let George out and I was changing his water. Brad couldn't hide his distaste for George. He just didn't get the appeal of a reptile for a pet.

"I don't understand why you couldn't just get a cat."

"A cat wouldn't like my weird hours."

"Cats don't care, they're independent."

"They aren't, really. Cats only pretend not to care because they're afraid of rejection. They have huge egos. After all, they trace their lineage back to royalty: to lions, tigers, and other kings of the jungle. Unfortunately, they're also well aware that they got the short end of the genetic stick. They can't roar or take down an antelope, they can only meow and chase down mice. Therefore, cats need to believe that they are the kings and queens of their domains. That means the humans must come to them, as proper servants do."

Brad grinned. "That's one of the things I love about you, Rainie. You're the only woman I know who can rattle off a complete psychoanalysis of a cat." He sat on the couch and started unwrapping the subs on the coffee table. He pointed at George.

"Still, we'll have to talk about him, come up with a compromise when we make more permanent arrangements between us."

"Uh...more permanent? Like what?"

"Like marriage." He said it as if there wasn't a question.

"Marriage?"

"Well yeah. Not next week maybe, but I thought that was where this relationship was headed. Didn't you?"

"Uh no. I mean, I never really thought about it."

"Never? You mean you never considered it?"

"I'm sorry. It just didn't occur to me."

"How could it not?" He looked genuinely surprised, and worse, hurt.

"Do you think about marriage with every woman you sleep with?"

"Is that all we're doing? Sleeping together? I thought I was more than a booty call."

I blinked, not liking where this was going.

"Are you calling me a slut or something?"

"No!" He looked aghast, whether at the accusation or my use of the word, I wasn't sure. "I'm just trying to figure out where you're coming from. I mean, this isn't just a casual fling, is it?"

Actually, I had kind of thought it was. Not that I engaged in such things often. In fact, Brad was the first guy I'd slept with since my divorce, which made him exactly third on my list of conquests. But hey, I was an adult, living in a free country, and I *had* dated him almost three months before we had sex the first time. Surely that didn't qualify me as a loose woman?

"Look Brad, I like you a lot, but I don't think I'm ready for marriage just yet."

"That's okay." He shrugged. "I haven't proposed yet. My point was that we were heading down that road. Aren't we?"

I blinked at him again, not sure what to say.

"Are you trying to tell me there's no chance you'll *ever* be ready to get married?"

"No! Of course not. I'm sure I'll be ready to commit at some point..."

"Well, there you go." Brad smiled. "Hey, I wasn't trying to pressure you. We have lots of time, and I know there are a few things we have to work on before we're ready to walk down the aisle."

Yeah, I thought but didn't say. Like your aversion to my beloved pet, and your penchant for pop music from the 90's. And how about the fact that you could sink in front of a TV set for twelve hours at a time when thirty minutes of that drivel makes me want to jump off a tall building?

On the other hand, Brad was a good looking guy, and always sweet and polite to me. He worried about me, and - most of the time - concerned himself with whether or not I was having a good time with him, in and out of bed. He was even a bit wealthy, and he didn't seem to have the slightest hint of hidden homosexual tendencies. All in all, a pretty good choice for a husband. So why had I never considered it?

I wasn't sure, but I really didn't feel like considering it now. I changed the subject and ate my sandwich, and sent Brad on his way within an hour without having to fend off an actual marriage proposal.

Chapter Sixteen

I was way too nervous to just hang around the house waiting for midnight, so I went shopping for new stealth clothes. I had thrown the others away. I didn't think it possible to get the swamp stink out of them. I chose straight legged black jeans, bravely buying ones that fit, rather than a pair one size larger like I usually did. I still bought an extra large sweatshirt, but hey, I'm a girl that prefers comfort to fashion.

Jack showed up promptly at midnight. He frowned at my black eye.

"Who do I owe for that?"

I felt a warm flush at his offer to defend me, while at the same time irritation that he thought I couldn't do it myself. Maybe it was true what men said, that there was just no understanding what women want. Hell, I obviously didn't understand myself.

"Ken did it, but Brutus took him down."

"Yeah? Maybe that dog isn't so dumb. Too bad he didn't rip out his throat while he was at it."

"Then what would we do for entertainment tonight?"

"I'd think of something." Jack's grin made me blush. Not for the first time I wished I could be like Belinda and have a snappy comeback ready for his off the cuff flirtations. It was like watching people play hacky-sack. It looked so easy, but then I tried to join the game and could never seem to kick the little bag back to the other person and I'd end up looking like a total klutz, a complete loser. I wasn't any better at tossing around witty repartee, especially of a sexual nature. Instead I pretended I'd missed his comment.

"Are we ready to go?"

"Almost." He handed me a small flashlight. "The lens is covered, see?" He turned it on, and it produced a thin stream of light. "You can snap the cover off if you need more light, but then people will see it from outside."

"Okay." I slipped it into my pocket.

"I brought gloves for you." He handed me a pair of black leather gloves, so soft and supple they might have been heavy silk.

"Nice."

"Very. Don't lose them. You ready?"

"I doubt it."

"Come on. I'll even let you get a punch in before I cuff him."

It all started out so easy. The apartments were only a few blocks from my house so we walked over, the only people on the street at this hour.

The elevator was scarred and had painted over graffiti, but it seemed to function okay. I was secretly terrified of elevators. They were on the same par as jail cells, tiny enclosed spaces I couldn't walk out of when I wanted. I was not, however, going to admit that to Jack, especially when I was on my way to confront a meth dealer. For tonight I was going to be brave.

The problem was I was shaking so bad I had to clench my teeth to keep them from chattering. It had to be 80 degrees in the elevator. If Jack noticed me trembling, could I possibly convince him I was cold?

The elevator stopped at the third floor. Only the service elevator went to the fourth, to allow access to the construction workers, and you needed a key for that one, so we got off and went looking for the stairs.

The stairwell door had a heavy looking lock on it, but it wasn't engaged. Damage to the doorjamb showed us why; probably a lot of people used the top floor for nefarious activities. Who would care? Until the state came off some money for the renovations is was just empty space, not making anyone any money.

Low wattage emergency lights provided enough illumination to make out the stairs. I followed Jack up, setting each foot carefully like he did, avoiding the bits of litter and construction waste strewn on the risers.

The fourth floor door was unlocked. Jack cracked it open and peeked through, standing in silence for a long moment. There was nothing to see or hear. At this hour most of the residents were asleep, and there was little ambient noise from the quiet streets.

Jack slipped through the door, and I slid out behind him. Jack flicked on his flashlight and carefully explored with its thin beam.

We were in a dark hallway, the walls stripped to bare slats, the floor a hazardous obstacle course of clumps of plaster, piles of wood still embedded with nails, and other construction detritus that I couldn't readily identify in the low light.

There were multiple doorways, at least ten, I would guess. The doors were removed from most of them, but I could see two still intact.

Jack started down the hall, shining his light at our feet. I turned on my own flashlight and followed closely, careful where I stepped, trying to control my breathing, which suddenly seemed to be coming in fits and starts. I started breathing in carefully through my mouth, slowly out through my nose, hoping I didn't start gasping and wheezing.

Jack paused at the first missing door and peered cautiously around the door frame. He used his light to check the corners. Nothing but a large empty space; all the apartment walls had been torn out.

We carefully crossed the hall and checked the door on that side. Again, nothing but a bare space.

Maybe Gina had been wrong. Surely if Ken was up here we'd hear something. I didn't see any particular path in the debris. If he were up here, wouldn't there be signs of his passing?

I was feeling calmer now as we got to the third door and found nothing but more empty space. I should have asked Gina where she'd gotten her information. Maybe the old gossip mill had failed her this time. After all, it was just a bunch of locals chatting over their back fences, not the CIA.

The fourth door was a little more problematic; the walls were still intact. We would have to go in and check each room.

Feeling more confident now, I tapped Jack on the shoulder and pointed to the right, then at myself, indicating that I would check that room while he checked the left. He hesitated only a moment before he grinned and nodded.

I still moved carefully, even though I had pretty much convinced myself there was no one up here but us. I peered around the corner, like Jack had done, and let the little beam of light proceed me into the room.

There were some signs of recent habitation here, but nothing sinister. An old twin mattress was in one corner, and the floor was strewn with beer bottles and empty potato chip bags. I spied a couple of used condoms and shuddered, glad for a change that I was wearing shoes. Just a party hangout, nothing I hadn't seen many times. In fact, I would have been delighted to find just such a place when I was a teenager, and those beer bottles might have been mine.

There was another door leading out of this room. I stepped around the trash and peeked in. Just a closet, empty except for mouse turds.

I went back to the main room, where Jack was waiting. He shook his head, and I shook mine. Nothing.

We went back to the hall and moved on to the next door. We had two more to check before we got to the apartments where the doors were still hung. If we were going to find anything, I supposed it would be there. I tapped Jack once again, this time indicating that I would take the whole apartment on the right side, he could take the left.

He frowned and shook his head. I put my hands on my hips and frowned back, conveying as much annoyance as I could in silence. It must have been enough. He shrugged and waved me on.

Once again the walls were intact here. I saw nothing in the first room, so I moved on to the next. I guess I was getting too confident; I wasn't as careful where I set my feet.

I stepped on a rounded chunk of concrete and my ankle twisted. I tried to jump back before I hurt myself, and instead fell against the slat wall with a loud *thunk*. A shower of plaster was dislodged from the ceiling, and several chunks hit with thuds that sounded preternaturally loud in the otherwise silent building.

I froze in place and killed my light, sure that Ken would materialize out of nowhere to shoot me.

Nothing. Complete silence.

After a long moment my thudding heart slowed and my breathing returned to normal. I moved on, my caution renewed.

This apartment was as empty as the others, showing no more than similar signs of teenagers drinking and groping in the dark.

I returned to the hall to find Jack waiting. Even in the dark I could see his scowl. He put his lips to my ear. "You okay?"

I nodded, glad he wasn't going to scold me for the noise. He turned to tackle the next apartment, one with a closed door.

He put his ear to the wood surface and listened. Hearing nothing, he stepped back, then leaned forward and slowly turned the knob. The door opened easily, and he gave it a gentle push. It swung back on surprisingly quiet hinges.

No one shot at us from the other side. Still nothing but silence.

Jack peered around the door, paused another moment, then stepped in. I came behind him, expecting another condom strewn room.

Instead I saw tables, and smelled the unmistakable odor of ammonia.

These were crude tables, much like we'd seen at the abandoned house. They were once again made from old doors. It seemed once Ken had an idea, he stuck with it. The doors were propped up by an odd assortment of wood piles and rickety looking end tables, as if he'd used anything he could find.

The tight beam of the flashlight reflected off an assortment of mason jars and cans of sterno. The windows were covered with black plastic trash bags; two of them billowed with the wind. Apparently the state wouldn't even pay for replacement glass.

Jack moved into the room and I followed, although I wasn't sure why. We'd obviously found the meth lab, but Ken was just as obviously not here. Why were we exposing ourselves to these fumes unnecessarily?

Jack moved over to the windows, but I stopped, not wanting to go any farther into the hazardous atmosphere. He peeled away the trash bag over one of the windows with missing glass, letting a blessedly fresh breeze into the room.

"You again!"

I froze, not so much at the voice as at the unmistakable feeling of a gun shoved into my back. I let out a squeak, just like a little mouse with its tail caught in a trap.

"What the hell do you want now?"

"We just wanted to talk to you, Ken." Jack spoke calmly, as if we'd just run into each other in a coffee shop. But he had his gun out, pointing at Ken, which unfortunately meant it was pointing at me, too.

"So talk."

"Let her go first."

"No way. This bitch stole my dog!"

The dog again. Sheesh. The dog didn't even like him, why was he so obsessed about it?

"She found him wandering in the road. She took him home for safe keeping."

As if just noticing Jack's gun, Ken abruptly pulled the muzzle out of my ribs and pointed it across the room at Jack.

"Drop it." He sounded just like Danno on Hawaii 5-0. Jack just grinned.

"Why don't you drop yours?"

I let them argue it out. As soon as he moved the gun I did a quick duck-and-roll under the table, out of the line of fire. It would have been a great move if I had ducked a little lower. Instead I smacked my head on the underside of the table and I heard glass rattling.

"Hey, watch that!" Ken shouted at me, but I didn't care. I scrambled out the other side and found myself crouched at Jack's feet.

I hadn't suddenly grown my own cajones, but on the other hand I felt pretty stupid cowering at his feet. I had to stand up. I stood next to him, trying to look like his backup.

"Nobody needs to shoot anyone here." Jack spoke calmly, as if he were saying, 'hey, why don't we go downtown for a beer?' I thought I'd try my hand at it.

"He's right, no shooting necessary. I didn't steal your dog, really. I found him out on Garr Road. I would have given him back, but you scared me, coming up on me like you did on the street..."

Okay, I might not have sounded as cool as Jack. In fact, I might well have been yammering, but Ken's eyes were flicking between me and Jack's gun now, his concentration broken. That was probably good.

Beside me, Jack was scanning the room, his head still, but his eyes moving side to side, taking it all in. He was tight as a coiled spring, and I was desperately hoping he had some idea of how to get us the hell out of this situation.

He shifted ever so slightly, moving closer to me. I kept talking, hoping to distract Ken from whatever miracle move Jack was planning - because there was no doubt in my mind we needed a miracle.

"Oh shit!" The exclamation exploded from Jack's lips simultaneously with his arm clamping around my waist. I was still in mid-nonsense-sentence when I felt myself propelled backward. The next sound I heard was breaking glass as Jack threw himself out the fourth floor window - with me in tow!

We landed hard on the iron platform of the fire escape. Seconds later the world erupted, and everything was crushing sound and blinding light and searing heat.

"What?" I would have screamed the word had the wind not been knocked from me by Jack's abrupt grab followed by the hard fall. Instead I produced a breathless squeak, a pathetic mewl of terror and confusion.

"Let's move!" Jack shoved me off and surged to his feet in one smooth motion. He was pulling me up, and I was still blinking and gawking, unable to figure out what was happening, what I was supposed to do.

The ominous sound of tearing iron intruded on my confusion. I didn't know what it meant, but it couldn't be good. Jack's urgency penetrated the fog in my brain and I scrambled to my feet.

There was a smoking hole where the apartment window had been. The fire escape was littered with broken, charred bricks and mortar dust. In a flash of (belated but brilliant) insight I realized the meth lab had exploded. Worse, the not-yet-renovated fire escape had been severely damaged. It was no longer attached to the bricks, which of course weren't there to be attached to, and the

281

section we were standing on was listing precariously.

"MOVE! MOVE! MOVE!" Jack sounded like a drill sergeant in a John Wayne movie, but I suddenly understood why those soldiers would storm a bullet riddled beach when they heard it. It was an urgent sound, one that got the blood going and initiated the flight or fight response.

Jack was reaching back toward the building, grasping a lead pipe that appeared undamaged. He swung out over the gap between the rapidly falling platform and the brick wall and snugged his feet tight on the pipe.

"Come on!" He shinnied down a few feet, leaving me room to make the same maneuver. I gaped at him. Was he kidding? He wanted me to hang four stories over a concrete parking lot on a three inch iron pipe? I couldn't...

There was another, louder screech of metal and the platform tilted precariously, almost pitching me over the side. I stopped thinking and instead reacted. I lunged for the pipe, my survival instinct recognizing its relative solidity even if my terror soaked brain could not. My hands gripped the rough pipe and I swung against the wall, my feet scrabbling for purchase on the bricks. Instead I found Jack's head and shoulders.

He was swearing mightily as the soles of my shoes scraped against his ears and cheeks.

"Stop kicking!" He shouted loudly enough to penetrate the top layer of my panic. I found purchase on one solid shoulder and then the other, and stood there, clinging to the pipe as if it were the love of my life about to march off to war.

Jack let me stay there for a breath, then two.

"All right, we need to move down." He sounded amazingly calm now, his tone demanding but far from panicked. "I'm going to slide down. Just hang on, slow your descent against the bricks."

Before I could protest I felt his shoulders shift, and abruptly I didn't have a muscular shelf supporting me. I frantically shuffled my feet against the rough brick, but there was nothing much there. I slid down the ice cold pipe. The thin leather gloves protected me for the first few feet, but it didn't take long for the rough pipe to tear right through them. I slid for an eternity, thinking my hands would be worn down to bare bones before I reached the ground.

The ground, apparently, was not Jack's intended destination, at least not yet. I felt his strong arm snatch at me, and I was no longer moving. I felt a narrow but miraculously solid ledge under my feet, and I was pressed hard between the wall and Jack.

We stood there a moment, my cheek pressed into the cold pipe, my backside form fitted to Jack as if I was welded to him, never to move again.

His breath was warm in my ear in contrast to the icy night. He spoke softly, a strange contrast to the screaming going on in my head. "I've got you, but it's probably best if you don't look down."

I wonder why people say that sort of thing, because of course the first thing I did was look down. Nothing but three stories of air between me and the hard asphalt of the parking lot. I clutched at his arm encircling my waist and threw my head back, belatedly taking his advice.

"Hah!" His bark of laughter was short but heartfelt. "Wasn't that a rush?"

A rush? What, was he kidding? I had almost been killed here. I'd had a gun pointed at me by a cranked up maniac and then I was jerked through a window. I'd been subjected to an explosion and nearly plunged four stories to a gruesome death. Now here I was on a narrow ledge, precariously clinging to a lunatic who thought this was all just a *rush*!

Then again, I was still alive, and relatively safe. My heart was pounding hard, pushing my blood through my veins with such a hard and fast rhythm I swear I could hear the thrum of the veins vibrating. Strangely, I realized I felt pretty damn good.

Abruptly I heard myself laugh.

He chuckled in my ear. "Hey, I think you get it!"

Yeah, I think maybe I did.

His voice went soft again, his head leaning close in to mine. I felt his lips brush the sensitive skin just below my ear. "Feels good to be alive, doesn't it?" He pulled me tighter against him, and I felt another kind of rush. God, could I really be thinking about sex here on the ledge?

Yes. I definitely was thinking about it.

In the distance I heard sirens.

"I think we'd better get going. I'd rather not explain my involvement here."

I nodded, thinking there were a number of gray areas of legality in our actions tonight, gray areas that might well land us in bright orange jumpsuits. Not only did I look terrible in orange, there was my absolute terror of being locked in small enclosed spaces, so it probably was best that we get scarce.

"Can you make it to the window?"

I turned my head to the right. There was an open window a couple feet away, but the only access was the narrow ledge. This morning my answer would have been a resounding "no!" but that was before I'd "gotten it."

"Piece of cake," I told him.

He loosened his grip on me and I edged toward the window, carefully stepping over his big feet, regretful for more than one reason when I no longer felt his hard body pressed against mine. Damn, did everyone who risked their life get this obsessed with sex? If so, I was beginning to understand the appeal of being an adrenaline junky.

I kept a grip on a handful of his shirt until I had my other hand on the edge of the open window. I ducked through and landed in a graceless heap inside.

He followed a moment later, without benefit of someone's shirt to cling to, moving with the supple ease of a tomcat letting himself into the house for the night. He offered me a hand and pulled me to my feet.

A woman stood staring at us, clutching a worn robe around her, her mouth hanging open.

"There's a fire, lady!" Jack spoke with some urgency. "Get your kids and get out!"

"Was that an explosion?"

"Yeah, on the fourth floor." Jack glanced up, and when he did I suddenly became aware of how hot it was getting it the apartment.

"Oh my god, the kids!" The lady suddenly ran from the room, and Jack followed her. I glanced the other way. That was obviously the front door, and shouldn't we be going?

A minute later Jack came back with a five year old kid in his arms. The mother was right behind him carrying an infant.

"Let's move!"

We hustled into the hall, where doors were opening, people peering out cautiously.

"There's a fire! Everyone to the stairwells!" Jack spoke in a loud, commanding tone that I much admired. It made me want to obey, but it didn't induce panic. Jack set the kid down and gave the mother a gentle push toward the stairs. "Go on, you've got plenty of time. Just keep moving."

He turned to me then. "Knock on every door, make sure everyone is moving."

I nodded and started pounding on the nearest door. So much for the plan of getting out before the cops got here.

Jack worked the other side of the hall, and now people were flooding out of their apartments in various states of undress, some carrying sleepy children, others sheparding them ahead.

"Let's go." Jack turned away from the last apartment on his side and headed for the elevator.

"Hey, you're supposed to take the stairs when there's a fire."

"No sweat, the fire's on the other end. We've got time, and the stairs are too crowded." He punched the down button and the doors opened. We got on even as we heard sirens winding down outside.

He punched the button for the first floor.

"You sure this is safe?"

"It's fine." Jack grinned. "I want to get out of here before I'm recognized. This didn't go exactly according to B&E policy."

A moment later the car was stopping on the second floor, presumably to allow another passenger on. Jack pulled me to him and kissed me, and when the doors opened the new passenger saw only a pair of young lovers.

I don't know if he only intended the kiss to be a ruse, but he was sure putting some effort into it. His hands were inside my sweatshirt, warm and welcoming, and I leaned into him, eager to enhance the rush I was already feeling. His thigh pressed against my legs, and I shamelessly let my own limbs fall open, letting his thigh press where it felt the best.

Now I've had promiscuous moments in my life, but this was ridiculous. If he'd pushed a bit farther, I think I would have done the deed right there in the elevator, audience and all. Then again, I don't think it was one of his guns I was feeling hard against my belly. I think maybe he was thinking something along the same lines.

The elevator stopped and the doors opened, and I heard a distinct "humph!" of disgust as the other passenger disembarked. I had never seen the other person. It could have been my mother for all I knew, and I still didn't care.

He gently pushed me away before the doors could close again. "We'd better go, babe. We can pick this up later."

Yeah, like maybe in the street. Behind some bushes. Or maybe…

I shook my head, trying to clear it of sexual thoughts. He put an arm around me and walked through the lobby, his head bent close to me, a smile firmly planted on his face.

"Here we go, just two young lovers out for a stroll. We'll walk right past them."

"Them" was the collection of cops collecting on the street out front. They were bounding out of their cars, eerily lit by their flashing lights. A couple of people poked their heads out of the first floor apartments.

"Hey, what's going on?"

"I don't know. Sounded like a train crash."

"I think there's fire on the fourth floor," Jack informed them. That got them moving, and within moments we had a group of people pushing toward the front door. We blended in and stepped out with them.

We strolled away from the chaos arm in arm, turned the corner and continued ambling with seeming nonchalance as more police cars and then an ambulance blasted past.

We turned onto a quieter street, and for the first time I let myself consider the explosion.

"You think Ken made it out of there?"

"No way. There was a wall behind him. We barely made it going out the window."

"So I guess he won't pay his back support after all."

"Nope, but I think his kids can collect some kind of Social Security benefits until they're eighteen. I think we did them a favor."

"That's a pretty callous way to look at a man's death."

"He was a pretty callous man. Even his dog didn't like him."

"True." I felt a shudder go through me, and for just a minute my knees felt weak. "Wow, I'm kind of shaky all of a sudden."

"It's just the adrenaline. It'll pass in a few minutes."

"Okay," I shrugged, taking his word for it. "So what do we tell B&E about this whole mess?"

"As little as possible. Did you tell anyone else you found Ken?"

"Nope, I just heard it today from a friend."

"Good. Just watch the news in the morning. If they've ID'd Ken, don't say anything. If they haven't, call Belinda first thing. Sound shocked if you can. Tell her you just found out yesterday that Ken Gripe was squatting up there, and you're wondering if it could be him. Belinda will tell Harry, and he can decide how to handle it."

"I don't know about lying to Belinda. I'm not a very good liar, and she's not stupid."

"You've got that right. I *am* a good liar, but she catches me at it all the time. The thing is, she'll know you're lying, but she'll pretend she doesn't,

289

because she won't want B&E involved any deeper than necessary. Just make it sound good, so she doesn't have to look stupid."

"What if I have to talk to the police?"

We'd reached my front door, and I stopped on the porch. My ardor had cooled with the draining of the adrenaline, and I no longer felt an immediate need to rip his clothes off. In fact, I was suddenly remembering who and what Jack was, and I was a little afraid I'd let him go too far. What if he wasn't the kind of guy who didn't listen to "no" once he got hot and bothered? Not that I thought he'd been told no by many women, but he was definitely the kind of guy who could take what he wanted.

He had a slight smile on his lips, and I wondered if he knew what I was thinking. He answered my question.

"Don't worry about the cops. I don't think anyone saw us, and they can't do anything without evidence. Don't let them intimidate you."

I nodded and finally turned to unlock the door, not sure what to do next. It seemed rude to just close the door on him, but if I invited him in that had to seem like a clear invitation to continue what we started in the elevator.

I opened the door and turned back to him, blushing, feeling more awkward than I'd felt since junior high.

My feelings must have been clear, and he decided to rescue me. He grinned and shrugged.

"I'd better get going. Mind if I come for poker Saturday?"

"That would be great!"

"I'll see you then."

He kissed me lightly on the cheek and bounded off the porch to his truck, as gentlemanly as if we'd just come back from dinner and a Disney movie.

Huh. Maybe it wasn't just women that were hard to figure out.

Chapter Seventeen

I set my alarm so I could catch the morning news, but then made use of the snooze alarm twice. When had I lost the ability to stay out to all hours and still bound out of bed first thing, ready for a new day?

Ten minutes later I hit the snooze for the third time and burrowed back under the covers with a groan. My back ached from slamming into the fire escape, my legs hurt from trying to cling to the brick wall, and my hands were burning from the slide down the pipe. Oh yeah, and my face hurt from Ken punching me and I was so tired I felt like I could sleep for three days.

I was just dozing off, having lulled myself with that little bout of self-pity, when my cell phone rang.

I poked my head out and glared at the phone, which was doing a little dance as it vibrated and played the tune from Dragnet. I'd put the ring tone on for a joke, but it sure wasn't very funny now.

Glaring at it didn't help. It kept on ringing. With a sigh I snaked one hand out from under the blankets and snagged the phone. I flipped it open one-handed and put it to my ear.

"What?"

I heard Jack's laugh.

"Not a morning person, are you?"

"I'll be up by noon, that's still morning."

"But by then you'll have missed the news. You're supposed to take care of some business this morning, remember?"

"I remember," I grumbled. "I was just getting up."

"Well, I can save you the trouble. They've identified Ken already, and tentatively ruled the fire as a meth lab gone awry. I doubt they're going to investigate very thoroughly. It looks pretty cut and dried."

"So I don't need to call Belinda?" My sleep fogged brain was beginning to function, maybe from relief that I wouldn't have to explain the previous night's activities.

"Nope. As far as anyone is concerned, we were nowhere near the place."

"Wonderful." I flipped the phone shut and tossed it on the bedside table. I was already burrowed back under when I realized how rude I'd been to Jack. I guess if I was tired enough, I wasn't scared of anyone.

The alarm blared again a few minutes later, and this time I realized I had to pay attention. I was due at Virginia's in a half hour.

I dragged myself out of bed, brushed my teeth, washed haphazardly and ran a brush through my hair. The front looked crinkly, and I squinted blearily at my reflection. Huh. Apparently my hair got singed while I was being blown out the window. I might have to get it trimmed at some point, but I didn't have time to mess with it now.

I stumbled to the kitchen for coffee. I tossed an ice cube in so I could drink it quick, and slammed the first cup while I checked on George. He was still snoozing under his nighttime heat lamp, oblivious to my presence.

"Good boy," I mumbled. I grabbed a travel mug full of coffee and left for work, arriving with two minutes to spare.

I perked up a bit as the day went on, but I was still pretty tired by the time I got home that night. Belinda had wanted to talk about Ken's unexpected and rather spectacular demise. I'm not sure if she realized how much I was trying not to say. At least I didn't have to pretend to be surprised, since his name had been splashed all over the news.

I let George out and fed him, then fixed myself a can of chicken noodle soup. It was not only easy to fix, it didn't require a lot of effort to chew, and I was saving all my energy just to stay up until a reasonable bed time. Like nine o'clock. Maybe eight thirty.

I had just flopped onto the couch and flicked on the TV to watch Jeopardy when my cell phone rang. I checked the caller I.D: Jack.

"Hey," I greeted him.

"Hey yourself. I'm right around the corner, you mind if I stop by for a minute?"

"Sure, I'm not doing anything." Actually, I was way too tired for company. Why didn't I tell him no? But it was too late.

"I'll be there." And he disconnected.

He must have literally been right around the corner, because he knocked two minutes later.

"Come on in. Want a beer?" What the hell was the matter with me? Wasn't I too tired for company?

"No thanks, I just stopped by to bring you these." He held out a pair of leather gloves, just like the ones I had trashed sliding down the drain pipe after being blown out of the window.

"Why?"

"Because you need a good pair of gloves for stealth missions."

"Oh." I wasn't sure what else to say. I mean, why was he bringing me gifts? And what made him think I was going on any more stealth missions, anyway?

There was another knock on the door.

"Geez, it's like Grand Central Station here tonight."

I opened the door. It was Brad.

"Hi! I was just in the neighborhood, thought I'd stop by."

Now here's the thing with just dropping by. Brad knows I hate it when he does it. He has a cell phone, just like most people with an income over five thousand dollars a year in this country, so it's not like it would be difficult to call before he showed up. That would give me the option of telling him whether or not I was in the mood for company.

The problem was he never could understand my need to be alone at times. He thought me wanting to be alone translated as "don't want to be with *you*." Therefore, he just dropped by whenever he felt like it. Never mind that I had just told Jack to come over even though I wasn't in the mood for company. At least he had called first.

"Hi Brad. Did you lose your phone?"

"Hey, I'm sorry, I know you like me to call, but I just decided at the last minute...oh, hello Jack." His tone went distinctly cooler.

Jack nodded curtly at him, and turned back to me.

"I'd better get going. Don't slide down any poles without me, okay?" And then he did a strange thing: he winked at me.

From the corner of my eye I saw Brad's eyes narrow. I closed the door behind Jack.

"What the hell was that supposed to mean?"

"What?"

"That wink, and that crap about sliding down poles. What did he mean by that?"

"Why didn't you ask him?"

Brad's head jerked back as if I'd slapped him and he didn't answer right away. He didn't really need to, because I could read it in his eyes. He didn't ask Jack because he was afraid of him. That really pissed me off. He was afraid to ask Jack so he figured he'd bully the information out of me.

"I'm asking *you*." He finally recovered.

"He just stopped by to bring me a new pair of gloves."

"Why?"

"I don't know," I answered honestly. "Jack doesn't always explain his reasoning to me."

"I don't want you hanging around with him."

"Why not?"

"Oh come on, Rainie! That comment about sliding down poles, and then that wink! Are you trying to tell me there's nothing going on there?"

"Don't be absurd, Brad. I'm not his type."

"I doubt that Jack is that discerning."

"What the hell does *that* mean?"

"I didn't mean it the way it sounded."

"Maybe you should go. I'm tired. Call next time before you come."

"Why? So you can make sure Jack is out of the way?"

"I don't care if you know Jack is here. There's nothing going on."

"Maybe not on your end, but I can guarantee Jack is interested in something more than a working relationship. Isn't the fact that it bothers me enough reason? Why can't you just do this one thing for me?"

"I have to hang out with him! It's my job!"

"Then quit the damned job! You don't need it. You make just as much money taking care of the old folks. Why can't you stick with that?"

I took a deep breath, seeking the reasonable tone that I knew was somewhere deep inside me. "First of all, because I can't survive on twenty-four hours of work a week. Secondly, as fond as I am of

Thelma, there's not a lot to challenge me in that job. I need a little excitement in my life."

"Excitement? Is that what you need?" He abruptly pulled me to him and kissed me. This wasn't a simple "hello" kiss, either. This was slow and deep, and his hands were under my shirt, one of them working its way down my back, the other one sliding around the side, working its way up. My anger was rapidly morphing into ardor.

His thumb brushed over my nipple and my insides turned to liquid. I leaned into him and his hand pulled me tighter to him, and I felt his own response digging into my belly.

He pulled his mouth away from mine and trailed it along my jaw line to my ear. He whispered, his breath hot on my skin. "So? How's this for excitement?" He gave my nipple another twitch and I gave up a tiny moan.

"You see?" He was still whispering in my ear, and it seemed like his words were traveling to the very core of me, heating me up from the inside out, reminding me why I really *liked* having a boyfriend. "I can provide all the excitement you need, and you won't be risking your life."

I made a noncommittal "mmm" sound and turned my head, seeking his lips, wanting to get back to the kissing part.

I heard amusement in his tone when he asked me, "So, is that a yes?"

"Yes to what?" I was still searching out his lips, but a part of my brain was already saying "uh oh!"

"Yes, that you'll ditch the job."

My passion ran to fury in .000 seconds. I pushed him away from me and stood with my hands on my hips, my eyes narrowed. My insides still felt like liquid heat, but now it was more like something along the lines of magma.

"How dare you! Are you really giving me an ultimatum? Who the hell do you think you are?"

He had the audacity to still look amused. "Don't think of it as an ultimatum. Think of it as a better offer."

"A better offer?" My voice had traveled a long way up the scale, nearing the point that only dogs could hear. It was the pressure, I supposed. The heat was building inside me like a teakettle set to boil with its steam release hole blocked. Another minute and my head was going to blow off like an aluminum pot lid.

"You really think I would give up a job I love just to have sex with you? I've already been there before buddy, and let me tell you, you're asking way too much for services rendered!"

He no longer looked amused. Nothing like attacking a man's sexual prowess to get him pissed off. His own eyes narrowed.

"You seemed to like it just fine!"

"Well sure, it was okay. I mean, I like McDonald's shakes, but they're no substitute for a hand-dipped malted from the Sweet Shop."

"Yeah? Are you saying Jack is the hand-dipped variety?"

"I wouldn't know. I only work with him."

"Yeah? Well tell me this: has he kissed you?"

Now if ever there was a good time for a lie, this was it. Unfortunately, his question triggered a flashback. Immediately I remembered the heat of Jack's kiss, and my face flushed in sympathy. I ducked my head, but too late. Maybe he saw the blush, or maybe he saw something in my eyes.

"Fine. I get it. My mother was right all along about your kind."

"My kind? And what kind is that?"

"Look in a mirror and ask yourself that question." His tone was venomous, and it stung.

He moved toward the door rapidly, as if being in the same room with me was suddenly intolerable. He jerked the door open and stepped through without a pause. Just before it slammed behind him he growled "Have a nice life!"

The slamming door was like the final powerful down stroke at the end of a symphony, the note that tells the audience that without a doubt the music is over. It's okay to applaud, to stand and shuffle toward the exit, to move out to the sidewalk for a smoke.

I didn't feel much like applauding. I was full of rampaging hormones. In the space of mere minutes I'd gone from exhausted to horny to furious to...

I wasn't sure what I felt right now, so I did the expedient thing.

I burst into tears.

I wasn't much of a crier, so the next morning I got up, washed my face, and tried to put the whole incident with Brad behind me. What the heck, I had known it wasn't going to last much longer, what with his talk of marriage and all. Better to get it over sooner rather than later.

Or so I told myself. I kept playing the whole scene over again in my head: Jack's pole comment, which in retrospect did sound a lot like a sexual innuendo, and his wink. What had that been about? Then the escalating argument with Brad. I wanted to put it all on him, but I had to admit he might have had a reason to be suspicious. Why *had* Jack done that? It was almost as if he had deliberately goaded Brad.

Maybe he had. I hadn't been kidding when I told Brad that I didn't always understand Jack's motives. He was a strange man, a bundle of contradictions.

Whatever. Brad should have given me the benefit of the doubt. It was time to move on.

Chapter Eighteen

"Does that black eye have anything to do with your bad mood?" Thelma jumped right to it, five minutes after I got to her house.

"I'm not in a bad mood."

"No? Then why the frown on your face? Why the grunted hello?"

"I suppose I do have the blues. I'm sorry. I'll get past it, I promise."

"Don't be sorry, we all get the blues. Here," Thelma thrust a big mug of steaming black coffee at me. "Sit down and tell me all about it."

"You want to be my therapist?"

"People with friends don't need to pay therapists. Now come on, tell me all about it."

"Well, to begin with I broke up with Brad."

"Oh. Well, I guess that's a bummer, but really, he wasn't right for you."

"How can you say that? You never even met him."

"That's partly my point. Why didn't I ever meet him? I wanted to, but he never seemed to be available. Does he have something against old people, or does he just not care about any of your friends?"

"He's met most of the guys. He stopped by for poker a couple of times."

"Okay, so he wants to check out possible competition."

"You might have a point."

"Sure I do. Anyway, tell me about the breakup."

I did that, which of course led to Jack kissing me, so I had to first explain about Ken and the dog, and meeting Gina in the parking lot, which in turn led to the meth lab explosion. Thelma hooted with laughter at that.

"I *knew* you had to be involved in that! I kept watching for you to pop up on the news."

"Jack and I ducked out before we could be questioned. He likes to keep a low profile."

"I think you should follow his lead." Thelma laughed again. "Blew that place right up! Did you do it, or was it an accident?"

"It was an accident!" I protested indignantly. "Well, actually Jack mentioned that I might have spilled some of the chemicals when I ducked under the table, and they might have run across the table to an open flame from a Sterno can..."

Thelma laughed again, and I couldn't help but join her. "Oh honey, you're good! Why, I've gone all my seventy-plus years without ever blowing anything up, and I had some pretty wild nights!"

"I don't know that we should be laughing though. I mean, a man died."

"Not much of a man. Didn't take care of his kids, and even his own dog didn't like him. Dogs will lick the hand that *beats* them. It takes a pretty bad guy to make a dog turn on him."

"I suppose you're right."

"Of course I am. Now, what I really want to know is how in hell you could have the blues...I mean, you got *kissed* by that hottie Jack! Forget Brad, I want to know more about that!"

She was right again. Thinking about Jack was a lot more pleasant than thinking about Brad, and a good laugh, as always, was better than a good cry. Maybe I should have been paying Thelma.

Over lunch Thelma asked how my other client was doing. Normally I don't talk about one client with another because of privacy issues, but Thelma, of course, was more than a client. Besides, she knew Virginia and Miss Ida in a roundabout way. They had all lived in Buchanan for most of their lives, and their paths had crossed from time to time.

"I still don't get the idea of Ida taking in people for charity. Now her older sister Beth, she might have done that. That girl was always taking in strays of the four footed variety, had a heart of gold. It's a shame she isn't the one who lived long enough to take care of her mother."

"Virginia thinks it's strange, too. But maybe Ida has changed. People do, you know."

"Sure, maybe." Thelma shrugged. "Maybe she's taken a long look at her immortal soul and decided she'd better make up for some of the evil she's done before she meets her maker. Somehow I doubt it though. I never thought Ida worried overmuch about God and sin and whatnot. She was always a live for the moment, do what feels good kind of person."

"That's what her mother says. Still, she is doing a good thing, for whatever reason, and she should be given some credit for that."

"I suppose." Thelma shrugged, and we let the matter drop.

Wednesday morning I went to Virginia's. It was a beautiful morning, so I wheeled her out to the front porch so she could work on her flowers.

I watched her work, slowly moving from flower to flower, pulling off the dead blooms with arthritic fingers that seemed to barely respond to her commands.

"There was a time I could have zipped through these boxes in a matter of minutes," Virginia commented as she painstakingly pulled another flower toward her. "Now it takes me half a day. Then again, what's the hurry? I don't have much else to do."

"I thought you might like to go for a walk around the neighborhood today."

"That might be nice," she nodded. "If you don't mind pushing my wheelchair all over the place."

She sighed and her hands dropped into her lap. She stared off across the street, or maybe across the galaxy and into the end of time.

I sighed, too, and sat down on the porch swing. Virginia was a lot of fun to be around, her quick intelligence and sharp wit a true joy. I hated seeing her drifting off into the no-where land of dementia. The only good part was that she often smiled when she "went away," so at least she was lost in good memories.

Her fugue only lasted a few minutes. She abruptly snapped out of it and went back to her flowers, speaking to me as if our conversation had never been interrupted.

"Scarecrow is gone."

"Scarecrow? You mean the homeless guy, Doug?"

"Yep. Ida says he just moved on, but where would he go? And why didn't he take his stuff? Not that he had much, mind you, but Ida threw it all out. What homeless guy gives up a roof and abandons his only change of clothes? Don't they usually wear them all at once? I'm telling you, that daughter of mine..." Virginia shook her head. "This is the third one that's gone missing overnight."

"The third?" Now that was interesting.

"First it was Bozo, some old guy with a huge red nose. Then there was Bob. He was always bobbing his head up and down, like a chicken, you know what I mean?" I nodded to encourage her to go on. "Then there was Hummer, always making this 'hmmm' sound down deep in his throat. Like to drive me crazy. He just took off a couple of weeks ago."

"Some people just don't like to stay in one place for long," I pointed out.

"Sure, I know the type. But these are obviously homeless men, and I know at least two of the others left their stuff behind, because I say Ida carry it out to the garbage. Why would they do that?"

306

That was a good question. Why would Doug have taken off? He said he didn't have any food. Maybe he went looking to cadge a meal and something happened to him.

"I sure would like to know what that girl of mine is up to." Virginia was frowning at the flowers.

"Well hey, if you want I could go upstairs and have a look around Doug's room, see if there's any indication of why he left." Listen to me, helpful little caregiver that I am. Never mind that my curiosity was about to cause my skin to burst open.

"Now, that might be a thought. I forgot you're a detective."

Well, a P.I.'s assistant, really, but I didn't correct her. After all, I thought she was about to give me permission to go upstairs.

"Why don't you do that? And while you're up there, take a peek at the bathroom. Ida's been doing all kinds of remodeling up there, but I told her not to dare touch that old claw-foot bathtub. That old thing has been here since the house was built, and I took many a lovely bubble bath in it. You let me know if she's done anything to it."

I wasn't sure if I should leave Virginia alone. When I wasn't here she was alone all the time in her room, but right now she was my responsibility. She must have seen my hesitation.

"Honey, I'm just fine. Ida leaves me alone out here all the time. The porch gate is latched, and you know I can't work it open with these twisted fingers of mine, so I'm not likely to wander away while you're gone. Now go on, check it out for me."

I only hesitated another moment. I took my caregiving responsibilities seriously, and I'd had plenty of clients in the past that I couldn't leave alone for a minute, but Virginia wasn't one of them.

"Okay."

"Ida's room is on the right, and after that is the bathroom. Doug's room is the first door to the left."

"Okay, I'll be right back."

"I'm not going anywhere." Virginia snorted her little laugh and went back to the flowers.

I hurried inside and up the stairs. Sure enough, there were six doors lining the hall, all of them closed.

Gee, what had Virginia said? Was Doug's room to the right or left?

I only hesitated a moment before trying the door to the right. Damn, it was locked. Of course, it was an old-fashioned kind of locked, where the key was just a long thin rod with a couple tongues on it. One key would probably work for every door up here. If I had one.

I glanced down the hall. People liked to lock the bathroom door when they were in there, and these locks worked from either side. I had to check the bathroom for Virginia anyway, so I scurried down to the next door and opened it.

There was no sign of Virginia's claw-foot tub. Instead there was a large, slope sided tub with Jacuzzi jets, a separate shower stall, and a sleek looking pedestal sink. The tile floor was black and so shiny it was almost reflective; the walls were a deep blue. There was nothing about the room to indicate it was in an aged Victorian relic.

Fortunately, they had not updated the door. As I hoped, the old lock was still there, the old key on the inside. I wiggled it out and practically scampered back down the hall to Ida's room.

I needed to be quick. Usually Ida and Frieda stayed out all morning, but that didn't mean they might not come home early. I worked the key in the lock and slipped inside.

The bedroom was huge, dominated by a four poster bed covered in frilly stuff. I can never remember what's what; duvets and shams and skirts, who the heck knows? But her bed was piled high with lots of flowery material and lace.

To one side was a small sofa that faced a 36 inch flat screen TV. Nice. Virginia's TV was an old 19 inch model, serviceable but nowhere near the quality of this. Neither was anything else in her room, come to think of it.

There was a big, well polished desk that was likely an antique. There was a short stack of paperwork right in the center. I couldn't resist a peek.

Huh, it was from an insurance company, and it had Doug's name on it. At least, I assumed it was his: Doug Harrison.

I wanted to read more, but just then I heard a door close somewhere down the hall.

I whispered a swear word and hurried to the door, keeping the key concealed in my hand. If it was Ida or Frieda, I would claim I wandered into the wrong room by mistake, and oh? Well no, the door wasn't locked...

I stepped into the hall. It wasn't either of the women, it was the other homeless guy. I wracked my head for his name, but all I could remember was Virginia's nickname for him: The Debater.

"You seen Doug?" The Debater asked as soon as he saw me. He didn't seem to think it was strange that I was coming out of Ida's room, so I casually locked the door behind me while I answered him.

"No I haven't. I was looking for him myself."

Debater had no better hygiene than Doug. There was a faint miasma of urine and cheap gin that hung around him. It was almost visible, like the little cloud that followed Pigpen in the Peanuts comic strip. His clothes were new but cheap, work clothes from a chain store's discount rack. He scratched at his crotch, then an armpit, and I couldn't help but back up a step.

"He was s'posed to play cards, but I can't find him."

I edged around him. "I'll ask around, let you know if I hear anything."

I quickly returned the key to the bathroom door and then came back to check Doug's room.

This one wasn't locked. It looked like an old-fashioned kid's room, with a narrow metal framed bed and blue striped mattress. The sheets and blankets were neatly folded on a bench at the foot of the bed. There was a strong smell of disinfectant.

"Not here, like I said." Debater was peering over my shoulder.

"So I see. Well, I'll let you know if I hear from him."

I pulled the door shut and hurried back down to Virginia, who was once again gazing off into space with a sweet smile on her face. Maybe she was ten years old again, enjoying a bubble bath with her dollies in her old claw-foot tub. I sat quietly and waited for her to come back to me.

How could Miss Ida afford to get health insurance for Doug? I mean, it was one thing to get him a cheap set of new clothes and give him a room to sleep in. Insurance was a whole different ballgame. And who in their right mind would insure an indigent alcoholic anyway?

Of course, I hadn't read the papers. Maybe it was just an application.

And maybe it was just none of my business.

Chapter Nineteen

I didn't have much time to think about Doug for the next couple of days. Thelma was in a snit because I'd hardly spoken to her other than my usual scheduled hours, and Tommy thought I was avoiding him. I suppose I was in a bit of a funk. I missed Brad a lot more than I thought I would.

So what, I asked myself. Do you want to call him?

No way. He was a controlling asshole with an iguana phobia. I could do better.

So why did I miss him?

My funk stayed with me right up to the weekend, but it lifted a bit on Saturday afternoon. It was poker night again.

I went shopping and got a little creative with the snacks, actually cooking up some little bar-b-q sausages and making up a chili dip for the nachos. It's not that I was feeling terribly domestic, but I seemed to have a lot of nervous energy to burn off.

I went for a bike ride late in the afternoon, and just for the hell of it I stopped at Casey's and got one of his big greasy cheeseburgers and a large order of fresh cut French fries to go. I don't know why I didn't eat it there. I guess it just seemed pathetic, having a lonely feeding frenzy in public. Some things were better left behind closed doors.

I ate every scrap, standing at the kitchen counter. Maybe I thought that if I ate it standing up it would fall all the way through and not land in my belly as excess fat.

I was relieved when Mason and Jeff showed up, as usual with contributions to the snack buffet. I sampled from the cheese and sausage plate Mason brought but ignored the beautiful veggie tray Jeff put on the counter. I set out my own contributions and ate several nachos dipped in the chili dip while we were waiting for Riley, Jack and Eddie.

I popped a little sausage in my mouth and licked my fingers, not wanting to miss one juicy, orgiastic drop. I froze with one finger in my mouth at that thought.

Damn. I recognized this behavior. It's how I gained seventy pounds when I was married to Tommy. I'd better take up mountain climbing or skydiving or even volunteer as a crash-test dummy. Anything would be a healthier alternative to deal with my depression than eating every fat-filled goody I encountered.

"I'd better get the cards out." I rinsed my hands at the sink, as embarrassed to have anyone witness my indulgence as if they'd caught me having solo sex. If the guys had noticed they didn't say anything. They were talking about some brawl that had broken out at a baseball game.

Eddie and Jack arrived at almost the same time, Riley a few minutes behind them. I was pleased to see that Riley hadn't been drinking tonight, and

Eddie looked a lot happier than the last couple of times I'd seen him. Maybe he'd concluded his mysterious business in La Porte.

Jack looked yummy, as usual. Huh, there I went again with the food references. I really needed to get a grip!

We settled down to play some cards. We got through only a few hands before I suggested a break to go out and smoke a cigarette. It wasn't that I particularly wanted one, but I couldn't seem to get my mind off the dip and the sausages.

"What's up, Rainie?" Everyone had stepped out to the backyard, even though only Riley and I smoked.

"What makes you think something's up?"

Mason laughed. "Come on, we could all see it. You've hardly smiled, and your mind isn't on the game."

"Yeah, a great night to take all your money."

"I'm never that easy, Jeff." I laughed. "It's no big deal. I just broke up with Brad a couple days ago."

"Hey, that's great!" Eddie grinned.

"I figured you'd think so."

"You really miss him all that much?" Jack sounded curious, as if he found that hard to believe. It crossed my mind to point out to him that he had contributed to the fight, but then I would have to repeat his pole comment in front of the guys. Nope, not gonna happen.

"I don't know." I shrugged. "Anyway, I didn't come out here for counseling, I just want to smoke. Let's talk about something else."

After a few awkward moments the conversation turned to the new healthcare bill, a hotbed of contention in our diverse group. The conversation didn't stop even after Riley and I put our cigarettes out and led the way back into the dining room.

"No one can afford healthcare the way it is except the most wealthy or the poorest poor who qualify for Medicaid. That isn't right." Jeff was all for national healthcare.

I was suddenly reminded of the papers I'd seen on Miss Ida's desk, the insurance forms for Doug.

"A lady I know took in an old homeless guy and is trying to get him health insurance."

"Really? She must be pretty wealthy."

"Actually, she's not."

Jeff frowned. "Then how can she afford it?"

"Besides, if he's old he should qualify for Medicare," Mason pointed out.

"The forms I saw weren't Medicare. They were for Owings Mutual."

"Maybe it was supplemental insurance," Riley suggested. "My mother has that, to cover some of what Medicare doesn't."

"Maybe it isn't health insurance at all," Eddie put it. "Maybe it's life."

"I can't imagine anyone giving this guy life insurance. Besides..." I cut myself off abruptly. A horrible thought had just occurred to me, but no way could I believe it of sweet Miss Ida. "Besides," I finished the sentence, "It's really none of my business, and I'm sorry I brought it up. Is it my deal?"

I spent Sunday afternoon at the library, going through the past week's papers.

I scanned through the usual crime beat stuff: a couple of shootings in South Bend, a couple of robberies in Benton Harbor and Niles, several one car accidents where "alcohol may have been a factor." I wondered how often they said that in the initial report, only to find it wasn't the case. There were rarely follow up articles to such crashes, so the public would be left with the impression that almost every one-car accident was alcohol related.

Long live freedom of the press, but save us from those who believe everything they read as gospel truth just because it's written in newsprint.

I went through Monday, Tuesday, Wednesday and Thursday's papers without finding what I was looking for. Then, in a one inch story in Friday's paper I found something promising.

The article simply said a man had been found dead in an alley behind the Kitchenette Diner on South Michigan Street in South Bend, cause of death unknown.

This isn't all that rare. There is a large homeless population in South Bend. In fact, they have a nationally recognized homeless shelter there that does a lot of good. Even so, there are rules for those who want to stay there, and not everyone is willing to follow them to stay off the streets. Therefore, now and then a homeless guy would end up dying in an alley or someone's doorway.

But it isn't so common that it didn't strike a chord with me. I wish they had included a description. Could it be Doug? If so, how did he get to South Bend? And what did he die from? As scrawny as he'd looked, he certainly hadn't appeared to be on death's threshold.

Then again, I wasn't a doctor.

I sat back and considered the problem for a few minutes. The only way to know if it was Doug was to get a description of him. I doubted if the coroner would give me that info if I just called and asked.

Then again, wouldn't they be looking for someone to identify him?

Uhg. That would mean going down and actually looking at a dead body. What fun.

Then again, I didn't have much else to do.

I went home to look up the coroner's number.

It didn't occur to me until I was dialing that maybe the coroner's office wasn't open on Sunday. Then again, what would they do with dead bodies until Monday? They must have someone to answer the phone for emergencies, and at least, pardon the dark humor, a skeleton crew.

Sure enough, a guy answered the phone after four rings, sounding a little rushed.

"Coroner's office."

"Hello, my name is...Sandy." I came up with the lie at the last minute. I was amazed by the ease with which the rest rolled out. It must be Jack's influence. I even managed to sound somewhat tearful. "I've been looking for my Uncle Max since last Monday, and I saw in the paper that you found a man...I mean, you know...dead..."

317

"Could you be more specific, ma'am?" His tone was kind enough, but it implied that they found a lot of dead people.

"This one was found in an alley…" I managed to sound like I was choking back tears. Or maybe I just sounded like I had swallowed a bug. "My uncle is schizophrenic, so he wanders sometimes, and his health isn't good…"

"Can you describe your uncle?"

I could picture the guy at the other end of the phone scanning his list of John Does, ready to match my description with one of them.

"He's older…in his sixties…gray hair, tall, very thin…"

"Do you know what he was wearing when he wandered away?" I could hear the slightest hint of excitement in his voice, and I thought I'd hit pay dirt.

"Brown workpants and a flannel shirt, kind of new but cheap. He didn't like to spend a lot on clothes."

"Well ma'am, I'm not saying anything for sure, you understand, but we do happen to have someone that matches your description. Would you be able to come down here?"

I swallowed hard. I probably already had my answer. Did I really need to go see him to be sure?

Of course I did.

I told the guy I could be there in an hour, and he somberly told me where he was located and which door to come in.

I thanked him in a false teary voice and hung up.

I suppose if I'd gone on a weekday the whole identification process would have been more formal. I was afraid they'd ask for my ID, but they didn't. They just took me back to a little room, asked if I was ready, and then opened a curtain so I could see the body on display on the other side.

Sure enough, it was Doug. I'd only seen him once, but his gaunt visage was unmistakable. I think there might even have been a smear of syrup left on his chin from the French toast I'd given him.

I shook my head and tried to look relieved and sad at the same time.

"No, that's not Uncle Max." I turned away. "Poor man. Do you know what he died from?"

"Not yet."

"Well, I hope you find his family."

"I'm sure we will." The young man was pretty good at the sympathy bit. It almost seemed like he really cared. "Have you filed a missing person's report with the police for your uncle?"

"Not yet. They make you wait a while with adults."

"They shouldn't make you wait when there's a history of mental illness. I'd check with them if I were you."

"Okay, I will." I gave him a grateful smile through what had become real tears. I was thinking about Doug, lying on that cold slab, waiting to be cut up and then embalmed and buried, and no one to mourn him because no one knew who he was. But I couldn't tell anyone that I knew him without giving them Miss Ida's name, but I wanted to talk to her

319

first, and I really didn't have enough information yet.

I headed home. This was a job for the internet.

I wanted to see if there were any other suspicious deaths in the past few months that might account for the other missing men Virginia had mentioned.

The search was tedious, even with my new experience with search engines. I changed the parameters several times, narrowing my search until I finally hit pay dirt.

Six months ago two young boys fishing from the bank found an unidentified man floating in the St. Joseph River. An autopsy revealed a blood alcohol well over the legal limit, and the cause of death was accidental drowning.

Four months after that a man known to the homeless shelter as "Henry" died when he passed out on the railroad tracks and was hit by a train. I remembered that one. It had been gruesome and tragic, and received a lot of press.

I couldn't find a third one, but I thought I had enough. None of this was real evidence, nothing I could take to the police. What could I tell them that they would believe? But it was enough for me, and I thought it was time to ask Miss Ida about Doug's whereabouts.

I rang the bell at Miss Ida's house and waited with what patience I could muster for one of the elderly women to get to the front door.

Miss Ida answered, as always with her heavy makeup fully applied and her hair helmeted into place. She blinked at me, clearly surprised.

"Why Rainie, what are you doing here?"

"I just wanted to talk to you, if you have a moment."

"Of course, dear." Miss Ida stepped out on the porch and shut the door behind her. "It's such a lovely day, why don't we sit out here?" She sat in one of the big rocking chairs, but I shook my head when she indicated the other one and leaned against the porch rail instead.

"So what is it, dear? Oh my, you're not quitting are you? Mother is so fond of you..."

"No, it isn't that. I was just curious: do you know what happened to Doug?"

"Doug?" she blinked rapidly, her false eyelashes fluttering so fast I was afraid her eyelids would take flight.

"Yeah, you know, the man you rent a room to."

"Oh, you mean Mr. Harrison! We were never so informal as to go by first names. That tends to make people so presumptuous, don't you think? After all, I wanted him to remember I was his landlady, so he would keep his proper place in the household."

"You're talking about him in the past tense. Has something happened to him?"

"Happened to him?" Miss Ida went pale under her thick layer of makeup, causing her red blush to stand out like circles painted on the cheeks of a clown. "What do you mean?" There went the blinking again, and she seemed to be searching for a place to look: at the sky, the street, the flowers...anywhere but at me.

"Well, is he here?"

"No, as a matter of fact, he isn't." Miss Ida seemed to physically get a grip on herself and she finally looked at me, her eyes steady now, almost steely.

"Young lady, perhaps you should get to the point."

"The point is Virginia told me Doug was gone, but she didn't know why, and you weren't talking. I wondered why he'd leave such a sweet situation."

"Well, not that I think it's any of your business, but how should I know why a man like that does anything?" Miss Ida stood up, pulling her indignity around her like a protective cloak. "He was an alcoholic, you know. I took him in, tried to help him, but some people just don't want to be helped! He took off without a word the day his check came, and took a few good pieces of my silver with him!"

"Did you file a police report?"

"No, I didn't. For one thing I didn't want mother to know what he'd done. She was already unhappy about the arrangement, and I didn't want to give her fuel to complain further. Besides, I feel sorry for the man." She assumed a saddened expression. "Addictions are a terrible thing, Rainie. They eat a man up from the inside out, and cause even good men to behave badly. Why my own dear Larry..." She trailed off and swiped at an eye as if wiping away a tear, but I didn't see any actual moisture. "Well, never mind. Just suffice it to say I have a

322

personal interest in trying to help the less fortunate."

Her behavior seemed so phony, yet I really didn't know her all that well. Maybe this was the best she could do at displaying emotions. I know I wasn't all that great at it myself. Besides, everything she said made perfect sense. It surely made more sense than what I was thinking: that she was running some kind of insurance fraud scam.

"I have some sad news, Miss Ida." I changed my tone, trying to no longer sound accusatory. Maybe I could still salvage my job; I did hate to leave Virginia in the lurch. "I saw where they found a homeless man dead in South Bend. I think it's Doug."

"Doug, dead?" She stared at me, wide-eyed, looking genuinely shocked. Of course, she could just be shocked that I knew. "How do you know?"

"I saw the article in the paper about an unidentified man, and I remembered your mother telling me Doug was missing. I called the coroner's office and gave a description. They think it's him." I didn't tell her I'd gone down there. That sounded entirely too aggressive.

"You called? Why are you so interested in Doug?"

"I'm just a curious kind of girl." I shrugged it off. "I thought you might like to know."

"Oh...well of course, I'm glad you told me. I guess I'd better go down there and identify the body."

"Doesn't Doug have any family?"

"No, not a soul." Miss Ida shook her head sadly. "He told me when he moved in that his wife had died childless years ago, and his only brother passed last year, also without children."

"Wow, that's sad."

"It is." Miss Ida sighed. "Well, I'd better call the coroner's office. Thank you for telling me, Rainie. I would have always wondered what happened to him."

"You're welcome." I reluctantly accepted a hug from her, not sure if it was intended to comfort me or her, or perhaps was just a gesture that seemed appropriate to the situation. I turned and went back to my car, dissatisfied with the results of our conversation.

Chapter Twenty

On Monday morning I woke to a dreary, rain soaked world. I watched the news long enough to catch the weather: rain all day, with periods of heavy thunderstorms later in the evening. Well, at least that was something to look forward to; I did enjoy a good thunderstorm.

I showed up to work with Virginia as if nothing had happened. Miss Ida seemed content to pretend the same thing. She gave me her usual cheery greeting before heading out the door with Frieda, both equipped with huge, bright umbrellas that contrasted nicely with the gray day. Our conversation might have been shorter and cut off more abruptly than usual, but otherwise it seemed like just another day.

Virginia was in her room, looking through an ancient photo album, the thick pages so aged they were almost crumbling. Many of the pictures were faded to sepia, a few so much so that they looked like photographs of spirits taken just before they'd vanished into the air.

"Oh, I love old pictures. Can I look with you?"

Virginia looked at me suspiciously. "You really like to look at them, or is that just a caregiver thing?"

I laughed. "Fair question. I was taught to do that as a good caregiver, but I found out I genuinely love it. There's something about them, the clothes and settings, the stories people tell me about them. Like a living history lesson."

"Huh. Okay, as long as you're not just humoring me."

I sat down with her and we spent a good hour slowly turning the pages as she commented on each one. She had something to say about everyone in there: a favorite uncle who had been lost in the war. An old beau who had been pushed aside by the man Virginia eventually married, but who had snagged Virginia's cousin as a consolation prize.

She pointed out pictures of two siblings who had died in childhood, one from small pox and another from TB.

"That happened all the time back then. Not that children don't die tragically now, but in the neighborhood I grew up in there weren't many families who hadn't lost at least one child before the age of ten."

She had photos of herself in her prom dress, in her wedding dress, and one with her all bundled up in a long coat and white scarf, her hands buried in a giant muff, her cheeks so stained with the cold that it was obvious even in the old black and white image.

She slowly turned another page, and a corner crumbled in her fingers like a fresh-baked cookie. A picture came loose and fluttered to the floor.

"Oh damn it." Virginia swore softly.

I picked up the picture and handed it to her. A single tear was rolling down her wrinkled cheek.

"This album won't be around much longer, but my fingers aren't nimble enough anymore to redo it. I've asked Ida to help, but she doesn't really care."

"I'd be happy to help you."

Virginia sighed. "I'm sure you would, but what would be the point, anyway? The only one who would care about these pictures is Ida, and she doesn't. Never will. She's a live-in-the-moment kind of woman, doesn't care about the past, and not too much about the future."

I didn't know what to say to that. Miss Ida was her only living relative. It was too sad to hear that there was so little affection there.

"I think I've had enough for this morning." Virginia closed the photo album and folded her hands on the front cover. She stared off into space, and I let her go for the moment.

I went to dust the pictures and knick-knacks on her dresser, a never ending job. The dresser, like her photos, told much of her life, a diorama depicting her childhood, marriage, her children's lives and even their deaths. I picked up a tiny plaster hand to dust it, and was almost startled into dropping it when Virginia suddenly spoke.

"Have you seen the new guy yet?"

"The new guy?"

"Sure, Ida couldn't leave that room empty for long. I can't figure what pile she found and how deep she's searching it to find these guys, but this one is about as aware as a potted plant. She thinks I didn't see him, but I still get around, you know. She led him upstairs by the arm, and I swear if she'd let go he would have just stopped moving, like a worn out wind-up toy."

"It's rather nice that she's taking these men in."

"That's my whole point: Ida simply isn't nice. She doesn't have a charitable bone in her body. Hell, she only keeps me here because she doesn't want my savings to go to some nursing home."

"But I thought you wanted to stay in your own home."

"I did, but this isn't my home anymore. She does what she wants with it, and I hardly go anywhere but this room and the kitchen. She has the heat shut off in the parlor, to save money she says. I say, what did I save the money for if not to be comfortable in my old age?"

I was silent for a long moment. What Virginia was describing was a form of elder abuse, not to be taken lightly.

"So you want to go to a nursing home?"

"Not a nursing home, really. I was thinking one of them assisted living places, like Brentwood in Niles. You ever see that place? Like a mansion, plush carpets and brocade furniture, table cloths on the dining room tables! And they do things there, play cards and go on shopping trips, why they even take a busload to the casino a couple of times a year."

"Wow, sounds pretty good."

"That's what I thought. I know sometimes I'm not with it, but they have people there who can help me to the bathroom or into the shower, and other old people won't much care if I don't know what day it is. But it's not cheap, and Ida says if I spend my money on that, in my last days I'll end up in some Medicare facility laying around in dirty diapers." Virginia shrugged. "Maybe she's right."

"But it's your choice, Virginia. Like you said, you saved the money. I could talk to her if you'd like."

"No, don't do that. She'll just get mad and fire you, and I kind of like your company. Besides, if I do run through all my money my care would fall to her. I guess she has a right to have a say."

Virginia fell silent again, her head drooping toward her chest. Some days it seemed she wandered in and out of dementia like a kid playing on a swinging door. But she wasn't drifting away this time. She lifted her head and looked at me.

"I'm doing all right here, Rainie. She's a pain in the neck sometimes, but she's my daughter, and I suppose in her own way she loves me. I think I'm just worried about these men she keeps bringing home. It all seems pretty strange to me."

"It is a little," I agreed.

"You want to have a run up to take a look at the new guy?"

"You think I should?"

"Why not? Besides, I think I'd like a little nap. These rainy days make my bones ache. Could you help me onto my bed first?"

"Of course."

She wheeled herself to the bed, but I could see the weariness in her. Depression could do that to people, and it was often more pronounced in the elderly. I might have a talk with Miss Ida one way or the other. Maybe she wasn't aware of just how much her mother was affected by the presence of the boarders.

Virginia lay back with a sigh and gave me the tiniest of smiles.

"Thank you dear. Just twenty minutes or so, I'll be right as rain."

I pulled the covers to her chin. She was already staring off at a point beyond the ceiling, her eyes drooping.

I wanted a look at the new guy, but even more I wanted another shot at searching Ida's room. Now, I know it's wrong. I know all about privacy and breaking and entering. I do watch *some* TV. Besides, I was curious, and as Jack said, doing bad things only counted if you got caught doing them. In which case, of course, I would be mortified and probably pass out from the humiliation, but I thought I was pretty safe. Ida and Frieda weren't due back for two hours.

So I headed for the stairs, figuring to take a short peek at the new guy and then a longer peek at Ida's desk. I was on the second step when the phone rang.

Ida had an answering machine set to pick up on the first ring when she was out, so her mother wouldn't be bothered. I think it was more that Virginia would sometimes forget to give messages, but whatever. I was halfway to the landing by the

330

time the brief greeting played out and I heard the beep indicating it was time to leave your message.

I don't know why I paused. Ida's messages were none of my business. But I did, and listened while a man's well-modulated voice, one obviously accustomed to public speaking, came softly over the speaker.

Damn, she had the volume down too far. I couldn't quite make it out...wait, did he say insurance?

To my credit, I froze in indecision for a long moment. I mean, I didn't just automatically hurry back down to snoop, I actually considered whether or not I should. Then again, wasn't I on my way to break into someone's bedroom?

I went back down and stood for a moment staring at the answering machine. Electronics are not exactly my forte. I couldn't program a remote for a TV or set up a DVD player if I were being threatened with evisceration. In fact, Mason had to show me how to use my own answering machine. I did know that on mine I could listen to the messages and then choose whether to delete them or save them. I assumed most of them would have the same options, but did the machine somehow indicate whether a message had been listened to already? There was a little red flashing number 3, which I figured meant there were three messages.

Oh well, out of the frying pan into the fire and maybe straight to the ash bucket, but I pushed play on the machine.

The first one was a hang up. I pressed save, and it moved on to the next one. The 3 was still showing. The second message was longer.

"Hi Ida, it's Barbara from Kuntz Travel. I have those brochures you wanted. Do you want to stop by or would you prefer I mail them? Give me a call and let me know. Thanks, and have a lovely day."

The third message was the great voice I'd heard from the stairs. "Hello, this is Tom Kelly from Kelly Insurance. I know this is a difficult time for you, but I wondered if you had a time frame on the death certificate for Mr. Harrison. Please call..." the rest was him leaving his phone number. I waited impatiently for him to finish his spiel, including another apology for intruding on her grief with business, then pushed save.

The little 3 was still blinking steadily. There should be no evidence of my having satisfied my curiosity.

That's how I'd chosen to term it, so take it or leave it.

I went on up the stairs. There was total silence on the second floor, no TV's playing, no water running, no signs of human habitation at all.

I went straight to the bathroom door for the key. It wasn't there. In fact, there was a shiny new doorknob in place of the old one, this one the kind with a little turn knob for locking the door.

I stared at the shiny gold-colored knob for a long moment. Why the change? Could Ida have possibly known I'd been in her room?

I went down the hall, looking at the other doors as I went. All of them had the new knobs on them, except Ida's and Frieda's. Theirs both had actual deadbolts installed, serious hardware to keep casual snoops out.

Well damn, so much for another look at her desk. I didn't have the slightest idea how to get past a deadbolt without a key, unless maybe I had time to use an ax or a chainsaw on the heavy oak door. Since that wasn't practical, I reluctantly gave up the idea of snooping.

I did stop at the door to Doug's old room, where the new resident was supposed to be. I knocked, but there was no answer. Virginia said the guy hadn't looked so good. I doubted if he'd gone out for a walk. He might be sick. I should check on him, right? I mean, it was the right thing to do.

I tried the knob, and sure enough it turned easily.

"Hello, anybody home?" I called out softly as I eased the door open a couple of inches. I didn't want to catch the old guy unaware, or worse, undressed.

"Hello?" I opened the door a little farther when there was no reply, and finally peeked around the door.

The first thing to hit me was the smell. A foul stench hung in the air, a combination of cheap booze, vomit, urine, human excrement and something I couldn't identify, a smell something like rotting meat. I pulled my head back and closed the door quickly, unable to stop a gag reflex.

I blinked my watering eyes and took a couple of deep breaths. Geez, was the guy dead? If not, he was surely unconscious from his own fumes!

I took a deep breath and held it while I opened the door a second time. There was a narrow lump on the cot, covered in a wool blanket. I saw the blanket rise and fall, accompanied by a wet snort. Okay, so the guy was alive. Still holding my breath, I crossed quickly to the bed and took a peek.

I only saw his face, but that was enough to make me grimace and want to gag again. It was filthy and gaunt, so much so I could clearly see the bones outlining his eye sockets. His beard was patchy, the hair missing in several places where there was only red, raw looking skin or open sores that were obviously infected. His mouth hung open, revealing a sore-covered maw devoid of teeth, and when I finally had to take in a fresh lung full of air the smell of his breath almost overwhelmed the stench in the air.

I backed away, horrified. Where had Ida found this man? If she was trying to help him, why hadn't he seen a doctor? Those wounds on his face needed to be cleaned and treated. I suspected there were more covered by the wool blanket, and likely the source of the smell of rotting meat. Who would bring home a man with gangrene and just leave him to lie in his own filth? There was no charity in that.

I backed out of the room quickly. I had to call the police, get this man some help.

I turned for the stairs, only to see Miss Ida step into the hall.

"I figured I'd find you up here snooping."

334

"I'm not snooping!" I could feel myself blushing. "Your mother just wanted me to check on the new boarder."

"Is that right?" Behind Ida I saw a short man carrying a black satchel. He looked vaguely familiar. "And how was he?"

"Frankly he's in pretty bad shape. He needs a doctor."

"And I've brought him one." Ida indicated the man behind her, who stepped forward and lifted his chin imperiously. It didn't help much. He was still short.

"This is Doctor Veldman. He's here to examine Mr. Bell."

"Veldman." I suddenly realized why he looked familiar. "I thought you were in jail for prescription fraud."

He glared at me with such pure loathing I actually backed up a step.

"Those were trumped up charges. I was exonerated, although the local news rags didn't give *that* the space they gave the accusations."

I supposed that was possible, but I remembered the scandal, and several people had come forward to say they'd been a part of the scheme to fill narcotic prescriptions for resale on the street. But now that I thought about it, I didn't remember hearing the final outcome.

"The real question is what are you doing up here instead of taking care of my mother?"

"She's taking a nap and…"

"She's taking a nap so you thought you'd take advantage to snoop around, maybe supplement your paycheck with a few baubles?"

"No!" I was outraged at the suggestion.

"Oh, I know all about your kind. I was warned to watch out for it, people who pretend to be so kind and caring but really just want to take advantage of the elderly once they're invited into their homes."

"That's ridiculous! I told you Virginia wanted me to check on this guy."

"Why would she do that? My mother hardly knows her own name half the time, why would she care about the boarders?"

"You know that isn't true. You're mother isn't nearly that bad off…"

"I should know my own mother better than *you*, a part time companion who apparently spends most of her time sneaking around where she doesn't belong!"

By now my palms were sweating, and I was afraid I might throw up. The fact was, although I of course had no intention of stealing from her, I *was* sneaking around where I didn't belong. I couldn't even vindicate myself by pointing out the sick man in the room behind me. Ida was bringing a doctor to look at him, even if that doctor had a questionable reputation.

"You need to leave right now, before I call the police and have you arrested."

"Arrested?" I stared at her, hoping I wasn't visibly shaking. "For what?"

"For trespassing and neglect. You'd better hope mother hasn't fallen out of bed while you were up here, leaving her unattended!"

That was ridiculous, of course. Ida left her mother alone in her room all the time. Yet I was being paid to be with Virginia. I didn't think it was possible to blush more than I already was, but I felt like I must have been lobster red all the way to my toenails.

"All right, I'll just go check on her..."

"No, you won't. Your services are no longer needed. You will leave the premises immediately."

"I need to get my purse."

"I'll escort you." Ida turned to Doctor Veldman. "Mr. Bell is in that room," she indicated the door behind me. "If you want to get started, I'll be right back."

Ida waved at me to go ahead so she could follow me down the stairs, I suppose so I couldn't snatch any valuables on the way out. I jogged down the stairs, wanting to end this as quickly as possible. I'd never been fired before, and I wasn't prepared for the sheer humiliation.

I was well ahead of Ida, who had to take the stairs at a more sedate pace. I hurried to Virginia's room to grab my purse. She was still sound asleep. I felt tears prick at the backs of my eyes. I wouldn't even get to say goodbye.

I grabbed my purse and stepped back out. Ida was there, breathing heavily from the effort of catching up to me. She didn't say a word, just followed me to the front door, staying close on my heels.

"I'll mail your final check." She slammed the door behind me.

I made it to my car and managed to drive away before I started to cry for the second time that week.

I managed to pull myself together with the aid of a chocolate shake for lunch. I know I would have been better off if I'd gone for a long bike ride or a brisk walk, but I'd promised Belinda I'd come straight into the office today. They actually had a backlog of reference checks that needed to be done.

I spent the afternoon at the computer, running names and social security numbers through one data base after another and compiling reports. For once I was glad for the mind-numbing tasks. I didn't particularly want to think today.

I went home and let George out. "Hey bud, how's it going?" He scrambled up to his shelf and stared at me. I took that to mean he was hungry, so I filled his bowl with fruits and veggies. "Look George, I got you some kiwi. Yum!" He shoved his snout into the bowl and started scarfing everything with equal enthusiasm. He didn't thank me for the special treat. That was okay. George had never been the demonstrative type.

I settled for a salad for dinner, remembering the past days' indulgences. I flopped on the couch and flipped on the news, letting the stories wash over me without really penetrating past the top layer of my brain. A half hour went by, and they started the same stories all over again. I kept staring at the TV, still not really listening, not really thinking.

Huh. I really had a bad case of the blues. I needed to shake this off.

Outside the weather was building into what promised to be quite a show. Thunder was rumbling, still far off but moving in, and lightning was flashing at a pretty steady rate. I've always loved storms, so I stepped out onto the porch to watch this one roll in.

It was prematurely dark, the sky a wondrous pile of black and gray clouds, pressing toward the earth with the weight of the rain they held, looking as if they might crush the old buildings of Buchanan if they didn't release their burden soon.

For the moment there was no rain, but the air was still thick with humidity, the ground dotted with puddles from the steady rain that had fallen most of the day.

I sat back and lit a cigarette, and spent a few moments playing with the smoke. It tended to hang in the air, holding its shape for long moments before finally dissipating. I blew a few rings, pleased with how well they formed.

Wow, was I easily amused, or what?

After a while I went in to collect a notebook and my favorite pen, one that was easy to grip, and had a nice rounded nib that seemed to flow effortlessly over the paper. A smooth writing pen seemed to pave the way for the words to flow easily from my brain. Or so I liked to think.

One thing about being in a blue funk, the mood lent itself to writing poetry. Not necessarily good poetry, but copious amounts of it. I sat and listened to the storm roll in and put my impressions of it on paper.

The first storms pushed south, never really giving me more than a distant light show, but around eight o'clock another one started rolling in, and I was pretty sure it would hit its crescendo right over Buchanan. I felt that strange excitement filling me, as if the electricity in the air was somehow infiltrating my bloodstream. I know storms can be dangerous, but I just couldn't bring myself to fear them.

Things were just getting noisy when I felt my cell phone vibrate and heard the little tone that indicated a text message. I slipped it out and looked at the read out: it was from Tommy.

"Car broke down at gym. Could you pick me up?"

Right then there was a particularly loud crash of thunder, and it was as if someone had drawn a sharp knife across the bottom of the swollen clouds. The rain was suddenly falling in torrents, blasting against the hot street, huge drops that seemed to bounce when they hit, creating a mist like low lying fog.

Get out and drive in this? I grinned. Sounded like fun to me.

I texted Tommy back to tell him I'd be there in 30 minutes. His gym was at the mall in Mishawaka, a few miles south of the Indiana state line. I grabbed my purse and my keys and jumped into the car.

Somewhere beyond all those dark clouds the sun had set, and the driving rain made for poor visibility. I kept my wipers on full, their loud *thwak* never quite hitting in sync with the songs on the radio. I sang along with Mellencamp and Styx, regretting that I'd forgotten my MP3 player when I was stuck listening to commercials.

In spite of the rough weather I made it to the mall by 8:35. The lot was still about half full, although many of the cars were parked in the back rows where employees were supposed to park. This late in the evening it looked like employees might outnumber shoppers, except near the movie theater, which was doing an excellent business on this rainy night. I drove around toward the back of the mall. Tommy's favorite gym had an entrance from inside the mall, but it also had a rather grand entryway direct from the parking lot. It looked more like a ritzy hotel than a gym. There was no big window displaying the exercise machines here. The patrons could sweat in relative private, the clanking of the weights and the whir of the exercise bikes muted by thick carpeting. I'd been inside before as Tommy's guest, but I'd been too intimidated by the sight of so many beautiful people in skin tight clothes. It seemed that only people who didn't look like they needed to exercise belonged there.

I cruised slowly through the lot, looking for Tommy's car, a little red BMW. It was an older model, but Tommy had lovingly restored it and treated it like it was his favorite son. I saw no sign of it now.

I stopped at the end of a row and scanned the lot again. Where the hell was it? If he'd gotten it started, surely he would have texted me to let me know.

As if summoned by my thoughts, my phone vibrated with the arrival of a new text.

"Saw you drive by. Car already towed. Waiting in blue van right behind you."

I twisted around in my seat. Sure enough, there was a blue van sitting at the back of the lot. Some good Samaritan must have let him sit in his vehicle out of the rain to wait for me. I drove on over and pulled in beside the van.

I was moving some items off my front seat to make room for him to sit and wasn't paying attention when he got out of the van. I should have been. If I had I wouldn't have been so surprised when my passenger and driver's side doors opened simultaneously. For the second time in a week I felt the unmistakable sensation of a gun muzzle, this time against the back of my neck.

Chapter Twenty-one

"So, here's the nosy little caretaker." I stared at the man leaning in the passenger side door, with another gun pointing at my nose. He seemed vaguely familiar, but I couldn't quite place him. He was big, maybe six feet tall but close to three hundred pounds, a mixture of fat and muscle, but plenty strong enough to keep me in line. Besides, there was that circle of metal digging into my neck.

"Wh...wh..." I couldn't seem to make whole words come out of my mouth. The guy behind me was not being gentle with the gun. He obviously didn't want me to forget it was there, not that I likely would.

"You been nosing around where you don't belong. Mama don't like that."

"Ma...ma?" I wasn't sure if I was repeating him or calling for my own mother.

The big guy eased into the passenger seat, no easy trick. He felt around for the seat release, grunting with the effort of bending over, and tried to push the seat back. I could have told him it wasn't going to happen. That seat had jammed years ago. I could have told him, except my tongue was firmly stuck to the roof of my mouth, and I couldn't work up enough spit to loosen it.

He finally grunted his way into position, his knees pressing against the dashboard, his gun once again pointed at me. The muzzle finally came away from the back of my neck as the second guy climbed into the back seat.

"Okay, drive."

"Wh...where?" Hah! I'd gotten a whole word out. I must be calming down. Good girl, I thought. Get control of yourself.

"Never mind where. Back out, I'll tell you which way to go."

"Wait, where's Tommy?"

"You mean the fruit? How should I know? We just borrowed his phone."

"Borrowed it?" For a minute I had a picture of Tommy loaning his phone to these thugs so they could lure me in.

"He might not know we borrowed it." The big guy grinned. "Now never mind him. Get moving."

"But why are you after me? What did I do to your mama?"

"You so stupid you can't figure that out?"

"Hey, there's no need to be rude!" I was outraged. I had a thick skin when it came to people insulting my weight or my lifestyle, but I hated people questioning my intelligence.

"Mama said Miss Ida caught you nosing around. She asked us to make you stop it."

"Oh." I assumed "mama" was Frieda, Ida's roommate. "Well, okay, I'll stop."

"Just like that, huh?"

I nodded, trying to look sincere. "I didn't mean to cause any trouble."

"Right. Stop talking and start driving." He waved the gun at me for emphasis, and my bravado drained away.

I got the car into reverse, only grinding the gears once in my nervousness. I glanced in the rearview and got my first glimpse of the guy behind me. There wasn't much light, just a glow from the big lot lights, but it was enough for me to recognize him.

"Hey, you're Bob Peck!" Even as I said it, I knew I should have kept my mouth shut. If there was any hope of getting out of this alive it wouldn't be increased by me admitting I could identify them.

"So?"

"Um...nothing." But it was something, all right. I hadn't seen Bob for a long time, and I'd rather have kept it that way. The Pecks were from Niles, and they had quite a reputation.

Back in the day it wasn't unusual to see the Peck name in connection with drugs, prostitution, car theft, robbery, even the occasional murder. Sort of a small town organized crime family without the organization. If that was Bob, then the guy next to me was probably one of his many brothers or cousins. There were a lot of Pecks in the southwest Michigan area.

Suddenly there was a little click in my brain, like a puzzle piece fitting into place: Frieda Peck, of course. She had done some jail time back in the day, for skimming the church offering if I remembered correctly. Her kindly grandmother demeanor was just a carefully cultivated front, and I had to admit she was good. She sure had me fooled.

I backed out of the parking slot and turned in the direction Bob's brother pointed me in. The van's headlights came on and it followed us out. Great, so there was at least three of them. How many guys did they think it would take to intimidate little old me?

I was fervently praying to every spirit and god my mother had ever invoked that they were only planning to intimidate me. In fact, I was willing to take help from the god of the Catholics, the Jews, the Muslims or even Zeus himself if they could keep me from getting killed tonight.

At least Bob no longer had his gun against my neck. His brother's gun was still pointing in my direction, but in a casual sort of way, as if he thought they had me well in hand.

Come to think of it, I suppose they did.

He directed me toward the back entrance. The road it let out on was busy enough, but if they had me drive north we would soon enough be on less traveled, even rural roads.

There would be plenty of places to shoot me and leave me dead in my car while they jumped in the van and sped away. I couldn't let them get me out of this lot.

Okay, that was a good thought. Now how was I going to follow through?

I thought about Jack. What would he do? Probably something really slick, like driving with one hand while he kicked the gun out of one guys grip and used his free hand to reach behind him and wrench Bob's gun away, all while grinning happily.

Okay, so forget Jack. I wasn't that athletic or as crazy.

I was moving slowly, keeping the car in second gear, trying to buy some time, but the parking lot exit was still coming up fast. I needed a plan, and I needed it now.

The rain had slackened for a while, but it was coming down in wind-blown sheets now, shimmering like a silver curtain where it was illuminated by the big parking lot lights.

The lights. Each one was planted in a huge concrete block, immobile obstacles placed at regular intervals across the lot.

It was do or die. Or maybe it was do *and* die. As I said, I wasn't that athletic, and the plan that had half-formed in my mind would require some measure of physical ability. Then again, the guy beside me was clearly in worse shape than I was. And I had the element of surprise.

I shifted down, causing the car to jerk when it tried to pop into first gear.

"Hey, knock that off!" The Peck next to me was shoved into the dashboard, and I felt Bob fall against the back of my seat.

"Sorry, I'm just nervous." I let it go into neutral, holding the clutch in so the car would keep moving.

"Just like a broad, can't handle a stick shift. You should get yourself an automatic."

"You're probably right." I tried to sound humble, though I was speaking between gritted teeth. It

347

wasn't bad enough these guys wanted to kill me, but they were sexists, too!

I surreptitiously snaked a finger into the door release latch and pulled gently, popping the door. The dome light on the Escort had burned out months ago, but the cover was rusted on and I wasn't able to change it. For the first time I wasn't unhappy about the inconvenience.

I turned the wheel sharply toward a light pole, while at the same time I shifted into gear and popped the clutch. I might not be an Olympic class athlete, but I sure knew how to drive.

The car lurched forward into the concrete base of the pole as I shoved my door the rest of the way open and rolled out of the car.

The car hit the base of the pole as my shoulder hit the wet pavement. It was easy to believe that the screech and bang of metal striking concrete was really the sound of my body hitting the asphalt.

I tried to duck and roll like they do in the movies, but instead I bounced, first on my shoulder, then on my face. I felt the burn of skin being scraped off my cheek, and wondered if I would be scarred for life.

I liked the sound of that: life. I decided a scar was a small price to pay.

I shoved myself to my feet and took off running. The other doors on my Escort had not yet opened. I didn't think the impact would have been enough to do much damage to the Pecks, but I figured the big guy in front would take a few minutes to pry himself out, and I hoped Bob was at least suffering from surprise.

The van skidded to a halt, and a voice shouted for me to stop. I didn't think it was in my best interest to obey, so I kept moving.

There was a loud ping and the echo of a shot. Someone had recovered from their surprise enough to shoot at me! I ducked down a row of cars and crouched between a Mercedes and a Pontiac, moving at a crouch, not thinking beyond move! Move! Move! I could even hear Jack's voice in my head, shouting those words, pumping up my adrenaline.

Jack. I sure wished he was here now.

There was more shouting behind me. The Pecks must have gotten out of the Escort. Someone was shooting again, the bullets hitting in front of me. I guessed that they didn't know for sure where I was, but they were anticipating where I was heading.

I was duck-walking past an SUV. I dropped to my belly and crawled under it, coming out the other side, and started off down that row.

The rain was pounding on me, hissing off the pavement, splashing off the parked cars, stinging as it ran into my eyes. If it came down much harder I was afraid I'd drown.

My legs were cramping from trying to run in a crouch, reminding me yet again of my lack of athleticism. It was hard to hear over the rain, but it seemed the shouting men were splitting up. I guess they weren't as dumb as they looked. It was only a matter of time before they surrounded me.

"She's got to be right here!" I heard Bob shout, and it sounded like he was right next to me. In a panic I dropped to my stomach and squirmed under the nearest car.

And I believe this is where my story began.

Here I was under a rusting car, waiting for that hand to grab me, for that bullet to end my life. My shoulder was throbbing, and my face felt like someone was holding a butane lighter to it. I needed another plan, and fast.

I needed help is what I needed. Professional help.

I reached for my cell phone and worked it out of my pocket with some effort. It was soaked, but I hoped it might still work. I hadn't heard any shouting for a few minutes, but that didn't mean the bad guys weren't nearby. In fact, I worried they might be sneaking up on me.

No talking then. I pulled up the text menu and hit buttons rapidly: "Guys trying to shoot me in mall parking lot. Help!"

I sent the message to Jack and stuck the phone back in my pocket. I couldn't think of anyone else who wouldn't be completely confused by that message. Even Eddie would waste precious time trying to call me to see if it was a joke. Jack probably wouldn't even be surprised.

That is, if he got the text, and it wasn't delayed by a high volume of calls. If the storm hadn't taken out any cell towers between here and Michigan.

He'd either get it or he wouldn't. He'd either come or he wouldn't. In the meantime I had to stay alive. Best time he could make was a half hour from Niles.

Thirty minutes.

It might as well have been thirty years.

The puddle under me was getting deeper, spreading under my body. I was rapidly getting flooded out of my refuge, which really didn't feel all that safe anyway.

I moved to the edge of the car and peered out. I looked left and right, and peeked under the cars as best I could, but between the dark and the pouring rain I couldn't see far.

No boots. Still no sound from the Pecks.

I crawled out from under the car and crouched in the lane, trying to breathe quietly, straining my ears for a voice.

Instead I heard the chirp of my cell phone telling me I had a message.

Damn, was I bad at this stuff or what? Sneaking around, trying to be quiet, but I forgot to turn off my cell phone ringer. If anyone called me...worse, if the Pecks remembered they had Tommy's phone, with my number programmed in, they could call and figure out exactly where I was.

I crouched as low as I could and fumbled with the wet phone, scrolling down the menu to the ringer options. Twice I hit wrong buttons and wasted precious seconds backing out of one menu to get back to the one I wanted. Finally I hit ringer off.

I glanced around again. Still no sign of my pursuers. I clicked to my messages, and there was one from Jack: "10 min." Ten minutes? Was he

351

close by? I supposed that was possible. There weren't many shopping or entertainment options in Buchanan or Niles, so a lot of people came down to the mall area on a regular basis.

I heard deep voices to my left, and crab walked carefully to the right. I peered down the row, but didn't see anyone.

I heard the distinct sound of high heels on pavement, running through the rain. At last, a shopper!

"Hey!" I stood up, shouted and waved at her. She hesitated, looking my way.

Ping! A bullet ricocheted off the roof of a car, only inches to my right. I ducked and scrambled under the car and kept moving, belly crawling out the other side and still moving until I'd cleared four cars. Twice I got stuck on mufflers and thought I was done for, but suffered only a large tear in my shirt as I forced myself to keep moving. I stopped when I was confronted by a low-slung Toyota. I was grateful I no longer weighed two hundred and twenty pounds, because I would never have made it under as many cars as I had, but even at I one-forty I wasn't going to get past that Toyota. Maybe Nicole Richie or the skinny Olsen twin could have done it, but I didn't have time to let anorexia win my escape.

So much for being saved by a random shopper. These guys must not care who saw them out here shooting.

In fact, did anyone care? I mean, where were the cops? Certainly everyone couldn't be ignoring the sound of shots being fired in the mall parking lot.

I wondered how much time had passed since I'd rolled out of the Escort. It felt like hours, but I suspected it was no more than ten minutes. Still, that should be enough time for the cops to arrive.

If anyone had called. The thunder was still crashing, the lightning periodically lighting up the night. Maybe the few people who'd heard the shots fired thought it was thunder.

"She's got to be here somewhere. Come on guys, find her!" The voice was unfamiliar, but I had to assume it was someone with the Pecks, and the "her" in question was me. I pushed back farther under the car I was hiding under. Something hard poked me in the back; I think it might have been the transmission. I couldn't go any farther. I waited, my head whipping left and right, watching for feet.

There was another crash of thunder followed closely by a brilliant flash of lightning. I saw a pair of feet, two cars away, a barely darker shadow against the bright light. At the same time I heard a voice shout behind me, and this time there was no doubt it was right there. In a panic I tried to squirm forward, but I was stuck! My pants had hung up on the transmission, and I couldn't get free no matter how hard I pulled.

I tried to back up, but I was stuck fast. I felt panic building in me, and I thrashed around like a rat in a trap. That analogy was too close to the truth. If one of the Pecks came around this side of the car, there I'd be, just my head sticking out, waiting for them to brain me like a cornered rat.

I was gasping for breath, little sparkles of light showing in my peripheral vision, and I feared I might pass out.

Think, Rainie, think! You don't want to die here!

Actually, I didn't want to die anywhere.

I squirmed an arm behind me and tried to feel for what was holding me. I tugged at my jeans, and my hand slipped off. I felt a sharp stab and almost cried out. Great; I'd cut myself on rusty metal. If the Pecks didn't shoot me I'd probably die of lockjaw.

There was only one thing left to try. I forced my hand underneath me, feeling the pavement scrape away another layer of skin. I unbuttoned my pants and tried to move forward again.

I pulled myself forward on my elbows like a commando, and fully understood for the first time why they always wore heavy canvas fatigues, even in the jungle. Bare arms were no good for dragging yourself across a rough surface.

Never mind that, I told myself. That's what skin grafts were for. Just get the hell out of here!

The pep talk must have worked, because I finally made it out from under the car, minus my pants and shoes, which were stuck somewhere in the pants legs. I was thoroughly scraped, but still alive. Score one for the good guys.

In the pool of light from one of the big overhead lamps I saw an elongated shadow. One of the guys was just coming around the front of the car. I ducked the other way and hurried down the next row. I had to be more cautious now. I was running out of real estate, getting to a point where there was a wide open area with no parked cars.

"Come on guys, she's gone already!" I froze at the sound of the voice, directly ahead of me. I saw the outline of a tall, thin man standing right in the middle of the row. In the heavy downpour I'd almost run right into him!

"She's got to be here, Gary. Keep looking."

"We won't find her in this mess. I'm soaked and I'm tired. She's probably home already, warm and dry and on the phone to the cops."

"Shut up your whining and keep looking!" I recognized the voice of the fat guy. I had to agree with him: Gary did sound pretty whiny.

I stayed where I was for the moment, waiting to see what Gary would do. He hadn't seen me yet, but all he'd need to do was turn my way and there I'd be. He was holding something in his hand, hanging down at his side. I didn't need any more light to figure out it was a gun.

Gary sat on the hood of a car, muttering to himself. He slipped the gun into his jacket pocket and pulled a handkerchief out of another pocket. He blew his nose and took a moment to peek at what he'd produced. Apparently not satisfied with the results, he put the cloth back up to his face.

Now, if I had taken any time at all to think about my next move it never would have happened. My knees would have turned to jelly and I probably would have thrown up every meal I'd eaten for the last week.

But I guess I was too exhausted and terrified and fed up with being chased to do much thinking. Or maybe I was overdosing on adrenaline.

I ran at Gary, nearly silent in my bare feet with the pounding rain for cover. I led with my uninjured shoulder and slammed into him full tilt. He fell forward and his feet slipped from under him at the same time, and he came down awkwardly, his head colliding with a solid *thunk* on the cars bumper.

He dropped to the pavement and didn't move.

I froze, stunned into indecision. I guess I had been expecting a fight of some kind, although surely I hadn't thought I'd win. I had just gotten tired of being the rabbit, and somewhere inside me that little voice had whispered that I should at least go down fighting.

But he was down instead.

I started to back away but remembered his gun. Yes! I could at least be armed.

I reached into his pocket, but it was empty. Damn, it must be in the other pocket, the one he was laying on. He was jammed up against the bumper of the car so I couldn't just push him over. Skinny or not the guy still had to weigh one-eighty, too much for me to dead lift. I was not, however, without skills.

In the course of caregiving I was often faced with a large client that had to be turned in bed for one reason or another. For that reason I'm not exactly a weakling, but even better, I have skills.

I squatted beside Gary and took a good hold on the bottom shoulder of his jacket and the waistband of his pants and heaved him onto his back.

With a client this was a gentle maneuver, accomplished by grasping the sheet underneath them, not their clothing. But hey, Gary wasn't a client, and I wasn't inclined to be gentle with him.

He started to moan, his head turning a little as his senses came back to him. I grabbed the gun out of his pocket and hurried away, down the next to the last row of cars.

I took a moment to look at the gun. My lesson with Eddie hadn't made me an expert, but at least I could look at it as more than a potentially deadly paperweight.

I was happy to see that this one was a revolver, and a pretty small one, at that. Not as much killing power, I'm sure Eddie would point out, but for my purposes I also thought it the simplest to operate. Point and shoot, just like my camera. Except of course my camera wouldn't buck in my hands, and snapping someone's picture wasn't likely to kill them.

I flipped the cartridge to the side: four bullets left. So, whiny Gary had overcome his apathy long enough to take a couple of shots at me. I was glad I'd knocked him out. It served him right.

I flipped the gun closed. It was slick from the rain, and I wondered if it was wet enough to misfire. I didn't know enough about guns to be sure how much wet they could take.

Now it was decision time. Should I take off across the empty space, maybe try to make for a mall entrance, or should I double back, stay hidden among the cars?

I wasn't sure what time it was. Maybe nine o'clock? My cell phone would have told me, but I'd left it behind with my pants and shoes. What time did the mall close? Nine or ten? And did they lock the outside doors right away, or did they have to wait for last stragglers to clear out? I didn't go to the mall very often, and I just didn't know the protocol.

I pictured myself, pounding on the locked glass doors, backlit from the lights inside, a perfect target for the Pecks to shoot.

No, better to stay among the cars, where I at least had some cover.

I dropped to my belly and looked carefully under the cars, searching for feet or shadows. There, two cars over, I saw someone moving slowly toward the front of the cars. Now where was the other one? They were being quiet now, and that made them a lot more dangerous.

I got into a crouch again and moved toward the back of the car. I stopped and peered around the bumper. No sign of the other guy, so I slipped around back to get behind the first guy. I looked down the first row, and there was nothing. I hurried across the opening to the next row, and there he was, doing the same thing I was doing in the other direction.

He was only one car length away from me. I weighed the gun in my hand and debated it. I remembered how startling it was to fire a gun, even when you were prepared for it, and how the gun tended to jump upwards when you fired. I wondered, first of all, if I could even hit him. It wasn't nearly as easy as it looked on TV. Secondly, did I want to shoot him in the back? That didn't seem fair, and besides, it might well get me arrested for murder.

So I waited until he moved on, creeping around the front of the car in the direction I'd come from, then I scurried across to the next one.

This was getting ridiculous. How long could I keep this up? I was tired and in pain and my legs were cramping from running around in a duck walk for so long. How long had I been out here? And where the hell was Jack?

As if my thoughts had summoned him, I saw his truck drive slowly past on the cross lane about twenty rows away. I was so excited I stood and started to run toward him, waving and shouting his name.

Ping! A bullet scraped across the hood of a car, so close I felt the sting of metal fragments hit my bare thigh. Then it felt as if someone punched me, hard, in my left arm. The blow knocked me forward and spun me around, and I expected to see the fat guy towering over me.

But he wasn't there. I hadn't been punched, I'd been shot!

I was flat on my back, stunned by the sheer force of the blow. I might have stayed that way until Bob Peck or the fat guy arrived to finish me off if not for the deluge of rain striking my face, running up my nose and into my open mouth.

I rolled to the side to keep from drowning, but I couldn't seem to get my body to do much else. The pain in my arm was blossoming into something epic. If I were a movie hero I'm sure I could jump up and fight Bob hand to hand, then steal a car and drive away like a Hollywood stunt driver on speed without ever missing a beat. But this wasn't a movie, and let me tell you, this hurt! How could my brain possibly get a message through to my limbs to move when its entire focus was on screaming "Pain! We have pain here!"

I heard running feet and shouting and managed to turn my head in the direction of the ruckus. It was Bob Peck rushing through the downpour, his gun out and ready to finish me off.

And suddenly I understood why maybe some of that hero stuff was possible after all.

Adrenaline shot through me as abruptly as if I'd been struck by a bolt of lightning. I sat up and then jumped to my feet. I was shocked to discover I was still holding Gary's gun.

Bob was only a few yards away and closing fast, the gun coming up in his hand, aiming at me. For a moment I wondered if he was planning to shoot me or stab me with it. How close did he need to get for a shot?

Whatever. I pointed the revolver at him and pulled the trigger.

There was a wet snap, but it didn't fire.

Bob finally stopped six feet away from me and lifted the gun still more. I was staring straight down the barrel, and I swear I could see the end of the bullet, like a winking eye, ready to blast out and punch a hole right between my eyes.

I pulled the trigger again and threw myself to the side in the same instant.

This time the gun fired, and I heard a cry of pain. Bob's gun flashed, the bullet whizzing by high, missing me by a good margin, but he was already lowering his arm, ready to take another shot.

Suddenly he was backlit by a pair of headlights, coming on fast. He turned to face this new threat, which I recognized as Jack's truck. It was flying down the lane like some glossy black steed from hell galloping to my rescue.

Galloping really fast. In fact, maybe too fast for conditions, and here I was, lying right in its path!

I scrambled out of the way, first on hands and knees, then finally getting to my feet and practically diving behind a parked car.

Bob just stood there like the proverbial deer in headlights, watching the truck bear down on him.

Jack hit the brakes hard, the rear end of the truck fishtailing first one way, then the other, never quite making contact with the rows of parked cars on either side. For a moment it looked like he might stop in time...but no.

He slammed into Bob, still moving about twenty-five miles per hour. Bob folded over the hood of the car and then lifted off, his arms spread wide like he was performing a trick on the high wire: *tad a*!! I had to suppress a giggle at the thought. This was certainly not funny.

He landed with a wet thump on the hood of a Buick and slid bonelessly to the ground.

Bonelessly. Ugh. I'd heard the word used before, but this was the first time I'd seen it in practice. It really did look as if every bone in his body had been pulverized to useless dust, and he slumped like a half filled sandbag.

I didn't have much time to be appalled. Jack was already out of his truck, a gun in his hand pointing at the fat guy, who in turn was leaning against a car and yowling like a cat in heat.

"Get out here, hands where I can see them!" Jack shouted at him.

"She shot me!" The fat guy yowled back. "The bitch shot me!"

The bitch? Did he mean me? How could I have shot him? I hadn't even known where he was.

"Get out where I can see you!" Jack commanded again in a tone that would not be denied. Even I wanted to come out into the open.

The fat guy staggered into the lane, his arms clamped across his ample belly.

"I'm gut shot. Call an ambulance!"

Gut shot? So he's the one who'd cried out when I'd fired the revolver. I guess my wild shot hadn't missed completely after all.

"Where's your gun?" Jack asked the fat guy.

"Back there. I dropped it when she shot me."

"Get on the ground."

The guy fell to his knees almost gratefully, seeming not to notice the deep puddle he landed in. I didn't see any blood, but then again I couldn't see much of anything between the dark and the rain. The downpour had lessened, as had the wind, and now it was a steady fall, the kind farmers preferred for their crops. The storm itself had moved off the southeast, now little more than an occasional rumble and distant flash to mark its passing.

I stepped into the glow of Jack's headlights. He had stepped between the cars to retrieve fat guy's gun, and he came back, tucking it into the waistband of his black jeans.

He looked at me closely, his eyes pausing for long moments on my face and shoulder, moving slowly down my torso and stopping again at my bare legs. As he did I imagined what he was seeing: the skin torn from my face and shoulder, the blood running down my useless arm, me dressed in nothing but a filthy, soaked T shirt and underpants, my knees scraped and bleeding.

Not a pretty sight.

"You okay?"

I nodded, not at all sure that I was. Finally, off in the distance I heard sirens. It seemed that at least one person was concerned about gun fire at the mall.

Jack glanced back at the fat guy, who was lying down now, holding on to his stomach like he thought it was going to break free and roll away.

Jack holstered his own gun and came over to me, slipping his jacket off.

"You don't look so good. Are you going to faint?" He slipped the jacket over my shoulders.

I tried to shake my head. No, of course I wasn't going to faint.

But then I did.

Chapter Twenty-two

The next few hours were a blur. I was moved from Jack's truck to an ambulance to the emergency room, all the while being poked and prodded until I wanted to scream at them to leave me the hell alone...until someone stuck something warm and soothing into my IV and then I didn't care at all.

I drifted in and out of my drug inspired happy place to answer questions put to me by nurses and doctors and other assorted people in hospital scrubs. There was one cute guy in a blue uniform who was very stern, and seemed disconcerted when I giggled at the phrase "gunshot wound."

I'm not sure what, if anything, I told him, but he went away and then I was being wheeled down a hall, staring up at the fluorescent lights. Jack was walking beside me saying something about surgery and he'd talk to me later. My bed stopped moving and someone covered me with a warm blanket that felt like it was fresh from the oven and then I drifted off to my happy place to stay for a while.

I was only in the hospital overnight, not even long enough for all my family and friends to stop and make a fuss over me.

Oh, they were there. My mother and Jedediah, my brother – thankfully sober - my sister in a brand new pair of shoes, my niece with a thick book to read in case waiting for me to die got boring, Eddie, Tommy and Jack all gathered in the surgical waiting room, as if I'd been shot in the head instead of the arm.

Unfortunately I was taken straight to the recovery room and everyone was told to go home, that I would sleep through till morning. I never would have known they were there if a nurse's aid hadn't told me all about it, sounding maybe just a little jealous.

There was a police officer at my bedside before breakfast was served. He'd taken Jack's statement and let him go, so I hoped I wasn't about to be arrested and handcuffed to my bed.

I told him the whole story, starting with the text from Tommy's stolen phone. Then I had to backtrack and explain about Ida and the homeless guys. The cop kept raising his eyebrows and saying "hmm" a lot, and I wasn't sure if he believed me. When I finished he asked a few questions for clarification.

"So you shot the fat...I mean, Gerald Peck?"

"I guess so, but not on purpose. I was trying to shoot Bob Peck."

"Who was trying to shoot you, but instead got run over by your friend."

"Yeah, but he wouldn't have gotten run over if he'd just *moved*. That's what I did."

"So your friend Jack was trying to run you over, too?"

"No, he wasn't *trying*. I think he was just trying to scare Bob so he wouldn't shoot me, but Bob just turned around and stared at him, didn't try to get out of the way at all."

"I see." I didn't think the cop saw at all, but I wasn't going to belabor the point. He finally left, promising he'd see me again (oh goody!) and advising me not to leave town. I thought they only said that on TV cop shows. It was pretty cool to hear it for real, and directed at me.

Before noon the doctor pronounced me ready to go home. I wasn't terribly surprised since I had no insurance, and they were probably wondering if I'd ever pay the charges I'd already incurred.

The good news was the bullet had lodged itself in fat and muscle, not shattering any bone. They cleaned me up and declared that no skin grafts were necessary for my many patches of road rash, but they sent me home with a healing ointment.

My hand required four stitches from whatever broken metal had cut me when I got my pants stuck, and I got a tetanus booster. Normally I would have been unhappy about the needle, but by that point one more jab meant nothing.

They gave me a prescription for pain pills which my mother reluctantly agreed to have filled. She thought I should stick to the more natural painkilling benefits of marijuana, but I pointed out to her that B&E required periodic drug tests, so maybe I'd better stick to the synthetic but legal kind.

When I got home I checked on George and then flopped on the couch, completely out of steam.

"Here honey, I brought you a pillow and blanket." My mother covered me up and fluffed a pillow behind me. "I'll stay with you today in case you need anything."

"No, please don't do that. All I want to do is sleep, I won't need anything."

"How can you know that?"

I sighed, so tired it was an effort to speak. But as nice as it is to be taken care of once in a while, I'd had enough of people fussing over me. I just wanted to be left alone to sleep.

"Mother, please..."

"Uh oh, it's mother now, huh?" She smiled and touched me gently on the forehead, a classic mother gesture that seemed to be a part of every culture. "I'll just sit here and read, you won't even know I'm here."

She settled into my only armchair and opened a book. I was going to argue, but it was too late. I was off to my happy place again.

When I woke up again it was already dark outside, and the living room was dim except for one small lamp burning in the corner. The house was completely silent; my mom must have relented and gone on home.

I sat up slowly, letting a wave of dizziness wash over me and then away.

I hurt everywhere. My arm, my shoulder, my legs, my face...in fact, I couldn't identify a single body part that didn't ache.

On the coffee table in front of me was a glass of water, my pain pills and a banana. Good old mom, watching out for me even if she wasn't here. I was surprised she hadn't left a joint and a lighter there as well.

I needed to pee, but I decided the pain was my first priority. I took a pill, then peeled the banana and ate it, amazed at how hungry I was. Fortified, I dragged myself off the couch to the bathroom.

When I came back I found Tommy sitting in my living room.

"How are you feeling?"

"What are you doing here?"

"Ah, grouchy. That's probably a good sign."

"Never mind that! Why are you here and how did you get in?"

"I'm here because your mother had to leave, and she didn't want you left alone. I guess she's decided I'm not trashing your aura, since she called and asked me to come. As for how I got in, you still keep a key taped to the back of the mailbox. Not a good idea, I have to say."

"Don't worry, I'll move it tomorrow."

"Okay. Well, if you're interested I have a few messages for you."

"Messages?"

"People have been calling and stopping by all day. I've been taking care of it so you could sleep."

"Oh. Well, thanks I guess."

"You're welcome." He pretended I hadn't said it sarcastically. "Let's see, several people called to see how you're feeling: the usual suspects, Mason and Riley and of course Eddie. Jack stopped by with your phone and your pants. He found them in the parking lot. Both are trashed, but he thought you might be able to salvage the sim card."

"That's cool. I hate having to reprogram all my numbers. Did you get your phone back?"

"Not yet." Tommy grimaced. "Cops say its evidence. By the way, I'm sorry they managed to get a hold of it in the first place. I've always been kind of careless with it, but it never occurred to me someone would steal it to use in a plot to kill you."

That got a smile out of me. "I'm sure it didn't."

"Your car has been towed for evidence, but they said you can probably have it back by the end of the week."

"Is it drivable?"

"I think so, but the front end is crunched, you need a new headlight, and the airbags will need to be replaced."

I hated to hear that, especially the airbags. They were damned expensive.

"So, next big thing: Thelma was here, and was she pissed!"

"Oh god, I never thought about that. I was supposed to work today."

"Right, and not only did you not show up or call, but when she tried to call your cell it said it was out of service. She tried the land line, but it was busy. One call after another, like I said. So she had her driver bring her over."

"I'd better call and apologize."

"Don't worry about it. When she heard the story she wasn't mad at you anymore, she was mad at *me*. I should have called her. Oh, and she left this." Tommy pulled a white envelope out of his back pocket. I peeked inside: five hundred dollar bills. "She said it was to help you out while you're off work."

"Great. Now I'm getting charity from my clients."

"Since when is Thelma just a client? Man, you are in a crappy mood. Well. One more message and I'm out of here. A detective from Indiana called, wants to set up a time for an interview."

"Why? I answered enough questions in the hospital this morning."

"That was about the shooting in Mishawaka. This detective is from South Bend."

"What does he want?"

"I don't know, he wouldn't say." Tommy put a business card on the table next to my meds and water. "He wants you to call and set up a convenient time. Do you want me to fix you something to eat before I go?"

"No, I'm fine." Actually, the pain meds were kicking in and I was feeling a little woozy, my stomach doing a slow roll. But I wasn't going to ask him to stay. I could take care of myself.

"All right then. See ya."

Tommy left, locking the door behind him. I put my head back against the couch. Yep, the painkiller was definitely doing its thing. I wondered if he had taped the key back onto the mailbox. I wondered if anyone else knew it was there.

I didn't wonder anything else. I fell asleep.

I woke up the next morning even stiffer and achier than the day before. I had slid down on the couch at some point until I was almost prone, but now I had a stiff neck on top of everything else. I was three days out from my last shower, and I felt grungy. My hair was still matted from being out in the rain.

I wanted a pain pill, but I was too nauseous to consider swallowing one. I had to eat something. I hadn't had anything yesterday but a bowl of cereal in the hospital and the banana Tommy had provided.

Moaning and groaning all the way - another advantage to living alone, you could indulge in such things as much as you wanted and no one was there to tell you to shut up already - I went out to the kitchen and scanned the fridge for a viable breakfast.

There was a dried out looking chicken breast left over from a few days ago, a wilted stalk of celery and a few apples. I slathered some mayo on a piece of whole grain bread that was a little stale but not moldy and slapped the chicken breast and half a stalk of celery on top. I folded it over and took a big bite. Yum, lazy person's chicken salad.

I ate it slumped at the counter, taking plenty of sips of water in between bites to offset the dryness. I was almost relieved when I was finally done with it, as if I'd completed a hated but necessary chore.

I took a pain pill, wondering how long I could keep up that pace without becoming addicted.

Now for the shower. I wrapped a trash bag around my wounded arm (a gunshot wound! I never would have expected one of those in my lifetime) and taped it in place. I washed my hair twice, no easy trick with one hand, and stood under the hot water until it ran to cold.

By the time I'd dried off and dressed in a T shirt and sweats I was feeling almost human again. I decided I'd call the detective from South Bend. Now that I was fully conscious, with my tummy full and my hair clean, my brain was able to focus on being curious.

I dialed the number on the card and asked for Detective Brian Miller. He came on the line after only a brief wait. His voice was deep and slightly accented, maybe a lingering southern drawl.

"Detective Miller."

"Hello. This is Rainie Lovingston. I got a message that you wanted to see me about something?"

"Yes, Miss Lovingston. Would it be convenient for me to stop by today?"

"Can't we just talk over the phone?"

"I'd prefer to come there if you don't mind."

"Um, I guess not. What time will you come?"

"Whenever it's convenient for you."

Hmm. Awful polite cop. I wondered if I was in trouble.

"I'm not planning on going anywhere today. I'm not supposed to drive. So I guess anytime is okay."

"I could be there in an hour."

"Okay."

"I'll see you then."

Detective Miller was a tall, narrow man. He was thin, with long arms and legs and a long neck. His face was long and narrow, his nose sized to match. It was as if he'd at some point been softened and stretched like saltwater taffy, then allowed to harden into sinew and darkly tanned skin. I wondered how such a narrow throat produced such a wonderful bass voice.

He came in, politely refused my offer of something to drink and settled comfortably in my side chair, a notebook open on his knee.

"Miss Lovingston, you told the officer in Mishawaka that you suspected that the same people who tried to kill you had killed a homeless man in South Bend, is that right?"

"Oh, I get it. I didn't think you guys talked across city lines."

Detective Miller gave me a thin smile. "Of course we do. Our cities are only separated by crossing a road. We don't have much choice but to cooperate. Can you tell me why you think they killed this man?" He glanced at his notebook. "Doug Harrison, right?"

"Right. But I told the officer I didn't know anything for sure, I just had suspicions."

"Why?"

So I gave him the short version, how I was a caregiver and my client's daughter had taken in some men who looked disreputable, how Virginia was worried. "I just happened to see an insurance form with Doug Harrison's name on it, and it made me wonder. I mean, Miss Ida isn't a wealthy woman. It was one thing to put a roof over a homeless guy's head, but quite another to insure him."

"So then what?"

I told him about Doug disappearing, and my search of newspaper articles. I was hesitant to tell him about my trip to the morgue to see Doug's body, but when I did he didn't act like I'd done anything illegal.

"So what did Miss Ida say when you confronted her?"

"She acted like she had no idea Doug was dead. She thought he'd just taken off."

"So you let it drop?"

"There wasn't much else I could do. I mean, I thought Miss Ida was a sweet old lady. She had me half convinced that I was crazy."

"But then?" Oh boy, this guy was good with the leading questions.

"But then she brought in another homeless guy, and this one looked like he was really on his last legs. I mean, he smelled like he'd died last week, you know? Well, Miss Ida caught me checking on him..."

"Caught you?"

"Well, I wasn't really doing anything wrong. Virginia asked me to go up and take a look, but it really pissed Ida off, and she fired me."

"Okay. So why do you think the men who tried to kill you at the mall were connected to Miss Ida?"

"Because they told me so. They said Miss Ida had told their mother I was snooping, and she said to make sure I kept my nose out of their business."

"And their mother would be?"

"Frieda. She lives with Ida and Virginia."

"Let me get this straight." Detective Miller folded his hands over his notebook and stared at me with narrowed eyes. "You think these old women were taking in homeless guys, getting life insurance on them and then killing them off?"

"Well, yeah, I guess."

"Just two old ladies."

"Well, and Freida's sons."

Detective Miller nodded slowly.

"I understand you've been working for a detective agency."

"Yeah, B&E. I'm a P.I.'s assistant."

"I spoke to the Buchanan police chief, and according to him you've already managed to piss a few people off. This wasn't the first time you were shot at."

"So what's your point?"

"Are you sure those guys weren't mad at you about some other business you were sticking your nose into?"

"Well hell, I don't know. I piss so many people off in a day it's hard to tell why one might be shooting at me. I practically have to wear a bullet proof vest in the shower these days."

"Sarcasm isn't going to help."

"If you're finished asking stupid questions, I have things to do." I stood up, ending the interview, but Detective Miller stayed where he was and offered his thin little smile again.

"I'm sorry if I offended you, Miss Lovingston, but you must admit this is an odd story, with pretty flimsy circumstantial evidence."

375

"Yet here you are."

"Right."

"Well, why? I mean, if the story seems so crazy why did you drive all the way up here to question me?"

"Because, Miss Lovingston, it just so happens that Doug Harrison *didn't* die of natural causes. He died of internal injuries sustained from an apparent hit and run. We had thought at first maybe a drunk driver had hit him and taken off, but then Mishawaka reported your tale. I was curious."

I sat back down. Curiosity was something I could relate to. Maybe Detective Miller wasn't all asshole.

"So, are you curious enough to look into it?"

"Actually, I am. If you could provide Miss Ida's full name and contact information..."

"Gladly. By the way, there's a doctor you might want to check out while you're at it. Miss Ida brought him home to see the homeless guys. His name is Veldman, and he has a history of getting involved in less than kosher activities."

"All right." The detective jotted some more notes, thanked me for my time, and left.

Jack called later that afternoon.

"Hey, how're you feeling?"

"Not bad. A little spacey from the drugs."

"You should try smoking pot. Kills the pain but doesn't put you to sleep."

"You think Harry Baker would approve of that?"

"What, you mean the drug tests? If you're wounded they expect you to test dirty."

376

"Did you call to give me medical advice?"

Jack laughed. "Tommy said you were pretty testy. No, actually, I have some news you might want to hear. First of all, none of the Pecks died."

"Really? But Bob looked pulverized, and the fat one was gut shot!"

"Bob has two broken legs and a mild concussion. The one you knocked out before I got there has a worse concussion. As for the gut shot, the bullet mostly went through his fat, didn't hit any vital organs. They'll all be around to stand trial for kidnapping and attempted murder."

"Does that mean I'm not going to be arrested for shooting him?"

Jack laughed. "You worry way too much. There *is* such a thing as self-defense, you know."

"Like defending yourself with a truck?"

"That too. Besides, that was an accident. I figured the guy would jump out of the way."

"Well, it worked, I guess."

"You did a pretty good job out there. Took one out, evaded the others...not bad for a caregiver."

"I'm not sure how good I did. Have you seen me?"

Jack laughed. "A little worse for wear, maybe, but you're alive and standing. That's more than you can say for the other guys."

I laughed with him, and it felt good to discover my sense of humor hadn't deserted me completely.

"So what's up with Miss Ida? You want to go snoop around a little over there?"

"No!" I was aghast at the suggestion. "I damn near got killed by those little old ladies. I think I'll let the cops handle this one."

"All right, I suppose that would be best. But maybe we can work together on something else when you've healed up a bit. Harry's pretty impressed. He'd probably support any efforts you wanted to make toward becoming a full time P.I."

"Yeah?" I felt a sort of warm glow all over at those complimentary words, or maybe I was just having a hot flash from the pain meds. "I'll have to think about that. Being a caregiver rarely means anyone will take a shot at you."

"And where's the fun in that?" Jack laughed and hung up.

The thing was, I didn't think Jack was kidding. He really did think getting shot at was fun. Strange man. But I liked him.

Chapter Twenty-three

Three weeks went by. I got my car back, replaced the headlight and airbags but left the dents. What the heck, couldn't make the old beast look much worse than it did, but the engine still purred along fine on all four cylinders. I had to drive one handed, a neat trick with a stick shift, but it was amazing how well a person can steer with their knees with enough practice.

I went back to work at B&E, spending all my time on computer searches and phone interviews. Harry Baker did ask if I was interested in pursuing a full time career with him, but I told him I needed to think about it.

Jack stopped in one afternoon while I was plugging away on the data bases.

"So Harry tells me you didn't say no. I have to admit I was a bit surprised."

"No one is more surprised than me. My road rash still hurts, and people still do a double take when they see the side of my face, which looks something like crusted over raw hamburger."

"It's not that bad."

"Ha! Not to mention my arm is still in a sling, and I have to go to physical therapy three times a week, where they torture me with apparent glee, smiling and clapping encouragement like demented cheerleaders. Do I really want to take a job that could put me in this condition on a regular basis?"

"Hey, don't blame this job. It was your caregiving that got you into this mess."

I stared at him, speechless. Damn, he was right. Why hadn't that occurred to me before?

"Hey, but still...this job got me shot at and blown out a fourth story window."

"Yeah, but you had me with you. It's a lot more fun to share the danger, don't you think?"

"There you go with that fun stuff again. You ever think about taking up a hobby, like bowling maybe?"

Jack just grinned and shook his head. "Let me know when you decide."

Another week went by and Miss Ida and Frieda, along with assorted relatives, were arrested for the insurance scam.

Virginia got her wish and moved to Brentwood, with its plush carpeting and card games and gourmet meals served in a dining room with real linens. Thelma and I went to visit her, and she was as happy as I'd ever seen her. She wasn't much surprised by her daughter's arrest, and shrugged it off. "At least she doesn't have to worry about money anymore. The state will take care of her."

The homeless man I'd seen the day I got fired died from gangrene, but not before Ida had bought a hundred thousand dollars of life insurance on him. Veldman had certified him as being in good health. In fact, he had certified seven homeless men in the past two years. All but two had died, a couple from natural causes, but the rest from "accidents."

According to statements read to reporters by their lawyer, the ladies didn't believe they'd done anything wrong. The insurance companies had lots of money, and the ladies needed a nest egg to supplement their woefully inadequate social security. As for killing five men, they pointed out that they had first taken them from deplorable conditions on the street, fed them, housed them and clothed them, vastly improving their quality of life. They insisted that all had died more cleanly and with less pain than if they'd been left behind a dumpster to freeze to death come winter.

I thought of Doug Harrison, hit by a car and left to die of internal injuries. Painless, right.

It was hard to believe those harmless, sweet looking old ladies had come up with such a sophisticated scam and pulled it off for so long. It was even harder to believe it was going on in a quiet little community like Buchanan. It just went to prove that you never really knew what was going on behind your neighbor's closed doors.

Was the guy two doors down really just a hobby hunter, or did he have a whole stockpile of weapons in his basement, ready to come out blasting one Memorial Day at the local parade?

Did the quiet little accountant on the corner have a collection of severed hands and feet fashioned as mobiles to adorn his bedroom ceiling? Maybe each toe and fingernail was painted a different sparkly color to catch the afternoon sunlight.

And how about the perky blonde that teaches your child's third grade class? After hours does she do ballet for exercise, or maybe pole dancing for cash?

You may never know. Or maybe a curious poet/caregiver/private detective living next door in quiet contentment with her pet iguana will find out for you.

9563576R0022

Made in the USA
Charleston, SC
23 September 2011